CORVUS

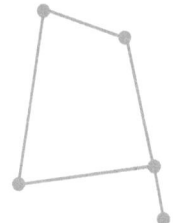

STAR-BLOOD

CORVUS

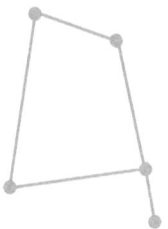

SOFI AGUILERA

Paperback ISBN: 978-1-63337-742-4
E-Book ISBN: 978-1-63337-743-1
LCCN: 2023915285

Printed in the United States of America
1 3 5 7 9 10 8 6 4 2

To my family: Mama, Papa, Caro, and Abu. Thank you for being the brightest stars in this constellation called life.

Chapter II

From the Egg the First One emerged, fed by the Light that remained.

He shone forth as the Sun, as the Divine Dragon of Wisdom.

The first Sound from this being came, one that vibrated to the ends of Space.

For Sound was the force that began Creation, and it shall cause the End.

Time its endless flight had commenced, and Night her reign had ended,

When the Eternal Breath of the Mother was first taken.

It shall expand when She exhales and contract when She inhales,

As the new cycle of Life takes place, one where the Seven are yet to take shape.

Time in a Wheel shall now rule to mark the Ages as they Begin and End,

For even if not yet born, the Luminous Ones shall soon rule each one.

The endless Sea in rage remained, until at last by Light it was claimed.

In Fire it burned, into the Seeds of the Eternal Breath it was transformed.

Darkness at last succumbed to the new being that had been born,

And a slave She became to the blinding power of Her Son.

Toward the edge Darkness was driven, away from the waters She had formed,

The same ones that Chaos had once roamed.

But Darkness freedom craved, the power of Eternity to regain,

Yet Her strength was not enough to defeat the Breath of Fire that now shone forth.

And into a deep Sleep She fell, embraced by the warmth of Her resplendent Son.

In an eternal Dream She remained, while a new Era of Light commenced.

CHAPTER 1

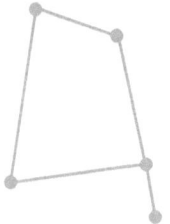

"CORVUS," *it whispered. "Child of Lies."*

The voice came from all around me, hissing like air. I opened my eyes, but my vision blurred. Only shadows swayed above me as I lay on the hard ground. Leaves swished loudly, with enough force to rip them off the branches—but there was no wind.

"Corvus," it whispered again. The voice rustled like the leaves. It didn't sound feminine or masculine.

I moaned. All of my body ached. I tried to sit up, but my muscles didn't respond. My head felt like someone had pried my skull open and then closed it again after stealing a chunk of my brain. I could feel it in my heart too—a piece was missing. I had lost something. But what?

I lay unmoving on the ground. Something prickled my neck and it took me a couple of seconds to realize that it was grass. I blinked several times, my eyes stinging, but could only see dark shadows. The leaves seemed to stir faster around me, more violently. After a few seconds I was able to make out words from that noise.

"The Prince of Darkness has awakened, the Demon inside him set loose," the swishing leaves said. A thousand whispers spoke at the same time. "So much innocent blood will be shed, so many lives taken."

Who was the Prince of Darkness? Fire burned inside my heart. I screamed out in pain.

"You have chosen to forget," the whispering voices said.

What had I chosen to forget? Whatever the voices were trying to tell me wasn't making any sense. The trees stirred again. I was sure they were trees now. I could smell them—that sweet smell of leaves after the rain.

"Where am I?" I tried to ask, but only slurred words came out of my mouth. "What am I doing here?" My tongue was numb, and I wasn't even sure I had spoken, but the trees still answered.

"You came here to forget."

"Forget what?"

The leaves swished louder, as if a tornado swept through them, but I could still feel no wind. I groaned again. What had I forgotten? And why couldn't I remember who the Prince was? I could feel it—a memory, but out of my grasp, like a vivid dream that you forget seconds after waking.

I sat up, a sharp pain seizing my head. I screamed.

"You have chosen to forget," the leaves said again.

I shut my eyes tightly, then opened them a few seconds later. My vision was clearer, and the pain from my head lessened a bit. Large oak trees surrounded me as far as I could see. They seemed to stretch up to the clouds.

"What did I forget?" I asked again, tasting blood in my mouth.

The leaves stirred with no wind, the whispering voices booming around me.

"You have chosen to forget your past," they said. "Because only the oblivion of your memories will lead you to the treasure."

I stood on trembling legs, but I was afraid to take support from one of the trees. Were they alive? How was it possible that swishing leaves could talk?

"You have done the impossible, Child of Lies," they said, this time softer, as if pitying me. "You have lied to yourself."

"*That makes no sense,*" I said, feeling my tongue again.

"*Your lie will lead you to your Prophecy,*" they continued.

I looked around, unsure of what I was looking for. I decided to walk to my right. The rustling of the leaves continued, the light blue sky peeking through them. I didn't know the time of day—it could have been morning or evening.

"*Every lie has a price, Corvus,*" the leaves whispered. *I covered my ears. I didn't want to hear what the leaves were saying, but their voices boomed louder.* "*The price to pay for this one will be high.*"

I walked faster. Those words meant nothing to me. The rustling continued, and even though there was no wind, I began shivering with the sudden cold.

"*You have chosen to forget,*" they said again, but this time it sounded more like an accusation.

The leaves continued to hiss, but more violently than before. I looked up and walked even faster. The leaves flapped wildly as if they were tiny wings. The branches moved randomly, like tentacles from an octopus with lives of their own.

"*You were so desperate that you would have paid any price,*" the angry leaves hissed at me. "*You thought that you could simply forget, that you could lie yourself into a new life—a new you.*"

The rustling became deafening. I ran, my heart racing as fast as my feet.

"*You will regret this lie,*" the leaves shouted.

I didn't know where I was going—there seemed to be no way out of that forest. I tripped on something and fell flat on my face with a grunt. So many whispers surrounded me, so many voices.

"*Leave now, Child of Lies,*" the leaves roared in unison.

Then they screamed. The whispers howled in rage, pain, anger, betrayal. Then they cried, lamenting something lost. Tears welled in my eyes. The screams engulfed me. I could feel their pain, their anger, their betrayal.

But stronger than all of that, I could feel the hole in my chest. I knew what I had lost. I felt it in every inch of my body.
I had lost myself.

●━━━━●━━━━●

The Gemini Twins sat side by side in front of me, their hands and feet bound tightly.

"Come on, Corvus," Pollux said. "You know we're on your side."

"Yeah. We're all friends here!" Castor said.

"You said that last time," I reminded them. "And I ended up with a knife at my throat."

"We were just playing around," Castor said with a mocking smile. "We wouldn't have actually cut your throat."

I huffed. The Twins knew I could *always* tell a lie from truth, so I didn't know why they kept lying to me.

I leaned against the wall behind me. The room was small, its concrete walls bare. On the left was the door that led to the hallway outside. On the wall to my right a twisting crack dripped like coils from the center of the wall to the floor. The crack let in fractured rays of golden light that cut in between me and the Twins like a blade and settled on the door at the opposite side. Outside, the street remained quiet, as it had been all day long. Rome had never been quiet before, but the earthquake two weeks ago had changed everything. Anger rolled through my body as I thought of the day of the earthquake again. We should have stopped Perseus before he could kill millions of people across Italy, but the others had barely made it out alive from the fight.

"We mean it this time," Pollux said as he widened his smile. "We do consider you our friend and—"

"Where is Perseus?" I asked for the tenth time.

"We don't know," they said simultaneously.

"You're the ones who let him escape," Castor said.

I clenched my fists. I hated dealing with the Twins. But at the moment we needed them—they were the only ones who knew where Perseus had gone, and we had to find him to steal the Prophecies of Alathea from him. At the moment, Perseus was the only person who had read all of the Prophecies, so he knew all the possible futures of all the Star Children. He would manipulate those futures to get to the one he wanted—one where the rest of us were dead and the world destroyed, all in pursuit of his delusional plan.

I looked back at the Twins, who continued smiling. The Twins had light auburn hair that sometimes shone golden with the light of the sun. Pollux wore his long hair tied in a bun, while Castor's was cut just above his ears. Their bright green and blue eyes sparkled like the sea. They had long oval faces with pointed chins, small noses, and high cheekbones. At nineteen, they were only two years older than me.

I heaved a sigh as I let the silence stretch between us. Even though they knew where Perseus was, they weren't working with him. The Twins only worked for themselves. That's what made them dangerous. They worked to sell and trade information between the Star Children, and whoever paid the highest price would get the most information. I was sure they had sold us out to Perseus before, telling him everything they knew about us—and now I needed them to tell me everything they knew about Perseus. But we had nothing to offer the Twins, so we would have to force the information out of them.

The golden light coming from the crack grew fainter, and the room darkened. The light on the door opposite to the crack seemed to melt as it slid down the wall and puddled on the floor. A truck rumbled outside, its engines loud and cranking. Once the truck had passed, a pair of voices began chatting, but I couldn't make out their conversation—my Italian was not that good. The voices faded out a couple of seconds later.

"You're not leaving until you tell me where he is," I said. "Don't make me force the truth out of you."

The Twins smiled unnervingly wider, their chins becoming more pointed. I hesitated. The Twins were never happy when I forced information out of them. Something was wrong—they seemed eager this time.

I took in a deep breath while Pollux anxiously twisted in his bonds. My scars began to ache. The ones on my calf and the back of my head hurt faintly, throbbing as if they were irritated. But the scars on my chest burned as if I had lit them on fire. My chest contracted, my breaths coming short, and beads of sweat began forming at the back of my neck.

"My friends." My voice sounded different in my head, like an echo, but to the Twins, it would have sounded the same as usual.

The Twins' eyes went blank, their expressions slack.

"Friends," Castor muttered.

"Yes, we're all friends." My voice deepened and rang inside my ears.

"Of course," Castor said. "We're old friends."

"We are." My voice bounced off the walls. "And you're here because you want to help me."

I clenched my teeth, the scars on my chest burning like lava.

"We always help our friends," Pollux said. His gaze was distant, the same as his brother's. Then he frowned, as if realizing that what he'd said wasn't really true. He stared confusedly at the floor.

"You *always* help your friends," I said. "Especially me."

"Of course," Castor said.

8

"You can help me by telling me where Perseus is," I said.

Castor looked at his brother, his face still expressionless. "Last night he only said he would go somewhere far."

Pollux nodded.

Last night? Perseus had been in Rome all along and had just left? I didn't have time to think of those implications. I needed to focus. Sweat drenched my back, and my chest tightened so much I struggled to breathe. I wouldn't last much longer.

Castor laughed. "He told us you would ask that."

"He . . . what?" I said. How had Perseus known that I would find the Twins?

"Did Perseus send you here?" I asked.

"No, my friend," Pollux said. "He knew you would come for us."

My chest blazed. Every breath felt like I had inhaled ashes.

"How would he know that?" My voice vibrated, distorted, within my bones.

Pollux smiled faintly. "It's in the Prophecies."

I let out a breath as I slid down the wall. My shirt clung to my sweat-drenched body. I took in deep breaths. The pain from my scars disappeared, as if they had never hurt—as if they were just normal scars.

Castor blinked a couple of times, and Pollux shook his head as if he were trying to get me out of his mind. Then Castor grunted, squirming against the ropes that tied him. Pollux closed his eyes for a few seconds.

So many thoughts raced through my head that I couldn't focus on a single one. I needed to talk to Virgo and Draco. I stood up and faced the Twins. They were still smiling at me.

"Friends," Castor said mockingly.

"I'll be back soon," I said.

Castor looked at his brother and laughed. "Perseus was right." He turned back to me. "So much potential in you, Corvus, but something's holding you back, isn't it?"

I clenched my jaw and walked to the door, my feet scraping the floor. I wouldn't let them hook me.

"Ever since you started recovering your memories you have been weaker, haven't you?" Pollux asked. I hesitated before opening the door. "Perseus did wonder how much you remembered from your past." I bit the hook. I turned around to face them. The Twins kept smiling. "Although I'm not sure why Perseus would be interested in your memories," Pollux said with mock speculation. "Unless there was something there that he needs."

Castor chuckled.

I turned on my heel and opened the door, then slammed it closed behind me. The temperature plunged as soon as I entered the dark hallway. The only faint light came from a broken window in the center of the left wall that had bits of broken glass clinging to it. Cold air streamed in, and even though my knitted sweater kept my torso and arms warm, the cold clawed at my hands and face.

I looked back at the closed wooden door, the room beyond it silent.

How had Perseus known about my memories? No one knew about them except me. I hadn't even told Draco and Virgo about them. My hands tingled and went numb as anxiety swelled in my chest. The Twins were right about one thing—if Perseus was interested in my memories, then that meant he wanted me to remember something. But what? My memories didn't even make sense to me, so why would they make sense to Perseus? I had recovered only a single memory from my past, and it made absolutely no sense.

I had tried to recover my memories by lying to myself, trying to convince myself that I wanted to remember my past. But it never worked, maybe because it wasn't a lie and I *actually* wanted to remember. I felt as if my memories had crossed through a black hole.

My chest tightened again, my heartbeat pulsing so violently I felt my veins would burst. I sat down on the floor. The cold air burned down my throat. A whimper sounded next to me, and I turned to see Sirius walking toward me. His big brown eyes seemed concerned as he arrived at my side.

"I'm fine, boy," I said.

The Dog didn't seem convinced. Sirius was a Boxer with white chest, belly, and paws, a black snout, and black hair around his eyes. The rest of his body was brown with dark stripes like a tiger's. He stood a head taller than me as I sat down.

He whimpered again. "I'm fine." I assured him. I took in several deep breaths.

Sirius glanced back the way he had come and growled. "No," I said as I stood, my head spinning. "You don't need to call Virgo and Draco."

Sirius blinked up at me.

I slowly walked down the hallway, away from the Twins. Sirius sniffed the spot I had been sitting on, probably smelling my sweat. A few seconds later he followed after me.

At the end of the hallway, I pushed the door open and walked through it. The stuffy living room was lit by only a few candles placed at the corners of the room. To the right, Virgo lay on the couch as she read a little book. I couldn't make out what the washed out title said, but wasn't curious enough to ask Virgo. I wondered how she could read with such faint light. On the floor next to the couch lay the two guns we had confiscated from the Twins. In front of the couch sat a large mattress that Draco and I had to share. We had found it a few blocks away, among the debris of a fallen building.

Draco sat next to the broken window on the left, staring at the orange and pink clouds against the blue sky. We had nailed blankets to the wall as makeshift curtains, and they mostly kept the cold out during the night. We had tied them to the sides, but we would probably untie them soon. On the opposite side of the room, directly in front of me, was an open door that revealed stairs leading down.

As soon as Draco saw me come out of the hallway, he stood up from the floor and walked over, his gaze questioning. Virgo put down her book and sat upright on the couch.

"I see the others haven't returned," I said.

The Lion was not sitting next to the stairs, where he usually slept, the Eagle was not perched on the opening, and the little black poodle was nowhere to be seen.

"Leo went to the butcher shop a few buildings away," Virgo said as she stood up. "I think there's still enough meat for him to eat for a couple more days. Maera went with him. I think he just wanted to go for a walk."

"And Aquila went to hunt for some squirrels," Draco said.

A few seconds of silence passed.

"What did the Twins say?" Virgo finally asked.

I heaved a sigh and sat down on the floor with my back resting against the wall. Sirius sat next to me and licked his paws. Virgo and Draco exchanged a worried glance. Virgo walked over to me and sat at my side. She pulled a strand of her brown hair behind her ear. Her warm brown eyes stared right into my own. The freckles splashed across her face were darker in the light from the candles. Her sharp cheekbones almost cut through her skin, and her cheeks concaved like hollow craters. Even though Virgo had gained some weight since I had met her, she was still incredibly thin, her body more bone than flesh. I wondered, for the hundredth time, how much power Virgo must have used for it to have consumed her the way it had.

Draco sat crossed-legged on my other side, his expression hard. Draco had reptile eyes—dark red and orange with a vertical black pupil cutting through the middle. His blond hair was disheveled, and a dark yellow bruise stained the pale skin on his neck. It scared me to think that he had almost been hanged during the fight against Perseus.

"So?" Draco asked.

"Perseus left Rome last night," I said. "They don't know where he went."

Draco's vertical pupils narrowed into thin lines.

"What?" Virgo's face paled. "He was here all along?"

Sirius rested his snout on Virgo's leg as he lay down. She absently caressed him behind the ears.

"Apparently," I said.

"He wouldn't have stayed in Rome unless there was something here that he wanted," Draco said.

The three of us exchanged a glance.

"Alathea's book of Prophecies," Virgo whispered. "He knew the first part of the book was hidden somewhere here. I thought we were the only ones who knew about it."

"Apparently we're not," I said. I shook my head slowly. My chest tightened again.

"If Perseus was here for two weeks and just left, I think it's safe to assume he found the book," Draco said.

My heart beat wildly, thumping against my ribs. Perseus now had two of the three lost sections of Alathea's Prophecy book. He had found the second part of the book weeks ago before he'd destroyed Rome. The second part of Alathea's book held the Prophecies about each Star Child—it contained all of our possible futures, which now Perseus controlled. The first part of that book had information about how and why the Star Children had been created. I didn't know how Perseus could use that against us, but we certainly didn't want him to have it.

My ribcage felt tight, as if my ribs were curling into my chest. I took deep breaths to calm down. The only reason *we* were still in Rome was to find that book. But again, Perseus had beaten us to it.

"The Twins said that Perseus knew we would find them and ask them where he had gone," I said.

Draco raised a brow. "How could Perseus know we would find the Twins? Did he send them?"

"They said that Perseus hadn't sent them." I took in a deep breath. "Perseus knew we would find them because it's in the Prophecies."

We sat silent for a couple of moments, listening to Sirius's snores as his head rested on Virgo's leg.

"So what do we do with the Twins now?" Virgo said.

"We should let them go," Draco said with a sigh. "I don't think there's a lot more they can do to help us."

"No," I said, maybe a bit too quickly. Draco and Virgo stared at me. "I want to lie again, see if I can get some more information."

Draco nodded, and his pupils expanded again. Virgo didn't argue either. The Twins probably wouldn't be helpful in finding Perseus, but I wanted to know more about what Perseus had told them about my memories. I had the feeling the Twins knew more than they had revealed today, and I would get the truth from them one way or another.

"We need to find Perseus," Virgo said, clutching the edge of her knitted purple sweater.

"And we will," Draco said. He looked at me, then at Virgo. "We'll find him."

"Maybe Orion would have been able to help us track him," Virgo said, "if he had ever come back with Andromeda."

I gritted my teeth. I hadn't thought of Andromeda and Orion for a couple of days, but at their mention fury rose inside my chest. Andromeda was responsible for the mess we were in. She had helped Perseus find Alathea's book, even though she hadn't known what he had truly planned to do with it—or that he had planned on killing her. She was the only person who could kill Perseus, the Prophecies said so, but she had failed to do it at the battle at Palatine Hill. Millions had died as a consequence—Perseus had caused the worst earthquake Italy had ever seen. Did Andromeda even care about that? After the battle she had just run away. We had sent Orion to find her, but he hadn't come back either.

They were both cowards, trying to escape their Prophecies as if the future was something they could run away from. Just as humans couldn't escape their Destinies, we couldn't escape our Prophecies.

My stomach began swirling, as if it were leaking acid, and I clenched my fists. I needed to find Perseus and get that book back from him. What would the Prophecies say about my past? Would they be able to fill in the gaps of my lost memories—that hole inside my mind? I had spent the last year not knowing anything about my past—my first memory was waking up in the hospital, shortly before Draco and Virgo found me. But before that, there was nothing—the first sixteen years of my life lost in the darkness. Except for that one memory that had resurfaced a couple of weeks ago . . . I tried not to think about it. That memory confused me more than it helped me.

I took a deep breath. Would the Prophecies also speak of my death? What would they foretell about my future? I didn't care if I was fated to die or be killed. The uncertainty of my future was worse than knowing for sure something terrible would happen. Whatever was prophesized to happen I could deal with it, accept it, but I *needed* to know—and only the Prophecies could give me an answer.

I wondered how humans did it, how they could live all of their lives without knowing what would happen. Some of them did look to the Stars to see their Fates and Destinies, to guide them toward their future. But most of them lived with uncertainty, walking blindly through life toward a certain Destiny that they were completely unaware of. I found living in uncertainty unbearable. I felt blind and lost, like an explorer without a map. I clenched my teeth. I would find those Prophecies.

"We don't need Andromeda and Orion," Draco said after a minute. "We can deal with this on our own."

Virgo pursed her lips. "I know we can deal with this. I just wish they would have stayed to help."

I looked out the broken window in the wall. The pink and orange clouds had disappeared from the sky, which had darkened into a marine blue. I rose to my feet, eyeing the room around us. The candle next to the couch flickered weakly. It occurred to me at that moment that we, the Star Children, were similar to candles. Our power was like a flame—the more we used it, the more it would burn and consume us. I looked back at Virgo, who stared at her scarred hands. Her fire had almost entirely consumed her, and again I wondered what she had done and if she would ever tell us.

Draco rose to his feet too. "I'm going to check on Leo and Maera. I'll be back soon."

"Check if there's anything at the butcher's shop that we can eat. Yesterday there was still some meat in the freezer," I said.

Draco nodded. He walked to the stairs and disappeared inside the darkness as he descended them.

Virgo stood and went back to the couch. From behind it, she pulled out the new sweater she had been crocheting and the metal hook she always used. I didn't know who the sweater was for. She lay the sweater out and began crocheting with yarn colored deep blue like the sea.

Virgo glanced up and noticed me looking. She smiled gently, and I smiled back. Virgo's sweaters, and everything else she knit, were special. Her sweaters always kept us warm, and nothing could break through them—not bullets, knives, or anything else. She had learned to knit from the Weavers, but that was a very sore subject, so we never asked her about it. But she had shared that the Weavers had taught her that weaving tied Fate and Destiny together.

I looked down at the olive green sweater she had made for me. I loved it—it was the only thing I liked to wear. It made me feel safer, and I appreciated that it kept me warm during the coldest nights.

Sirius got up from the floor and climbed onto one side of the couch, curled himself into a ball, and closed his eyes to go to sleep. I envied the Dog sometimes. He could fall asleep so easily.

I sat on the mattress a couple of feet away from Virgo. Her fingers hooked into my curls. "You need a haircut," she said.

"I'll get one as soon as I find a barber shop." My hair now curled below my ears. I didn't mind it much but knew it would start to irritate me once it grew a bit more.

"You could also ask Draco to cut it with his dragon claws," Virgo suggested.

I laughed. "I'll consider it."

Virgo pulled her hand away from my hair. "You should go to sleep."

"It's still early," I said as I looked out the window. I didn't have a clock but I assumed it couldn't have been later than six.

"But you didn't sleep last night," she said. I bit my tongue. "Yes, Corvus, we do notice when you wake up and walk out of the room."

"Sorry I woke you up again," I said, turning around to face her. She looked intently at the sweater as she knit.

She shrugged. "I don't mind. I'm just worried about you." She paused. "I think your insomnia is getting worse."

"I'm fine," I said. "It's just trouble sleeping, Virgo. I don't know why you worry about it." Virgo stared at me with her lips pressed together, but I meant it. I did feel more tired sometimes, but my body could function properly. It wasn't that bad.

"Maybe you could try taking pills?" she suggested.

"They don't work," I muttered.

She bit her lower lip and nibbled on it for a few seconds. "I think that your problem may be more emotional or mental." I wondered if she had read a psychology book or something. "Your thoughts are keeping you awake. What are you thinking about when you go to sleep?"

"I try not to think about anything."

That was a lie, of course. My thoughts were always the loudest at night. I thought about everything. I thought about my Prophecies and what they would say about me. I thought about Perseus, wondering if he would kill us all. But mostly I thought about myself, wondering who I really was.

My thoughts went back to what the Twins had said. If Perseus was interested in my memories, then that meant he knew something about my past that I didn't. But what could it possibly be? I heaved a sigh. Tonight would be another long and restless night when I would get to ponder this question. Virgo began to hum, and after a couple more seconds she started singing.

When the night arrives, their souls awake again,
A new moon dark above them, and below the earth barren,
The flames they all follow, for fire is what Stars are made of,
Of home the memories they try to remember, but in the end forget.

I closed my eyes. Was Virgo trying to lull me to sleep with a song? It was working. The knots in my muscles relaxed, and my heartbeat slowed.

Without purpose they roam,
but with a hope they walk,
Soon they will be born again into a flesh of flames.

I wondered where Virgo had heard that song—she liked to sing it. It seemed to have a prophetic air to it. Maybe the Weavers had sung it to her. I wouldn't ask her about it though. Virgo would tell me if she wanted to. We all had our dark pasts, and while I knew Virgo tried to forget about hers, all I wanted was to remember mine.

I could feel myself drifting away, but just then Draco's footsteps echoed up the stairs. Virgo stopped singing, and I opened my eyes again to see Draco walking into the room. He held one large brown bag in each hand.

"Where are Leo and Maera?" I asked.

"They're still at the butcher shop," Draco said. "Leo hasn't finished eating. He's going to wait for nightfall to come back. There's still a couple of people on the streets, so it's better if he waits a while."

I didn't like that very much. With the Twins here, I would have preferred Leo to be with us in case something went wrong—as it usually did. Draco set the bags down in front of the mattress and pulled a small box out of one of them.

"What's that?" I asked.

19

Draco handed me the small plastic box and I held it. "It's chamomile tea. It helps to have a more restful sleep."

I clenched my teeth, putting the little box down next to me. "I'm fine, guys. I really am." How had he even found chamomile tea in a butcher shop?

"*Thank you* would have been a better answer," Draco said. "No problem, Corvus, just trying to take care of you."

"Thanks," I said. "But I'm fine."

Virgo shook her head. "Sleeping three hours every night is not fine."

I stood up from the mattress and walked toward the broken window, then sat down next to it to look outside. The sky had turned dark blue, and the clouds had drifted over to the horizon. The third floor of the building was high enough to see the destruction around us. This building had mostly withstood the earthquake, probably because it was made out of stone and only three stories tall. On the other side of the street, one building had completely crumbled. It must have been an apartment building in the upper floors. Within the rubble I spotted a ragged couch, a broken plasma TV, a white bathtub, and some blankets and pillows. I was surprised no one had stolen the pillows yet. Those were in short supply. I also assumed that the first floor had been a clothing store. White mannequins poked out of the rubble, and a few lay on the sidewalk. The first time I had looked out the window I had thought they were real dead people, and it had taken me a second to realize it was just plastic.

The rest of the buildings on the street hadn't fared much better. The ones that still stood had cracks on every wall, and most, if not all, windows were shattered. On one building down the street, the roof had collapsed inward, but the walls still stood. In the distance I could see several other ruined buildings. Rome had been such a vibrant city before, with throngs of people on the streets, colorful buildings tightly packed together, the smell of food drifting through the air, and art displayed on almost every block and plaza. But only the skeleton of that city remained—ragged and crooked bones that held no more life.

The streets were mostly empty. All tourists had left the city, fleeing north to cities like Milan and Turin or south to Naples. A lot of citizens had left too. Rome was mostly uninhabitable now, like a lot of cities in central Italy. Rome had suffered most of the destruction, but other cities around it had also been ruined. The Italian government had spent a lot of money clearing the debris and restoring the cities, but I hadn't seen much progress. Hospitals were still overcrowded and morgues too full to take any new bodies, so the government had to divert some funds there as well.

Once or twice a day, police cars would pass by slowly, but aside from those and the trucks that removed debris, I hadn't seen other cars driving through the streets. We didn't have electricity, and Internet access was down, so we barely knew what was happening in the country. We didn't care much either. Only Perseus mattered. What he had done here was only the beginning. He would only grow more powerful, killing millions more. But the Twins didn't know where he had escaped to, so now we would have to figure out another way to find him.

Maybe I could have stopped him, I thought. I was still angry that Draco hadn't let me fight Perseus because the fight was "too dangerous." I didn't have the physical strength or speed that Draco had, and I wasn't such a good fighter. But still, I had wanted to do something helpful. All I had done was hide with Virgo, Sirius, and Maera, carrying the black poodle as it trembled in my arms—not very heroic.

21

Sometimes I felt like the team didn't need me. I just lied. That was useful when we wanted to get free food at restaurants or to interrogate someone, but I couldn't really fight to protect us. I felt close to useless.

Behind me, Draco and Virgo talked about the different meats Draco had found. We would have sausages for dinner and a few cookies Draco had stolen from a store. I risked a glance behind me. Draco and Virgo sat next to each other on the couch, looking into each other's eyes as they talked about cookies. Virgo kept tracing circles over the cover of her book. The blue sweater lay abandoned on her lap. Draco seemed nervously tense, as if sitting too close to Virgo made his muscles contract. Sirius snored peacefully at Virgo's other side, curled into a ball. Then he farted, and I heard it all the way from the window. Virgo and Draco didn't seem to have noticed though, and if they smelled something neither of them said so. I turned to look outside again.

"Hey," Draco said, pulling my attention back to him. "What cookies do you want for dessert?"

"Which ones do we have?" I asked.

Draco looked inside the bag. "A few different ones. I also got some cheese. And how many sausages do you want?"

"I'll eat three," I said.

I stood up from the opening and walked over to Draco, to see what else he had brought for us.

"I'll have two sausages *per favore*," one of the Twins said from behind me.

Before I could turn around, a hand clasped over my mouth and the cold kiss of a blade bit my neck. It wasn't a white carved knife, so it wouldn't kill me, but even so, I would prefer not having my throat slashed.

Draco pulled the white knife from his back. Virgo let the

22

book fall from her lap and bolted upright. Sirius jumped from the couch, standing protectively in front of her. A growl rumbled out of his chest.

"No, no," said Castor as he tightened his grip on my mouth. "Put that knife down, Draco, or we'll cut Corvus's throat. We mean it this time."

Pollux stood next to me—a smile plastered across his face. He had pulled his hair into a tight ponytail. "Sorry, friend."

Castor's sweaty hand gripped me so tight that I felt he would crush my teeth. He sniffed next to me.

"Oh man! What's that smell?" Castor asked. "Is someone dying here?" I was absolutely sure that was Sirius's fart.

"Walk over to the window, Draco. You too, Virgo," Pollux said.

Without dropping the knife, Draco slowly stepped to the left side of the room. His flaming red eyes never left the knife at my throat. Virgo followed after him, and so did Sirius. Why did the Twins always threaten to hurt *me*?

Once Draco and Virgo stood in front of the window, Pollux rushed to the couch. I realized, too late, that he had just wanted to get Virgo and Draco away from the guns. Draco must have realized that, too, because a deep growl escaped from his mouth.

Pollux picked up both guns and pointed them at Virgo and Draco. Sirius barked like a mad dog, snapping his snout, and Draco pushed Virgo behind him. I struggled in Castor's grip and he held the knife closer to my throat.

"Calm down," Pollux said. "Do you seriously think we would shoot you? They're just dart guns."

"What?" Virgo asked as her head peeked from behind Draco's shoulder.

"According to Perseus, tranquilizing darts are very effective

23

on Star Children," Pollux said as he admired both guns.

Then he pulled the trigger four times. Draco and Sirius lunged forward. Sirius was a few feet in front of Pollux when he whimpered. One of the darts had hit him in the neck. He swayed and then landed on his side with his eyes closed. Draco managed to knock Pollux to the ground. They fell in a tangle, Draco on top of Pollux. Then Pollux kicked Draco away from him. Draco fell on his back, two darts sticking out of his chest. Draco stayed on the floor with his eyes closed and his breathing slow. In front of the opening, Virgo already lay on her back, a dart sticking from her arm. Pollux then pointed the gun at me.

"Sorry, friend." He paused. "Actually, I'm not sorry for this." He smiled and pulled the trigger. I grunted as I felt a pinch in my chest. "No more lies."

Chapter XXXIX, Verse II

His words believed by many, even if lies they may become.
The Liar's past now forgotten and a new future to forge.
By the Trees he has been warned, and by the Seven Sisters advised,
But from the Demon Prince to hide, to escape his plans.
Lies to him are spoken, even if truths they shall turn into,
To escape his cruel heart, or to die by valiant deeds.
Only the turbulent Sea may save him from his fall.

CHAPTER 2

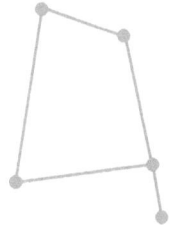

WHEN I WOKE UP, my head felt heavy. I opened my eyes. A floor-to-ceiling window faced me. Outside, the ocean stretched to the horizon. The water shimmered like tiny stars covering the surface as it reflected the sun. The tranquilizing dart must have knocked me out for hours. I realized that this was probably the first time in weeks that I had slept for more than three or four hours during the night, although I would have preferred that it had happened under different circumstances.

Someone moaned to my right. I turned to see Virgo and Draco tied to separate chairs, Virgo in between us. Tape covered their mouths, and their hands were bound behind their backs. A rope around their chests tied them to their chair. I was tied the same way. My wrists itched from the rope when I moved. I tried to pull my hands apart but the rope painfully dug through my skin. I groaned. Virgo and Draco just stared silently at me.

I glanced around the room. Behind us was a closed door. Next to the door sat a long glass table and three other chairs. So we were trapped in a dining room? Where had the Twins taken us? And where was Sirius? I thought about Leo, Aquila, and Maera too. They must have realized by now that we were missing. I could only hope that they found us, wherever we were, and that Leo bit off the Twins' heads.

Dizziness suddenly overtook me, and the whole room began to sway. It took me a couple of seconds to realize that the room *was* indeed swaying. Were we in a ship? I stared out the window again. We were at least a few stories above the ocean surface, and the floor slightly shifted up and down as we cut through the water.

I cursed the Twins inside my head. How had they escaped? And where had Castor found the knife? It didn't even matter anymore, but it angered me that they had taken us by surprise. But I mostly worried that we were on the ocean. The Twins could manifest their full power at the sea. They could materialize storms and shipwrecks—two things that I wasn't very excited about experiencing.

The door creaked open, and both Twins walked in. They closed the door behind them, walked toward the window, and stood in front of it. Pollux now had his hair tied in a small braid, and Castor had combed his back with gel. Their dark blue eyes reflected the color of the ocean outside.

"Before you ask," Castor said. "Your friend Sirius is fine. He's in another room."

Virgo sighed in relief.

"We would never hurt a dog," Pollux said. "Especially not a famous one."

"How's Sirius's new movie going by the way?" Castor crossed his arms. "We're excited to see him on the big screen again."

None of us answered.

As the main Star in Canis Major, Sirius was the luckiest Star in the Heavens. It gave wealth, riches, and fame. Sirius the Star Child had always attracted attention wherever he went, and we had taken advantage of that. Sirius's acting jobs gave us enough money to live comfortably. We hadn't talked to directors since the earthquake in Italy, but Hollywood was a problem for another day.

"Now," Pollux said. "You must all be wondering what you're doing here."

Again, we didn't answer.

Castor walked over to Virgo and removed the tape from her mouth. She spat on his face.

Pollux chuckled. "Ha! That's the second girl that's spit on you today." Castor simply wiped the spit from his cheek. "You're building yourself a bad reputation on this ship. How do you expect to find a girlfriend here if all the girls keep spitting on you?"

Castor ignored his brother as he stepped back.

"Are you working with Perseus?" Virgo asked.

I knew they would only let her talk because if they took the tape off my mouth I would lie and Draco would probably burn them to ashes.

"When have we ever worked with Perseus?" Pollux said. A couple seconds of silence passed. I squirmed in my bonds, but they only seemed to tighten around my chest. "No, we're not working with him."

"We're simply *doing business* with Perseus," Castor said.

"That's the same thing as working with him!" Virgo groaned in frustration.

"No," Pollux said, pulling a stray strand of hair out of his face. "We made a deal—an exchange really. He gives us something and we give him something in return."

What could Perseus possibly have offered the Twins? And more importantly, what had they offered to give him?

29

"What did Perseus offer you? You can't trust him. Didn't you see the destruction he caused in Rome? The earthquake killed millions."

"We don't care how many he kills," Castor said.

"We're fine as long as he doesn't kill *us*," said Pollux.

Virgo muttered something under her breath.

Castor pulled a sheet of thick yellowish paper from his jeans pocket, unfolded it and held it up toward us. It had jagged edges, as if it had been burned. Seven lines of text were written in dark red ink at the very center. "This is what he offered us."

"One of Alathea's Prophecies," Virgo said, her face pale.

"*Our* Prophecy," Castor said.

"He gave us this one as down payment," Pollux said. "He'll give us the other two once we have given him what he wants."

"Only three?" Virgo asked. "I'm pretty sure you have more than three Prophecies, and I'm guessing Perseus will only give you the least important ones. He'll keep the others." The Twins stayed silent. "Can't you see he's using the Prophecies to manipulate us all into the future he wants?"

Pollux shrugged. "Don't worry too much about our Prophecies, Virgo. For now, we're happy to have this one."

"How do you even know it's real?" she asked.

Castor looked down at the paper, reading it. "Looks legit to me."

Virgo glanced at Draco and me, desperation swimming in her eyes.

"What will you give Perseus in exchange?" Virgo asked.

The Twins looked at the three of us. "Rest assured, he doesn't want you," Castor said. He folded the Prophecy again and put it inside his pocket.

I let out a breath I didn't realize I had been holding.

"Perseus just wants what you're prophesized to find," Pollux said with a smile.

My gut clenched.

"Apparently the three of you, and the Dog, are prophesized to find a very important treasure," Castor said.

Something about that didn't sit right with me. Why would Perseus send the Twins to kidnap us instead of doing it himself? This meant Perseus wanted to find a treasure but didn't want to hunt for it himself—either because it was too dangerous or because he was just too lazy. My gut told me it had more to do with the former, but that didn't fit with Perseus's character. He would never send someone else to do work for him. He wouldn't risk any treasure getting away from his possession. I was missing something about his plan, and I had no idea what it was.

"Perseus was very clear that he wanted to keep you all alive, including the Dog." Castor turned to me. "Especially you, Corvus. Like we told you before, Perseus seemed very interested in your memories." He stared intently at my face. "I can't imagine what could be so important about them."

Draco and Virgo both turned to look at me, their gazes questioning. I avoided looking at them and kept staring at the Twins.

"Don't give me that face," Castor said to me, then turned to Virgo and Draco. "Come on, friends. This will be a fun adventure. Just the five of us, and Sirius, going treasure hunting."

"This will be fun," Pollux agreed.

They walked around us and exited the room.

"What memories?" Virgo asked as soon as they had left.

Draco raised a brow at me.

"Mmmm," I said, indicating that I couldn't really talk with the tape on my mouth.

Virgo didn't seem to consider that a worthy excuse as she stared questioningly at me. I leaned my head back so I could stare at the white ceiling. *We're doomed*, I thought. How would we escape the Twins? And how would we escape Perseus's plans? This was why he was so dangerous with those Prophecies. He had already started to manipulate the Star Children like chess pieces to get the exact outcome that he wanted. But we couldn't know how to escape his game if we didn't know what the game was. If we were prophesized to find some sort of treasure, then we probably would, but I wondered why it would be so valuable to him. I knew how Perseus operated; he didn't want treasures just to have them. This would give him more power.

I detected movement next to me and realized that Draco had stood up. He pulled the tape from his mouth.

"Mmmm?" I asked.

Draco showed me his hand. His fingers had elongated, becoming twisted like gnarled tree roots, and his nails had turned into deadly long claws. Virgo smiled at the sight of them, although I was sure no one else on the planet ever would. Draco used his claws to undo the ropes binding Virgo, and then he walked over to me. Virgo removed the tape from my mouth and Draco cut the ropes around my chest and wrists.

"Nice," I said as his hands shifted back to normal.

I stood up. My legs felt stiff, and I wondered how long I had been sitting on that chair. I turned to the door behind me. I hadn't heard the Twins lock it. Virgo walked over to it, and Draco and I followed her. She looked at both of us, nodded, and turned the handle.

Draco and I burst into the next room, which was a bedroom. The Twins weren't there, which was a relief. A muffled bark drew our attention to the left side of the room. Sirius had a muzzle and was chained to the wall. As soon as he saw us, he wagged his short tail.

Draco knelt at Sirius's side, removed the muzzle, then cut the chain with his claws. Sirius licked Draco's hand as his tail wagged even faster. Virgo hugged Sirius's neck.

"Let's leave before the Twins come back," I said.

Draco nodded and got to his feet. He extended a hand to Virgo and she stood too. I opened the outer door and peeked out, then walked into the red-carpeted hallway with wooden doors on each side. Draco, Sirius, and Virgo came after me, closing the door behind them.

The hallway had bright white lights next to every door. I decided to walk to the right, and the others followed. At the end of the hallway, I turned left. A small group of people waited outside a glass elevator, and opposite to that, wide stairs curled to the floors above and below.

"Is this . . .?" Virgo asked.

"I think we're in a cruise ship," I said.

How had the Twins gotten us inside a cruise ship? I decided not to waste time thinking about that.

"We have to get out of here," Draco said. He turned to me. "You could lie to the captain and tell him to take the ship back to Rome."

"Why Rome?" Virgo asked.

"Where else could we go?" Draco asked.

"We could go to the house we rented in Spain," I suggested. "To lay low for a while."

"What about Alathea's book in Rome?" Virgo asked.

My stomach twisted with a pull of anxiety, and my hands went numb. Virgo was trying to hold onto the last string of hope that the book may still be there—but going back to Rome would be a waste of time. "At this point I think it's safe to say Perseus has it and is looking for something new." I sighed.

"Corvus is right," Draco said with a nod. "We should lay low for a while and plan what to do next."

"Fine," Virgo said with a sigh. "But we don't even know where we are. And how will we get to the captain so Corvus can lie to him?"

"My guess is that we're somewhere in the Mediterranean," I said. "Let's just try to find some crew members. They should know where the captain's cabin is."

Virgo glanced nervously around us. "The Twins must be nearby. Let's stay alert."

As if her mention of the Twins had invoked them in the flesh, a yell came from behind us: "Hey!" one of the Twins shouted from the hallway.

I didn't turn to see which one it had been. "Run!"

The four of us broke into a sprint, Sirius leading the way. The people at the elevator made way for us. We exited through a sliding glass door, then ran through the side deck as fast as we could. We raced parallel to the railing. Below it the sea stretched as far as I could see. Sirius's big ears flapped with the wind as he led the way, and the salty air blew cold in our direction. Several people walked through the side deck as well, but as soon as they saw us, they moved out of our way. I risked a look back, but the Twins were nowhere to be seen.

We raced up the metal stairs at the end of the deck. I stopped to catch my breath at the top of the stairs. Directly in front of us, dozens of people played volleyball in the pool with a colorful beach ball. Under the shade of a curving roof, people ate and drank at a poolside bar.

Sirius looked around, his posture tall and alert.

"Where are the Twins?" Draco asked.

"They weren't following behind us," I said.

"I don't like that," Virgo said.

"Me neither," I said.

Most of the people on the upper deck didn't spare us more than a glance, but some of them did stare at Sirius for more than a couple of seconds. Draco pointed toward the bar.

"I'm pretty sure we can ask one of the bartenders if they know where the captain's cabin is," he said.

I nodded and walked over to the bar. Draco, Virgo, and Sirius stood behind me, keeping watch in case the Twins came back.

I glanced at the name tag pinned below the bartender's shoulder. "Alex," I said. My scars burned, but the pain felt much fainter than when I had lied to the Twins. Lying to humans was always easier. "Where can I find the captain?"

"Excuse me?" he asked.

"You just want to tell me where I can find the captain of this ship," I said. My voice sounded as if I had spoken underwater.

The bartender's stare went blank. "Yes, of course." He looked at his watch. "The captain must be in the control room right now." He pointed in the direction away from the bar, somewhere behind the pool. "If you walk past the pool and go down the stairs you'll find a hallway. At the end of that hallway, you will find the control room. But you won't have access to—"

"Thank you," I said and turned away.

The four of us walked toward the pool. I couldn't see any stairs leading down. Maybe we just had to get closer.

The ship swung to the side, as if we had hit a giant rock. I fell forward and landed on top of Sirius. The dog barked, and screams erupted around us.

"Sorry, boy," I said as I jumped back to my feet, my heart racing. "What the hell just happened?" I asked no one in particular. Sirius shook himself.

The boat had stopped moving. People gathered at the side of the ship and looked down. A woman pushed herself away from the railing and shouted in panic.

"The ship is sinking!" she screamed.

I could feel my stomach twisting as if it had tied itself into a knot. "I really hate the Twins."

CHAPTER 3

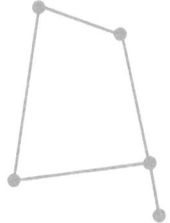

"WE'RE SINKING!" the woman shouted again.

She rushed down the stairs, still screaming, and disappeared from sight. People inside the pool rushed out in panic as if they'd realized that the water had poison in it. A man hugged the colorful beach ball as he rushed away toward the glass doors behind the bar. A pair of children cried for their parents, who rushed into the pool, fully clothed, and pulled them out. People from the bar raced back inside the ship, most of them still holding their cocktails.

My heartbeat went into a full race. What would we do now? Where were the Twins? Could they be reckless enough to sink the ship? I knew the answer to that last question already. Panic pulsed inside my veins.

Calm down, I told myself. *You can fix this. Every problem has a solution.* But how would I fix a sinking ship? I cursed the Twins inside my head again. How could they be so stupid? How would sinking the ship help them achieve anything?

The speakers turned on, and a voice shouted for us to go to our muster stations, whatever that meant. The upper deck emptied in less than a minute.

"Shouldn't we go to the muster stations too?" Virgo asked nervously.

"Yes," I said.

Sirius agreed with a bark.

"That's what the Twins would want us to do," Draco said.

"We don't really have much of a choice, Draco!" I said, feeling my heartbeat pulsing at the tips of my fingers. "It's either that or we drown!"

Draco shook his head slowly. How was he always so calm? "The Twins obviously caused this," he said. "They'll expect us to get into the lifeboats. We should do something else."

"Like what?" I demanded.

"We don't really have any other option besides getting into the lifeboats." Virgo shifted her weight from one foot to the other.

"I'm not sure," Draco admitted. "I just know that when it comes to the Twins, we shouldn't be so predictable."

"There isn't a lot we can do in a *sinking ship*," I said.

I could feel the ship lowering slowly and shifting to one side, so I had to plant my feet on the floor to avoid sliding away.

Draco looked at the empty stairs curling down. "The Twins could be waiting for us."

"This is a big ship, Draco," Virgo said. "I'm sure we can blend in with the crowd."

I wondered how the Twins had materialized the ship to sink. Maybe the engines had blown up? Or a giant crack had suddenly materialized at the bottom of the ship? We were in the middle of the Mediterranean, so we likely hadn't crashed against anything.

"How is waiting here better than being in a lifeboat?" Virgo asked.

Draco seemed to consider that. "Fine," he said. "Let's get to the lifeboats, but I still think that's a bad idea."

"We have no other ideas," I pointed out.

I breathed in relief as we headed to the stairs.

38

"Anyone know where the muster stations and lifeboats are?" Virgo asked.

"No idea," Draco said.

We descended to the floor below, then advanced through the cruise ship slowly. Draco wouldn't let us round a single corner before peeking at the next hallway to ensure that the Twins weren't there. It was eerily quiet inside the ship, but the silence was interrupted at irregular intervals by the creaking of metal as the ship continued to tip to the side.

After a while we arrived to one of the lower decks which I assumed was one of the muster stations. As soon as we stepped into the crowd, the noise overwhelmed me. People shouted random names that blurred together. Everyone around us already had bright orange life vests and waited their turn to get inside the boats.

My chest continued to tighten, as if my ribs were compressing my organs into a sandwich. My breaths were short and my hands twitched. Everything would be all right. I just had to get us inside one of those boats and we would be away from the sinking ship. But what would we do after? Where would the boats take us?

Draco grabbed my shoulder and pulled me forward. He had somehow found a pair of sunglasses to hide his reptile eyes. The deck was so crowded that I couldn't walk a single step without having to push past elbows, arms, and people's backs. I caught pieces of people's conversations.

"Will we die?" a little boy asked his mother.

"I should have stayed home," a young man said to my right.

"You see, Nadia," a man with a receding hairline told a middle-aged woman. "I told you *Titanic* wasn't a ridiculous movie. Cruise ships *do* sink."

We made our way around everyone to get to the front of one of the lines.

"Hey!" A bearded man complained behind us.

I turned around. The crowd glared angrily at us for cutting the line, as if ready to fight us or push us off the ship.

"We were next in line!" I shouted. My voice sounded shrill inside my ears, and my scars burned. For some reason the scar on my leg hurt more than usual. I bit my tongue.

The crowd relaxed at once, their expressions slacking. I turned around again just in time to see Sirius jumping into a raft.

"Where's the lifeboats?" I asked as the raft wobbled under Sirius.

"There's no more space in them, we only have these rafts left," someone said behind me.

Virgo climbed in after Sirius. A man in an orange vest with a large radio in his hand eyed the dog suspiciously.

"Miss," the man said to Virgo, who was hugging Sirius. "Animals can't—"

"Animals can go inside the rafts too," I quickly said to the man, who went quiet.

I climbed onto the circular raft, and Draco came last. We squeezed ourselves in the back of the raft. A few more people climbed into the raft after us. We were the only ones not wearing a life vest, but it was too late to get one now. The raft began descending. Thick cords slowly lowered the raft onto the water. The small circular windows from the side of the ship slid past us. They brightly reflected the light from the sun, so I couldn't see inside.

What if the raft sank too? What if I got tired of swimming and drowned? What if—?

"We'll be all right," Draco said as he patted my shoulder. He hooked an arm around Virgo and looked out at the sea. "Everything will be fine."

Everything wouldn't be fine. I knew that. How could things be *fine*? We were in a raft in the middle of the Mediterranean Sea. That was far from *fine*. The Twins must have been somewhere close—I could almost feel them—and I knew they wouldn't let us go that easily. Below us was a cluster of many bright orange lifeboats and rafts floating on the water.

Our raft landed on the water a bit roughly, making me jump a few inches then drop back down. Multiple groans and screams burst around me. The raft began to move away from the ship, toward the open sea. Were there strong currents at the open sea? Our raft seemed to be moving quite fast. We floated past other rafts and boats. A little girl on a raft to my right cried next to her mother, holding a monkey plush toy to her orange vest.

I couldn't spot anything around the cruise ship that could have possibly sunk it. I was sure it had been the Twins. A sudden gust of wind blew around us, howling as it ruffled my hair. It seemed to have a life of its own, pulling at my shirt, pushing against my skin, moving in random directions.

"Why is our raft moving so far from the ship?" A woman asked in front of me.

She seemed too small for her vest, as if she had shrunk inside it. Her bulging brown eyes darted around us. We had drifted at least twenty yards from the closest lifeboat, and we continued to float away. Why were we still moving so fast?

"Hey!" a man from one of the lifeboats waved his arms at us as he stood by the railing. We kept drifting away, the wind pushing us along. We were at least thirty yards from the rest of the cluster of boats. The cruise ship continued to sink deeper into the water.

The woman who had spoken screamed. "We're sinking!"

Then she jumped out of the raft a second later. People around us screamed, and they quickly jumped into the ocean one after the other, splashing into the water. I wasn't sure that was the best option, but they all seemed to be driven by panic instead of logic. A man next to me stood. Water pooled around his shoes. He pulled his phone from his jeans pocket, held it high above his head, then jumped into the water, keeping the phone above the surface.

"You've got to be kidding me," I muttered under my breath.

"We should have stayed on the ship," Draco said in a quiet voice.

"We would have sunk anyway!" I said.

Sirius barked at the water, as if that would make it go away. He pressed himself further to the side, where the water hadn't reached yet. The remaining people inside the raft jumped into the ocean too.

"Should we jump?" Virgo asked.

Before Draco or I could respond, the raft shot forward with a blast of wind. Virgo screamed and Sirius howled. I slid across the raft, through the cold water, and hit my back against one of the edges. I groaned, my gaze set on the clear sky above us. The wind howled louder—I could have sworn it was laughing at us.

Then the raft abruptly stopped a few seconds later. I shot to the other side of the raft again, gliding over water until my back collided with Sirius. He barked at me.

"Sorry, boy," I said as I struggled to my feet, which were completely submerged in the ice-cold water. The soft floor wobbled underneath me, making it hard to remain standing.

In the distance, about a mile away, the cruise ship continued sinking. Orange spots floated around it. How had we traveled so far away?

"We should have stayed on the boat," Draco said again as he stood with his arms outstretched at his sides to maintain his balance.

The wind died down as the cold water gripped my ankles. Sirius barked at the water again. The raft was sinking on one side. Virgo tried to walk backward, away from the water, but slipped, and would have fallen on her back if Draco hadn't caught her waist.

"Thanks," Virgo muttered as she looked up at Draco's eyes.

"Anytime," he said with a smile.

They stared at each other for a second before breaking apart. Sirius climbed onto the edge of the raft so he could stay above the water. He must have had great balance, because he stayed upright on the thin edge even as the raft wobbled below us. His claws embedded into the raft like a bird with its claws gripped tightly on a wire.

"Now what do we do?" I asked, once again feeling the surge of panic.

We didn't have any life vests. We could drown. Were there sharks in the Mediterranean? The cruise ship was so far away. I looked around us. There were no other ships, and I couldn't spot a strip of land. We were literally stranded in the middle of the sea.

"I think we're going to have to swim," Draco said dully.

He jumped into the water. His head disappeared for a second, and Sirius barked at the spot where he had disappeared, trembling.

Draco's head bobbed up. He didn't have the sunglasses anymore. He chuckled. "I haven't been in the ocean in so long."

The numbingly cold water rose up to my knees. I took in a deep breath. *Better sooner than later,* I thought, then jumped into the water. The cold wrapped around me, and I kicked my legs to swim upward, but just then a slicing pain broke through my skull.

I groaned, trying to hold my breath. For a second, I couldn't feel my body.

"Corvus!" someone shouted my name. I was drowning, sinking. No matter how many times I tried to get to the surface, the waves crashed above my head and pulled me back down. I was drifting, floating within the endless cold. My chest was warm, blood flowing out of it.

"CORVUS!"

The flashback ended abruptly, and the ocean embraced me back into the present. Something had changed inside me. I could feel it. Like I had opened a black box I hadn't known had been closed. I opened my eyes, and for a split second spotted something moving below me—a dark blur. I shut my eyes tight and opened them again, but the blur was gone. I kicked upward and my head broke the surface. I took in a gulp of air. Virgo wasn't in the raft anymore. Her head popped up a few feet away from mine a couple of seconds later, her brunette hair floating around her. Her freckles had turned a shade darker.

What had just happened to me? Had that been one of my other memories? I guessed it had been just a sliver of one. The scars on my chest burned. Had I gotten that while in the ocean as that strange memory suggested? But how?

"Come on, Sirius," Virgo said to the dog, pulling me out of my thoughts. "It's all right, boy."

I turned back to the raft that still floated a couple of feet in front of me. Sirius's head floated inches above the water. His dark brown eyes bulged out of their sockets, and his ears were thrown back. He looked at each of us in turn.

"It's all right, boy," I said. "It's just water."

His eyes seemed to bulge out even more, as if I had told him that he had to swim in lava. He extended his paw, grazing the surface, then pulled it back with a low growl.

"It's all right, Sirius," Virgo said sweetly. "It's not that cold."

The dog swallowed.

"Come on, boy," Draco encouraged him. "The water's not that bad."

"I'll let you sleep in my bed if you jump in," said Virgo.

Sirius stared at Virgo for a second, then jumped into the sea. Water splashed all around us. Sirius's head bobbed up from the water. His ears were still thrown back, and his eyes were wide with terror. Virgo moved closer to him.

"It's okay, Sirius," she said, then gave him a kiss on the head.

The howling wind began to blow around us, softly at first. Then it intensified, the wind blasting at my face, creating sharp waves around us. Sirius howled too. A small wave crashed against me and my head submerged for a moment. Another stab of pain shot through my head.

"I think he's dead," she said.

"No!" another person shouted. "Come on, Corvus. Don't leave me. Please don't leave me."

Frigid air surrounded me. My whole body was numb. Something crackled in the distance, thunder roaring in rage.

"Come on, Corvus," another female voice said, her tone sweet like honey. "We can't lose you too." Her voice cracked like glass.

The voices were fading. Only the cold remained, peeling my skin away until it reached my bones. My chest was tight, as if someone was sitting on it. Then I felt something warm on my lips. A rhythmic pressure began to throb in my chest, just like the faint beat at the tips of my fingers.

"WAKE UP!"

I breathed.

My head broke the surface again, and I spat out water.

The wind abruptly died down. Virgo gasped somewhere to my right.

"Quickly! Get on!" one of the Twins shouted behind me.

45

I turned around, kicking my legs to keep my head above the surface. Castor and Pollux were on an orange raft. They both knelt at the edge. I expected to see them smiling, but their eyes were wide with fear.

"I'd rather drown," I hissed. The raft came inches away from my face.

"You don't have to be dramatic, Corvus." Pollux leaned down, grabbed me under my arms, and pulled me into the raft before I could even protest. He let me fall with a grunt. A puddle of water began to form around me as my clothes dripped. A large backpack sat at the edge of the raft, and I wondered what it had inside. I looked down at myself and realized that my sweater wasn't wet, but that wasn't very helpful because the rest of my body and clothes were soaked. Sirius barked, and Pollux pulled him out of the water. Sirius stayed still as a statue as Pollux carried him, and once Pollux set him down, he shook himself. He came over to my side. His ears were still thrown back, but at least his eyes were normal again as he glared at the Twins. I pushed myself to my knees.

Castor pulled up Virgo, holding her by the waist, while Pollux extended his hand to help Draco climb on board. Once Draco was sitting on the floor next to Virgo, Castor nodded.

"Let's roll!" he said. The raft shot forward as if propelled by an invisible motor. I was thrown to the side. The wind howled around me.

"Where are you taking us?" I demanded as I pushed myself into a sitting position. "And why would you be stupid enough to sink an entire cruise ship?"

"People could have died!" Virgo screamed through the wind.

"That was quite an unfortunate event," Castor said, his teeth clenched as his gaze locked on the horizon. "I had been looking forward to karaoke night on the upper deck."

"But we weren't the ones who sank the ship," Pollux said, his eyes also narrowed in concentration.

"Oh really?" I said as the air buffeted my face. "If it wasn't you, what was it? An iceberg?"

"It was that damned Monster again," Castor said. Virgo and Draco looked at me. That had not been a lie. I shook my head.

"What Monster?" Draco said.

The Twins didn't answer, their focus sharp ahead, as if the Monster they had mentioned was chasing us. After a few minutes of riding in silence, we slowly came to a stop. The Twins both heaved, as if they had just run a marathon. They sat down next to each other on the edge of the raft, a few feet away from us.

"You're welcome," Castor said as he looked at each of us in turn, including Sirius.

"For what?" I asked.

"For saving you from that Monster," Pollux said in between breaths.

"What Monster?" Draco asked again.

"Cetus?" Virgo asked.

The name sounded familiar. Cetus was another Star Child, a hybrid of many different sea creatures.

Pollux nodded. I still detected no lies.

"Why would Cetus sink a cruise ship?" Draco asked.

"Because we were on it," Castor said.

"That Monster has been chasing after us for years," Pollux kneeled again. "It didn't attack us directly though. He could have easily destroyed that ship and eaten us."

"It's taunting us again," Castor said.

I didn't care about the sea Monster at the moment, although I briefly wondered if it had been the blur I had seen underwater. I only cared about getting our Prophecies back from Perseus.

"You both just want to tell us the truth." My voice rang inside my ears. The Twins turned to look at me, their gazes distant. "You want to tell us all the truth because you can't bear to keep it a secret any longer."

"We can't," Castor said.

"It's unbearable," Pollux agreed.

Draco stepped closer to me. He pulled his dripping hair back with his hand as he stared at the Twins. The vertical slits in his red-orange eyes narrowed.

"Then tell us *all* of the truth," I said. "What were you planning to do with us?"

"The cruise ship was supposed to take us to Egypt," Castor said, his stare blank as he looked at the horizon. "We tried using our Ship but it didn't want to show up. Maybe Cetus drove it away."

My chest was so tight as it crushed my lungs, but I knew I had to hold this lie.

"How did you get us all into the ship?" Draco said.

"Perseus gave us the tickets. We smuggled you in suitcases," Pollux said.

Sirius growled in indignation.

"I don't even want to know how you did that," Draco said.

My entire body burned, but my thoughts were clear enough to understand that Perseus had planned this through. He seemed very desperate to get whatever we were supposed to find.

"What's in Egypt?" Virgo asked.

"He didn't say," Castor said. "He just told us to go to a temple in Egypt and that you guys would find something there."

"He asked us to take the treasure back to him," Pollux said.

"Why are you really working with Perseus?" Virgo asked them.

48

"You want to answer her," I said, my voice strained.

The Twins looked at each other. The scars on my chest felt like they were bleeding acid, burning all of my skin and bone.

"We need our other two Prophecies," Castor said.

"Why?" Virgo asked.

It took Pollux a second to answer. "One of us will die." His tone was flat and emotionless.

"Perseus didn't say how, or which one of us it would be," Castor said. "If we give him the treasure, he'll give us our Prophecy so we will know how to avoid it."

I couldn't hold it anymore. I coughed wildly as I let go of the lie. I felt like I had breathed in ashes.

"Damn you, Corvus," Castor muttered.

I rested my back against the edge of the raft. I didn't know if I was soaked with sweat or seawater. At least I didn't feel cold anymore.

"Well," Castor said as he glared at me. "Now you know the truth. Happy?"

I was in fact *not* happy. But now we knew why the Twins were really working with Perseus. Pollux surveyed the open water, which was completely calm. Tension clouded his eyes, as if at any second the Monster would emerge from the waves and our raft would need to shoot forward again. I wasn't sure we could be safe from the Monster while still at sea, but the Twins didn't seem to sense any immediate threat. Was sensing danger at sea even one of their powers? I hoped so.

Pollux looked at Virgo. "You said that Perseus might be hiding the rest of our Prophecies. But do you think the one about our deaths is real?"

Virgo sighed. "Perseus doesn't give empty threats or offers. I'm sorry, guys, this Prophecy must be true." Castor hung his head low, but Pollux still stared at Virgo. "And yes, each Star Child has at least five Prophecies, from what I know. Perseus probably won't want to give you the rest because they may help him manipulate you in the future."

"I don't really know how one of our Prophecies could be more important than the one about our death," Castor said.

"Your deaths are probably the least of Perseus's worries," I said. "He has other important things he cares more about. Like how to destroy Fate and Destiny and let Darkness rule the Universe." I shook my head, and more water dripped from my hair. "You really shouldn't trust Perseus."

"One of your other Prophecies must have something important about the future—a certain event Perseus may want to avoid or maybe an event he wants to get to." Virgo sighed. "He has his own agenda. He'll manipulate us all with the Prophecies to get to a specific future he wants. We can't trust him."

Castor laughed, then pointed at me. "*He's* the one we shouldn't trust."

"*Me?*" I asked. I looked at Draco and Virgo but they just shrugged, as if arguing with the Twins was just useless.

"Your Constellation represents the Liar, the cheater, the deceiver, the betrayer," Castor hissed. "How are we supposed to trust *you?*"

I didn't know how to respond to that.

"Corvus and Virgo are right," Draco said, ignoring what the Twins had just said. "Perseus doesn't play fair. He never has. He'll kill everyone in his path to achieve his goals."

"He will," Castor said. "But he's also the only one who has the Prophecies. If *you'd* found them—as you promised us you would—none of this would have happened."

"Yeah," Pollux agreed. "If you guys had found the Prophecies first, we wouldn't be here right now."

I gritted my teeth and cursed Andromeda inside my head. This was all her fault. And *we* were the ones who had to pay the price for her mistakes.

"We didn't find them," I said, trying not to let my anger filter through my voice, "but we can get them back from Perseus. We can recover all of our Prophecies."

Pollux huffed. "Will you just steal them from Perseus?"

"We'll try," Draco said with a smile.

"That's the stupidest idea I've heard," Castor said. "You can't just steal from Perseus. I think we'll follow through with his plan."

"That's not a very good idea either," Draco said as he crossed his arms.

The Twins didn't answer but only stared at us.

"Think about it, guys," Virgo said. "Why would Perseus send *you* to take us to Egypt? Why not kidnap us and take us himself?" Castor opened his mouth, but then shut it again. "Whatever he wants us to find, he doesn't want to be there when we find it." Virgo looked at both Twins. "My guess is that finding this treasure will be dangerous. Perseus doesn't want to risk his own life, or else he wouldn't have hired you."

The Twins remained silent.

"Virgo's right," Draco said. "I'm betting Perseus doesn't want to risk his own life finding . . . whatever it is we're supposed to find."

Pollux sighed. "I hate it when you guys make sense."

"Maybe if your peanut-sized brains had thought about this for a little longer, you would have known there was a catch to Perseus's offer," I said.

"We want our Prophecy," Pollux said. "Even if it's just the one that talks about one of our deaths." His lower lip twitched.

"We *will* get our Prophecy."

"What if we worked together?" Draco said. The Twins turned to look at him. "We all want the same thing. If we made a plan together, I'm sure we could steal our Prophecies back."

The Twins exchanged a glance.

"If something fails, then we risk losing our Prophecy," Pollux said. "And one of us will die."

"But if our plan works, then we could get *all* of your Prophecies, not just two more." Virgo said. "We could get the Prophecy of every single Star Child."

The Twins considered this. I knew that they had met other Star Children—Centaurus, Ophiuchus, Capricornus, Hercules, and several others we didn't know about. The Twins worked in trading information between Star Children. If they had the Prophecies of every Star Child, then they could trade those for anything they wanted. Though their blank expressions didn't betray any emotion, a malicious spark danced in their eyes. They shared another look between them, as if they could communicate telepathically.

"All right," Castor said. "What would be our plan?"

"I have an idea," I said.

Everyone turned to me. A very reckless plan began to unravel inside my head—one that would very probably get us killed, but it was worth a try.

"Hopefully it involves food," Castor said. "Because I'm very hungry. The ship sank before we ate lunch."

I ignored him. "We're going to follow through with Perseus's plan."

Chapter LII, Verse I

In the Sea they dwell, inside the prophetic Ship of oak.
The Ship that was once sailed by the Generations of Old.
The Twins the ocean will traverse, following the orders of the Prince,
To find the treasure that has long been lost, the one hidden by the King.
The power of the waves and wind they command, and the blue fire as well.
But they will obey the Ship only after an utterance has been made,
For the Ship knows well how their Fates will end.

CHAPTER 4

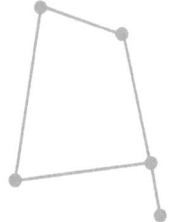

PAIN SHOT UP MY LEG, *and I bit back a grunt.*

"Maybe you should sit down again," Virgo suggested as she held my arm tighter, her grip barely keeping me upright.

"No," I managed through clenched teeth. "I'm fine. I need to start walking."

Virgo remained silent as I took a couple more steps on the cold hospital floor. The boot encasing my leg and foot thumped as I stepped forward. I hobbled toward the TV hanging from the wall, looking intently at the screen as I tried to ignore the pain. I pulled my hair back with my hand, away from my eyes. The screen showed Trafalgar Square in London. People walked on the street, right between the plaza and the National Gallery. I stopped walking. Virgo also stared intently at the screen. We had seen this video before—I had seen it so many times I had memorized certain things about it. The little girl jumping over a puddle as she held onto her mother's hand. A man in a suit reading from a tablet, an umbrella tucked under his arm.

I never made an appearance in this video, or any other video, but I knew that I had been somewhere to the left of this scene, close to the statue of James II—or at least that's where I assumed I had been, since that's where the paramedics had found me unconscious.

My heart drummed against my ribs, and my eyes darted toward the lower right corner of the screen.

My heart lurched. A young man with fiery red hair flashed into sight, trotting toward the National Gallery. Perseus looked around the plaza, as if trying to find someone he had lost. He stopped abruptly, as if he had collided with an invisible wall. Two seconds later, the explosion blasted out of the National Gallery. The screen burst with bright light, then the video cut out. I let out a breath I didn't realize I had been holding, and Virgo slowly guided me back to the bed. I sat down with a groan, all of my muscles sore.

I had been lucky—I had a broken leg, a cut in my calf, bruised ribs, a sprained wrist, and a concussion. But I was alive. Thirty-two people hadn't been so lucky.

"You should drink some water." Virgo walked to the small table next to the bed and grabbed the glass, then walked over to me again and put the cup to my lips. The cool water flowed down my throat, and Virgo pulled the glass away from me.

I looked back at the screen, but the news anchor was speaking now, and I couldn't tell what she was saying.

"None of them will ever suspect this was Perseus's fault, will they?" I asked, my voice almost a whisper.

Virgo shook her head. "They don't have any reason to." She placed the glass on the table with a loud thud. "They don't know the truth."

My tongue tasted like iron.

The truth.

Virgo had explained it to me, but I still had trouble wrapping my head around the information she had shared. Had I known that truth before? My memories still hadn't returned, even after two weeks, and I was beginning to worry. The doctors suspected that the concussion had caused amnesia, but when they had conducted a few brain scans, everything seemed normal. I let out a breath—I just needed to give it some time. And while I waited, I had Draco and Virgo to take care of me.

I was incredibly thankful they had found me. I didn't know what I would have done if I hadn't met them when I did—confused, in pain, and utterly alone. It was a miracle, I thought, a combination of coincidence and luck. They had been tracking down Perseus for months, following the terrorist attacks he had caused throughout Europe. It wasn't hard to know which attacks he had been responsible for—the demonic symbol of Algol, one of the Stars in Perseus's Constellation, always appeared near the attack site. Humans thought that the symbol belonged to some terrorist organization, and they would never have guessed the more sinister truth—Perseus was using Algol, the most dangerous and destructive Star in the sky, to kill thousands of people.

"I wonder what his end game is," I said. "I wonder if he's just practicing for something bigger, for something more destructive."

Virgo shrugged. "Maybe." She sat down next to me. "But only with the Prophecies will we be able to learn the truth."

"Right," I said. "The Prophecies of Alathea."

I still found it a bit hard to believe that a book of Prophecies existed out there, detailing the future of every Star Child.

"Has Draco found the translations we need?" I asked.

"We'll have to ask him when he comes back from the library."

Currently, we were looking for ancient Greek translations that contained the name Alathea, hoping that they would lead us to the mysterious prophet who had written the book and hidden it.

"*The sooner we get those Prophecies the better,*" Virgo said with a sigh. "*Perseus is becoming more dangerous. We need to know what he's planning, and we need to know how to stop him.*"

"*Are you sure the Prophecies will help us stop him?*"

Virgo nodded. "*All the Star Children have Prophecies that detail the different futures they might encounter, depending on their choices. We can't stop Perseus if we don't know what he's really planning, so the Prophecies will be able to detail that information. They might even reveal who and what can kill him.*" She looked at her hands, which were cracked with scars. "*He's up to no good. He already killed Cepheus, and he tried to kill Leo and Aquila, so we might be next.*"

Saliva flowed down my throat like lava. "*Do you think he was targeting me with the attack?*" I asked. "*Do you think he knew I was there?*"

"*I don't know,*" Virgo admitted.

Even if he hadn't known I was there, he had nearly killed me with that bomb. This was personal to me. It was his fault that I was stuck in this hospital, his fault that I had lost my memories and still hadn't recovered them, his fault that I had spent sleepless nights moaning in pain. Perseus hadn't placed the bomb and detonated it himself, but he had used Algol to manipulate people's minds into violence, causing them to kill others. He had indirectly caused thousands of brutal deaths around Europe.

My head spun with pain, and I closed my eyes.

"*You should lie down for a bit,*" Virgo suggested. She grabbed the boot and slowly lifted it up to the bed, then I swung my other leg up. With some effort, I lay down and stared up at the white ceiling. "*I should probably look at your leg again.*"

I just nodded.

Virgo slowly removed the boot and unwrapped the bandages from my leg as if she were peeling off layers from my skin.

"How's it looking?"

"The cut on your calf is healing well." Virgo's warm hand settled on my knee. "Your leg it's still swollen around the broken bone but much less than before."

She stood from the bed and walked to the other side of the room, opposite from the TV. The metal drawer creaked as she slid it open. She walked back to me a few seconds later, and I remained still as she wrapped the new bandages around my leg.

Virgo had provided most of my care over the past couple of weeks. I had lied constantly to keep the nurses and doctors away. I didn't trust them, and I feared they would see my scars shining in the dark and realize I wasn't human.

I sat on the edge of the bed again once Virgo had put the boot back on my leg. Hopefully I would be able to take that thing away soon. My walks around the room were becoming less painful, but it would probably be another few weeks before I could walk normally again.

Virgo stepped closer to me. "Your hair is a mess." She walked over to the table next to the bed and retrieved a comb from one of the drawers. She knelt behind me and slowly began combing my tangled and knotted hair. I could have combed it myself, but I didn't say anything. It would have felt awkward to have anyone else do that, but I felt a calmness with Virgo that made it seem like a simple gesture. "It looks like you haven't cut your hair in a year."

"That may be true."

"I might cut these knots myself if you don't," Virgo muttered.

I chuckled. My hair fell several inches below my ears now, and I constantly had to push it away from my face. I wondered when I had last gotten a haircut or if I had liked wearing it long.

Virgo finished combing my hair and set the comb down on the table, then sat on the bed a few inches to my side.

"Can you explain it to me again?" I asked after about a minute. "The difference between Prophecy, Fate, and Destiny?"

The concepts Virgo had shared were a bit confusing, and I was still wrapping my mind around them.

"Of course," Virgo said with a smile. "Destiny is given to each being at birth by the Stars. It cannot be changed or altered." She paused. "Fate is how you arrive at that Destiny—it's the different paths that lead to the same destination. Fate is governed by the Weavers, the Three Sisters at the bottom of the Celestial Ocean. They weave Fate into Destiny."

"But we don't have Destiny or Fate, right?" I asked. "As Star Children, we only have Prophecy."

Virgo nodded. "Humans also have Prophecies—it's a way for them to look into their futures and take a glimpse at their Fates and Destinies. But Prophecy is different for us. It's somewhere between Fate and Destiny. All Star Children have different Prophecies, and depending on our choices, we will arrive at a specific one."

"But no matter what we choose, we can never escape our Prophecies, right?"

Virgo shook her head, scratching her freckled cheek. "No. Any choice we take will eventually lead us to one of our prophesized futures. But if we have the Prophecies, we can make sure to choose our best future—one where we're safe from Perseus and Algol."

I wasn't sure how to feel about that. To a certain extent, we had free will but only as long as it remained within the bounds of our prophe-

sized future. So our choices did make a difference, but how much of a difference? I lay back down on the bed as my head started pounding.

"How did the Constellations even make us?" *I asked.* "How were we born out of the Stars?"

"I don't know." *Virgo stood up and extinguished the overhead light. In the partial darkness, my headache became a faint echo.* "The Book of Alathea supposedly says how that happened. But I imagine the Stars, with their power, materialized us into life and we inherited some of the power associated with the Constellation that created us."

"Why would the Stars and Constellations create us in the first place?"

"I don't know." *Virgo sat on the bed again.*

I could still see Virgo's freckled face, which seemed even more skeletal in the dark. Shadows moved across her face, and it took me a couple of seconds to realize that blinking light from my scars faintly flickered through my very thin robe.

The long scars on my chest were old, which meant I must have known I wasn't human for at least a few years. Contemplating this brought forth a myriad of questions about my past—how had I gotten my scars, where was I from, why was I here? More questions poured through my mind, but I had no answers to any of them. What if I never recovered any of my memories? Fear flooded inside my chest, weighing me down.

"Virgo? Do the Prophecies say more than just our futures? Do they explain who we are?"

Virgo didn't answer right away. She gripped the edge of her knitted sweater for a few seconds. "Possibly," *she said.* "I'm assuming they detail the decisions we've made to get to a specific future, so to a certain extent they must speak about our pasts." *She shrugged.* "Maybe this attack was one of your Prophecies. Maybe meeting each other and becoming friends was another Prophecy." A smile spread across her face.

I couldn't help but smile back. "Yeah, maybe."

My chest blazed with a renewed fire—a determination I hadn't felt since waking in the hospital. I would find those Prophecies. I needed them. If my memory failed, then the Prophecies were the only resource I had left that would reveal the truth to me.

Warmth filled my open palm, and it took me a second to realize that Virgo was holding my hand. She had never held my hand before, but I didn't pull back.

"You'll be all right, Corvus," she said with a gentle smile. "We'll figure out everything together."

I closed my hand around hers. "Thank you, for everything. I don't know what I would have done if you hadn't found me."

"You should go to sleep," she said. "We can talk more about Prophecies later."

I nodded. Virgo squeezed my hand for a second, but didn't let go. I closed my eyes, feeling the heavy warmth of her hand in mine. Virgo had insisted that we had never met before, but if she hadn't said that, I would have sworn that we had been friends before. There was an easiness between us that simply felt natural, but there was something more—something I knew in my heart I hadn't felt in a long time. I realized what it was then—when I was around her and Draco, I felt safe. I didn't remember anything from my life before, but I was sure I hadn't felt safe in a long time.

I gripped Virgo's hand a bit tighter, holding it as if it were my lifeline. Slowly, sleep began to come over me. The pain dissipated, and soon I was floating in a sweet darkness.

"What?" Virgo asked, squeezing water out of her hair.

"We want to steal our Prophecies back, right?" I said.

"Yes?" Draco said. "But how does that tie into following Perseus's plan?"

"Didn't you just say Perseus's plan was dangerous?" Castor said.

"Yes," I said. "But unless we have the treasure, Perseus won't come out of hiding. Whatever this treasure is, he's desperate to find it. He'll do anything to get it."

"This may be too dangerous, Corvus," Virgo said.

Draco huffed. "When have our plans been safe?" The vertical slits in his eyes expanded as he looked at me. "What do you propose we do?"

"Okay," I said as I straightened my back, happy that Draco was willing to listen to my plan. "We go to Egypt and find the treasure Perseus wants us to find. Then, the Twins act as if they're going to give it to Perseus in exchange for their Prophecies. My guess is that Perseus will keep *all* of the Prophecies he has near him. So, when the Twins go to Perseus, we'll know where he is, and while they exchange the treasure for their Prophecy, we could try to find all the Prophecies."

Pollux nodded slowly.

"A lot of things could go wrong there," Virgo said. "We could die finding the treasure or maybe Perseus doesn't have the Prophecies with him or Perseus could send someone to give the Twins their Prophecy and we don't know if he'll want to meet in person."

"He'll meet us in person," Castor said. "We can convince him of that."

"Still," Virgo said. "If you go to Perseus, then how will *we* be able to find the Prophecies? We don't know where he's hiding them."

"But as Corvus said," Draco said, rubbing his chin, "knowing Perseus, he'll want to have the Prophecies nearby—he would never leave them behind. Even if he does, once we know where he is, we could track him down to wherever he's hiding the Prophecies." He turned to me. "This may be a good plan."

"But what about the treasure?" Virgo asked. "If we want to go through with this plan, then Perseus will expect the Twins to give him the real treasure. I don't think that will be a good idea. I'm guessing this treasure is something important, something that will give him more power. We can't let him have it."

"I don't think any treasure is nearly as important as our Prophecies," Castor said. "I don't mind trading."

Virgo looked at Draco, then at me, then at the Twins. "You guys can't possibly think this plan is going to work out."

The Twins smiled devilishly. "It's the best plan we've had so far," Pollux said.

Virgo's gaze hardened as she stared at him. Draco placed a hand on her shoulder. "We'll be fine. We always are." Virgo's shoulders slumped as she sighed. "And the Twins are right, we—"

"Did I just hear Draco say we were right?" Castor asked.

"Trading our Prophecies for the treasure is worth the risk," Draco finished.

"I guess . . .," Virgo muttered.

"We just have one condition," Pollux said.

"What?" I asked.

"You give us the *real* Prophecies," Castor said with a smug smile. "You guys can keep copies of them so you can reference the Prophecies and everything they say. But we want the original ones."

"No," Virgo said.

At the same time Draco responded, "Yes."

Virgo glared at Draco. "Are we really going to let them have the real Prophecies?"

Draco shrugged. "We only need to know what they say. We don't really need the originals."

Both Twins smiled widely.

Virgo opened her mouth as if to complain again, but then just gave another sigh. We had no other choice, and Virgo knew that. We couldn't let Perseus be the only Star Child who knew the future.

Draco looked at me and nodded. I nodded in return.

"So now what?" Draco asked. "How do we get to Egypt?"

I looked around us. The cruise ship was a miniscule dot in the distance, the life rafts and boats reduced to orange particles scattered around it. The ocean stretched all around us as far as I could see. Without a compass and some idea of where we were or what direction we needed to go in, finding Egypt would be all but impossible.

"We could try calling the Ship again," Castor said to his brother.

"You think it'll listen?" Pollux asked.

"It's worth a try," Castor said.

Castor crawled to the edge of the raft, then he looked out at the ocean.

"Argooooo!" He shouted. "Heeeeeeelp!"

"Argo?" Virgo asked. "As in the Argo Navis?"

"Yes," Castor said.

"Argo Navis," I muttered in reference to the Constellation—another Star Object—that represented the mythical Ship that had first set sail in the ocean.

"Argoooo!" Pollux shouted as he kneeled close to the edge of the raft.

"I had no idea you guys had found it," Virgo said.

"We found Argo a while ago," Pollux said. "But the Ship has its own personality, so it shows up only when it wants to."

"The Ship is alive," Castor said. He scratched his hair, which was now disheveled. "I mean, as alive as any ship can be."

"So, we could be stranded at sea for days until it decides to show up?" I asked.

"We'll be fine," Castor said as he waved his hand. "He'll come rescue us, and if not, we'll use the wind to take us to Egypt . . . although that would be a long ride."

I looked across the ocean again. There was no sign of any ship. Besides, if the Ship hadn't picked up Castor and Pollux in Rome, then why would it show up now?

"Argoooo!" the Twins kept shouting. Meanwhile, Virgo came to sit at my side. Draco crouched next to us.

"Do you really think we can pull this off, Corvus?" Draco asked.

"This is quite a bad plan," Virgo said.

"I never said it was a *good* plan," I said. "It's just the only way we have a chance to get our Prophecies back."

I needed those Prophecies. No matter the cost.

Draco's red and orange eyes trained on me, his vertical pupils narrowing again. "I don't trust the Twins," he whispered. "We'll have to be careful, but . . . you're right. I don't see another way we can steal our Prophecies back and get the rest of Alathea's book."

"What about the treasure?" Virgo asked. "Are we truly willing to give it to Perseus?"

I shrugged.

"We'll cross that bridge when we get there," Draco said. "For now, let's just worry about finding it."

"Argoo—oh, there it is!" Castor said.

The three of us got to our feet at once. I looked ahead, following the Twins' gaze. A sleek black figure swam closer to us, and an entire submarine broke through the surface. Waves smashed against our little raft and sent me crashing on my back. A wave of cold seawater washed over us. I spat out some of it, then coughed. The strong taste of salt lingered on my tongue, and nausea overtook me. I breathed deeply for a couple of seconds, then sat up again, dripping water from every inch of my body, except the sweater.

Castor laughed hysterically, his hair plastered to his face.

The black steel submarine before us seemed to be half the size of the cruise ship.

"I thought Argo Navis was a ship," I said.

"Like we said, it has a personality of its own," Pollux said. "It can shift into any marine vehicle it wants."

"Sometimes it turns into a luxury yacht," Pollux said.

"Hello, Argo!" Castor said. "Did you miss your favorite Twins?"

A hatch opened at the top of the submarine. A loud growl echoed inside.

"Hmmm," Castor said. "That's not the answer I was hoping for."

Before I could point out that the growl sounded very similar to Leo's, the Lion jumped out of the hatch and into our little raft, knocking the Twins down. Leo's giant paws pressed down on their chests as he glared at them. The Lion was a head taller than me. He had gleaming golden fur and a mane that was a few shades darker. His eyes blazed like two bright suns. Leo still had bright pink scars on his ribs, face, and chest—the remnants of his battle with Lupus. The Lion took up most of the space in the raft, forcing the rest of us toward the edges.

"Leo!" Virgo said with glee.

Sirius barked and wagged his tail. Draco smiled. A comforting warmth spread through my chest at the sight of the Lion. The Twins, however, did not seem happy at all. Leo growled in their faces as they tried to squirm away.

"It's all right, Leo," Virgo said. "You don't need to kill them."

Leo growled again but stepped back. The Twins crawled to the other side of the raft, about three feet away from Leo, and looked at him with pale faces. I worried that the Lion's weight would sink our little raft, and I was about to suggest we all get inside the submarine, but Castor spoke first.

"You treasonous Ship!" he shouted at the submarine as he stood up. "You showed up to help the Lion but not *us*?"

The submarine said nothing, as I expected.

Virgo turned to Leo. "How did you even find us?" she asked.

I was more curious about how Leo had found the submarine. Had Leo summoned the Ship? Or had the Ship appeared to Leo? I had so many questions but knew they probably weren't worth my full attention.

Sirius shook himself, spraying drops of water all around him.

"We should get inside the submarine," Draco suggested.

"Good idea," I said.

The Lion went first, jumping back to the top of the submarine, then dropping into the hatch. Sirius went next, mimicking the Lion. Pollux grabbed the backpack I had seen earlier and strapped it across his shoulders. He nimbly jumped on top of the submarine and offered Virgo a hand. We boarded the ship one by one. The metal ladder was cold to my touch as I stepped down. The Twins came after me and the hatch closed itself on top of us.

I expected the submarine to look as they do in the movies—a lot of pipes and tech-looking stuff along the sides, metal floors and ceilings, everything grey and cold. But as soon as I turned away from the ladder, I realized that the inside of the submarine looked like I had entered a house. In front of us stretched a large hallway. It *was* made from shiny metal, but it had small paintings and a red carpet. The Twins led the way, and we followed them. The small paintings featured random images—one had a palm tree next to the ocean, another one showed books stacked in the corner of a room. Others depicted flowering trees, an empty meadow below a clear blue sky, a forest, and some colorful butterflies.

At the end of the hallway, stairs curled down to the floor below. We descended them and found ourselves in a large room that extended two stories above us. It seemed as if we had entered a museum. On both sides were glass displays with the skeletons of several aquatic animals. Sirius growled at one to our left, which looked like a large water snake. To my right was a skeleton of a creature that looked like an octopus with large tentacles, but it had no head. The twisting tentacles were just bound together in the middle.

"Are these creatures real?" Virgo asked as we walked past more displays.

"We assume so," Castor said. "We don't know who put them here."

Leo emitted a low growl at one of the creatures ahead of us. It resembled a thirty-foot-long crocodile, but it had two tails instead of one. At the end of the room was another set of stairs that led farther down, but instead of descending to the bottom floor the Twins turned right before reaching the stairs, passing by more display cases—one showed a small fish with large fangs.

A wide metal door with a wheel in the middle of it greeted us at the corner. With a grunt, Pollux began to turn the wheel. The veins in his forehead popped out as he strained to move it. His brother helped him, and seconds later the wheel rotated fast as the door slid inward.

The animals stayed outside. It was dark inside the new room, but as soon as we walked in, the lights turned on.

"What in the Stars?" Draco gave a low whistle as we entered the room.

My jaw dropped. The room was full of weapons, and not just any weapons—Star Weapons. At least that's what we called them. We had found only a few up until now and had lost a couple in the battle in Rome. But this room held dozens.

Star Weapons were all made from bone, and they were the only weapons that could kill us, aside from Star Objects or Star Animals. Mortal weapons could harm us but never kill us, though drowning, choking, and burning were still real threats to us. I glanced over at Draco, but his jacket hid the bruises on his neck.

I turned back to the weapons as a chill curled down my spine. Swords hung on the wall to our right. Like the weapons we'd had before, the hilts had carvings of Constellations or other mythical creatures, and their blades were all different. Some were double-edged and as long as I was tall; others were curved or ragged.

The wall in front of us featured spears and lances of all sizes and shapes. Most spears had long shafts. Some were smooth while others were decorated with carvings. Some of their points were shaped like large arrowheads, others like a curving and twisted blade. Many more were too intricate to describe. On the left wall hung knives and axes.

Castor walked over to the swords. He picked a large one with a double-edged blade and another with a curved blade. Pollux made his way toward the axes and knives. He picked up a big axe with two heads as big as his own that were arched like crescent moons.

"How the hell did you find all this?" Virgo asked.

"We didn't," Castor said as he admired his two swords. "They've always been here."

"Who put them here?" I asked, wondering who could have had so many Star Weapons.

The Twins shrugged again. "We weren't the first ones who found Argo," Pollux explained. "This Ship was owned by someone else before."

"This Ship is very old," Castor said.

I wondered just how old the Ship could be. We hadn't met any Star Child older than thirty-five.

"Feel free to grab whatever you want," Castor said.

I walked over to the swords and picked up one that had a blade as long as my arm. As soon as I held the handle, the carvings seemed to twist beneath my hand, as if they were alive, but when I looked at them, they hadn't moved. The weapon was very light, so I didn't struggle carrying it.

Draco grabbed a long spear with an arrowhead point, and Virgo held a large knife in her hand. She seemed uncomfortable touching it, as she always did whenever she held a Star Weapon.

Conveniently, Castor and Pollux had leather scabbards and belts so we could tie our weapons to our waists and backs. The sword I had chosen hung from my back. Draco's spear was held at his back too sticking up a foot above his head, and Virgo tied a belt to her waist for her knife.

"Now, let's go downstairs so we can talk," Castor said, his two swords crisscrossed on his back. We left the weapons room and the metal door closed behind us. Sirius and Leo eyed our weapons as we descended the stairs we had passed on the way to the weapons room.

We arrived at a living room. On one side was a wall with a large painting that displayed a swirl of red and black. I thought I could make out a shape of a dancing woman with flowing red hair. In front of us, a ceiling-to-floor window showed the depths of the ocean. The dark water seemed to be unmoving, even though I knew we must have been moving fast. We must have been very far below the surface.

"Make yourselves at home," Pollux said.

In the middle of the room were three large, navy blue couches arranged around a glass table. They were all angled to face the window. Below them lay a fluffy white carpet.

The Twins walked over to the right where an oak table stood against the wall with food on top of it. My stomach growled. How long ago had I eaten? Draco, Virgo, and I joined the Twins and discovered sushi, pizza, some roasted salmon, and even a basket of tacos. Where had the food come from?

"Oh right. Argo!" Pollux shouted with a mouthful of meat taco. "We need you to take us to Egypt."

I didn't know if the Ship had understood, but I hoped it had. Sirius barked next to me, looking at me with his big brown eyes. I picked up four tacos and placed them on the floor for him. Tacos wouldn't have been a very healthy meal for a normal dog, but Sirius always ate the same food we did.

Leo sat down next to the window and stared out at the ocean, his tail wagging slowly. Virgo walked over to the Lion and sat next to him on the floor, setting her plate full of sushi and tacos next to her. She talked to Leo while she ate, probably filling him in on what had happened. Leo's face was unreadable, but he stared intently at Virgo.

The Twins sat on the couch that faced the food table to devour their meal. After serving myself two slices of pizza and two tacos, I walked with Draco toward another couch on the other side of the table, a few feet behind Leo and Virgo.

A bark and a screech came from the stairs and I turned. From the stairs, Maera came rushing down and Aquila flew into the room. The Eagle screeched again and settled next to Draco, perching on the top of the couch. He looked at the Twins with his bright yellow eyes. Aquila was a Golden Eagle with a wingspan of ten feet. His left wing had healed after the battle of Palatine Hill, and he could fly again, but the scar shaped like a crescent moon had remained.

Maera, with his curly black hair, walked over to Sirius, who was wagging his tail. They smelled each other, as they usually did, and then ate tacos together. Castor looked at the dogs, while Pollux eyed the Eagle warily, as if he would poke out Pollux's eyes with his beak. We ate in silence for a while. After finishing my plate, I served myself more food and gobbled it down.

"So, how did Perseus even get the Prophecies?" Castor asked after about ten minutes. "He didn't tell us that."

"That's quite a long story," Virgo said as she leaned back on Leo.

"You guys missed a lot," Draco said.

"We noticed," Castor said. "A 'terrorist attack' in New York, the city of Rome and most of Italy destroyed . . . I'm glad we missed all of that."

"We know Perseus was responsible for all of that. But what actually happened?" Pollux gave his taco a huge bite.

"It was Andromeda's fault," I said.

Virgo's head snapped to me. "It wasn't. Perseus tricked her."

"It's still her fault," I said.

"Wait, hold on, you found another Star Child?" Castor asked.

"We found three more," I said.

"You remember how a month ago we were tracking down Perseus?" Draco said.

"Yeah," Castor said. "We're the ones who told you he was in New York."

"We weren't the only ones who had found him," Virgo said from the floor next to Leo. "Cassiopeia found Perseus about a year ago, but she never approached him directly."

The Twins were silent, and something about the way they slightly tensed made me think they had already known about Cassiopeia being in New York.

"She kept close watch on him though," Draco said. "Perseus managed to find a couple of Prophecies, although we're not sure where. He told Andromeda he had found them in Greece, but that may have been a lie to mislead anyone also looking for those Prophecies." Draco took a bite out of his pizza. "Cassiopeia stole those Prophecies from him a few weeks ago."

"And then we stole them from her, although she had destroyed the originals, so we only read the copy." Virgo took a bite of her sushi.

"What did those Prophecies say?" Castor asked.

"They talked about Algol, the Demon Star," I said. "Basically, Perseus will use Algol to murder millions and kill most of the Star Children."

Castor pulled his hair back with his hand. "Yeah . . . we knew that last part already."

"And you're still willing to help him?" I asked.

Castor shrugged. "Look man, we don't care if he destroys the entire Universe as long as he tells us how to avoid our own deaths and leaves us alone."

"If he destroys the Universe, you'll die too," Virgo said. "So maybe you should start caring."

Castor shrugged again. "What's the worst that could happen without Fate and Destiny?" he asked with a mouthful of pizza.

"Oh, I don't know," Virgo said. "The Universe would just fall into Darkness and Chaos, shattering all structures that support Life. We would all die."

"But Perseus believes that he can eradicate Destiny, Fate, and Prophecy without destroying Life," Pollux said, crossing his arms.

"And you believe him?" I asked.

"I don't believe he would destroy all Life. What's the point of killing everything?" said Castor.

"Even if we didn't die, a world without Fate, Destiny, and Prophecy would still bring Chaos," Virgo said. "It's like living in a world without rules and laws. Destiny and Fate are the laws that keep the Universe balanced."

Castor shrugged again.

"Perseus just believes what Arianna tells him," Draco said. "She convinced him that it was possible. Whatever lies Perseus believes . . . they will end up killing us all."

"Wait," Pollux nearly choked on a sushi roll. "Arianna? As in the Physical-Manifestation-of-Darkness Arianna?"

I nodded. The Twins exchanged a glance. I wasn't surprised that they didn't know of Arianna's return. We had only found out about it two weeks ago.

"Huh," Castor said. "Well, I'm not sure how that's going to turn out."

A couple seconds of silence passed.

"What happened after Cassiopeia stole the Prophecies from Perseus and after you stole them from her?" Castor asked. Pollux remained quiet, holding his head in his hands. I looked at Virgo and Draco. How to explain all that mess?

"In short," Draco said, "Perseus and Andromeda are bound by Prophecy. One of them will kill the other. So, Cassiopeia sent Andromeda to kill Perseus, but she didn't. And instead, he tricked her into helping him retrieve the Prophecies."

"If she was sent to kill him, then why didn't she kill him?" Castor asked.

"That's the million-dollar question," I muttered.

"And how did he trick her into helping him with the Prophecies?" Pollux asked.

"She can open any lock or safe with her power," Virgo explained. "Perseus knew that. He used her to open a chest in Delphi, Greece, where all the Prophecies were hidden."

"And what about Rome?" Castor asked. "What happened there?"

"Algol," Draco, Virgo, and I said simultaneously.

Leo growled at the mention of the Demon Star.

"A single Star caused all that destruction?" Castor asked.

"Have you been listening to what we've been telling you for the past day?" Virgo asked. "Perseus used the Star to kill millions and will continue to do it."

"We had seen his attacks before," Pollux said. "All those terrorist bombings and stuff that Perseus had caused using Algol. But what he did in Italy is something else . . ."

"He practically destroyed all of central Italy," Castor said.

"That was Algol's first rising," I said. "Algol is prophesized to rise to full power three times. The first rising already happened, the second one will be in a few more weeks—"

"And we have no idea when the last one will be," Virgo finished. "All we know is that when Algol rises to full power, its destruction is absolute—worse than what happened in Italy."

"How do you know about the three risings?" Pollux asked. "Was that one of the Prophecies you stole from Cassiopeia?"

I nodded. Unless we found a way to stop Perseus, his next two risings would bring even more destruction and death. But the Twins wouldn't care about that. All they wanted was the Prophecies so they could trade them for more information, money, and whatever else they wanted.

"So where is Andromeda?" Pollux asked. "Please tell me Perseus didn't kill her."

"If he had killed her, we would probably be dead too." Draco rubbed his neck where the bruises still tainted his skin. The Twins eyed Draco's neck, then exchanged another glance between them.

"She's alive, but after the attack she and Orion left us," Virgo said.

"Wait, you found Orion too?" Castor asked.

"Yes," I said, remembering the tall guy. We had sent him to find Andromeda and come back for us, but he never had. I had never liked either of them. They were too unreliable.

"Hmmm," Pollux said. "Is Orion as handsome as the myths say?"

Virgo pondered that for a second. "Yes."

Draco's black pupils narrowed.

Pollux turned to his brother. "I want to meet him."

"They'll come back," Virgo said. I knew she hoped that Orion and Andromeda would just show up suddenly and help us. But I knew better. It would be a while before we saw them again.

"Oh, I forgot," Pollux said. He rose from the couches and rushed up the stairs out of sight. He came back a few moments later holding the backpack I had seen earlier. He sat down and opened it. "I believe this is yours." He threw a wallet at me, and I caught it before it hit my face. I opened it and found our credit cards intact inside. We had a couple million dollars in our bank accounts from Sirius's movies. It hadn't been of much use in Italy after everything was destroyed, but I knew it would come in handy later. I pocketed the wallet.

Pollux pulled a dark blue sweater from the backpack. Virgo immediately jumped to her feet. She snatched the knitted sweater from Pollux and examined it. Then she folded it and hugged it to her chest, walking back to Leo. "Thanks," she muttered.

"I'm afraid we ate all of the sausages and cookies you had for dinner." Pollux set the backpack down. "But we saved the chamomile tea! Let me know if you want some."

I almost asked for one, but then decided not to. With a long sigh, I looked at everyone gathered around me—Sirius, Maera, Aquila, Leo, Virgo, Draco, and the Twins. It was up to us to stop Perseus now.

CHAPTER 5

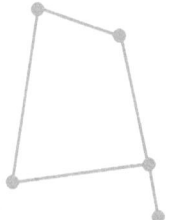

I STOOD AT THE TERRACE, *watching the sunset. The sun reflected its orange and red light in the windows of the buildings around me; it had almost disappeared below the horizon. The clouds were dark orange on the blue sky. The wind ruffled my short hair and my open shirt.*

Dread rose inside me like a slow tide. My hands had gone numb, and my mind spun with different thoughts. You could die, *I told myself. I tried to ignore my thoughts, but they kept telling me to stay home, to ignore everything I had learned in London.*

There was no going back now. I had made my decision.

I stayed on the terrace for what seemed like hours. The sky grew dark, but the Stars didn't come out. The Stars never came out in big cities. I walked back inside my room. The scars on my chest shone brightly. The white light that came out of them pulsed in tune with my heart. The mirror next to my desk reflected the light from my chest as I stood in front of it looking at myself.

Would I recognize myself in a few days?

The white light from my chest illuminated my face, casting pulsing shadows on my cheeks. The ragged scars ran from the top of my chest to my belly button. I looked back at my face in the mirror— would it be a stranger's face soon? My skin had become more tanned during the summer, and now it looked a darker shade of brown. I had let my dark beard grow again—I had always been too lazy to shave it, but maybe I would shave it before I left. I met my gaze and my own dark eyes stared back at me, reflecting the terror that curled in my heart.

The door to my room opened and Merope walked in. She closed the door behind her and turned on the lights. The white light from my scars extinguished. I turned to face her.

"What are you—"

"So you're leaving," she said with a sigh.

I stared at her blankly for a second. "How would you know that I'm leaving?"

Merope chuckled. "Maybe because I'm your sister, and I've known you most of your life." She crossed her arms on her chest. Her ebony hair flowed in loose curls, reaching her waist. "I know you better than you think, Corvus."

"You can't tell the others about this," I said quickly.

"I haven't, yet . . ." Merope sighed, her sapphire eyes staring at me like a turbulent ocean. "Why? Why are you leaving?" She leaned against the wall next to the door. "Ever since you came back from London you've been acting very strange. What did that Star Child tell you?" She paused. "What did she tell you that you didn't tell us?"

"I can't tell you right now," I said. "I have something to do first . . . something I need to do alone."

"And why would you need to do it alone?" she asked. "Come on, Corvus. You've never done anything alone before. What's really going on?" She looked into my eyes as if she could pierce my soul. "I'm not sure you're prepared for whatever it is that you're planning."

Her words hit me like bullets. That was exactly why I had to go alone, why I couldn't tell the others. All my life I had only lied and let everyone else do the rest—let everyone else be the hero. They had never let me fight, never let me go on dangerous missions. Not since we had

82

lost Darren—the day I had almost lost my own life. And the one time I had *been allowed to go on a mission alone, it had been disastrous. Although I had never told that to the others*. I had failed my family the day Darren died, but I wouldn't fail them again. Soon, I would become strong enough to keep them safe, and they would know that I was just as powerful as they were.

I looked away from Merope's eyes and turned back to the mirror. My eyes seemed to have turned a shade darker. I could do more than just lie. I would prove to the others that I was as capable as them.

"I have to do this on my own," my voice didn't quaver.

"I won't let you kill yourself on this foolish mission," Merope said. Her voice had softened—I knew she was angry.

"You don't even know what I'm planning," I argued.

Merope stayed silent for a moment. I turned around to face her again, her gaze intense as a storm. She walked over to the nightstand next to the bed and opened the second drawer. She pulled my red notebook from it. My heart squeezed painfully as she opened the notebook. Merope shifted through the pages for a few seconds until she found the one she was looking for. Anger stained my cheeks with heat. How had she dared read my personal notes?

"I just want to forget," Merope said in her honey-sweet voice. "I want to forget who I am. I want to forget everything that I've ever been, everything I've ever done. I just want to remember my name, remember how to use my power, remember that I am a Star Child. I will remember I am looking for the Cup, and I will remember where it is. Everything else will be gone from my memories."

"You have no right to—"

"As soon as I find the Cup and hold it, I will remember again who I am, not before." She finished reading and looked up at me. "How is erasing your own memories going to help in anything? And what Cup are you talking about?"

"You had no right to read that," I hissed.

"Why would you want to erase your own memories? That's dangerous. Something could go wrong," Merope said, her voice still as ice. *"You're willing to lose everything you are just for a stupid Cup? Seriously, what did that Star Child tell you that you kept to yourself?"*

"You don't understand," I said.

"No. I don't. You're willing to forget us, your own family, just to find a stupid Cup. I don't understand why a Cup would be more important than us."

"It's not about that. You don't understand," I repeated. *"You'll never understand."*

"I won't understand unless you explain." Merope let the notebook drop into the drawer. I didn't answer. I had explained it before, but they had never understood. *"Stay here, Corvus,"* Merope said slowly. *"Don't make an impulsive decision that will hurt everyone. We can do this together."*

"Together?" I asked. *"You mean you and the others do everything and leave me in the car because it might be 'too dangerous' for me to come with you?"* I huffed. *"We've never done anything together. I'm just a spare part here. I just lie, and once that's done there's nothing else I'm useful for."*

Merope narrowed her eyes. *"Is that what this is all about? Haven't we talked about this before?"* She paused. *"Do you really believe that? That you're a spare part?"* She took a step back, hurt. I was the one who deserved to be hurt, not her. *"You think we don't consider you useful for anything else?"*

"You don't," I said. *"You said it a minute ago. I've never done anything by myself and if I try to do it, I'll get hurt or killed."*

"I never said that."

"You clearly implied it."

"That's not . . ." She took in a deep breath, rubbing her eyes. "All we want is to keep you safe." She didn't meet my gaze.

"Keep me safe so I don't die like Darren did."

Merope startled, as if I had slapped her. I knew this had been a low blow, but I didn't care anymore. My anger was boiling hot. "Everything that doesn't involve me lying to others is too dangerous for me. It always has been. My lies are the only skill you think I'm good at."

"That is what you're best at," Merope said, meeting my gaze. "Your best weapon is your lies, Corvus, not a gun, not a knife, not your fists. But you can't see that, can you?" I turned away from her, looking at my bare feet. "Being able to fight, doing dangerous things like the rest of our reckless family . . . that doesn't make a person braver, it doesn't make one stronger." She shook her head. "We all have our strengths, and yours is different from ours."

"You mean I'm weaker," I said.

Merope raked her hair with her hands. "Did you listen to anything I just said? You're as strong as the rest of us. Each of us has a different strength, that's what makes us powerful. That's what makes us who we are. You don't need to erase your memories and go on a stupid, dangerous, mysterious mission to prove you're as strong as the rest of us." Merope shook her head again, her curls swishing from side to side. "This is madness! Where are you getting these ideas from? When have we ever told you you're not strong enough? When have we ever made you feel less than you are?" I didn't answer. Merope gave a soft chuckle. "Your mind is your best weapon but also your worst enemy. These poisonous ideas . . . I don't know where you get them from."

"They're not ideas!" I shouted, the words spilling out of my mouth like a waterfall. "You're the ones who didn't let me go to Africa with you because it was too dangerous! You're the ones who left me in *the hotel in Greece because you didn't want me getting hurt on the mission! You're the ones who didn't let me meet Centaurus because if he decided to attack us, he could kill me! I am never enough to do the same things you can do. No matter how much I train, no matter how much I improve, I'm never enough for any of you!"*

Once I let it all out, my chest lightened.

Merope didn't speak for a few seconds, and I could feel the tension extending between us like an electric wire.

"You're confusing two very different things," she said. "Being enough has nothing to do with our missions being too dangerous for you to join us. You're a good enough fighter, and you have improved a lot, but we don't want you getting hurt. If something happens to you, if you die, then all the lies you've told will disappear. We'll lose everything that we've built the last six years."

"So that's it," I said. "You don't care about me. You just want my lies because without them we wouldn't have anything."

"No! That's not what I'm saying." She walked to my side and held my arms. She had surprising strength. The girls had always been stronger than me. "You're just hearing what you want to hear! We do care about you. You're our brother, now get these mad ideas out of your mind and tell us what you learned in London so we can all work on this together."

"No," I said. For the first time, I had found something that could change our future and turn the tide completely in our favor. I knew how to find the Cup, one of the most powerful objects in the world. And I had learned secret information about the most ancient and most powerful Star Child ever born. After I had the Cup in my possession, I would have enough power to keep the others safe, and I would never let them down again with my weakness.

"What do you mean no?*" she asked.*

"We're home!" Maia shouted from downstairs.

"We brought donuts!" Electra said.

They must have come back from their trip to the mall.

"If you won't tell them, then I will," Merope said.

She let go of me and walked toward the closed door.

"Merope," I said, *my voice echoing inside my ears.*

She turned on her heel, her eyes staring daggers at me. "You wouldn't—"

"You want to forget about everything we just talked about," I said, *my voice so deep it sounded alien. My chest blazed as if it were melting. My heart burned, my bones crumpling to ash. I wanted to scream in pain, but I somehow held it back. The light from my scars twinkled frantically.* "You just want to forget I've been acting strange and that I'm planning to leave. Forget you read my notebook." *Merope's bright eyes went blank, and the light from them seemed to extinguish. My chest pounded like a hammer smashing through it.* "You want to forget that I will erase my own mind." *Merope's empty gaze stared at me.* "You just want to go downstairs to eat donuts and pretend nothing happened here."

"I want donuts," *she agreed.*

She walked out of the room and closed the door behind her. As soon as she left, I collapsed to my knees, gasping for air. The physical pain had stopped, but my heart twisted with a different type of pain. I had never lied to any of my siblings—ever. I had promised them years ago that I would never use my lies on them. The guilt tore at my chest, and I tried to push it away. I wouldn't lie to them again, ever, but this one lie had been necessary. I couldn't let Merope tell the others the truth.

I trembled as I pushed myself up and I looked at myself in the mirror again. What if I didn't remember who I was? I would, I assured myself. The reason I had written down my lie in the notebook was to read it every day, to know it by heart so I didn't leave anything out. The lie would work, and I would become one of the most powerful Star Children.

Finding the Cup would probably take me a couple of weeks. I already knew where it was, so the hard part would be to actually get it. It wouldn't be that bad, I told myself. I would go to Egypt, find the temple, get the Cup, and come back.

I could make this work.

Would my siblings even care when I left? Would they miss me? Would they try to come after me? Even if they did, they wouldn't be able to find me. I would leave no trace of where I was going. I wondered what would happen when I woke up without my memories. How would I feel if I didn't remember anything? Maybe it would be good, to get a break from everything I knew, to have a clean mind for a couple of months.

The door to my room opened, and Maia walked in. She had tied her fiery red hair in a messy bun at the back of her head. Her face was long and thin, her nose big. She had thick eyebrows above her forest green eyes. Even though she was only three years older than me, like the rest of the girls, she stood half a head taller.

"Don't you want donuts?" she asked.

"I do."

She stared at my bare chest. Her eyes trained on the two scars. She bit at her lip and probably noticed my trembling hands.

"Did you have a flashback or nightmare?" she asked. "About . . . Darren?"

"I've always had the nightmares," I said with a shrug. I had gotten used to them. Maybe erasing my memories wouldn't be so bad. I would finally be able to get some sleep. I felt the cold ocean wrap around me, and I shivered, pushing my memories away.

Maia stood behind me and gave me a soft hug. Then she kissed my cheek and pulled back. I looked at the small scar on her chin.

If the room had been dark, her scar would have shone with pulsing white light.

"Whenever you have your nightmares, just remember that you're safe," she said sweetly. "Remember that we'll never let anything happen to you."

"I know," I said. They had focused so much on protecting me that they had taken it to the extreme. I sighed, looking down at my scars again. They had realized on the day of the attack that I wasn't enough. I hadn't been able to protect my siblings. Darren's death had been my fault—I should have been able to protect him, to take us back to the shore before it was too late.

"I'll be down in a few minutes," I said to Maia.

"You better," she said as she pulled away and walked to the door. "Those donuts will be gone in less than ten minutes."

She left the door ajar, and I could hear Merope talking to Electra.

I looked at myself in the mirror again and traced the old scars with my own fingers. I stared into my own eyes again.

"I am enough," I repeated to myself. "I. Am. Enough."

I would get that Cup. I would find the most powerful Star Child, no matter the cost.

I woke up sweating, my shirt almost soaked through. I sat up in the bed, taking in deep breaths. Tremors shook my body. My fuzzy mind whirled at the new memory. How long had I slept? Maybe a couple of hours. I could feel the submarine swaying with the waves, or maybe I was just dizzy.

Dim light bled in from the edges of the closed curtains. That was strange. I hadn't seen the curtains last night when I walked into the room. The metal wall had been bare. I slowly stood from the bed. The floor was cold under my bare feet. I walked over to the curtains and slid them open, surprised to see the ocean surface outside the large window. How had that happened? Weren't submarines supposed to be underwater?

I opened the door and peeked outside. The hallway had shifted too. The wooden floor reflected the dim yellow lights that lined the walls. They looked like old lanterns, but instead of a flame they had a little orange lightbulb. Argo must have shifted into a boat, or maybe a large yacht, while I was asleep. I closed the door behind me—I wasn't going to get any more sleep tonight—and walked down the hallway.

"*Child of Lies.*"

I stopped abruptly, nearly stumbling forward. That voice, I had heard it before. It sounded like . . .

"*All lies have a price.*"

The whisper sounded like swishing leaves. I picked up my pace and shook my head, trying to wake myself fully. The voices were similar to the ones in my memories, but there weren't even trees around me. At the end of the hallway, I stepped outside through a sliding glass door. Cold wind swished around me, making me shiver. The main deck, which was empty, looked similar to the one from the cruise ship, but smaller. It had a square pool at the center and a couple of wooden chairs to the side.

I walked over to the railing and looked down at the smooth, black ocean. Dread curled inside me, and I took a step back. The crescent moon stared at me from the top of the sky. It looked like a smile, which was mildly encouraging.

Half of me wanted to consider the implications of the new memory, and the other half of me was terrified about what it implied. Why had I recovered another memory now? The first memory had come back randomly, a couple of months ago.

Had the ocean triggered this one? I had felt something inside of my mind open up when the cold water had wrapped around me. That feeling had triggered the ghost of a memory, but something had also opened inside of me—a black box. I felt terrified of what I would find inside of it.

"Another nightmare?" Virgo said from behind me.

I startled and turned around. She stood a few feet behind me with Draco at her side.

"Something like that," I said.

They both moved closer to me, trapping me against the railing.

"Or was it one of your memories?" Draco asked, folding his arms.

The vertical slits in Draco's eyes narrowed, but Virgo's eyes were warm as always.

"Don't you think we deserve to know?" Draco asked. "We're your friends."

"I have always trusted you," I said. "It's just that . . ."

Virgo placed a warm hand on my shoulder. If she noticed that my shirt was still sweaty, she didn't mention it.

"I don't know who I am," I said. "I barely remember anything about myself."

After a moment of silence, Draco said, "You know who you *are*." His pupils expanded. "You just don't know who you *were*."

"What's the first thing you remember after losing your memory?" Virgo asked.

"I . . . the terrorist attack in London over a year ago. I remember the day you found me in the hospital. That's my first *real* memory." I turned and looked out at the dark sea again. Virgo's hand remained warm on my shoulder, and that warmth diffused through my shirt and oozed into my skin. "At first I thought that my memories were missing because of the concussion. I always hoped that my memories would return but they never did."

Virgo hugged my back, her arms wrapping around my own. For a second, her warmth spread through the rest of my body. Then she let go.

Draco patted my back. "You never told us that."

I shrugged. "I expected my memories would eventually return." I didn't turn to look at them and instead took a deep breath. "Then we started tracking down Perseus and . . . well, my memories didn't seem important anymore."

"They *are* important," Draco said. "At least Perseus seems to think so, according to the Twins."

"Do you remember anything before the attack at all?" Virgo asked, pulling me around to face them again.

"I started recovering pieces of my memory a couple of months ago, when the insomnia started," I said. "Just pieces."

"What do you remember?" Draco said.

I tilted my head to one side, then the other. "That's the problem. Those little pieces of memory seem . . . troubling, and they have only left me with more questions than answers."

Draco turned to Virgo, but she just stared at me with her eyes narrowed, as if I were a puzzle she was having a hard time putting together.

"I'm sure we can find answers inside your memories," she said.

"What do you mean by *troubling*?" Draco asked. "Are they bad memories? You don't have to share them if you don't feel ready."

"It's not that," I said as I faced them both.

I took a deep breath. "I had thought that my memory loss came from the attack in London, but . . ."

"But . . . ?" Draco asked. "I'm not enjoying the suspense here."

"I purposefully erased my own memories."

Virgo blinked and Draco looked dumbfounded.

"What?" Virgo asked.

"Why would you do that?" Draco said at the same time.

"I . . . I don't know," I admitted. "I remember waking up inside a forest. The leaves were speaking to me and—"

"How can leaves speak?" Draco asked.

"I don't know, they just did," I said with a shrug. I was sure that had been a real memory and not a dream. I could still hear their whispering voices.

"Dodona," Virgo said.

"What?" I asked.

Virgo's gaze was distant. "The Oracle of Dodona in Greece."

"I think I read about that somewhere," Draco said, pensive.

"The priestesses who worked at Dodona interpreted Prophecies by hearing the rustling of the leaves," Virgo explained.

"What were you doing in Dodona?" Draco asked.

I shrugged again.

"Do you remember why you erased your own memories?" Virgo asked.

"Or do you remember anything else at all?" Draco asked. "I'm sure Perseus is not very interested in talking to leaves. Not unless they said something important."

"The leaves told me that I had lied to myself and chosen to forget to find what I most desired, or something like that," I said. "They told me that every lie came with a price and that I would regret the price I would have to pay for this lie."

"How does erasing your memories help you find what you most desired?" Draco asked. I shrugged. "And what *is* what you most desired to find?"

I shrugged again. "I forgot."

Virgo raised a brow.

"How did you even erase your own memories?" Draco asked.

"I think I lied to myself," I said. "I've tried doing it again, to convince myself that I want to remember, but it never works. It's as if I purposefully didn't want to recover my memories so I made myself immune to any lie that could help me recover them."

As I said those words, I realized they made sense. If I had lied to myself to forget and had gone through so much trouble to do that, then I must have done something to prevent myself from recovering my memories with another lie.

"So you erased your own memory to find what you most desired and then you forgot what that was?" he asked.

"I'm pretty sure that's what happened," I said. "Which is very stupid, I know."

"It is kind of stupid," Draco agreed.

"What else do you remember?" Virgo said. "There has to be something that gives us a clue."

"I remember . . ." Part of me tried to fight against my new memory. I sighed. "I was back home, at least it felt like home. I was talking, arguing really, with Merope, a girl who was one of my sisters." Draco's pupils narrowed. "I'm sure they weren't my biological sisters, but maybe I was adopted or something."

"How many sisters did you have?" Virgo asked.

"I . . . I'm not sure." I tried to recall the names I had remembered. "Merope, Maia, and I think Electra?"

"Well, that's—" Draco began.

"I know those names," Virgo said. She held her head in between her hands, as if that would make her remember. I could almost see the gears spinning inside her head. "Electra, Maia . . . Merope," she muttered under her breath. She looked up abruptly, her eyes wide. "Those are the names of the Pleiades."

My mind reeled for a second. "The Star Cluster in the Constellation of Taurus."

The Pleiades made up the most well-known Star Cluster in the sky, but I didn't know the names of all seven Stars.

"But they're just Stars," Draco said, "not a Constellation. We've never met any Star or Star Cluster that can materialize into Star Beings like us."

"Not that we've met," Virgo said. "The Pleiades form arguably the most powerful Star Cluster, so it wouldn't surprise me that they are also Star Children."

Draco turned to me. "And you remembered the Pleiades were your sisters?"

"I—yeah, we lived together. I think we had been together for years," I said.

"Hmmm," Virgo said. "I know a bit about the Pleiades, but they have so many myths and stories that I can't be sure of what they can materialize here—what their powers are."

"They *are* Star Children, I'm sure of that," I said, going through my memory again. "Maia had a scar on her chin. I remember thinking that if the room had been dark, her scar would have shone."

"So, they *must* be the Pleiades," Virgo said. "This is interesting. If a Star Cluster can materialize into Star Children, does that mean that other Clusters or individual Stars can too?" She paused, pensive. "The Pleiades belong to the Constellation of Taurus, the Bull, but from what you're saying, Corvus, they seem to be independent of their Constellation."

A long silence stretched between us.

"Do you remember what you were talking about with Merope?" Draco asked.

I sighed. "She was trying to convince me not to erase my memory because it was dangerous and something could go wrong."

"It looks like Merope was right," Draco said.

"Unfortunately," I admitted. I remembered something else from that piece of memory, something we had both said several times. "I told Merope that I had to erase my memories to find a Cup . . ." My voice trailed off as my muscles went stiff. "I was supposed to remember that the Cup was in Egypt, hidden inside a temple."

Draco tensed, his pupils narrowing into very thin lines.

Virgo stood very still. "You were searching for a Cup in Egypt . . . and now Perseus has sent us to Egypt to find a treasure. This can't be a coincidence. How could Perseus know you were searching for a Cup?"

I shrugged.

"Maybe Perseus assumed that you remembered where it was?" Draco asked. "But how would he know that?"

"I didn't remember that until tonight," I said. "I guess I wasn't the only one looking for the Cup." I started connecting my thoughts. "The Prophecies must say that I erased my own memories to find the Cup, so maybe Perseus knew that."

"Crater," Virgo whispered.

"What?" I asked.

Virgo shook her head slowly, then pulled a strand of hair behind her ear. "Crater is the Constellation of the Cup, and it comes from the same myth as Corvus."

I looked at Draco. "Remind us of that myth please," he told Virgo.

Virgo just looked back and forth between us, as if she had expected that we already knew the myth, then sighed. "The god

Apollo sent his messenger, Corvus, to fill his cup, Crater, in a sacred lake," she began. "But the white raven got distracted eating fruit. Once he realized that he was late to meet the god, the raven quickly filled the cup. When he arrived back with Apollo, he lied to the god and said that a giant serpent had prevented him from filling the cup. Corvus even brought a real serpent as evidence." Her eyes glistened as she told the story. "But Apollo saw through the lies so he put a spell on the raven and turned it black. Then he threw the Serpent, the Cup, and the Raven into the sky as Constellations."

"What's the Constellation of the Serpent?" I asked.

"Hydra," Virgo said.

I remembered the myth now and wondered if it could be related to my memories. I made a mental note to study the Constellation myths better once I had the time.

"Could it be possible that you were trying to find Crater?" Draco said. "Star Objects are incredibly powerful. Whoever owns them can manifest the power of the object, just as we can manifest the power of our Constellations with a thought."

"It could be," I said.

"I can't think of any other Cup that could be *that* important," Virgo said. Then she shook her head. "But I still don't know why you would think that erasing your own memories would lead you to the Cup."

"You couldn't even remember you were looking for a Cup," Draco said.

"I think I was supposed to remember the Cup," I said.

I tried to search through my new memory again, but I really didn't know why I had erased my memories to get to the Cup.

"So that's why Perseus is interested in your memories," Virgo said. "He knows you set out to find Crater and wants it for himself."

"What can Crater actually do?" I asked.

"There's a lot of myths associated with it," Virgo said. "There's the Greek myth, which I just explained. But there's others." She pulled another strand of hair out of her face. "Some people associate it with the Holy Grail or the Cup of immortality that belonged to the Gods."

"That seems powerful," I muttered.

Perseus would definitely want to have immortality. I breathed out, thin mist coming from my mouth. A moment of silence stretched between the three of us.

"So," Draco said. "In summary, you and the Pleiades were working together. You somehow knew where Crater was and erased your memories because you believed that was the only way to get to it."

"Yeah." I was pretty sure that's what had happened.

"But where are the Pleiades?" Virgo asked. "I mean, you left them about a year ago, and we've never seen them. Could they be hiding?"

Pain twisted in my chest. My sisters hadn't found me yet, or maybe they hadn't wanted to come find me. What if they didn't really care about me? I tried to convince myself that wasn't true. They could be trying to hide from Perseus, or maybe they had no idea where or how to find me. I hadn't wanted them to find me before I found the Cup and had left no trace of where I was going . . . but it had been over a year now.

"We're still missing something," Draco said after a minute. "This whole erasing your own memories thing doesn't sit well with me."

"It doesn't sit well with me either," I said. "But I don't remember why I did that."

A sudden gust of cold wind blew around us.

"We should go inside, guys," Virgo said. "We can talk in my room."

We made our way to Virgo's room while my heartbeat echoed in my ears from my dread over those whispering voices.

A few silver rays of light filtered through the large windows. Leo slept with his head in between his paws in front of it. He raised his head when we entered, but then lowered it again and began snoring. Virgo's room was a lot bigger than mine. Maybe Argo liked her better?—with an L-shaped couch with white throw pillows and a king-sized bed. Someone slept in the bed, and it took me a second to realize it was Sirius. The dog lay on his side, and the blankets covered him completely, only leaving his head out, which rested on a pillow. Maera slept next to the larger dog.

Aquila perched on the nightstand next to the bed, watching us with his bright yellow eyes. I had never seen him sleep. Virgo sat on the couch, then Draco and I sat to her sides.

"Is there anything else you remember?" Draco said. "Anything that should be important?"

I thought of that for a second, then nodded. "I remember that I had information about a Star Child—the most powerful Star Child. The Cup was supposed to lead me to that being."

"Who could that be?" Virgo asked. I shrugged. She sighed. "We need to take this one step at a time. Let's focus on finding the Cup first. I'm sure now that Perseus sent us to find Crater in Egypt because he thinks Corvus is the only one who knows how to find it."

I nodded. This mission had a new meaning for me. The reason my memories were missing was because of Crater. I had been willing to lose everything to find it. We couldn't let Perseus have that Cup. We would have to find another way to trick Perseus out of hiding and make him think he would exchange the Cup for the Twins' Prophecies.

"And we need to stay very alert," Draco said. "I don't trust the Twins, and I have the feeling they may turn on us once we have the Cup."

"It's a possibility," I admitted.

"For now, let's go to sleep," Virgo said. She moved to the edge of the bed. "You boys can sleep on the couch if you want."

Draco smiled. He stretched out on one side of the couch, me on the other, resting my head on one of the pillows. Even though my eyelids felt heavy as iron curtains, I just couldn't sleep.

When the night arrives, their souls awake again,
A new moon dark above them,
and below the earth barren,

Virgo began singing very softly, but I could hear her perfectly.

Soon they will be born again into a flesh of flames.
Flames that burn white like their souls.
Flames that burn out the brighter they shine.

I began drifting away, the song the only thing I focused on. My breaths seemed to come more easily to me, and soon I was asleep.

Chapter XIX, Verse III

In the field the wounded soldiers lay sleeping,
The roaring Lion did wake them from their slumber.
A new battle to be fought, or else to ruin they shall fall.
The Golden King rises once again, to rule a realm not his own.
Lending his strength to the fallen, so they shall rise once again.
Betrayal then shall await, from the one that was once his friend.
The wasted land he will then roam, until the new generation is born.

CHAPTER 6

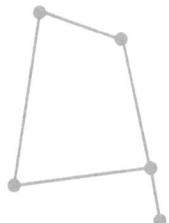

I STOOD LOOKING OUT from the terrace of the hotel. We had docked at Alexandria, the coastal city closest to the temple we needed to visit. The sun shone through the cloudless morning sky and glimmered off the ocean. The sunlight's reflection created an opaque effect on the water, as if sand were suspended on the surface. Waves rolled as they approached the rocky shore, and the fresh breeze smelled of salt. I took a deep breath and closed my eyes for a moment. I felt a bit better rested than most days.

"Corvus, come on," Virgo said behind me.

I pulled myself from the glass terrace and walked back into our hotel suite. It was expensive, but we had enough money in the credit cards to pay for it. Leo sat next to the terrace door, wagging his tail slowly as he observed the Twins. He didn't trust them either and looked at them like mice he might eat for dinner. The Twins pointedly avoided looking at the Lion.

Sirius and Draco sat on a large couch below a mirror, facing Virgo who sat on a chair next to a wooden desk.

At the far end of the room was the kitchen, where the Twins sat talking to each other in hushed tones. In between the kitchen and living room was a hallway that extended to the right with two doors that led to the Twins' room and the one I shared with

Draco. Opposite from that, next to the desk, was the door that led to Virgo's room.

"We should get going," Virgo said as she set Maera down and stood up. The Twins also stood and walked over to us.

"All right then," Pollux said as he rubbed his hands together. "The temple we need to go to is a few miles away. It's very close to the Nile."

"What temple is it?" I asked.

Castor and Pollux both shrugged. "We don't know what it's called," Pollux said.

"How could you not know?" Virgo asked.

"Perseus gave us the exact location," said Castor. "But the temple doesn't seem to be well known. We tried looking it up online but found nothing."

"That's strange," Draco muttered.

"Yeah," Pollux said. "We couldn't find any information about it."

That certainly was strange.

"It's not a particularly impressive ruin either," Castor said. "It's pretty small, from the pictures Perseus showed us."

"But still," I said. "Why would it have no name or information about it?"

"There are a *lot* of ruins in Egypt," Virgo said. "So if this one is not frequently visited, it makes sense that it would slowly fade to the background while people visit the most popular ruins."

"I guess," I said.

"It would also make sense that if there's a treasure hidden in the ruins, it should not be a popular place to visit," Draco said. "Someone must have hidden it in a temple they knew wouldn't attract much attention."

I looked at the Twins, who stood side by side. "And Perseus didn't tell you what kind of treasure we were supposed to find?"

"Nope," Pollux said.

"It's supposed to be important. And Perseus assured us it would be there somewhere." Castor waved his hand vaguely, as if *somewhere* could mean anywhere in or near the temple.

"According to Perseus," Pollux said, "one of the Prophecies said we would find it. So I'm positive we will . . . somehow."

Virgo shot me a quick glance, and I knew she was remembering the conversation we'd had with Draco earlier in the morning. Everything seemed too coincidental—Perseus sends us to find Crater at the same time I begin to recover new memories. And the treasure that he wants us to find just happens to be part of the memory I recovered most recently. I knew the ocean had triggered that memory—but it could have triggered any memory. The pieces of the puzzle fit together too smoothly, and I couldn't help but think that there was something terribly wrong with the timing of the memories I was recovering. But I didn't know what I could do about it.

It scared me that Perseus knew more about my past than I did and that he was using it to his advantage. Could he know about my sisters too? Did they have their own Prophecies? That thought terrified me, but I would have to worry about that later.

"So," I said, "our plan is to explore the ruins or temple or whatever and see what clues about the 'treasure' we can find."

"Pretty much," Pollux said.

"We should hire a tour guide," Virgo said. "None of us are proficient in ancient Egyptian so we'll need some help."

"Perseus didn't give you a deadline on this, did he?" I asked. The Twins both shook their heads.

"He just said to get it back to him as soon as possible," Pollux said. "We have time, but let's try to get it as soon as we can."

I nodded. I looked at Sirius, Maera, and Leo. "I think you guys should stay here for now. We're only going to see the temple and then come back." Finding a van big enough for Leo was always a challenge, not to mention the lie I had to tell everyone who saw us to make them believe he was only a cat.

Leo growled.

"Corvus is right," Draco said. "You can come with us to the temple next time we go there. Right now, we'll just be looking for clues."

Leo didn't seem very happy. He simply stared at the Twins again, his golden eyes cold as a distant sun. The Twins strapped on their weapons. We all knew that finding the treasure would be dangerous—dangerous enough that Perseus himself didn't want to be here. I hung my sword from the scabbard at my back. Draco's spear was too long for him to strap it to his back if he wanted to walk through doors without ducking, so he just held onto it. Castor had his two swords at his back, and Pollux his axe. Virgo strapped the knife at her waist.

Before leaving, Draco put on a pair of sunglasses that the Twins had given him. After exiting the room, we rode the elevator to the ground floor. The hotel was two stories tall. At the center it had a circular garden with beautiful plants that rose up nearly to the domed glass ceiling. The floor and pillars around the small garden were made of red marble. The reception desk sat on the opposite side of the room.

The few people in the lobby eyed us suspiciously as we walked through. One man to our left, dressed in shorts and a white shirt, stood still as he watched us pass by. The janitor, who was mopping the floor on our right looked up and stopped for a second, then went back to mopping. We walked around the garden and stopped a few yards away from the reception desk.

"I'll go convince the receptionist that we need a tour guide," I said.

"I'll go with you," Draco said.

We walked together to the receptionist's desk.

"Good morning," I said to the young woman sitting behind the desk. She looked only a few years older than us. When she saw us, she eyed our weapons carefully.

"They're fake," I lied, and her expression softened.

"What can I help you with, sir?" she asked.

I wasn't sure I looked old enough to be called *sir*.

"Could we get a tour guide?" Draco asked.

She pressed her lips into a thin line. "You can only get a guide if you book it in advance, and—"

"We did book it in advance," I said, my voice distorted as if I had spoken underwater. The scars on my chest began to burn, and my pulse raced inside my veins. "We should have a tour guide ready for us right now."

Her eyes went blank for a second, then widened. "Sure," she said. "I remember you guys coming yesterday. Give me a few minutes and I'll get your tour guide."

She rose from the chair and quickly walked away from us.

"What should we do with the Twins?" Draco said once she was out of earshot. "I don't believe they'll be so friendly once we find Crater. I'm also sure they know exactly what we're looking for but don't want to tell us." I nodded. "For now, your memories give us an advantage."

I wished I could remember more, but for now we would have to use the few pieces of my past that we had.

"They'll try to take Crater and leave us behind," I said. "And they'll try to steal all the Prophecies from Perseus on their own."

"There's a lot of ways this could go wrong," Draco said. "When we find Crater, we have to keep it away from the Twins."

"Perseus will expect the Twins to give it to him," I said. "We need a plan to make Perseus believe the Twins have the Cup without actually giving it to him."

Draco nodded. "We'll think about that once we have the Cup. In the meantime, let's just focus on finding it and be careful around the Twins." He sighed. "The worst part is that we already know they'll betray us, but we don't know when or how. And I hate to admit it, but we need their help to find Crater and get to Perseus."

"We'll worry about that later," I said as my stomach swirled with anxiety.

I hated feeling that uncertain—having to watch our backs every second because we didn't know what would happen next. If we had the Prophecies, we would be more prepared to face the future. I trusted that the Prophecies said we would find Crater, or else Perseus wouldn't have sent us here. That gave me a string of hope to cling to.

Draco sighed. "Our biggest problem for now is that Cup. If Perseus isn't here, it's because he thinks finding Crater is too dangerous."

"But Perseus is very powerful, and he's never backed down from anything dangerous," I said. "Either this is *extremely* dangerous, or we're not seeing the full picture."

"It might be both," Draco said. "But we don't have much of a choice. We need to get those Prophecies back and this is our best chance to do it before Algol's next rising."

I nodded. That was our priority. If we knew Perseus's future, then we might find a way to defeat him once and for all. Even if Andromeda was the only one who could kill him, the Prophecies would be able to tell us what we could do to defeat his allies and bring Perseus to his death.

The receptionist came rushing back toward the counter. "Your tour guide should arrive here shortly."

"That's great, thanks," I said.

"He'll meet you at the entrance of the hotel," she said.

"Thank you," Draco said.

We walked back to the others. The Twins were talking to Virgo. Draco tensed at my side but said nothing. We all walked out of the hotel together. Despite the bright sun above us, chilly air greeted us outside. For some reason I had expected Egypt to always be warm, but I realized that at least in the late fall it isn't.

We waited in silence next to a fountain—a black marble cobra spitting out water—for a couple of minutes until a middle-aged man walked out of the hotel. He had a hat that made him look like he was about to go on a safari. He wore light brown pants, a white shirt, and a dark brown jacket. The man gave us a warm smile. He didn't stare suspiciously at our weapons, which was a relief.

"I hope you're all ready for the greatest adventure of your lives!" His clear eyes shone with excitement.

The Twins frowned. "I guess?" Castor said.

"Good!" The tour guide spread his arms wide in a dramatic posture. "Because today we will walk the streets that the ancient gods once walked through, we will enter their forbidden temples, we will observe the dead mummies, and we will discover their long-lost secrets!"

"Actually," Pollux said. He pulled out a crumpled map from his jacket. "We only want to go to this temple right here." He pointed at the map.

The tour guide's smile dropped from his face, and he deflated like a balloon. I guessed there were no dead mummies at the temple we planned to visit.

"But there's nothing interesting there," the tour guide said. "That temple is not even in our tourist brochures." He paused. "I'm not even sure it's open to the public anymore." I wondered why that was so. "Instead, I could take you to the catacombs of

Kom, the Roman Amphitheatre, the Sarapeum, or the Anfushi Tombs!"

"We just want to go there," Pollux pointed at the map again. "That's the only temple we want to visit."

The tour guide just looked at all of us, blinking, then forced a smile. "Well, all right then! Since you're the ones paying, then I guess that's where we'll go!"

He motioned a few feet behind us to where a white car had just pulled up. Draco, Virgo, and I got in the back together, with Draco's spear crossing through the car and in between the Twins who sat on the seat in front of us. The tour guide sat next to them, without mentioning the spear tip that lay less than a foot from his face.

For the entire ride, the tour guide didn't shut up, rambling random facts.

"Oh, and look! Right on that street there is a traditional food restaurant . . . Five miles north of that light post is where we found a mummy buried in one of the temples . . . Did you know that all the pyramids of Egypt are built west of the Nile River . . . The Egyptians used to have more than two thousand deities!"

I considered telling him that he preferred to be quiet, but then I realized that the Twins were so annoyed at hearing him that I let him keep talking just so they would feel more irritated.

We arrived at the temple after two long hours. The van stopped fifty yards away from it, although it could have probably driven closer. We all climbed out and stared at a strange, roughly triangular hill made of light brown stone before us. The steep hill stood about two stories tall and looked completely out of place in the otherwise flat terrain, almost, but I wouldn't have called it a pyramid. Something was definitely odd about it, and I wondered why it hadn't drawn more attention. The temple was carved into the side of the hill, and two stone statues guarded the rectangular entrance.

My pulse quickened. Next to me, Draco had gone tense, like a tight coil about to spring. Virgo grasped the hilt of her knife. In front of us, the Twins shifted uneasily, and for the first time in two hours the tour guide had gone quiet. It was as if the place emitted a strange vibration that made people want to be away from it. Andromeda had told us that when she and Perseus had found Alathea's book in Delphi, Greece, they had entered a cavern that no archeologist had been able to discover before. Maybe there were places that only Star Children could access? That was plausible.

"All right, kids," the tour guide said. "Welcome to the temple!" He didn't mention the name of the temple. He had clearly recognized it from the map, so he knew about it. I would have assumed that at least archeologists had named the temple, but perhaps not. "To your left, in the distance, you'll be able to spot the Nile River." I could indeed see the river flowing parallel to us about half a mile away. The water was dark blue, and the river seemed wide enough that Argo, as a small boat, could have fit through it.

I couldn't spot anything else of interest in the flat terrain. The tour guide started walking forward, and we all followed him. The barren ground was hard beneath my feet, and small pebbles crunched as we walked. I could feel the dread around me like a current of wind.

As we got closer, I studied the statues guarding the entrance. They had human bodies, but the heads had been smashed off. Both statues seemed male, based on their build. In one hand they each held a broken staff, and in the other an ankh—an Egyptian cross.

We stopped at the entrance. Draco held his spear so tightly his knuckles had turned white and his hand red. Next to him, Virgo eyed the statues suspiciously, as if they would burst into life. The Twins stood close to each other.

"All right," the tour guide said before we walked in, forcing a smile. He glanced at the statues, which towered at least two feet above him, even without the heads. "This temple was built in the Third Intermediate Period, about six hundred years before the Common Era. Archeologists don't know who built it or why." He cleared his throat as he looked uneasily at the statues. "It is also not known to which god or goddess this temple was dedicated." He motioned to the entrance. "Now if we walk inside, we can see some inscriptions on the walls." He disappeared through the entrance.

I hesitated for a moment, my stomach knotting. The Twins walked in first, and Draco followed right after them. A screech echoed in the sky. I looked up, smiling at the sight of Aquila flying above us. Knowing he was there made me feel a bit safer, but without the Lion I still felt anxious. I stepped into the temple. It was more spacious than I expected. The rectangular room was at least twenty feet wide and thirty feet long. The ceiling was fifteen feet above us. It had cracks that looked like spider webs.

At the opposite side of the room wide stairs led upward. The steps were broken and cracked, more like a pile of stones than actual stairs. A statue stood on each side of the room, right in the middle of the wall. Both statues had human bodies, and like the statues outside, the heads were missing. One of the bodies seemed female and the other male.

The male statue on the left had his arms crossed on his chest, and he seemed to have been holding something in each hand but those objects had broken off. At his waist he had some sort of belt or ribbon. The female statue had one of her hands crossed over her chest as she held a thin staff. Her other hand dangled below her waist, holding an ankh.

The tour guide cleared his throat and looked at the walls. Next to the statues were many hieroglyphs and some large drawings. I couldn't make out anything the hieroglyphs said and tried to look at the drawings instead.

Since we were looking for the Cup, I had expected to see at least one drawing or inscription that showed a cup, but there were none. I focused on a drawing where the paint had mostly peeled away, but I could still see some colors. It showed a goddess dressed in red with faded yellow skin and black hair. In one hand she held an ankh, and a five-pointed star crowned her head.

"Scholars have long debated the meaning of these hieroglyphs," the tour guide began. "They are written in a combination of old Egyptian hieroglyphs and Late scripts, but they seem to have been inscribed around 100 CE, which makes most scholars believe that they're a forgery—not originally Egyptian."

Virgo walked toward the stairs, looking carefully at the drawings. The Twins inspected the statues, while Draco looked at the tour guide, paying attention to the explanation. I was glad at least one of us was listening. I zoned out of the rest of the explanations, lost in my own thoughts.

Someone had tried to leave a clue on how to find Crater, I was sure of that. It must have been another Star Child—no ordinary human would have been able to hold a Star Object. But which Star Child had been alive nearly two thousand years ago?

My mind buzzed. I thought of all the weapons and strange marine animal bones we had found in Argo. The Twins had said those had been there before they found Argo and that someone had owned the Ship before them. Argo, the inscriptions—they seemed to indicate that long before we had materialized into existence, other Star Beings had been alive and active.

"What does this drawing mean?" Virgo asked as she pointed at the drawing of the goddess I had just seen.

"That is the goddess Sopdet. A few archeologists believe that the temple was dedicated to her, since she is the only goddess represented on the walls," the tour guide said as he narrowed his eyes at the drawing. "The inscriptions next to her haven't been found anywhere else, and they don't seem to represent any myth or incantation. We believe these are also a forgery, but the drawing itself seems to be an original."

"What does the inscription say?" I asked.

The tour guide walked closer to the wall. "It doesn't make any sense," he said as he shook his head. "As I just mentioned, we believe these were forged in later times, as they don't resemble texts normally written in temples. But I will translate it anyhow: *In all of its might the Star shines bright. The Cup remains below the temple, only found in the river that flows plentiful. When the broken god drowns below the rushing waters. Death awaits below, unless the empty Vessel endures the brimming power. Then to—*" He paused. "The whole middle part is damaged so I can't make out what it says . . . *In the end only betrayal awaits, and the loss of everything once gained.*"

Virgo's eyes went wide as she stared at the wall, and Draco began fidgeting with his spear, running his fingers over the carvings. I knew we were all thinking the same thing—someone, nearly two thousand years ago, had inscribed one of Alathea's Prophecies onto that wall, leaving a clue on how to find the Cup. The Prophecy was confusing, as they usually were, but one thing was clear—the Cup was here, hidden somewhere beneath the temple. Or maybe somewhere in the Nile? The Prophecy said *in* the river, but at the same time it said underneath the temple. Maybe an underground river?

Andromeda had told us that to find Alathea's book, underneath Delphi, they'd had to enter a secret cavern under the ruins. She said that Perseus had somehow found it. Maybe we were dealing with something similar here—a hidden place underneath these ruins that only Star Children could find.

"Is that all?" Castor asked.

"Pretty much," the tour guide said. "The rest of the inscriptions are just random hieroglyphs drawn in the walls, written by someone who clearly didn't know Egyptian—this is the only part that can be read."

"Who was the goddess Sopdet?" asked Virgo. "You said that the temple may have been dedicated to her."

"Well, we don't know if it was dedicated to her," he pointed at the headless statues. "Without the heads it's hard to say which gods the statues represent. Scholars believe the ones outside could be Anubis and that these two are Osiris and Isis . . . but we're not absolutely sure. That's just based on the objects they hold and the way their bodies are positioned. Egyptian gods are most easily distinguished by their heads, which are all different."

"But whoever forged all these drawings clearly showed interest in Sopdet," Virgo said.

"I believe so," the tour guide said. "She is the goddess most prominently drawn here, and several inscriptions have her name. Although archeologists also believe that there might have been other inscriptions here before that were purposefully destroyed or erased to inscribe these new ones."

"So, who was Sopdet?" Virgo asked again.

"She was a very well-known goddess," the tour guide started. "Usually identified with Isis, Osiris, or Anubis. But she was mainly a star goddess, of—"

"Star goddess?" Castor asked.

The tour guide didn't seem happy to be interrupted. "Yes, some stars and constellations, the most important ones, were represented by gods or goddesses." I felt my stomach swirling. The tour guide pointed at the drawing of Sopdet. "Her consort was Sah, personified by the constellation Orion." I could feel my heartbeat like hammers pounding in my ears. "And Sopdet herself represented the Dog Star, Sirius."

The room grew unnaturally quiet.

"Sirius?" I asked, my voice a bit shriller than I intended.

The tour guide nodded. I turned to Draco and Virgo, and the three of us shared a knowing look. The Twins also exchanged a glance. They didn't seem surprised, and I wondered if Perseus had shared this with them. In turn, the tour guide eyed us suspiciously, as if he knew some sort of understanding had passed between us that he was not part of.

"All right then," Castor said after a couple of seconds. "Thank you so much for the tour. You can leave now."

"But—" The guide seemed offended and surprised at the same time.

"Thank you so much for the wonderful tour," I said as my scars burned slightly. My voice sounded much deeper inside my ears. "You enjoyed giving us this tour and are happy to return to the car and wait for us there."

The tour guide smiled. "It was indeed very fun to visit this temple. I hadn't been here in almost a decade! I'll go wait in the car now to give you some time to take some pictures."

He walked out of the room, and I took in a deep breath.

"So," Pollux said. "Looks like we're in the right place."

"And it seems that we're looking for a Cup," Virgo said, pensive.

"I guess so." Castor eyed the two statues without meeting her gaze.

"Now we have to figure out how to actually get the Cup," Draco said. "Perseus didn't say anything about that, did he?"

The Twins both shook their heads. "He said we would find the clues here, which we have."

"But as always Alathea's Prophecy is cryptic," I said. "The Cup is found in the river that flows plentiful? That has to be the Nile, but then how is that related to the first line of Prophecy about a star shining bright, which I'm assuming is Sirius? And the broken god drowns? Is that a reference to a specific god? Are there any Egyptian gods who drowned?"

"We'll need Sirius," Virgo said. Everyone turned to her. "Whoever made these inscriptions mentioned Sopdet several times, and she is prominently drawn on the walls. If Sopdet represents Sirius, then he might be the one to provide the next clues on how to find the Cup." She paused for a second, whispering the lines of the Prophecy to herself. "I think I might know how everything is related."

"How?" Pollux asked.

"In ancient times, the Star Sirius signaled the flooding of the Nile. It was seen shortly before sunrise a few days or weeks before the annual inundation of the river. The Star defined the Egyptian new year," Virgo said. "The flooding usually started in August and in December the waters went back to normal, but I think this doesn't happen anymore. In any case, the Star Sirius has always been associated with the Nile."

"The Prophecy says that the Cup is found in the river that flows plentiful," Castor said. "Could that mean that the Cup is hidden in the Nile instead of here in the temple then? And that Sirius can find it?"

"If it's hidden at the bottom of the Nile somewhere, then that technically still counts as being below the temple," Pollux said.

"Should we be looking in the Nile instead then?" Draco asked.

"With Argo we could sail this area of the Nile to look for the Cup," Castor said.

"I'm not completely sure that it's in the Nile," Virgo said. "But we can be certain that Sirius, the Nile, and the Cup are related. And maybe Sirius is the only one who can find the Cup."

Is that why Perseus had sent us? Because he knew we would need Sirius to find the Cup? I had the feeling I hadn't known that before erasing my memories. I had been sure that I could do this by myself, but I had been wrong.

The image of Sopdet stared back at me from the wall. I found it strange that the Prophecy appeared right there on the wall, giving us instructions. Humans wouldn't have been able to decipher what it actually meant, but the fact that it was in plain sight bothered me. Someone had hidden the Cup and left clues on how to find it. Had that Star Child known someone would need the Cup in the future? And why had they hidden it in the first place?

"We should get back to the hotel," Castor said. "And then we could come again tomorrow morning with Sirius and all the others. Although I'm not sure how much the dog will be able to help. I mean he's just a dog."

"A very smart dog," Virgo said defensively. "For now, bringing him here seems like the best thing we can do. Maybe Sirius will be able to find something we haven't been able to."

"Wait a second," Draco said as he slapped his forehead with his free hand. "Stupid," he muttered under his breath. He removed his sunglasses, revealing his dark red-orange eyes. He looked at the floor, scanning it, his eyes narrowed. The Twins exchanged a look, but I knew what Draco was doing. I sometimes forgot that Draco could see more of the electromagnetic spectrum than we could. He could see X-ray, ultraviolet, radio, and other wavelengths that we probably weren't even aware of. "Yep," he said. "There's a large hollow chamber below this temple." He squinted his eyes. "I—it's blurry, but I can see it clearly." He looked over the rest of the floor. "I don't see an entrance though."

"Maybe we could break through it," Castor suggested.

Draco shook his head. "There are many layers of rock before getting to it." He looked wildly over the floor, as if trying to follow a very fast-moving spider with his gaze. "I've never seen anything like this. It's as if the chamber is purposefully diverting light rays to hide itself."

I didn't know what that meant, but I knew that it probably confirmed my earlier suspicions. There *were* certain places only Star Children could access, which were invisible to humans.

"So at least we know where we need to go—below this temple," Virgo said. "Now we only have to find an entrance, and I have a feeling Sirius is the only one who can help."

"We should get back to the hotel and speak to Sirius," I said.

Draco looked away from the floor. He seemed dazed, one vertical pupil thinner than the other. He blinked a couple of times and put his sunglasses back on.

"Sounds like a plan," Pollux said. "And if he doesn't find anything, I would suggest we search the Nile with Argo. Maybe the entrance is there."

"Could be," Draco said.

"Wait," Pollux said as he turned to Draco. "Isn't the Constellation of Draco the one that guards treasures and secrets? So shouldn't *you* be able to find the Cup, Draco?"

Draco tensed, and even though he had his glasses on I knew his pupils had thinned into a line. He didn't like talking about that. Even if his Constellation ruled over lost treasures, he had never been able to materialize finding them or knowing where they were. He should have been able to do that, but instead Draco was just half-dragon and didn't seem to have powers related to his Constellation other than breathing fire and seeing alternate wavelengths. I sensed Draco was hiding something from his past. He had briefly mentioned that his other powers weren't available to him anymore, but I didn't know what that meant.

"I can't do that," Draco said simply.

"We should just follow the Prophecy." Virgo pointed at the wall. "It will surely lead us to the Cup."

The Twins nodded, although they eyed Draco suspiciously, as if we had an advantage that we weren't sharing. None of us mentioned the rest of what the Prophecy had said—about how death, betrayal, and loss awaited us along with the Cup.

We could worry about that part later.

CHAPTER 7

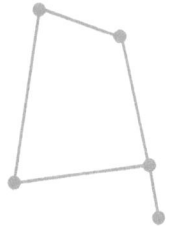

SIRIUS WAS SLEEPING on the couch and didn't wake up when we came into the hotel room. The evening sun warmed the room as it filtered through the window. Leo raised his head from his paws as he lay next to the clear terrace door, staring at us with interest. Maera just wagged his tail from the carpet. I couldn't see Aquila, so I guessed he was still outside flying. Maybe he had gone sightseeing.

We all crowded around the couch. Sirius kept snoring.

"Sirius," Virgo said softly.

The dog cracked one eye open, saw us all standing above him, and raised his head. He blinked a couple of times.

"Hey, boy," I said. "We need your help."

Sirius stared at us, then stood up, shook himself, and stretched. He sat on the couch, facing us. Virgo told him what we had found at the temple, and the dog listened quietly. Leo was listening too—his gaze never left Virgo and his tail went still.

"So, we need your help figuring out how to find the entrance to the secret chamber where the Cup is hidden," Virgo said.

"Can you help us, boy?" I asked.

After a couple seconds of silence, Sirius extended his paw to me. I took it and smiled, then I let go. Virgo scratched him behind the ears.

"Now we have a plan for tomorrow," Castor said. "We go back to the temple and hope Sirius finds a secret entrance hidden somewhere."

My stomach swirled with anxiety. We still didn't know how Sirius would be able to help or what dangers awaited us. The Prophecy said the Cup was below the temple, but that didn't mean it would be easy to find it.

"Not a very elaborate plan but still a good one," Pollux said. "In the meantime, I could use some rest." He and his brother retired to their bedroom.

"Some rest sounds good," Virgo said.

I nodded, although I had the feeling that, as usual, I would not be getting much of it.

●———————●———————●

I stood looking at the wooden door at the end of the hallway, lightning flashing into the house from the tall window at my side. Outside, rain pelted the backyard and dark clouds covered the sky. It was around midday, but it looked dark enough to be night. I hated the weather in London.

I walked down the hallway toward the door. It had taken me days to find her and trapping her hadn't been easy, but she was here now. That was all that mattered, and I planned on getting as much information as I could—that's what I was really good at.

The others had sent me to London alone. We had found another Star Child—Centaurus—in Africa. We knew he was probably more dangerous than this one, so instead of letting me go to Africa to find Centaurus, I had been sent here. I was always sent on the less dangerous missions. I hated that. But part of me appreciated being alone with no one around to tell me what to do. Even though interrogating this Star Child would be far less exciting than fighting a Centaur.

I sighed. Someday. If I kept training and proved I was as brave and strong as the others, they would let me go with them. I stopped before opening the thick wooden door at the end of the hallway, simply holding the cold handle. I would find a way to prove myself, but for now we needed information from this Star Child.

I walked through the door and closed it behind me. The only window was at the top of the room to my left, and it barely let any light through. It took a second for my eyes to adjust to the darkness. I realized that she had moved to the corner of the room, her arms hugging her legs.

"What do you want now?" she hissed.

The chains that bound her wrists and ankles clanked against the floor as she stood up. I knew the chains wouldn't let her get close to me. At her full height, Cassiopeia was a few inches shorter than me.

"You haven't answered my questions, Cassiopeia," I said. "Or should I call you Zia?"

Even in the dim light I noticed how her face paled. Cassiopeia's blond hair was tied in a messy ponytail. Her light blue eyes were cold as ice. She had a thin face with a straight nose and full lips. Her cheeks were rosy, her brows thick. Cassiopeia looked to be around thirty, but I didn't know her exact age.

In my head, I went over her myth again. She was the Queen of Ethiopia, wife of King Cepheus. She had once boasted that she was more beautiful than the Nereids—the Sea Nymphs. So Poseidon punished Cassiopeia for her boastfulness. The Sea God sent the Monster Cetus to ravage the coast of their kingdom. The only way to appease the Monster was for Cassiopeia to sacrifice her daughter Andromeda. They had left Andromeda chained to a rock, until Perseus had seen her on his way back home and had killed Cetus using Medusa's head.

At Perseus and Andromeda's wedding, Perseus accidentally killed Cepheus and Cassiopeia with Medusa's head when a fight
broke out among the guests. Not the happiest of endings for the royal
couple. Cassiopeia, Cepheus, Andromeda, Cetus, and Perseus were all
Constellations. But we weren't sure what Destiny the Constellation of
Cassiopeia controlled or what she could materialize as a Star Child.

I didn't care about that right now though.

"I didn't get to introduce myself yesterday," I said. "I'm Corvus."

Cassiopeia pressed herself against the wall. "The Liar," she whispered. "The cheater, the traitor, the deceiver."

I smiled. "The Queen," I whispered back mockingly. She had lived
most of her life in hiding, lying low, trying to avoid the rest of the Star
Children. She earned money by selling secret information between governments and intelligence agencies and trading weapons on the black
market. I didn't know how she had found that particular job. I took a
few steps to the right, still out of her reach. Her eyes never left me.

"What do you want?" she asked again.

"It's not about what I want," I said. "It's about what you want."
Her eyes narrowed at me. "And right now, you just want to stand very
still, without moving."

The two scars on my chest began to ache. Cassiopeia's mind was
strong. She moved farther back into the corner, pressing herself against
the wall.

"You don't want to move," I said, hearing my voice distant, as if
it were coming from the end of a long tunnel. "You just want to stand
still, very still, like a statue."

It took a couple of seconds, but Cassiopeia became still. Only her
chest rose slowly up and down as she breathed. I walked closer to her.
Her stare was blank, looking at the wall behind me, and her expression had softened. I pulled her blouse down a little, and immediately
white light pulsed into the room. I stared at Cassiopeia's scar. It was

right over her left breast, as if someone had tried to stab her in the heart. The bright light pulsed in tune with her heart.

I let go of her shirt and walked away from her, making my way to the opposite side of the room. I let the lie drop, and Cassiopeia shook her head wildly. Her eyes became razor sharp.

"You little b—"

"You want to stand very still again."

Her words died on her lips. I stepped closer to her again. The muscles in my arm tensed in anticipation. I slapped Cassiopeia hard across the cheek, the sound echoing across the room, and stepped back as I dropped the lie. Cassiopeia's hand immediately went to her reddened cheek, and she let out a low hiss.

"I'm sorry, you were saying," I let my back rest on the cold wall.

Cassiopeia remained silent, her eyes glaring daggers at me.

"You know what else you want?" I asked. Cassiopeia breathed faster, although I wasn't sure she had noticed. "You want to tell me the truth. You want to start by telling me how you got that scar. It seems old."

I had come to realize that older scars shone brighter, but I wasn't sure why that happened.

My scars burned again. Cassiopeia gritted her teeth, and she groaned. A few seconds passed, but she didn't answer. I let a minute pass and still she remained silent. I still found it strange that some Star Children fell easily for some lies yet struggled to resist others. But Cassiopeia was something new—no one had ever fully resisted one of my lies. It usually took others a few seconds to finally yield, but they always did.

"You want to stand very still again," I said as I walked back to her. Cassiopeia's hand remained on her cheek. I pulled out a small dagger from my pocket. Cassiopeia's eyes darted to the flashing metal, but she remained unmoving. I had found that my lies were more powerful when people were in pain—it weakened their minds, as

their thoughts only focused on stopping the suffering instead of trying to resist the lies.

I stood right in front of Cassiopeia, holding the little dagger tightly in my hand. It wasn't a Star Weapon—it wouldn't kill her— but it would hurt the same. I dove the knife into her belly. Cassiopeia didn't make a sound, but her blue eyes flooded with pain. I pulled the knife out. Blood splattered on the floor between us.

"You want to tell me about that scar," I said.

But she didn't yield. Her eyes flared with anger, and if she hadn't been frozen, I knew she would have smiled.

I clenched my jaw. All right then. I placed my hands over her stomach, feeling for her ribs. Then I placed the tip of the dagger right in front of one. Cassiopeia didn't say anything. I dove the dagger forward until I felt its tip hitting bone. Cassiopeia moaned, but she still didn't talk. Blood flowed freely from her white shirt. Maybe Cassiopeia had been tortured before—it wouldn't have surprised me given her current occupation.

I pulled the knife out, and her breaths became more ragged. I let the dagger drip blood for a few seconds as I looked at her now avoiding my gaze. Why wouldn't she tell me about the scar on her chest? I hadn't been particularly interested in it at first—it was the first question I had thought of as I evaluated her mental strength. But now I was intrigued about it.

Cassiopeia remained silent for another minute. She didn't seem to mind getting stabbed in the torso. I looked at her face—her skin soft as a white petal. A smile crept up my cheeks. Some of us had inherited the personalities from our Constellation myths, and I was curious to find out if Cassiopeia was as vain as in her stories.

I placed the bloody knife on her cheek, and her breath caught. "It would be a shame to leave a scar here," I said. I pulled the knife back. I hadn't cut her, but the blood that had clung to the knife stained her skin red. "Or here," I placed it on her lips. I pulled the knife back, then pressed the tip to her chin. A thin line of blood oozed down her neck.

Cassiopeia's mind snapped.

I took a step back as I let go of that lie. Cassiopeia collapsed on the floor, her fingers tracing her face. She let out a hiss when she touched the little cut on her chin. Only then did her hands turn to her torso, and she moaned in pain as blood stained her palms.

"You want to tell me how you got the scar on your chest," my voice was slow and deep.

"Cepheus did it," she finally said after a couple of seconds. Cassiopeia hugged herself, her blank stare glued to the stone floor. "He tried to kill me."

I considered that. We had never heard of anyone who knew Cepheus. But since he had been Cassiopeia's husband in mythology, it made sense that they knew each other. Although many Star Children who shared myths had never met.

"Why?" I asked, still wondering why she would refuse to tell me that.

"We had a fight," she said.

"How long ago was this?" I asked, pondering if Cepheus was worth finding as well.

"Why does that matter?" she asked. I could feel her mind rebelling against me. She began slipping out of my lie. I gritted my teeth, my scars burning like fire.

"Because you just want to tell me," I said, feeling the echo of my voice reverberate in my bones.

Cassiopeia slid down the wall and sat on the floor. "This was around ninety years ago . . . maybe a hundred."

Now that was truly interesting. Cassiopeia was a lot older than I had guessed, even though she didn't look it. I considered the implica-

tions of this new revelation. Maybe coming to London had been better than going to Africa after all.

"How is it possible that you've lived that long?" I asked.

My scars kept burning, but I ignored them. I was in control now.

"Star Children are immortal," she said. "We grow until a certain age and then stop aging. We live until we are killed."

I had known that already, but every other Star Child I knew had been born around the same time I had. I didn't think there was anyone older than twenty-five. Until now.

"Are you the oldest Star Child?" I asked.

She shook her head. "There are older ones," she said. "We are normally born spontaneously, materializing into life every few centuries or so." She paused, her eyes trained on a distant horizon. "But a few years ago, a burst of Star Children materialized. At least fifteen of you were born almost at the same time." She looked at me. "But I don't know why."

She must have been talking about me and all of us who were around the same age. I was almost seventeen and knew of others who were a couple of years older than me.

"Do you know who these Star Children are?" I asked.

She looked at me. "You look around their age. And I know of others." She shivered. "Perseus is one of them," she whispered, and I could hear the fear in her voice. "He has Algol within him. That will lead us all to destruction. He needs to be stopped."

So, Cassiopeia wanted to stop Perseus. That was one of the main bits of information I had wanted to know from her. I felt she had much more to share, so I pushed on.

"Who else?" I asked.

She cocked her head again. "I have heard of the Pleiades. The Seven Sisters are also here among us." My heart skipped a beat. How had Cassiopeia found out about them? It seemed like someone had snitched their existence, and I was sure I knew who that had been. "They are unique, born from Stars instead of Constellations. And their power is very destructive. I also know of the Gemini Twins and . . ." She paused. I could feel her mind trying to rebel again, to break free from the lie like a caged animal that had been sedated but was regaining consciousness.

"Cassiopeia," I whispered. "You just want to tell me the truth and to keep nothing for yourself."

"Orion and Andromeda," she whispered. "My children."

I placed my index finger on my upper lip, thinking. Cassiopeia wasn't working alone, as we had already guessed. Orion and Andromeda were powerful Constellations, and I wondered what these two Star Children were capable of materializing.

"Why have you been hiding them?" I asked.

She looked up at me, her face emotionless but her words full of anger. "They are mine,*" she said. "I won't let anyone else have them."*

"Fair enough," I said. "Where are they now?"

"I sent them away, to foster homes on the outskirts of New York City," she said, and I could feel the regret in her tone. "This was too dangerous for them."

"What was too dangerous for them?" I asked.

I could feel it again, her mind trying to break free, trying to hold back a secret she had been hiding for so long. But her mind was weak, already wounded.

"I tried finding Cepheus again," she began. "Orion tracked him, although he didn't know who he was tracking. Even after all those years I still loved Cepheus, and I knew he loved me too." She paused. Her face was still blank but a tear fell from her eye. I wasn't interested in hearing any dramatic love stories but knew that this was leading to something important. "But when I found him, he was dead. A Star Child had killed him."

"Which one?" I asked.

Cassiopeia hugged her legs again, her stare void. "A monstrous one," she whispered. "There are many Monsters among the Constellations but none that could have done that.*" I could feel her mind again, but this time it wasn't trying to break free. I felt her stark fear, even though I had never been able to feel anyone else's emotions. I was suddenly cold. "This Monster is not any Constellation we know of." She turned her empty eyes toward me. "This Constellation is one that has been lost in time, hidden on purpose, too dangerous to gaze at."*

"How could it be a Constellation that we don't know of?" I asked.

All the Stars had been charted in the sky. A Constellation couldn't just disappear. Sometimes Constellations varied from one culture to another, but the forty-eight original Constellations were always accounted for.

"I don't know," Cassiopeia admitted. "But it's a Constellation more ancient than humanity. A Constellation that cannot be seen in the sky anymore."

"Are you sure this is another Constellation, separate from the forty-eight Constellations that the astronomer Ptolemy charted?"

She nodded. "Cepheus left a message for me." She paused, as if the words slashed her throat as she spoke. "He knew I would find him." She paused again. "This was not any Star Child that we know of. This creature comes from a Constellation we have never seen in the sky."

I scratched my growing beard, trying to make sense of what Cassiopeia had just said. The Stars in that Constellation must have been very ancient if they had extinguished long before humanity had begun staring at the sky. Every Constellation controlled a different Destiny. My Constellation controlled the Destiny of lies, betrayal, and cheating. So, if a Constellation simply disappeared or was destroyed, then what happened to the Destiny it controlled? Did that Destiny just disappear? Would people be given free will in that particular area of their lives without Fate to guide them?

And what could have destroyed so many Stars at the same time? Had Darkness swallowed that Constellation? It was a possibility— after all, Darkness was the only force big enough to destroy Stars. I also wondered, if the Constellation had been destroyed long ago, did that mean that the Star Child born out of that Constellation had been here for millennia? Every Constellation had manifested into a Star Child, so if this Constellation had gone extinct long ago then that Star Child must have been born long before that. How was it possible that the Star Child could still exist without its Constellation?

"This Star Child is the oldest," I said slowly.

"And more ancient than humanity, yes," Cassiopeia said.

"And that's why you left your children behind?" I asked. "Because this Star Child is too dangerous?"

"I won't risk them getting hurt."

I leaned against the wall, the cold seeping through my shirt. "Why did you choose to live in New York?"

"Because Perseus is there," Cassiopeia said. "I want to know what he's planning."

I had already guessed that, but I'd wanted her to confirm it. I knew we could use that to our advantage. But for now, that piece of information seemed insignificant compared to everything else she had just told me.

"How much information have you found out about this . . . Lost Star Child?" I asked.

She was silent for a couple of seconds. "Cepheus didn't leave much. He captured it, but the creature wounded him and he died." The shadows on her face made her eyes seem hollow. "The Monster won't stay captured for much longer. It's very dangerous and the only way to defeat this creature is with the Cup."

"*The Cup?*"

"*Crater,*" she said, "*the Constellation of the Cup.*"

"*Why would that be the only way to defeat the Lost Star Child?*"

"*The Cup has many powers, and whoever holds the Cup can use them as they wish,*" she said. "*Whatever liquid is poured into the Cup can be converted.*"

"*Converted into what?*"

"*Into poison, to kill any living creature. Or it can be converted to heal others, maybe even bring back the dead and grant immortality. Whoever owns the Cup owns its power.*"

"*And you want to find the Cup so you can defeat the Lost Star Child,*" I said.

"*Yes,*" Cassiopeia said. "*That Monster must be destroyed and water converted to poison in Crater is the only thing that can kill it. Cepheus knew that . . . but he never managed to recover Crater.*"

I wondered what Monster or creature could possibly be so powerful. I knew I had to find it. But first I needed Crater. It wouldn't be smart to go near that Monster without a weapon to kill it. I thought about the Cup. If I owned it . . . I could become more powerful than my siblings. But I needed to be the one who found it because Star Objects could only be used by a single Star Child. I may have been the most selfish brother ever, but I wanted that power for me. My siblings were powerful enough already; they didn't need the Cup. And if I had the Cup, I could use it to protect all of us.

"*Where is Crater?*" I asked.

"*In Egypt,*" she said. "*In a temple, but I'm not sure which one.*" She paused. "*I do know that there is a price for holding the Cup.*"

"*What price?*" I asked.

She shrugged. "*I don't know. That's what the Oracle of Dodona said—for one to hold an empty vessel, one must become an empty vessel.*"

"Hmmm," I said.

I would have to investigate that further. Now I knew where I would go first—to the Oracle of Dodona in Greece. It would be a nice little vacation. What about my family? *I thought.* They would want to know about this. But I couldn't tell them, not yet. If I told them about the Cup, then they would want to hold it and own its power. I couldn't let that happen. I needed to be the one who found the Cup and the Lost Star Child. If I did that, then the others wouldn't think me weak anymore. This was my chance to prove to them that I was strong enough and just as brave as they were. I wouldn't fail them again.

I glanced back at Cassiopeia. She had given me enough information, much more than I had hoped for. I had a plan now, going to Dodona in Greece to ask what that cryptic message about an empty vessel meant, then going to Egypt to find Crater.

"Where is the Lost Star Child?" *I asked.*

I could feel Cassiopeia's mind rebelling again and electricity ignited my veins. She had made a blood promise never to say where the Lost Star Child was hidden—I could feel it. Cepheus must have made her do that in the message he left behind. My lies were powerful, but I couldn't force someone to divulge something they had promised with blood.

"I'm not sure where," Cassiopeia said, although she knew exactly where it was. "The only way to find it may be with Alathea's Prophecies."

I considered that. A lot of Star Children were trying to locate the Prophecies, including my siblings and me, and we were close to discovering the location. We believed Alathea's book to be in either Greece or Rome and were trying to narrow down the location. If they could find those Prophecies and I did the rest, then we would know where the Lost Star Child was, and I could defeat it with Crater.

I smiled. What Cassiopeia had just told me changed everything. There was a forty-ninth Constellation, and the Star Child it had created was the most ancient, powerful, and dangerous one of us. We needed to find it and destroy it.

I walked over to Cassiopeia's side and held her bloody chin. I forced her eyes to look into my own. I was planning on telling her to just walk out of the building and forget about me, but an idea formed in my head.

"Cassiopeia," I said. "After I unchain you and leave the room you will just want to forget you ever met me. You will want to forget everything that happened here."

"Yes," she said. "I just want to forget."

"And," I said, "you will forget the existence of the Cup, the Lost Star Child, and the Lost Constellation, and you will also forget about the Pleiades. You just want to forget about all that. It's too dangerous to remember."

"It is dangerous," Cassiopeia agreed.

"You just want to go back to your normal life," I whispered. "Go back and forget about everything I have told you to forget. You will believe that Cepheus was killed by . . . Perseus. Yes, Perseus used Algol to kill Cepheus."

I knew that was plausible. Algol was the most powerful Star in the sky and he the most powerful Star Child. For the first time, Perseus might have a rival, a creature more dangerous than him. That thought made a shiver run down my spine.

"I just want to go back," Cassiopeia said.

"And you will believe that the stabs in your torso came from a mugging on the street as you walked alone at night."

"I was attacked," Cassiopeia agreed.

I smiled again. I would find that Cup, I decided, and then I would find the Lost Star Child. I looked back at Cassiopeia, who *still stared emptily at me. I didn't care what the price was to get that Cup.*

I would pay whatever price was necessary.

I woke up with a start, sitting up in the bed. The cold sweat on my chest made my shirt cling to my skin. My heart thundered. I took a couple of deep breaths, but my pulse didn't slow down.

The curtains had been left open, and light from the street illuminated the room. I realized Draco wasn't in his bed next to mine. I stood up and walked toward the living room. Leo was fast asleep in front of the front door behind the dining table. I assumed Sirius and Maera were with Virgo. I wondered where Draco was but didn't worry too much about him.

I made my way to the terrace door and silently slipped out. Cold air swirled around me, but I didn't care. Why couldn't I have a single restful night? And why was I recovering so many new memories now?

The ocean was as dark as the night above, reflecting the moon that still smiled in the sky, but today it had thinned. The ocean surface seemed undisturbed, flat as far as I could see.

I took in a few deep breaths, trying to clear my head. I had recovered a completely new memory, and I had so many questions about it. The image of Cassiopeia's bloodied face flooded back into my mind, and I shivered. I had stabbed her without any remorse and slapped her too. My entire body shook. I wasn't sure what I had expected from my past, but that was certainly not who I had expected to be—cold, violent, merciless. Dizziness washed over me, and I almost threw up. I gripped the terrace railing to keep myself from collapsing. Who was I? I would never have imagined torturing someone to get information out of them—not even the Twins. But that had felt natural in my memory, as if I had done it many times before.

I breathed through my mouth for a few seconds, and the nausea slowly faded. But my arms still shook as I held onto the railing. I pushed the image of Cassiopeia's bloodied face away and thought about what she had told me about the Cup and the Lost Star Child. Now I knew that the reason I had wanted to find the Cup was to kill that Star Child. But who or what could that Star Child be? I must have learned more in Dodona, and that information must have convinced me that I needed to erase my memories to get to the Cup. That meant I must have gone there at least twice—the first time to follow Cassiopeia's lead, when I found out I needed to erase my memories, and then to actually do it. The first memory I had recovered made a bit more sense now—I had chosen to erase my memories in Dodona and had woken up there without them. I wished I could remember what had happened the first time I went to Dodona. That would explain my strange decision to erase my memories.

I also thought about the Pleiades, apparently my sisters. Cassiopeia had said that their power was very destructive. Maybe destructive enough to help us beat Perseus. But where could they be hiding? And most importantly, why had I used my lies to hide them? Maybe I had tried to hide us all. It seemed possible. I didn't have any memories of Perseus, but I clearly knew who he was. That meant we must have been hiding from him, knowing how dangerous he was.

Now that Perseus had all the Prophecies, however, he must have known the Pleiades existed, if he hadn't before. Another realization struck me. If Perseus had the Prophecies of every single Star Child, then he knew about the forty-ninth Constellation. He knew of the existence of the Lost Star Child, and he must have known, too, that the only way to defeat it was with Crater.

The floor beneath me began swaying, and I held so tightly to the railing my hands hurt. Could that be the reason Perseus needed the Cup? To destroy the most powerful Star Child that rivaled his own power?

I heard a noise behind me and turned around. Draco walked out of Virgo's room and headed toward the hallway when he stopped, noting the open door to our room. He turned to the balcony and found me waving at him through the clear terrace door. He walked over, slipped onto the terrace, and slid the door closed behind him. He glanced back at Virgo's door.

"It's not what you think," he quickly said. His face was as red as his eyes. "Nothing happened."

"I wasn't thinking anything," I said. "And I'm surprised nothing has happened."

"What do you mean?" he asked as he tugged at one of his sleeves.

I smiled. "You guys have known each other for how long? Two years? She's pretty and she's smart. You would make a nice couple."

"I . . . I don't know about that," he said. I huffed. I couldn't believe that after all this time neither of them had made a move. "It's just that . . ." He looked into the distance, his face a normal color again. "She has a really dark past. Even after all these years I don't know much about her. I don't know what she can material-ize. I don't know where she got any of her scars . . ."

"Does starting a relationship imply that you have to know *everything* about her?" I asked.

"No, not at all," he said quickly. "It's just that every time I try to get close to her, she pushes me away. Something in her past . . ." He shook his head sadly. "I know she has many scars.

I've seen some of them. She's been hurt before, so she built a wall to protect herself from everyone around her." Draco turned back to me. "And she's scared of tearing down that wall. And frankly so am I."

"Well, I'm not an expert on romance, but you could try inviting her out to dinner . . . if we survive all of this. Or just invite her out for a walk, give her a flower, a book, some chocolate. I honestly don't know what else girls like."

Draco shrugged. "I don't know either."

I was quiet for a second, pensive. "You could buy her a lot of yarn so she can knit more."

"I'm sure she'd like that." He stepped closer to me. "Have you ever liked someone?"

The question took me by surprise. "I . . . I don't know," I admitted. "I don't remember liking someone, and if I did . . . well, now I've forgotten that person."

I thought that maybe I had liked someone in my past but that I had never loved anyone, not romantically at least. Even though I didn't have my memories, that was just something I could feel.

Draco nodded.

"You look paler than normal." His pupils narrowed at me. "Are you all right? Is it the insomnia again?"

"I'm fine," I answered, maybe a bit too quickly. "It's just everything that's going on."

Should I tell Draco what I remembered? Even as that thought crossed through my head, something stirred in my stomach, holding me back. He and Virgo already knew about two of my memories, but this one felt more intimate, more personal. I was terrified to tell him what I had done to Cassiopeia, afraid he would think I had been a psychopath. And I had been so protective about the information I had learned that I didn't feel comfortable sharing it.

"It's completely fine to have insomnia," Draco said, pulling me out of my thoughts. He was silent for a few seconds, and I didn't dare meet his gaze. Instead, I looked out at the moon.

"It's just . . . ," I said. "I'm afraid of who I was." That was a reality I hadn't wanted to even think about until it crossed my lips.

"I think that's normal," Draco said. "You're probably similar to how you were, but maybe you have changed a bit. And that's all right."

"I remembered something important," I said in a low voice. I didn't want to think about who I had been. I had more important things to worry about.

"There's a Lost Constellation, a Lost Star Child," I began, "whose Constellation disappeared in very ancient times, but he, or it, still materialized in this world. It's the most powerful Star Child, even more dangerous than Perseus and Algol. And the only way to kill it is with the Cup. Virgo said that a liquid poured into the Cup could be used to gain immortality, but from my memories I know it can also be used to kill any living creature."

Where I had learned that information or from whom didn't seem important at the moment. I suppressed a shiver when the image of Cassiopeia's bloody shirt flashed back into my mind.

"It makes sense. Perseus must know all this," Draco said after a few seconds, his eyes set on the moon, his black pupils wide. "He must want to destroy that Star Child, since it rivals his power, and to do that he needs the Cup."

"That's the same thing I thought. But why would he send *us*? Perseus would want to be here to make sure no one else has the power of Crater. It doesn't make sense."

Draco took a deep breath. "Perseus obviously knows something we don't."

"The Prophecy inscribed in the temple wall talked about death and betrayal," I said.

"We already know where the betrayal part comes from," Draco said as he looked toward the hallway where the Twins would be sleeping inside their room. "And death has always followed us wherever we go." He didn't seem very worried about that, which made me feel calmer. Draco turned back to me. "But memories aside, are you feeling all right?"

"That isn't important," I said.

I had more important things to worry about, namely stopping the most powerful Star Child from destroying Fate, Destiny, and Prophecy and making the Universe fall into Chaos.

"This is a stressful life, Corvus," Draco said. "And we all deal with it differently."

"I'll be fine."

Draco was silent for a moment. "I should tell Virgo what we just discussed." He looked at her closed door. "She said she would be awake for a little while longer."

I smiled but said nothing.

Draco pulled away from the railing and walked back inside. I stayed outside for a little longer, looking at the dark sky. I could even make out some Constellations. At that point I knew them all. Above me was, ironically, Andromeda, as if she were making up for her absence by showing up in the night sky. Cassiopeia was a bit fainter, but she was still there, close to Andromeda. Cepheus was there, too, at the side of his Queen. I knew Perseus stood nearby, too, but his Constellation was hidden somewhere behind the hotel. I wondered what happened once a Star Child died. Would our Constellations know about it? Would they care? Did

Constellations have consciousness?

I took a deep breath of cold air.

"A pretty night," someone said behind me. I startled and turned around to find Pollux. His long hair was disheveled, reaching a bit below his shoulders. His dark blue eyes were alert as always, and for the first time I wondered why the Twins' eyes always seemed to be the same color as the ocean, changing with it as night and day passed by.

Pollux wore only pants, showing off his lean and muscular chest. A bright scar shone on his right shoulder. He caught me looking and I turned away with warm cheeks.

"Yeah," I said quietly.

Pollux walked over to the railing, his bare shoulder brushing my arm. My heart beat faster, and I leaned away.

"It was about a year and a half ago," he said, referring to the scar. "One of our negotiations didn't turn out as we expected it to."

"How so?" I asked.

Half a smile lit up Pollux's face. "We underestimated the power of our new friend."

"You didn't expect him to fight you?" I asked.

Pollux chuckled. "He didn't fight us. He can hurt people without even lifting a finger."

"Sounds like a dangerous Star Child," I muttered, curious about who it had been. Someone who could kill other Star Children without the need to fight was dangerous indeed.

"He is," Pollux said almost in a whisper. We were silent for a while, and I felt how the silence grew awkward after a few seconds. "Why do you care so much about defeating Perseus?"

That seemed like a random question. There were a thousand reasons why I would want him dead, but I knew he was asking why I would personally care.

"I don't want to live in a world without Destiny, Fate, and Prophecy," I said.

His brows knitted together. "Why?"

"It's just . . ." I didn't really want to talk about that but felt I had no choice. "I don't like living without knowing what's going to happen in my future."

"Hmmmm," Pollux said pensively.

"I kind of wish we had Destiny too," I said.

Pollux looked out at the sea. "Why would you want that?"

"I wouldn't want to make a wrong choice," I said. "With Destiny, there never is a wrong decision. You know that every choice you make will eventually lead you down the path you're supposed to walk." I sighed. "If we had Destiny, then I could know what's going to happen and deal with it. I want to know what the future holds for me." I paused. "Without knowing my future, I feel I'm walking blindly."

Pollux nodded slowly. "So, you're afraid of the uncertainty that the future holds."

"I—" I cut myself off. "I guess I am." Part of that fear came from my memory loss. I was walking through the world, mostly oblivious to who I had been—but as long as there was Prophecy, I could find myself again. Fear clutched my chest—did I really want to find out who I had been? That question had never even crossed my mind until now. The bloody dagger flashed into my view.

"You're afraid of deciding what you want your life to be," Pollux said.

"I'm afraid of making wrong choices that may endanger my friends," I admitted. "I'm afraid of letting them down."

I was exhausted of not knowing what came next, of not knowing what my Prophecies said about me. I was terrified that we would fall into Perseus's trap that would lead to my friends' deaths—that I would be powerless to stop it. I found it ironic that I had felt almost the same in my memories.

"It's all right to be afraid, Corvus," Pollux said, his gaze breaking away from the ocean. "If you're scared, that means you care. You're scared of where you and your friends are going to end up, and that's perfectly valid."

If we had the Prophecies, I wouldn't have to be scared—we would know how to face the future together. We could plan for whatever came our way. But how does one plan for the unknown?

"Are you afraid?" I asked. "That one of you may die?"

That may have sounded a bit harsh, but Pollux didn't seem offended. He simply let his shoulders drop.

"Prophecies, unlike Destiny, can be altered," he said. "We're sure that once we know our Prophecy, we can escape it."

"Yeah," I said, although I knew that we could escape one Prophecy but still face another one that might still be terrible. I didn't say that out loud though.

"Before Perseus told us of that Prophecy, I had never been afraid of the future," he said, once again looking out at the ocean.

"So you're not afraid of not knowing what the future holds, where you're heading or where you'll end?" I asked.

He shook his head and smiled. "Castor and I lived with humans in our early years, and we learned a lot from them." He sighed. "Some humans seek out their Destiny in the Stars, but most of them don't." He pulled his hair back with his hand. "I found that I like their way of living. Part of the thrill of life is not knowing where it's going to take you." He turned to me. "You live every day fully, and you make your own path."

"And how do they deal with the fear of uncertainty and failure?" I asked. "How do they live not knowing how their lives will end?"

Pollux shrugged, as if it was not a big secret. "You just make your best effort every day. And doing your best sometimes doesn't get you where you want to be, so you just keep trying until you get there."

I wasn't sure that completely answered my question. "What if you still fail?" I asked. "What if you end up hurting the people around you?"

"If you did your best, then you have to accept that there is nothing else you could have done," he said gently. "All we can do in life is our best and nothing else."

I nodded. I wasn't sure I liked his philosophy of living.

"You should try to get some sleep," Pollux said after some time. "You too."

He walked inside without another word. I waited outside for a couple more minutes. I never thought I would have a deep conversation with one of the Twins. For a moment I wished we could work with them without worrying that they would turn their backs on us. We all would have made a very good team against Perseus.

I quietly walked back to my room and got in bed. Draco came back around twenty minutes later. He closed the curtains and got in his own bed.

I took a deep breath, knowing that the next day would be intense. I was still bothered by the fact that Perseus had sent us here. Even if Sirius was the only one who could find the secret entrance, he could have kidnapped us himself and forced us to find the Cup.

He had decided not to come for a reason, and that terrified me. Perseus was no coward, so I wondered what he had read in the Prophecies that had made him stay behind. We would find out the next day. I had the feeling that whatever it was, it would lead us close to death—just as the Prophecy had said.

Chapter XIII, Verse I

The White Throne occupied by the Queen that no one can resist.

Golden threads her hair resembles, so vain her beauty to use it as a weapon.

With sweet words to inflict harm upon those who know no better,

And to the enemy a promise made, one to disguise the curse born of love.

The world she shall then roam, looking for what her heart knows not.

When the Old King she finds murdered, a new enemy she will pursue.

The Forgotten One will be remembered, only to be forsaken once again.

CHAPTER 8

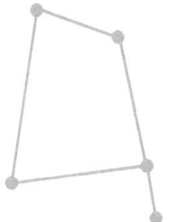

WE'D DECIDED that all of us would go to the temple. I had to lie to the receptionist again so she could get us a van big enough to transport Leo, and after that Draco had driven us to the ruins using the van's GPS.

I knew that Sirius would be able to find something that the rest of us couldn't. If his Star had been mentioned several times in the temple, that meant he had a connection to this place. Maybe he would be able to find the secret entrance to the underground chamber Draco had seen.

Once we stepped outside of the van and stood facing the temple, dread clutched my chest. We'd brought our weapons too, preparing for whatever dangers we might face. I had my sword strapped at my back.

Sirius emitted a low growl and threw his ears back. That was not a good sign.

"What is it, boy?" I asked, but he only growled in return.

I couldn't speak dog but guessed that whatever he said wasn't good. Sirius looked intently at the Nile River.

"He's feeling something," Draco said. I didn't know if *he* knew how to speak dog, but for some reason he always understood the Star Animals better than Virgo and I did.

"What's he feeling?" Virgo asked as she patted his side.

Sirius growled again, this time as if he were in pain.

"Let's go inside the temple," Castor suggested.

We walked over the rough ground. Sirius kept growling, shaking his head as if he were trying to get rid of a fly buzzing around him. He barked a couple of times at the ground. At the entrance, I stopped for a second to look at the decapitated statues. Leo entered the temple first, then Aquila flew in, followed by Sirius and Maera. The rest of us followed after. Luckily, we all fit inside the temple, with Leo closest to the stairs and the rest of us near the entrance. Leo looked at the walls so intently I wondered if the Lion could read hieroglyphs. I was about to ask Sirius if he still felt strange, but he barked before I could say anything. The sound echoed off the walls, startling all of us.

"What is it, boy?" Virgo asked.

But Sirius only whimpered, staring at the ground with his ears thrown back.

"What's happening with him?" Pollux took a step away from Sirius. "Did he find something?"

Leo growled at Sirius, and Sirius barked back at him. Draco frowned, so I assumed he hadn't understood that particular conversation. Sirius growled and whimpered, like the time he had stepped on a nail. Was he in pain? He barked louder.

"Sirius," Virgo said as she knelt next to him. "What is it?"

Sirius was quiet for a couple of seconds. Leo gave a growl that sounded like a sigh, and Sirius only whimpered back. Then he began barking madly, as if a poisonous snake had bit him. Leo retreated further back into the room, pressing himself against the wall. Aquila flapped his wings like a crazed chicken, and Maera hid behind Leo, trembling.

A rumble boomed outside, as if a thunderstorm was about to start. I ignored the sound and knelt next to the dog. I tried to calm him down, patting him on the side. That usually worked, but at the moment he seemed mad, about to bite off my hand if I touched him. I took a couple of steps away as he began howling loudly.

"Sirius, please calm down," Virgo pleaded.

"Guys!" the Twins shouted simultaneously from outside.

Virgo stayed with Sirius while Draco and I rushed out.

My heart shrank with dread.

"Didn't Virgo say that Sirius indicated the inundation of the Nile?" Pollux asked.

"She said that it didn't happen anymore," I said.

A wall of dark clouds moved toward us like a marching army. Lightning twisted inside of them like white veins in a formless black figure. The thunder rumbled over the desert, shaking the ground. Rain began to pour out of the clouds like a violent waterfall. In front of us, half a mile away, the Nile began to swell outward, spilling onto dry land.

I rushed back into the temple, where Sirius howled at the walls.

"Sirius!" I said. "Stop! You're going to make the Nile overflow!"

"What?" Virgo asked. "How?"

"Didn't you say that Sirius announced the flooding of the Nile?"

"I said that happened in ancient times," she said. "And that the Star *announces* the flooding, not *directly causes* the flooding."

"It looks like the Star may have the power to do just that," I said, my heart galloping wildly. "Sirius is materializing the flooding of the Nile."

Virgo turned back to the dog. "Sirius, you need to stop this right now!"

The dog howled, and for a split second my gaze met with his. I understood what he was trying to tell us—the power of the Star Sirius was out of his control.

The Nile was going to flood.

Virgo must have understood that, too, because she stopped shouting at him. Had the temple triggered something in him? Or was being so close to the Nile causing his power to awaken? Stars could sometimes mean different things for different cultures? Did our power change geographically?

Draco, Pollux, and Castor charged back into the temple. A second later a blast of wind shot inside with such force it nearly tumbled me over. The wind died down a second later at the same time the curtain of rain washed over the temple so strong that the temple shook and water began dribbling inside.

Sirius stopped howling. I could see his ribs protruding from his sides. He looked like he had lost a few pounds in minutes—he had materialized something very powerful. Draco knelt next to Sirius and carried the big dog. Sirius growled in complaint, but only for a few seconds before he rested his head on Draco's shoulder.

More water rushed into the temple, covering the ground completely. Leo rushed up the stairs with a growl. Maera raced up after him, and Aquila flew behind them. Draco, carrying Sirius, climbed the broken steps, the Twins right at his heels. I was about to do the same when Virgo held onto my arm.

"I think this is what the Prophecy meant," she said over the roar of the storm outside as our ankles became submerged under the icy water. "*The Cup remains under the temple, only found in the river that flows plentiful.* A flooding river has water flowing plentiful, and it's now flowing *into* the temple. This will somehow lead us to the Cup."

"So the secret entrance that will lead to the Cup is only activated by the flooding of the Nile?" I had to speak loudly, nearly shouting, to hear myself above the battering rain.

"I'm not an engineer, but there could certainly be a locking mechanism that only opens with flowing water," she said, her eyes wide.

That was plausible. Although flooding an entire river to open a secret entrance was a bit extreme. Maybe whoever had hidden the Cup had done this on purpose, knowing that the Nile didn't flood annually anymore, so only Sirius would be able to cause a flood big enough for the entrance to open. That meant someone had gone to great lengths to keep the Cup hidden and had made it nearly impossible for others to find.

"But what about a broken god drowning?" I asked. "What does that mean?"

Outside, the rain became so heavy that I couldn't see anything beyond the entrance, just the rain like a grey curtain that hid the rest of the world behind it. Water kept pouring in, rising halfway to my knees.

"I don't know . . . yet," Virgo said. She grabbed my hand and pulled me toward the stairs. We splashed through the water, then quickly climbed the steps.

The room above was the same size as below, but there were no statues and the walls were completely bare. On the left wall was an opening, but the water was angled away from it so it didn't spill inside. I couldn't see anything beyond the rain. Thunder boomed outside.

The Twins huddled together in the far-left corner. Leo, Maera, and Aquila stood on the opposite corner. Draco was in between them and the Twins, with Sirius lying next to him, breathing heavily. Draco patted the dog, who seemed to be asleep. I rushed to Sirius's side. He was breathing, which was a relief. Virgo gasped as she ran her hand over the dog's protruding ribs.

"He'll be all right," Draco said over the pounding rain.

I looked out the window again, the rain diving into the ground like sharp daggers. How much land would flood? Was it raining only around this area or throughout all of Egypt? Would the flooding affect other people? I didn't have time to ponder about those questions. We needed to find the Cup, and I wouldn't leave without it.

"We have to find the entrance to that secret chamber," I said.

Draco nodded. "We should go downstairs again and look for it."

"And preferably let's do that before we all drown," Castor said.

Virgo patted Sirius on the side and gave him a kiss behind his ears. "We'll be back soon, Sirius."

The dog opened his eyes in acknowledgement.

"All right, let's go," Draco said as he stood up. He looked at Leo. "Take care of Sirius."

Leo growled. Draco left his long spear on the floor next to the wall. It was too long to maneuver in the flooding temple.

Pollux, Castor, Draco, Virgo, and I descended the stairs, leaving the animals on the upper floor. The water was now up to my knees, and it was painfully cold, numbing my muscles. I tried to wade around the room in search of . . . what was I even looking for?

Only dim grey light came from the entrance, bathing the temple in an eerie and misty glow. Water splashed against the statues, sloshing back and forth in the room. Dust fell from the cracks in the ceiling and dropped into the already murky water that poured in from the entrance.

Castor and Pollux slid their hands along the wall on the left, as if their touch would discover something that their eyes couldn't. Virgo examined the statue on the right—pulled an arm, pushed the torso—probably hoping something in the statue would open the entrance, which was nowhere to be seen.

I looked down at the dirty grey water. If the secret chamber was underground, then maybe the mechanism to open the entrance was on the floor. I still didn't know if the water itself would cause the entrance to open or if we had to do something ourselves.

I dropped to my knees and inhaled sharply at the biting cold. I pressed down on the rough ground to see if that would do anything. The water kept rising, and I had to close my mouth to avoid swallowing it. My hands slid over the coarse surface, but I couldn't feel anything distinctive.

"I'm not finding anything!" Pollux shouted.

"Me neither!" Castor shouted.

The water continued to rise, and I had to stand up. I trembled from the cold, feeling like my skin was being peeled off with knives. The Twins moved closer to the stairs, but Draco kept passing his hands along the inscriptions on the right wall. Virgo swam to the other statue and began inspecting and pulling at it. The water was now up to my waist.

"We might end up drowning, guys," Pollux said.

"What are we even looking for?" Castor asked.

"Anything!" I shouted, not feeling the lower part of my body anymore.

We needed to find that entrance. I needed to find that Cup. I could feel the pull of it. Maybe as part of my memories returned so did everything I had felt. I had been searching for that Cup for so long. It had to be *mine*. I wanted it. I needed it.

The water kept rising as I looked at the statues and the hieroglyphs at their sides. The water rose to my chest. I took a gulp of air and swam downward. The cold water wrapped completely around me. I opened my eyes but couldn't see anything. The water was so murky I couldn't even see my hand in front of me. My lungs began to ache. I didn't even know what I was looking for as I reached the floor and began to touch it with my hands again, hoping the secret entrance would just open to my touch. The floor was coarse and cracked, biting into my palms.

A hand tightened on my shoulder. Draco pulled me out of the water. I took in a gulp of air, my hair plastered to my face. I brushed the water out of my eyes.

"What the hell are you doing?" Draco demanded. "You could drown!"

"Trying to find a hatch or something!" I shouted back.

The Twins seemed to have fled to the upper floor.

"We don't even know what we're looking for!" he shouted.

He was right. I had no idea what I was doing. Then why did I keep frantically searching the floor? Because the Prophecies had said that we would find that Cup. If it was in the Prophecies, then we would find it, one way or another. That thought gave me an odd sense of determination. We *would* find that Cup.

"I have to keep looking!" I shouted.

I took in another gulp of air and swam underwater again. I reached the floor again. There had to be *something*. My lungs screamed at me, and the cold numbed my muscles. My hands blindly swept across the floor as I swam around with my eyes closed. Draco grabbed my shoulder and pulled me up again. As soon as my head broke the surface, I took in a gulp of air and coughed. I realized that my feet no longer touched the ground, and I struggled to stay afloat. The entrance to the temple was gone, completely submerged underwater, and our heads were dangerously close to the ceiling.

Draco grabbed my arm and swam toward the stairs, pulling me with him.

"No! Wait!" I shouted. "We still haven't—"

Draco pulled me along harshly. Dripping with water, we both crawled up the stairs to the room above. The water was steadily climbing up the stairs and would soon reach the second floor.

The black clouds outside made it seem like it was night already. Lightning crackled violently, twisting inside the clouds like snakes. Water covered the ground as far as I could see.

"Did you find anything?" Pollux asked.

"Does it look like we found anything?" I shouted.

Sirius was up again, his ears thrown back and his eyes bulging as he looked at the water slowly climbing the stairs. I found it ironic that he had always hated water so much. I walked over to him, my clothes hanging heavily on me.

"It's all right, boy," I said gently. He gulped, trembling. "You couldn't have known this would happen. None of us could have known."

Sirius looked at something behind me. I turned around just in time to see Virgo gasp for air as Draco dragged her up the stairs.

"*When the broken god drowns below the rushing waters,*" Virgo said. "I know what that means! The broken god is the statue of the god!"

She jumped back into the water before Draco could pull her back. "Virgo!" he shouted, although I was sure she couldn't hear him underwater.

"I have to go back too!" I said as I looked at the stairs.

Draco stopped me with an arm across my chest. "This is madness!" he shouted. "We don't know for sure the Prophecy is referring to those broken statues!"

"We have to try!" I said.

Castor walked to my side and looked dubiously at the water. "You know, there could be crocodiles or snakes in the water."

I looked back at the water. "I don't care."

I pushed Draco's arm away. I rushed down the stairs until the water was up to my waist. Then I took a deep breath and dove into the water, which was still painfully cold. We *would* find that damned Cup. Prophecies didn't lie. If Virgo thought that she had found something on the statues, then I needed to help her. I swam to the right. My left hand slid across the wall, but when I got to the statue I didn't bump into Virgo. My hands only grasped the hard and cold outline of the statue—the arm, the broken head. I set my feet against the wall and pushed myself to the other side of the room. My lungs burned, and I didn't know how much longer I would last.

"Watch out!" Electra shouted somewhere behind me. "It's coming!"

My vision went dark as the waves pounded at me. I drifted farther into the open ocean.

"Corvus!" Several voices shouted in horror.

I tried to hold onto a rocky wall to my right, to stop the current from pushing me farther away into the ocean. The stone was slippery with seaweed and moss, and my hands slipped away as the current pulled me.

"Help!" I shouted, just before a wave washed over me and I went completely underwater.

I shook myself, trying to escape my memories. I didn't want them right now. I needed to find Virgo. The entrance had to be here. Perseus wouldn't have sent us here to drown. Or would he? I reached the other statue, but Virgo wasn't there either. I held onto the statue's shoulder and waved my arm, expecting to brush or bump against her. Panic flooded into me. Where was she? My lungs burned, and my head felt like it would explode.

A hand gripped my shoulder and pulled me up. I struggled in Draco's grip, but after a second, I thought better of it and let him drag me toward the stairs. My head broke the surface and I breathed, my lungs sore and relieved at the same time. The Twins stood at the top of the stairs, dripping puddles. The water had climbed even higher. It only had around five more steps until it reached the second floor.

"Where's Virgo?" I asked.

"I don't know!" Draco shouted desperately as he looked back at the water. He dove in and disappeared under the surface. I breathed raggedly, staring helplessly at the water. Seconds passed and Draco didn't come back. Virgo had to be down there, she had to be all right. More seconds ticked by and neither of them came back. I dove back into the water. The Twins shouted something behind me, but I didn't hear them. The cold felt like a sheet of needles stabbing my skin, but I ignored it.

I swam frantically, my arms extended before me to see if I could feel them. I opened my eyes, but the water was so opaque that I still couldn't see anything. A current pulled me to the side. I instinctively tried to swim against it, but it was too strong. It pulled me backward. I screamed and realized a second later that I had air in my lungs to scream. It took me another second to realize I was falling through the air.

My back hit something hard—it slammed into my muscles and bones. Cold water was around me again. I frantically swam upward. As soon as I broke the surface, I coughed wildly, trying to keep my face above the water as it slid from my hair into my eyes, making me shut them again. Water splashed loudly somewhere nearby, like a waterfall, and I could feel it spraying on the back of my head.

Screams echoed above me. A splash sent a wave of water over my head. I coughed out more water and used my hands to wipe it out of my eyes. Back water spread all around me. The sound of the waterfall came from a column of water dropping from a square opening in the ceiling above. Dim light from the opening lit the room. I swam away from the column of water. The ceiling was at least three stories above me.

I coughed again, my throat raw. We had found the secret chamber—or more like an underground cavern—and the water cascading from above must have come from the temple. Probably half of the temple floor had opened into the cavern. Next to me, one of the Twins came out of the water, coughing. I recognized Castor's short hair. Pollux's head bobbed to the surface a second later, coughing too.

"Come on, Virgo," Draco said.

I turned around. Draco was kneeling on a small island made of black rock, about ten feet in diameter, a few yards away from me, and I quickly swam toward it. I pushed myself from the water and crawled over the rough surface, kneeling at Virgo's side. White light pulsed very slowly from the scars at the back of her hands. Draco pressed his mouth against Virgo's, then pulled back and pressed his hands on her chest. Virgo spat out water and gasped, then turned to her side and coughed out more water from her lungs.

Draco muttered something under his breath. He pulled Virgo into his arms, and she shakily hugged him back. I just knelt there, not knowing what to do. The Twins climbed onto the small island. Pollux's hair had come undone, so it looked like a soaked mop had been placed over his head. Virgo looked into Draco's eyes. He smiled shyly, and she returned the smile. Castor cleared his throat, and both of them turned to him.

"It's too dark," Pollux said.

Deep blue light snaked above his right hand. It took me only a second to realize he had called on St. Elmo's fire. In Greek myths, when sailors saw St. Elmo's fire, it indicated that they had the blessing from the Twins and were safe from storms. But I hadn't known the Twins could materialize it. The name was misleading though. What Pollux had over his palm did not resemble fire. It looked more like blue lightning twirling on his hand.

Pollux swung his hand upward, and the veins of blue light hung in the air a few feet above us, illuminating the chamber. The cavern was made completely out of black stone, and the water was the same color, reflecting the deep blue light. I couldn't tell how deep it was. From above us, water kept cascading down. I hoped that with all the water flowing down here it wouldn't reach the second floor where we had left our friends. I wondered how we would get out of here once we had found the Cup but guessed we could worry about that later.

"We actually found it," Virgo whispered.

"*You* found it," Draco said.

"How?" Pollux asked.

"I didn't do anything," Virgo said. "Maybe the water activated a mechanism to open the floor."

"All right," Pollux said as he stood up and pulled his long hair back with his hand. "Now what?"

I noticed that behind the cascading column was a circular opening. The water flowed in that direction like an underground river. I couldn't see where the river led, but I knew that we had to follow it.

"Now we find that damned Cup."

CHAPTER 9

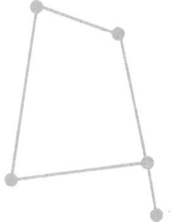

"I DON'T KNOW about the rest of you," Castor said as he looked at the black water. "But I don't really feel like swimming."

"I don't see any other way that we can—" I started.

Virgo screamed and all of us huddled together at the center of the tiny island. Something was coming from underneath the water, making the surface bubble. A figure broke through the surface, and it took me a second to realize it was a wooden raft. It had a strange shape, like a canoe, but to me it looked like a floating wooden coffin without its lid.

"Argo?" Pollux asked.

The raft didn't answer, although I hadn't expected it to.

"Argo!" Castor exclaimed in glee. He laughed. "I knew you still cared about us!"

I wondered how Argo had found us but realized that wondering how a magical boat had found us was useless. The raft floated closer to us.

"Ladies first," Castor said as he motioned toward the raft.

He helped Virgo on, then Draco, then me, and the Twins climbed in last. I sat down as soon as I stepped on the raft. I was afraid of losing my balance when the raft started to move and falling into the water. Once we were all settled, the raft began to move toward the opening. It circled the cascade of water. I wondered what would happen to the others who had stayed in the temple. I hoped they would be fine. If the water was flowing down here, then it probably wouldn't reach the second floor. Would the storm still be raging outside?

Argo moved slowly, as if he had all the time in the world. Even though we had no rush, dread built up inside me with every thump of my heart. The blue light from above extinguished, and neither Pollux nor Castor created more of St. Elmo's fire. Only the light from the scars on Virgo's hands remained, illuminating her face in ghastly light, but after a few seconds she covered them with her sleeves. Argo swayed slightly as it broke through the water.

I suddenly remembered part of my conversation with Merope. I had planned on getting back my memories once I recovered the Cup. Would I finally remember who I had been? Part of me wanted to remember everything, but the other part of me felt terrified. What if I didn't like my other memories? Or maybe I wouldn't remember anything. After all, my plan to erase my memories while still remembering certain things had failed.

"I can't believe Perseus didn't want to get a little wet to get the Cup," Castor said somewhere at my side.

"Maybe he's scared of drowning," Pollux said.

For some reason that didn't click right inside my mind. Perseus wouldn't shy away from swimming, would he? If drowning was what he was afraid of, then he was more of a coward than I had thought. I balled my fists in anger. Perseus must have known that Sirius wouldn't be able to control his power once he got here and that the Nile would flood.

Our surroundings became darker as we moved further away from the main cavern. I could make out figures along the sides, carved into the walls. They looked like statues standing on water, but I couldn't be sure.

"Well, this is creepy," one of the Twins said.

"Very creepy," the other one agreed.

A burst of blue-violet light appeared next to me, over Castor's palm. The figures along the walls did look like statues, but they seemed to have been disfigured by gravity melting the black rock over the ages. Castor extinguished his light a couple of seconds later.

We rode on for what seemed like hours. I held onto the edge of the raft, feeling like I was slipping forward. But then I realized that the river angled slightly downward, leading us deeper underground. None of us spoke a word as we moved forward. Did the Nile somehow flow into this subterranean chamber? The Prophecy had said that the Cup awaited in the river that flowed plentiful below the temple. This was what it must have meant.

When Argo finally stopped, I couldn't make out anything in the pitch blackness. Two bursts of blue light, one more violet than the other, materialized behind me, one from each Twin. They swung their hands upward at the same time and a small net of blue light expanded above us—like lightning suspended in the air like a twisting net.

My eyes immediately settled on the Cup. It sat in the middle of the cavern on a small, roughly circular island made of black rock. At fifteen yards in diameter, the island's surface was uneven, like sharp waves in a violent storm. In the middle it had spiraled steps leading up ten feet to a platform where the Cup stood.

The cavern around us was bigger than the one we had dropped into—it was at least six stories up and as large as a football field. The walls were black, the surface hard but at the same time sleek as an eel, reflecting the blue light. On the far side of the cavern was a roughly rectangular platform that rose out of the water. It seemed to be about fifty feet in length and about twenty feet wide. Its terrain was flat, but there was nothing on top of it.

The raft took us closer to the island and stopped right at the edge. I scrambled out of the raft, the others right at my heels, and we rushed up the tiny spiral steps. At the top, we stood together, pressed shoulder to shoulder in a circle as we all looked down. My heart beat so hard my chest hurt. The Cup was made of gold and resembled a small chalice. It had no jewels or inscriptions. It was just pure, beautiful, shining gold, but for a mythological cup I would have expected it to be bigger or more ornamented. No one reached down for it. The Twins looked at me.

"So," Pollux said. His voice echoed through the silent cavern. "Who gets to touch the Cup first?"

"I think it should be me," I said.

"Hmmm," Pollux said. "I don't trust you enough for that."

"We don't trust you enough either," Draco said to the Twins.

The Twins looked challengingly at us.

No one made a move for the Cup.

"The Prophecy did say betrayal awaited us," Castor said.

Draco emitted a low growl, and my breath hitched. I had only heard that sound a couple of times. He considered it an animal trait and hated doing it because it made him sound like a beast. But when he was really mad, sometimes it slipped out.

"You better be careful about what you say or do next," Draco said, his calm voice scarier than that growl.

The Twins both gave a step back, standing at the very edge of the platform.

"We don't plan on stealing the Cup from you," Pollux said. "We would only prefer if Corvus didn't have it."

"Why do you distrust me so much?" I asked. "I have never done anything to you."

The Twins didn't respond.

"Do you trust *me* enough?" Virgo asked. "I can take the Cup."

I trusted Virgo with my life, but even as she said those words, I felt a savage instinct to just grab the Cup myself, regardless of what anyone thought. I had wanted the Cup to be *mine* for so long. But more than that, I had erased my memories for a reason, and that reason hadn't become clear yet. We had found the Cup without needing anyone else to erase their memories. So then why had I done so? I was missing that little part, that piece of the puzzle that seemed so crucial but didn't fit in anywhere.

The Twins exchanged a glance. "Fine," Pollux said. "We trust Virgo to hold the Cup."

Virgo knelt down, but Castor held her arm. Draco pushed him back and he nearly stumbled off the platform. He regained his balance quickly.

"Wait," Castor said quickly. "What if it has some sort of trap?"

"A what?" Draco asked.

Castor looked around us. "I don't know. I've just seen enough movies to know that finding treasures is never this easy. What if the Cup has a trap and as soon as one of us grabs it, the cave collapses or the statues we saw earlier come to life and kill us!"

Draco's brows furrowed. "I think you've just watched too many movies."

"And finding the Cup was *not* easy," Virgo complained. "We nearly drowned."

Without further argument, she reached down and scooped up the Cup. I didn't realize my hands had been clenched until Virgo grabbed the Cup and nothing happened. Had I expected something to happen? I didn't feel the tug of my memories coming back. I felt nothing, and that made me very uneasy.

"See," she said as she motioned at the Cup. "Everything is— *Aaaaaa!*"

She let go of the Cup as if it had burned her hand. Crater clattered on the hard ground. Draco held onto Virgo before she could collapse. The Cup began to roll toward the edge of the platform. Before I could react, Pollux threw himself forward. He landed on his chest and caught the Cup as it began to fall. He scrambled to his feet again. After a second of silence, Pollux doubled over and screamed in pain as if someone had stabbed him. The Cup fell from his hand and clattered hard, then rolled off the platform.

I jumped from the platform. My feet and ankles felt like they had been crushed by a hammer, but I ignored the pain. The Cup kept rolling, and I jumped forward, falling to my knees and catching it mere inches before it fell into the black water and disappeared. I held the gleaming Cup in my hand, not quite believing I had managed to catch it. Crater was warm, despite having been in a cold cave for millennia.

I wondered what the Cup had done to Virgo and Pollux, but just then I felt it, like a pull, as if the Cup were sucking my soul through my hand. I screamed, feeling every cell inside me burn, but I didn't let go of the Cup. I held it tighter. Someone was calling my name, but all the sounds around me cut off abruptly.

I opened my eyes, not remembering that I had closed them. I was not in the cavern anymore. I was back in the forest at the Oracle of Dodona, where I had woken up without my memories. The place where the leaves had spoken to me. Except now the oak trees were still, and none of the leaves spoke even a whisper. I knew I wasn't really in that forest. Everything around me was too still, as if I were standing inside a picture.

"Who are you?" someone whispered.

The whisper was different from the one I had heard from the leaves. It was as if someone were trying to talk to me from across the galaxy, shouting, but so far away I could hear only a faint echo.

"I'm Corvus," I held the Cup tighter. "Who are you?"

"Crater," it answered.

I looked down at the Cup. Had it actually talked? Was that even possible?

"I have a conscience too," the Cup said with its distant voice. "It is simply different from yours."

"Where are we? Why did you bring me here?" I asked. "What did you do to my friends?"

"I have done nothing," the Cup replied.

But I was sure that Crater had done something to me, taking me away from the cave. Had Virgo and Pollux seen this forest too?

"What did you do?" I asked again.

The Cup was silent for a couple of seconds, as if it were pensive.

167

"Only an empty vessel shall hold an empty vessel," Crater said. "A full vessel cannot receive my power."

"What?" I asked.

Why did everything have to be so cryptic? I was about to ask Crater to be a bit clearer, but just then the answer came to me.

"An empty vessel," I said.

"Yes, Corvus," the Cup said. "You are empty."

"I am empty of memories," I realized as I spoke.

My tongue tasted metallic, as if I had swallowed blood. It all clicked together.

"You are empty just as I am," the Cup said, and I could sense relief from it.

"Is that good?" I asked.

"It is wonderful," the Cup agreed. "If a vessel is full of Essence, then my power cannot flow into that vessel. I can only let my power flow into an empty vessel."

Now I understood why I had erased my memories. Only without memories could I receive the power Crater had to offer. But why memories? Why did that make a person full or empty?

The Cup seemed to understand my thoughts. "Memories are the Essence of the Soul. They are the only thing the Soul takes with it after Death."

That must have been the information I learned the first time I went to Dodona.

"But you are filling again," Crater said. "I detect a sip from your Essence."

He must have meant the memories I had been recovering plus my memories from the past year since I had woken up in the hospital.

"What would happen if I recovered my memories again?" My heartbeat pulsed in my hands, and I wondered if Crater could feel it too.

"Then you would not be able to use my power anymore," the Cup responded.

My body turned cold, as if the temperature had suddenly dropped. "I can't have my memories back then?"

"I never said you couldn't," Crater said in its strange voice. "I just said that if you do, you won't wield my power anymore." Had I known that before? I was almost sure I hadn't, because I had certainly planned to recover my memories. "True power always comes with a sacrifice. As long as you are willing to lose a part of you, I will give you a part of me."

I wasn't sure what to make of that. A mix of emotions swirled through me—anger, sadness, regret. But did I regret losing my memories? How could I regret something I couldn't even remember? Could I live the rest of my life not knowing who I was or who I had been? And if I wanted to keep Crater's power, did that mean that eventually I would have to erase my memories again? Was that I sacrifice I was willing to make?

I decided not to think of that at the moment. "What did you do to my friends?"

"I did nothing," Crater said. "They were full, so when they touched me, they overflowed." He paused. "Their taste was bitter, their Essence strong."

"You saw their memories?"

"Yes, I was filled with their bitter taste," Crater answered, as if it had been a horrible experience. "I drank from their Essence, it flowed into me. The boy, he was a strange flavor, but the girl, she was like acid. Never let her touch me again . . . her taste was like nothing I have experienced before. So much death. So much blood. So much regret." The Cup gave a long pause. "But you, Corvus . . . your Essence is barely anything. I like that."

I was pulled out of the forest. My skin turned itself inside out. Then I felt the cold and hard ground underneath me. I groaned.

"Corvus!" Draco said. He knelt over me, his face hovering anxiously above mine.

"I'm fine," I said as I sat up. My head felt fuzzy.

We were still on the island. A small cluster of snaking blue veins hovered a few feet above us. I looked down at my hand and realized I was still holding the Cup. It had shifted. Now it looked like a golden thermos. It even had a lid and everything. *What in the Stars?* I wondered. Had the Cup decided to modernize?

I heard a moan and looked away from the thermos. Virgo and Pollux lay on their backs a few feet behind me. Castor knelt over Pollux, holding his brother's limp hand. My heart beat up my throat at the sight of Virgo's pale face. She moaned again as if she were in pain. Draco rushed to her side. I crawled toward her, not letting go of Crater. Relief washed over me as Virgo's chest moved up and down in a steady rhythm. Pollux also seemed to be breathing. Argo, still looking like a coffin-raft, waited for us at the edge of the island.

"What happened?" I asked.

Draco shrugged. "They've been moaning in their sleep." He turned to me. "You were moaning, too, but you woke up after a while." He looked back at Virgo and Pollux.

As I leaned closer to Virgo, I noticed something else—she had a white strand of hair at the side of her head.

"Where did that come from?" I asked.

"Pollux has it too," Castor said as he motioned to his brother. Even though his hair was much lighter than Virgo's, the thin strand of white hair was noticeable.

"It happened after they touched the Cup," Draco said.

I looked back at the thermos in my hand. It had taken a lot more than just their memories. Had it taken part of their lives too? Their Souls? Crater had said that their Essence had overflowed into him, or something like that. But I didn't see how that was related to getting a strand of white hair. The only thing I knew for sure was that holding the Cup would be lethal to anyone but me.

"What happened to *you*?" Castor asked.

I didn't feel comfortable sharing the information I had just discovered. I didn't mind telling Draco and Virgo, but I still didn't trust the Twins. Knowing that I was the only one who could hold the Cup gave us an advantage.

"I'm not sure," I said. "How long was I out?"

"Like twenty minutes," Draco replied.

Something inside my chest nagged at me—another piece that didn't fit the puzzle. If Perseus knew that I was the only person who could use Crater's power, then why had he sent me to retrieve it? Maybe the Prophecies were confusing enough that Perseus didn't know the full truth. He probably knew that I was the only one who could successfully retrieve Crater from its hiding place. But I was sure that Perseus had no idea that I was the only Star Child who could use Crater's power. I smiled. For the first time, we had an advantage over Perseus. I didn't know how we would use it against him, but I felt happy knowing we had information that Perseus didn't.

"Let's get out of here," I said.

Draco carried Virgo in his arms—she looked delicate, about to break like a twig. Castor carried his brother.

Virgo stirred. Her eyes fluttered open and she looked up.

"Draco," she whispered.

"It's okay," he whispered back with a smile. "I've got you."

Virgo fell asleep again.

I climbed onto the raft. Draco climbed after me holding Virgo, then Castor with Pollux. Argo began moving slowly away from the island. I let out a breath, leaning back to rest.

Then the world exploded around me. I was screaming, flying through the air, then I was falling, my insides churning inside me. The cold water enveloped me once again, like knives of ice stabbing me. My head broke through the surface. The cavern was pitch black for a few painful seconds until small veins of blue light appeared to my right. The light coiled next to the cavern wall, on top of the large platform I had seen earlier. Draco was swimming toward it, dragging Virgo. Castor was already there, pulling Pollux up from the water. I swam quickly to the platform, which was not as easy with the Cup. Draco pushed himself onto the platform, and I pulled myself up a couple of seconds later. Castor dragged his brother away from the edge, and Draco did the same with Virgo.

I had just pushed myself up to my feet when a shriek erupted behind me. It was like metal grinding against metal, making an electric shiver race down my spine. I turned around.

I felt as if the water dripping from my clothes had turned to ice. I stared at the giant Snake that had come out of the water yards away from the platform. Its body was slimy black, like a giant eel's, but it had scales that unmistakably belonged to a Serpent. Its eyes were yellow and green and its teeth as long as my arms. The snake's body extended to the top of the cavern, its body dripping water. The Snake stared intently at us. It hissed, its black tongue slithering out of its mouth. Argo was nowhere to be seen, and I hoped that the Ship was still alive. I couldn't see any wreckage anywhere, which I hoped was a good sign. The twisting blue light intensified above us, illuminating the cavern better as the light reflected off the walls around us. The Snake looked at the blue light curiously.

"What in the world?" Castor wondered out loud.

But I knew exactly who that was. It had been in my own myth. The story of Corvus had always involved the Raven, the Cup, and the Water Snake.

Draco became very still. "Hydra," he whispered.

Chapter XLII, Verse I

The Black Snake awaits below the dark waters,
Imprisoned by the King after a brutal battle between them fought.
The Snake shall guard the treasure that brought the King so much pleasure,
But now the Cup lies abandoned, after the King a curse has suffered.
In the river the Snake shall await the arrival of the new generation,
A battle shall follow, with power and death waiting in the shadows.
The curse of the King will be nearby, to plague the Young Ones that now fight.

CHAPTER 10

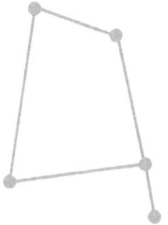

THE SNAKE lunged forward. I threw myself to the left, my arm brushing the Snake's slimy side. I landed on my back, still holding Crater. I jumped to my feet at the same time the Snake retreated, hissing angrily.

On the opposite side of the platform, Draco had placed Virgo behind him. Both seemed unharmed. Next to him, Castor held a bloodied sword in one hand. Draco dragged Pollux, who had been at his brother's feet, and placed him next to Virgo.

"We need to get that Snake away from them," Castor breathed.

I nodded.

The Snake hissed at us again. Castor extended his free hand and another cluster of blue, lightning-like light appeared hovering above it. He swung his hand upward and the light flew high above us, creating another net. It wasn't as bright as the one the Twins had created together, but enough to illuminate the whole cavern, even if a bit dimly. The Snake hissed as it looked at the light above its head—it seemed transfixed by it. The blue light reflected on its slimy body as if the Snake itself had blue veins curling through it.

I pulled out the short sword I had strapped to my back. Draco had left behind his spear, but he was just as deadly without any weapons. Castor pulled out his other sword.

The Snake turned back to us, its vertical pupils narrowed at the golden Cup in my hand. I had to distract the Snake and guide it away from the platform.

Argo had returned, although now had shifted into a wooden plank floating silently on the water.

"Protect Virgo and Pollux," I said to Draco.

I rushed forward and stepped on top of Argo, which immediately sped forward, away from the platform. I was somehow, miraculously, able to keep my balance by bending my knees. The Snake, seemingly confused at first, just stared at me as I sped past it and toward the little island. Then it shrieked and lurched after me, cutting through the water like a knife.

I was almost at the island but knew that I wouldn't get there before the Snake swallowed me whole. Argo must have known, too, because it swerved to the left, directly away from the island. The Snake, which didn't have time to stop, raced past me. I slashed the sword in front of me, cutting through the side of the Snake, which was like cutting a very hard piece of gelatin. The Snake let out a shriek that made me want to cut off my ears.

Then I was in the air again. The twirling blue light flickered above me. I held the sword and Cup in a death grip as I fell down screaming. Ice cold water greeted me.

I thrashed my feet, trying to swim upward as fast as I could. My head broke the surface and I took a gulp of air. I opened my eyes but everything was blurry. A second later my surroundings came into focus. Directly in front of me was the island. I frantically swam toward it, hauling myself up as I coughed. I put the sword down for a second to wipe the water from my eyes, then picked it up again.

Behind me, Hydra chased Castor, who stood atop the Argo board. I marveled at Castor's ability to keep his balance as the board moved swiftly. The Snake's head bit into the water but it missed Castor, swallowing a mouthful of water instead. The Snake pulled up and opened its mouth, then bit down again, missing Castor by a yard. Castor slashed both swords forward and cut the snake's side. Hydra shrieked, thrashing wildly. A surge of water threw Castor from the plank and he splashed into the water. His head bobbed up, and he coughed.

"Hydra!" I shouted. The snake's head snapped my way. "You just want to stay still!"

My chest was on fire. I had never felt that kind of pain before. I could feel the fire consuming me from the inside, burning away my flesh. The Snake stayed still, its green-yellow eyes staring at me blankly. It had a deep gash across its front neck that oozed dark red blood into the water.

Castor got back on the wooden plank. He shouted in rage as he slashed one of his swords and cut the Snake's neck. Hydra broke free of my lie, but it was too late for the Snake now. The head hung loosely to the side, only attached to the neck by a thin piece of skin. Its thick inner skin was a swirling mesh of red and black.

The Snake hissed blood. The plank moved closer and Castor slashed off what was left of the head, which dropped into the water. The Snake's green-yellow eyes were open in surprise as they disappeared below the surface. The rest of the body slowly drowned below the black water.

Castor knelt on the wooden board, looking down at where the head had disappeared. He pulled back his dripping hair. Draco was still on the platform behind me. He had moved Virgo and Pollux farther away from the water, placing them both against the wall. He stood at the edge of the platform, looking at the still water. The only movement was the reflection of the twisting blue light above us.

"That wasn't that bad," Castor said.

"Wait . . . ," I said. Wasn't Hydra also part of a myth with Hercules? As I recalled that myth, red foam started bubbling from the water where the body had disappeared. The Snake's severed neck slowly resurfaced. The skin was misting, as if it were burning. Castor moved backward with the plank, closer to the entrance, gagging. A second later the smell hit me. My eyes watered and I coughed. It smelled as if rotten meat were being dissolved by a very strong acid.

The mist coming out of the neck faded, and light red blood dripped from the neck. The drips of blood formed chunks of skin, as if the liquid blood had solidified. The newly formed skin was light red, but with the blue light above, it looked purple. It seemed slimy and delicate, with black veins forming through the skin like cracks in a ceramic pot. Then the skin grew black scales that formed like leaves sprouting from a branch. The neck diverged into two different chunks, the solidifying blood forming two necks that grew out of the main one. The new necks were raw like meat from a butcher shop, and they too began growing those ugly black scales.

I realized too late what we had done, and judging by Castor's ghastly pale face, he knew what we had done too. The two new heads formed simultaneously, first just two big blobs of pinkish skin. Then bones came out of the skin, giving shape to the skull and fangs. The eyes were white orbs, but a second later the dark pupils grew, then the yellow-green irises, as if someone had dropped paint and it had spread on its own. One of the heads turned to Castor as the black scales grew over it, and the other head fixed its gaze on me. Once the two heads were full of scales, they hissed at the same time.

The head looking at me lunged forward. I threw myself behind the black pillar where we had recovered the Cup and felt the island shaking from the impact as the Snake crashed against the pillar. Small pieces of black stone flew in all directions, and one hit me in the back of the head. I grunted as I crouched behind the pillar.

"Hydra!" I shouted, my throat ragged. "You just want to stay still!"

I moved away from the pillar and gave a startled jump back. Five feet in front of me, one of the Snake heads looked at me blankly. Agony seared through my muscles as I held the lie.

Twenty yards to my left, the other head had its jaws open, inches away from swallowing Castor as he stood on the plank. I fell to my knees as pain cut through the two scars on my chest.

Something splashed behind me. Draco was swimming toward the island. Castor and Argo moved to the side of the head, and Castor swung his sword down, severing the head. The head, still with its jaws open, splashed into the water and sank below the surface. What was that idiot doing? Two more heads would sprout from that.

"Draco!" Castor shouted, his voice resonating across the cavern. "Burn the neck!"

Draco pulled himself up on the island and raced past me toward the edge a few yards away from the Snake's sinking neck. The Snake I held with my lie still had that blank stare, and I grunted as the pain cut through me. Draco inhaled, puffing up his chest. Castor wisely rode away from the Snake. When Draco exhaled, a column of fire exploded from his mouth, extending about ten yards in front of him. A burst of orange and red light illuminated the cavern, reflecting off the walls and the skin of the Snake-head in front of me. The eyes of the snake seemed to swim in fire. Just as the other neck was slowly submerging under the water, the fire hit it. The slimy skin of the Snake turned white and cracked, as if it had been burned to stone. Around it, water boiled and mist formed.

The head in front of me hissed. I felt as if my ribs had ripped out of my chest, but I didn't have time to think about the pain. The lie was gone. The Snake turned toward Draco. I forced myself to my feet, pushing the pain away. I threw myself at the Snake before it could lurch toward Draco, plunging my sword into its neck, right behind its head. The Snake shrieked. I tried to pull my sword back but it was stuck. My feet left the ground. I gripped the hilt of the sword with all the strength I had as the Snake's head rose into the air, reaching toward the ceiling. The veins of blue light twisted mere feet above me. Castor and Draco shouted below me, but I couldn't make out what they were saying.

Hydra snapped its head around as if trying to bite me, but it couldn't reach me. My arm strained as I held onto the sword, my body swinging wildly in the air. The black walls, ceiling, and water, all reflecting blue light, blurred together. The noise, too, became a single clamor of screams, shouts, shrieks, and hisses. The wild movement stopped just as I felt I was about to fly away. The Snake began swimming to the side, and it took me a second to realize it was going to crush me against one of the walls. I let go of the sword and fell into the water. Again. An abrupt wave of silence hit me, but as soon as my head broke the surface the commotion blared all around me. I wiped my eyes with my free hand. I was a few feet away from the island, and I quickly swam toward it.

At the other side of the island, partially visible behind the broken stone pillar, the Snake shrieked, shaking its head as it tried to dislodge the sword in its neck. Castor was a few yards in front of it, trying to cut its head. But the Snake was moving so quickly from side to side that Castor missed, slicing empty air instead. He swung his large swords wildly, but merely managed a few cuts. I pushed myself on top of the island as the Snake shrieked again. It thrashed so violently that it created a wave that knocked down Castor. He screamed, then splashed into the water. The blue light above us extinguished, plunging the cavern into darkness. Fear wrapped around my chest. The Snake shrieked again, the sound echoing off the walls. I couldn't tell where the Snake was, but from the water swishing around me I knew it was moving closer.

A roaring shriek echoed through the cave, but I knew that one hadn't come from the Snake—it was a lot deeper. For a couple of seconds I heard only my thundering heart. Orange light exploded before me, so close that the wave of heat scorched my face. The flames reflected off the walls in a dancing swirl of orange and red. Draco's fire engulfed the Snake's head in front of him as he stood at the top of the broken pillar.

The fire stopped, and darkness spread around me like black ink. I breathed heavily, Crater clutched tightly in my hand. Could I use it to kill Hydra? Hadn't Cassiopeia said in my memory that the Cup could kill any creature? A net of blue light near the ceiling lit our surroundings again, seconds after the fire had extinguished. The blue veins seemed to hover more loosely this time. The Snake was still alive, its neck standing out of the water about fifty yards to my right. Half of its face was scorched a dark shade of grey, and blood oozed from the raw skin around it.

The Snake turned its head to stare at Draco with its remaining eye. Draco breathed heavily. Hydra lunged, but Draco jumped off the pillar, falling into the water.

"Hey, ugly!" Castor shouted from the opposite side of the island. I couldn't see him behind the pillar.

The Snake hissed.

I looked down at Crater. It had shifted into a large chalice. I knelt down at the edge of the island and filled it with water. Maybe it would work. The Snake head snapped back to me.

"You want this?" I shouted.

The Snake shrieked as it got closer, then stopped at the edge of the island, its face yards away. I screamed as I threw the water from the Cup onto its head. The Snake didn't move. It simply stared at me for a second, seeming a bit confused. I knew I had done something wrong. The Snake wasn't dead, although it looked mildly irritated. Using the Cup probably wasn't as simple as that. I felt stupid for a moment but realized I had distracted the Snake long enough for Castor to sneak around it and swing his sword through its neck. The head came off, plunging into the water. The neck rapidly sank down.

"Draco!" Castor shouted.

But Draco was just pulling himself onto the island. He looked at the Snake's sinking body and jumped to his feet, coughing up water. He inhaled, but the neck had already sunk below the surface.

A couple seconds of dead silence passed.

"I've never liked Snakes," Castor muttered.

The water began bubbling again, but the neck was not resurfacing. Castor came closer to us, the board stopping right at the edge of the little black island. The three of us stood side by side.

Castor held his swords in front of him. Crater shook in my trembling grip. The water foamed red and white, but the severed neck didn't emerge. Moments later, two more heads bobbed up from the water, already fully formed. They looked murderously at the three of us.

Draco and I jumped behind the black pillar, and Castor sped away. A splash and a choked shriek echoed behind me. I motioned to Draco with my head. He nodded. His blond hair was plastered to his forehead, and his eyes seemed purple with the blue light above. Draco inhaled, then exhaled as he peeked around the pillar. I rushed to stand behind him.

The Snake emitted a piercing shriek, but it didn't recoil. Instead, it waved its head madly, hitting Draco on the side. Draco flew away from the island and sank into the water. The burnt Snake turned to me. The other Snake, which had been facing the other way, also turned. Castor wasn't riding the board anymore. Argo floated away from the Snake as fast as it could. Castor's head bobbed up in the water a few feet to my right, looking disoriented. He wasn't holding his other sword.

"Hydra," I said. "You want to remain still." But my voice sounded completely normal. My scars burned with an intensity I had never felt before, and I knew my power was exhausted.

I wasn't sure if snakes could smile, but both heads bared their teeth mockingly. I stepped back, and the heads followed me slowly. Draco hadn't resurfaced, and Castor clung to Argo and coughed loudly. My heart lurched into my throat as I nearly fell backward into the water. I came one step away from the edge of the island. Three yards in front of me, the burnt Snake head opened its jaws with a hiss, revealing a dozen rows of sharp teeth extending into its throat.

"HEY!" Virgo shouted behind the Snakes.

The island shook beneath me, and a crack thundered above me. The burnt Snake head clamped its jaws shut, looking at the cracks spreading on the ceiling. The island trembled again, and I fell to my knees. A piece of rock from the island broke off and submerged below the water. Draco pulled himself onto the island, looking at Virgo as if she had gone absolutely mad. She stood at the edge of the platform, shivering. Her fists were clenched, and her brown eyes held a fierce intensity I had never seen before.

The Snake head leaned closer to Virgo.

"No!" Draco shouted as he scrambled to the edge of the island. Panic rose in my chest. The burnt Snake head turned back to me, its green-yellow eyes fixed on the Cup. It opened its mouth wide once again.

Virgo screamed, and a boom blasted through the cavern.

CHAPTER 11

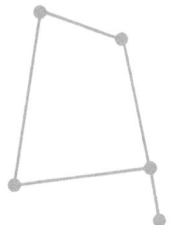

I HAD HEARD Virgo scream before, but that sound was something else—it came from the depths of her soul. The scream echoed across the cavern, vibrating inside my bones. Hydra shrank back, hissing. The Snake shook itself wildly, the two heads twisting in pain.

The cavern trembled as Virgo continued to scream. The ceiling cracked, roaring loudly. The cracks crept through the cavern, sliding down the walls and disappearing into the water.

A piece of ceiling broke off and landed in the water ten feet in front of me. I covered my face just as the water splashed over me. Virgo stopped screaming, but the cavern continued to shake. A large piece of rock broke free from the ceiling and fell on the Snake in front of me. As soon as the rock made contact with the head, a loud crunch echoed across the cavern and made my stomach churn. The limp head, and the rock, silently disappeared below the surface.

The other head shrieked at Virgo. She fell to her knees, breathing heavily, not even paying attention to the Snake. Draco stepped in front of me and stood at the edge of the platform. He inhaled.

"Hydra!" I shouted, raising the Cup above my head. The Snake snapped its head to me and locked its eyes on the Cup. Draco exhaled, and the largest column of fire I had ever seen escaped his mouth. It engulfed the giant head completely, and the Snake shrank to the side. Another piece of ceiling broke free and fell right on top of the head. Hydra's last remaining head broke into grey pieces, as if the fire had turned it to stone and the rock crushed it to dust. It all sank into the water.

"We need to get out of here!" I shouted as the cavern continued to tremble.

As if it had heard me, Argo came up at the edge of the platform with Castor inside. Draco and I jumped into the raft and Argo raced toward the platform on the right. Small pieces of rock broke free and dropped into the water.

As soon as we got to the platform, Draco grabbed Virgo, who seemed about to pass out again, and hauled her into the raft. Castor carried his brother and hurried back to us. Once everyone was seated, Argo raced toward the exit, going around the island in the middle of the cavern. A tall piece of wall broke off next to us and crashed into the water, surging Argo forward. I grabbed onto the side, afraid the raft would turn over.

The cavern continued cracking, and more pieces of the ceiling rained like black hail. The blue light on top of the cavern extinguished as we entered the river. The raft wobbled. The force of the falling rocks made Argo sway underneath us. A few seconds later the raft surged forward and we screamed. My breaths were too loud inside of my ears. Someone else was moaning. Water swished at our sides. I calmed my breaths, holding on tighter to the Cup.

"Virgo," I said, looking around wildly in the dark, unable to spot her.

"I'm all right," her voice came from behind me. I turned and felt her hand take hold of my soaked shirt. I took her hand in mine and realized both of us were shaking. I held onto her tightly.

"What?" Pollux asked.

"It's okay," Castor responded.

"What's okay?" Pollux asked, then he moaned again. "Do we have the Cup?"

"Yeah."

A moment of silence passed.

"Why is it so dark? AM I BLIND?"

Castor laughed. "You're not. We're back in the tunnel."

In a low voice, Castor explained what had happened. When he mentioned Hydra, Pollux only moaned in response.

"What did you do?" Draco whispered at my side. He wasn't asking me.

Virgo squeezed my hand tighter, and I squeezed back. She had saved me, but I wasn't entirely sure of what she had done. I had studied the myths related to her Constellation in depth but had never truly deciphered what she was able to do. The rest of our Constellations were easier to interpret—Corvus was the Liar, Draco the Dragon, Orion the Hunter, Argo the Ship, but Virgo had many different myths.

There were only three female Constellations in the sky. Cassiopeia was the Queen, Andromeda was the Princess, and Virgo was the Goddess. But it wasn't clear which specific goddess she represented. The Greeks associated her with Demeter, the goddess of harvest and fertility, with Persephone, the queen of the Underworld, with Athena, the goddess of wisdom and military strategy, and with Dike, the goddess of justice. Sometimes Virgo was depicted with wings, other times with wheat in her hands. She was also associated with Astraea, the goddess of justice, innocence, and purity. In Egypt she was associated with Isis, the goddess of love and magic. In Babylon she was associated with Ishtar, goddess of love and war, and to the people of India she represented the goddess Kauni, the maiden. Her main star, Spica, represented prosperity in most cultures.

Whereas other Constellations remained constant in different parts of the world—like Canis Major, usually seen as a dog, or Taurus, seen as a bull—Virgo didn't have that consistency. She represented a powerful Goddess—there was no doubt about that—but she seemed to represent all goddesses at once, which made her powers hard to interpret.

"I didn't do much," Virgo finally whispered with another squeeze of my hand.

If that hadn't been much, then I didn't want to be around when she actually did much. I tried to think of how any of her Constellation's mythologies could tie into making an entire cavern collapse, but I couldn't see any direct links.

I went over the small details that Virgo had revealed to us about her past. She had been kidnapped when she was a child. We didn't know what had happened during that time, but she told us that after escaping she had been left for dead. Then the story got confusing. She had been rescued, and then she had lived for some time with the Weavers, which made little sense.

The Weavers were the Three Sisters who controlled Fate. They weaved into every single person's life strands of Fate that took the person directly to their Destiny. Although I didn't know how that actually happened. All I knew for sure was that they were extremely powerful creatures and as ancient as the Universe itself, they were immortal, and they lived at the bottom of the river Eridanus, another Constellation. But no one knew where Eridanus was located as a physical manifestation on this planet, or how to find it.

Thinking about Virgo finding these powerful creatures and living with them scrambled my mind as I tried to make sense of it. All I really knew about that time was that shortly after she'd left them, Draco had found her.

She had also told us that the last time she had used her power had been when she was kidnapped. I assumed she had either used it to escape or kill her kidnappers. But whatever she had materialized had consumed her entirely and nearly killed her. She had never fully recovered from that. That's why she looked so thin, because she had literally consumed her body with her power. This must have been the first time in years that she used it.

I let out a sigh, feeling the warmth of Virgo's hand in mine.

"Corvus."

I startled. The raft swayed a little underneath us, but no one said anything. I realized that the Cup had spoken to me.

Yes? I said inside my head.

The Cup didn't answer immediately, but I became aware of its presence. My body vibrated slightly.

"You emptied yourself on purpose," it said.

I did, I responded.

"Interesting."

My body continued to vibrate, and warmth spread in my chest.

Can every Star Object form a bond with Star Children? I asked.

"Yes," Crater answered. "Without a bond we have no power, no true purpose. Once we are linked to a Child of Light, then we become alive."

Castor and Pollux must have bonded with Argo. But I wondered if other Star Objects had bonded with Star Children. There were several Star Objects in the Constellations—Crater, Argo, Ara, Corona Austrina, Corona Borealis, Lyra, Libra, and Saggita. Draco had burned Ara in Rome after the battle at Palatine Hill, so it was probably dead, and the Twins had Argo. I wondered where the other five objects were and if we would ever find them. Could you bond with more than one object? For some reason I felt that we couldn't. I looked down at the chalice, even though I could barely make out its shape in the darkness. I owned the Cup and its power now.

Crater stayed silent for the rest of the ride, and I wondered when it would speak to me again. The Cup had said nothing while we fought Hydra, although there was not much it could have said. I wondered what I would be able to do with Crater. I would have to learn how to truly use its power. Cassiopeia had said that if I filled it with water, I could decide to turn that to poison and kill any creature, but as Virgo had suggested earlier, I was sure I could also use it to heal.

I held the Cup tighter. Who had hidden Crater in an underground cave with Hydra? Obviously someone had. It had probably been the same person who had written the Prophecy on the temple wall. But that had been thousands of years ago. Had Hydra and Crater been waiting in that cave for millennia? And why had the Cup been hidden in the first place? My head spun. I was missing something but didn't feel confident I would find answers anytime soon.

Sometime later, I heard the unmistakable sound of splashing water. It soon became louder. A couple of minutes later we returned to the cavern where we had first entered the subterranean river. Water still poured from the hole in the ceiling. In the dim light, I was able to see Pollux sitting up, his hair tied in a messy bun at the bottom of his head. Next to me, Virgo lay with her head on Draco's lap.

I thought of Sirius, Maera, Leo, and Aquila, and a knot formed in my stomach. I hoped they were all right and that the water hadn't reached the second floor. Argo moved toward the tiny island in the middle of the cavern. Pollux and Castor climbed onto it.

"Why are we getting out?" I asked.

"Argo needs to shift to get us out of here," Castor responded.

Draco helped Virgo climb off the boat, and I walked out after them.

Pollux and Castor both eyed the Cup with a wary glance. Crater had turned into a thermos again. The Twins had probably figured out that they wouldn't be able to hold it.

Argo disappeared under the water. Everyone was quiet as we waited for it to resurface. We were all still wet, but no one seemed to care. Pollux and Castor stood close to each other, looking at the dark water. Virgo leaned on Draco, who had an arm around her waist to help her stand upright. Meanwhile I held onto the Cup, which was still warm.

Argo came back up a couple of minutes later. It had transformed into a small metal submarine about twenty feet in length and ten feet wide. The small hatch at the top opened, and the Twins climbed in first. I went after them, descending the metal ladder. Draco and Virgo came inside last.

Once in the submarine, I looked at our new surroundings. The light inside was entirely blue. At each side of the submarine were side by side seats with an aisle down the middle, similar to the seats of an airplane. I didn't know if this was how small submarines looked but guessed Argo had set this up.

"We have to go back to the temple to get the others," Virgo said as she stood next to me.

Seeing her in the blue light made me clench my hands unwillingly. She looked thinner than she had before, her cheeks a bit more sunken, the skin on her face clinging more fiercely to the bone.

"Virgo, what—" I started.

"I'm fine," she said sharply.

Draco helped her sit down. Virgo put on her seat belt, as if we were going for a roller coaster ride.

"Yeah," Castor said. "Argo will take us back up."

The rest of us sat down and put our seat belts on. Draco sat next to Virgo. The seat next to me was empty, and in front of me were the Twins. There was no control panel at the front or any other sort of buttons or radar that I expected a submarine to have.

After we were all buckled in, the submarine began to move. I assumed that there were underwater tunnels that somehow led to the Nile. Castor began to hum in front of me, and soon his brother joined him. I didn't recognize the song, but it seemed like a depressing tune, which didn't make me feel any better.

I had so many questions rolling inside my head, but instead my brain decided to shut down and focus on that stupid tune. It seemed like only a few minutes had passed when Argo surged forward, and I was pushed back onto the seat. The Twins groaned, but neither Draco nor Virgo made a sound. Argo went still. I undid my seat belt and walked to the back of the submarine. The hatch opened above me, and I climbed the ladder to take a peek outside.

A ghostly fog surrounded me. The humid cold stuck to my skin. Murky grey water stretched all around us. There was a bark to my right. The boat began moving in that direction. After only a few seconds, a roughly triangular structure materialized in front of me. Sirius peeked out from the rectangular opening in the second floor. He barked louder when he saw me. Behind him I spotted Leo, so I guessed Aquila and Maera were there too.

"Hey, boy!" I shouted. Sirius barked back. "We'll get you out of there."

I descended the ladder again. Virgo and Draco stood directly in front of me, and the Twins leaned against one of the seats.

"Everything is still flooded, but the second floor of the temple seems to be all right," I said. "But the opening is not big enough for Leo."

"Hmmm," Draco said. "We could try to—"

Argo spun, nearly making me tumble down. I held onto the metal ladder. Then the submarine stopped.

"What was that?" Virgo asked.

Pollux climbed the ladder. "Argo is directly facing the temple." He muttered. "Ohhhh . . . smart Ship. Hey guys! Step as far away from the opening as you can."

"Why would they need to—" But then I realized what Argo was planning. The others must have realized it too. We all rushed back to our seats as Argo moved away from the temple. I put my seat belt back on.

Argo stopped, then surged forward. I was pushed back against the seat. I braced for impact. A deafening sound boomed outside as I shot forward, the seat belt nearly cutting me in half.

Argo was still again, and the hatch opened. Draco and Virgo, being closest to it, climbed out first, then me and the Twins. We stood inside the second floor of the temple—or at least what remained of it. Argo had literally blasted through the opening, creating a large hole on the side. Part of the roof had collapsed, and pieces of it lay strewn on the floor. Our friends were huddled in the far corner. Leo's muscles relaxed as soon as he saw us, and Sirius barked. The dog seemed better, but he was still thin. Virgo rushed to Sirius and hugged him tightly, and the dog licked her ears. Maera jumped into Draco's arms, and he laughed. There was no fog inside the temple, as if even the mist knew better than to come into this place. To the right, water sloshed against the steps. It was lower than before, but I still couldn't see the first floor.

Argo retreated into the water, maybe to shift again into a bigger submarine or boat. Leo emitted a low growl when his eyes settled on Crater. The Lion's gaze was fierce, as if he recognized the Cup. But how could Leo recognize Crater, which had been inside an underground cavern for millennia? I held the Cup tighter.

"We should get going," Pollux said behind us.

Argo waited for us outside, this time as a big white yacht. It moved as close as it could to the opening, and one by one we all climbed out of the temple and into the yacht. I didn't realize I was cold until the warmth from inside the yacht wrapped around me like a blanket. We were in a small living room with large windows on each side that showed the gloomy water and fog. Directly in front of me were two semicircular couches that faced each other with a round table in between them. Behind those were narrow stairs that led down to what must be the bedrooms.

The warmth unknotted my muscles and I sank down on the floor, without enough strength to make it to the couches. How much of the Nile had flooded? Had people lost their homes or drowned? A shudder went down my spine. I didn't want to think about that. If all the Nile had flooded, then we may have crippled an entire country. Were we no better than Perseus then? Willing to flood one of the largest rivers in the world for our selfish purposes? But this had *not* been selfish. We had been forced to retrieve the Cup. We had never intended to harm anyone.

Leo let out a tired growl as he walked to the window on the right and lay down on the floor. Aquila perched on the couch. Draco was still carrying Maera. Virgo and Sirius walked side by side into the room, Virgo leaning on the dog for support.

"So, what happens now?" Pollux asked as he walked to the window on the left. The fog swallowed the temple as Argo moved away. "How do we get the Cup to Perseus and steal all the Prophecies?"

"How about we sleep first," Castor suggested. "Then we make a new plan tomorrow."

As soon as Castor said *sleep* my eyelids felt as if they were made of iron, and my eyes stung. Sleep seemed like a good idea. My brain felt burnt. Even if I wanted to come up with a new plan, I simply couldn't. I still didn't trust the Twins, but since I was the only one who could hold the Cup, they couldn't steal it from us and take it to Perseus. And the Twins were outnumbered two to seven, so trying to turn on us now wouldn't be a good idea—they surely knew that.

"Sounds like a plan," Draco said as he stepped around me.

Virgo only nodded. She seemed about to collapse and weakly managed to push the strand of white hair out of her face. I looked down at the Cup. Could I use it to help Virgo heal?

"Virgo," I said, my voice hoarser than normal, as if I had swallowed glass. I cleared my throat. I motioned at the Cup. "Maybe this could help."

Virgo opened her eyes wide. "No," she said immediately. Her voice was so firm it startled me. The Twins eyed her curiously. "You could consume yourself, Corvus." Draco stepped a bit closer to Virgo. "No," Virgo told him before Draco could argue. "That Cup has incredible power, and we can't use it any time we want, not unless we want Corvus to die."

"Why would I die?" I said as I looked down at the Cup.

"The Cup could completely consume you." She paused. Her eye sockets were caved into her face. "Unless it's life or death, don't use it." How did she know so much about the Cup's power? What wasn't she telling us?

"It *is* a life-or-death situation," I argued. "I would be dead if you hadn't saved us from Hydra. I'm pretty sure all of us would be dead. Let me heal you. I can—"

"No," Virgo cut me off with a wave of her hand, as if slicing the idea in half. "Save the Cup's power for when we actually need it."

Before I could keep arguing, Virgo turned on her heel. She walked toward the stairs and climbed down, holding onto the railing with a tight grip. The Twins remained silent. Draco and I exchanged a glance, and then he followed after Virgo. Why wouldn't she want me to heal her? She looked worse than she had when I had met her. I would talk to Draco later so we could find a way to convince her to let us help her. I didn't think I would die if I only healed her a little.

I forced myself up to my knees and then somehow found the strength to stand. Castor said something about five rooms, so we could each get one. I nodded absently.

I welcomed the fatigue, thinking I might have my first night without insomnia. But something in me was still restless. How would we fool Perseus to get the Prophecies back? I reminded myself that we had the advantage over him—Perseus didn't know I was the only one who could hold Crater. He would *never* have let another Star Child hold a weapon as powerful as Crater, so he must have assumed I was the only one who could find it and that the Twins could then give it to him. We would find a way to use that to our advantage—we *would* get those Prophecies.

•————•————•

Celaeno and I walked side by side on the beach. The sun was beginning to set below the horizon. It tainted the clouds pink, red, orange, and dark yellow. The color from the clouds reflected on the ocean, making it look like the sea was bleeding.

The foaming white waves gently washed over the sand a few feet to our side. I tried to stay away from the water. I didn't like swimming, or the ocean, but Celaeno had insisted we come to the beach for a while before we each set out on our missions. I had tied my shoes together so I could swing them around my shoulder. The tips of my shoes bounced against me as I walked.

In one hand I held the small shells we had found along the way. "Look at this one, Cela." I knelt down and brushed sand away from a white conch shell. It was intact. "This one is for Maia."

"She'll like that one," Celaeno said.

I smiled at her. The setting red sun cast an unnatural glow on her golden skin. She had midnight black hair tied into a large braid at her back, which accentuated her narrow face, and her eyes sparkled like silver stars. She smiled as we kept walking. Her steps were light as always, her ballerina's grace present even here on the beach. She began to hum a song, and I almost expected her to start dancing.

I looked down again, trying to find more shells. I already had five shells for Maia, Electra, Taygete, Alcyone, and Sterope. I had given Celaeno her small pink shell and was missing one for Merope. I also had some money to buy the girls some plush toys. We weren't kids anymore, but I knew they liked to have their plush toys on their beds. I had seen some cute sea animals at the aquarium store next to the hotel. I would have to go buy them before leaving.

We continued walking in silence for a while. After some time, I found a spiraled shell that I knew Merope would like. I pocketed all my shells and wiped the sand from my hands. I would wash the shells with clean water once I got back to the hotel. Even though I already had seven of them, I kept looking for more, in case I found a prettier one. My bare feet sank into the sand with each step as I kept my gaze down.

Something hit me on the chest, and I realized it had been a sand ball.

"Hey!" I shouted as I looked at Celaeno, who ran away from me like a gazelle.

I picked up a handful of sand and raced after her. Half of the sand spilled out of my hand, but I threw whatever I had left. It hit her in the back of the head and her braid dripped sand.

"Argh!" Celaeno stopped running. Before I could stop myself, I crashed into her back and we both tumbled down, falling side by side.

Celaeno laughed hysterically next to me. "I think I have sand in places I shouldn't have sand in," she said.

I laughed too. "You started this."

"You just looked too serious," she said as she continued laughing.

Celaeno stood up, shaking the sand away from her clothes. She extended her hand to me and I held it. She pulled me to my feet. For a moment I worried about the shells in my pocket, but when I retrieved them, they all seemed intact. I pocketed them again. I also picked up my shoes, which were full of sand now, and swung them around my shoulder again.

"We haven't had a sand fight in years," I said as we started walking again.

"Not since we were little children." Celaeno kicked sand to the side. "I think this is the first time we've been at the beach since—"

I bit my tongue. She was right. We hadn't been to the ocean since then. I looked out across the sea, which still looked like it was bleeding red. The sight of it made dread curl through me like sharp claws.

"Do you still have nightmares?" Celaeno asked.

I looked down at the sand, spotting a couple more buried shells—they all seemed broken, so I didn't bother picking them up. "Sometimes," I admitted.

It had been years since the attack, but I still dreamt about it. Those nights it felt like the attack had only happened weeks ago.

"I sometimes have nightmares too." Celaeno walked over the wet sand as a wave pulled back. "I sometimes speak to him." She paused, and I didn't dare interrupt. "It sounds strange, I know. But I do feel Darren is still here with us, watching over us, protecting us . . . even though we couldn't protect him."

My heart tightened as if I had plunged a ragged piece of glass through it. I wanted to say something to make Celaeno feel better. I wanted to tell her that we did everything we could. At least they did everything they could. I had almost died with Darren, but I couldn't even bear to think about that.

"I can't help but feel that any time we're near the ocean it's waiting for us," I said, "ready to kill us."

"I don't like being in the ocean either." A shadow passed over Celaeno's eyes. "But right now, we don't have a choice."

We continued walking. My meeting would start in about an hour. What if something goes wrong? I wondered. What if it ends up in a fight? My heart began to race faster. This was the first mission where the others were letting me meet new Star Children alone. I usually stayed behind unless someone could stay with me. I couldn't mess up.

I wasn't supposed to have come. But we needed to be very careful about what information we let other Star Children know about us, especially knowing some of them would come after us once they figured out what we were trying to find. We definitely didn't want others to know about the existence of the Pleiades. As far as we knew, they were the only Stars that had materialized into beings. That left me as the only candidate to come on this mission—the only spy our family could use.

But the meeting I had scheduled wasn't the only reason we were here in Riviera Maya, Mexico, so far away from the others. We had heard rumors about a strange sea creature that had appeared here. Some called it a mermaid, others said it was a mutant fish, and a *couple had seen the horned, fury face of the creature. If our instincts were correct, then Capricornus might be roaming the underground rivers and caverns in the area. Celaeno's mission was to follow up on those leads to see if she could find him.*

"Do you think they'll be all right?" I asked after some time. Celaeno and I had gotten the easy mission, and I worried about the others.

"They'll be fine," Celaeno assured me, although she sounded like she was assuring herself. She looked out at the ocean. "They won't have to fight—they just need to gather information from the witnesses."

I nodded but still felt that old twist of fear in my heart. A week ago, we had heard that a cruise ship had been shipwrecked in the Black Sea. It wouldn't have been a problem for us to investigate, except that the only two survivors had claimed that a giant Monster had attacked them—a giant Monster that seemed to have no describable shape.

My chest tightened—it had to be Cetus. No other sea Monster could match that description. Our other siblings were already in Turkey to investigate. They'll be fine, I told myself. They won't go into the ocean. I took a deep breath. You will all be together eating hot dogs for dinner in less than a week. It also made me feel safer that Cetus had last been seen in the Black Sea and not the Atlantic or the Caribbean Sea, so most likely I wouldn't find it here. I would be fine—the worst I would find here would be a couple of sharks and maybe some crocodiles.

A while later, the docks came into view. I could see some yachts in the distance, but we were still far enough away that they were only white dots edging the beach.

"Okay," Celaeno said. "You're up, Corvus." I stood straighter. I wouldn't fail. "I'll see you back at the hotel tonight."

"Good luck," I said.

Celaeno flashed a smile. "You too."

Celaeno walked away from the beach toward the towering hotels in the distance. She would be fine. I wasn't worried about her. I was more worried about myself. I had taken up this mission simply because I was the only one who could, and I felt that pressure weigh heavily on me. The others had trusted me with this, and I couldn't let them down. I wouldn't.

I was early for the meeting but I decided to go to the docks anyway. As soon as I stepped on the wooden planks, I wiped the sand off my feet and put my shoes back on. I paced back and forth, the wooden dock swaying a bit as the waves washed against it. I looked out across the ocean, which had turned a very deep dark blue. Even though Cetus had been spotted in the Black Sea, I still feared that somehow it would know I was here and travel all this way just to kill me.

I had to keep reminding myself that I was safe. I kicked a pebble and it splashed into the water below. Would the others be all right? They had promised to stay away from the ocean, but that didn't make the fear go away. I knew that the other reason they had sent me here was because I would be far away from Cetus—far from the Monster that had almost killed me.

I sighed.

I decided not to think about Cetus anymore. I had an important meeting coming up and I needed to focus. The full moon was less than halfway up the sky, its reflection rippling on the sea as the hot wind swept at the waves. The night sky was now clear of clouds, dotted with a few stars. I wondered if humans traveled to the Stars once they died, as so many mythologies claimed.

"Hey, Darren," I said as I looked at the twinkling stars. They were jewels scattered on a velvet veil. "It's me, Corvus. Just thought I'd say hi . . . I usually don't say hi." That seemed like a stupid thing to say. "If you're listening, I just wanted to tell you I miss you . . ." I heaved a sigh. I really did miss him. "I'm sorry." I hung my head low. "I'm sorry I failed you. I'm sorry I couldn't save you."

The smell of seawater burned into my nostrils, and I had the urge to vomit. I took a few deep breaths, which didn't help. I couldn't break now. This was an important mission. I looked back toward the ocean and noticed a yacht moving directly toward me. Its white surface gleamed as it reflected the light of the moon, and it seemed as big as some of the houses we had lived in.

My heart drummed inside my ears.

The yacht was yards away now, getting closer every second. Less than a minute later, it stopped right next to me. The glass door on the lower deck opened. No one came out. I took a deep breath and slowly walked inside.

The wooden floor was polished smooth, and the right and left walls were floor-to-ceiling windows. In front of me were two couches in the shape of a semicircle that faced each other, and behind them were stairs leading down.

On the couch facing me sat the Gemini Twins.

Chapter XLI, Verse I

Once a beautiful Queen but then transformed into a Dog,
The power of the bright star shall still be in her command.
In love with the Golden King but now both doomed into solitude,
The Lion and the Dog will lose most of their power,
Confined to mainly observe the new war turning into Chaos.
The howling will announce the flooding of the Nile,
For the river shall recognize the true power of the Dog Star.

CHAPTER 12

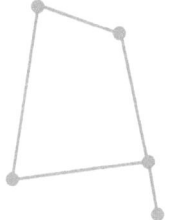

I HAD NEVER MET *the Gemini Twins. As we had expected, they were indeed twins. They would have been identical except for their hair. One of them wore his hair long, tied in a braid, while the other Twin had short hair.*

As always, when meeting new Star Children, I had gone over the mythology of their Constellation. While Pollux and Castor were twins and had the same mother, Queen Leda, they had different fathers—Castor was the mortal son of the king Tyndareus and Pollux was the son of the god Zeus. They were known to be good horsemen, and Castor excelled in sword fighting. Their Constellation, Gemini, had been important to sailors since ancient times. They believed that the divine Twins could rescue ships and sailors that had been shipwrecked by the mighty god Poseidon. As far as we knew, the Twins could cause sea storms and sink ships.

"Ahhh." The Twin with short hair smiled. "Welcome, friend! I'm Castor."

"What is your name?" Pollux asked.

"I'm Aaron."

"Oh, I see," Castor said, dropping his smile. "We'll figure out which one you are." Castor seemed pensive. "Hercules? No, you're not that strong. Orion? No, you're definitely not handsome."

I clenched my teeth.

Pollux looked at me with an intense gaze, his eyes boring into me. "Hmm," he said. "You're just a little bit handsome."

I felt my cheeks flushing with heat. Pollux smiled, and I slid my gaze back to Castor.

"Why don't you take a seat?" Castor motioned at one of the couches. I walked slowly and sat in front of the Twins.

"We have crab cakes, shrimp soup, and ceviche," Castor said.

"I already ate dinner," I said.

"Well, we hope you don't mind us then." Castor stood up and walked to the back of the room toward a table filled with food.

"Have you been enjoying your trip to Cancun?" Pollux said, scratching his cheek. "Did you go to the pyramids?"

"I arrived today," I said. "Haven't had time to go on any tours."

Pollux raised one of his brows, then chuckled. "All work and no play then?"

Castor came back, holding two large bowls in each hand. He handed one of the bowls to his brother. Castor sat back down, and both Twins began eating.

"So," I said. "You told me you had information about the Star Child called Cassiopeia."

She was one of the Star Children we had never been able to locate. Although Cassiopeia wasn't such an important Constellation, she was still worth investigating. Star Children were rarely alone, so maybe she would lead to more powerful Star Children. The more we knew about other Star Children, the easier it would be to learn if they were our friends or our enemies.

"We do," Castor spoke between mouthfuls. "We have a lot of juice on Cassiopeia, but first we want to hear your juice."

My heartbeat intensified, hammering into my ribs. "My juice on what?" I asked.

Castor swallowed his food and laughed. "You know we trade

information." He smiled. "Depending on how much information you give us, we'll decide how much to tell you."

"What do you want to know?" I asked with a sigh.

"You could start by telling us your real name," Pollux said as he picked at his food.

"How about I tell you about other Star Children I know of," I said.

"No, no, no," said Pollux. "We want to know about you."

I smiled. "I'm not that interesting."

Castor smiled back, a piece of fish hanging from his fork. "That's our price, friend." The fish fell back into the bowl. "You want to know about Cassiopeia, tell us about yourself first. And you better make it interesting."

I leaned back on the couch, acting as if I was considering what to tell them, although I perfectly knew what I was going to say. I had gone over this dozens of times with the girls. This meeting was less about gaining information than it was about giving information we wanted the Twins to know, and share, with the rest of the Star Children. The Twins had control over what most Star Children knew about each other, and we wanted to be able to direct that flow of information to cover our tracks.

"What if I told you about Perseus?" The Twins went very still. "I promise he's a lot more interesting than I am."

Castor set his bowl down on his leg. "And how would you know about Perseus?"

I didn't answer.

Pollux laughed. "No one knows much about Perseus." He smiled. "I would be very surprised if you knew anything about him."

Castor eyed me suspiciously.

"I have a spy close to him," I said with a smile. "Perseus was adopted into a rich family and has a couple of foster siblings."

The Twins eyed me in silence for a few seconds. I wasn't lying about that. I smiled at the Twins. I had realized that the best way to manipulate people with information was to tell them lies wrapped around pieces of truth.

"Where does Perseus live?" Pollux asked.

"Tell me about Cassiopeia," I said.

"That's not how it works," Castor said. "You give us information first."

I bit my tongue, but this was information that I was willing to trade. The more information I gave them about Perseus, the better we could hide ourselves. We needed to lead others directly to Perseus to know exactly who was his ally and who wasn't. I leaned back again, staring at the Twins. I let the silence stretch for a few seconds.

"Perseus lives in New York," I said. The Twins listened attentively, their food forgotten for a moment. "He's the adopted child of Andrew Wood."

"The mega-multimillionaire?" Castor asked with wide eyes.

"Yes," I said.

"He has other adopted siblings who live with him," I said. "Although you won't find much information about them. The Wood family is very private. Their kids even changed their last names in school so they won't attract attention."

"And which one of them is the snitch?" Castor asked with a smile.

"It doesn't matter," I said.

"That's not a lot of juice, friend," Pollux said. "You're going to have to tell us more about Perseus if you want information on Cassiopeia."

I smiled. My sisters and I had all the juice on Perseus, much more than any other Star Child. But I wouldn't tell the Twins everything about him. Some things we wanted to keep to ourselves.

"Algol has awoken inside Perseus—that's what's been causing the strange terrorist attacks in Europe," I said. "Algol will make him the most destructive, dangerous, and powerful Star Child."

The Twins were silent for a second. "Now that . . . is juicy juice." Castor chuckled.

"*Cassiopeia also lives on the outskirts of New York,*" *Pollux said. I didn't detect a lie. That couldn't be a coincidence. Could Cassiopeia be after Perseus? Was she his friend or enemy? I would have to ask her myself.*

"*We're not sure what she can materialize.*" *Pollux picked up his bowl and ate some more fish.* "*But she's still dangerous.*"

"*Why?*" *I asked.*

"*We very strongly believe that she was trained as a Russian spy and worked for the government for some time,*" *Pollux said.* "*But now she works for herself. She trades information between powerful governments and sometimes she trades weapons too. That's how she makes a living.*"

"*A Russian spy?*" *I asked. I still didn't detect any lies. The Twins may have been known for being a tricky duo—but their information was always truthful. That's what made them so good at what they did.*

They shrugged simultaneously.

"*What else do you know about her?*" *I asked.*

"*Tell us more about Perseus,*" *Pollux said.*

I clenched my jaw. I couldn't reveal a lot more, not without endangering my sisters.

"*As I said, Algol is very destructive,*" *I said,* "*and Perseus doesn't seem to know how to control it. With it, he could cause more terrorist attacks or simply gruesome accidents and deaths to people around him.*"

"*Why did Algol awake all of a sudden?*" *Pollux said.* "*Every Star Child is always able to use the power of the Stars in their Constellations.*"

I shook my head. "*We're not sure, and we believe he's not sure either.*"

"*Hmmm,*" *Castor said as he continued eating.* "*What else do you have on him?*" *I glared at Castor.* "*Just one more, friend, I swear.*"

I had gone over this with the others. This would be the little bit of information that would help us cover all of our tracks.

"Perseus has been travelling a lot to India," I said. "Mostly to the south. He's looking for something there, but I don't know what it is."

The Twins considered this. Pollux seemed to believe it, but Castor's brows knitted together.

"I'm pretty sure he'll be there in a couple of days, in the city of Kanniyakumari on the southern tip," I said. "If you don't believe me, go look for him there. I heard he's interested in the city's temples."

"Is there a specific reason why he's interested in the temples in India?" Pollux asked.

I shrugged. "I just know he's looking for something."

Castor didn't break his gaze away from me. I didn't want to be explicit about it, but knew the Twins were smart enough to figure out Perseus was interested in the mysterious Prophecies of Alathea and that he was hunting them down in India. The Twins would want proof that Perseus was actually there, so they would go to India—and they would actually find Perseus there, roaming the temples. The Twins would then tell other Star Children they had spotted Perseus and that he was looking for something important. Then the other Star Children would start searching the temples in India, too, far away from us.

"Cassiopeia is not working alone," Pollux said. "We know she's with other Star Children, but we don't know who they are."

"Where can I find her?" I asked.

"Like we said, she's usually on the outskirts of New York City. Not sure where." Castor bit into a big piece of fish.

"New York is a big city," I said. "You need to be more specific."

"Well . . . ," Pollux said. Castor glared at him, but Pollux ignored him. "Cassiopeia has been visiting London a lot. She spends her time in the British Museum. She flies to the city almost every weekend and visits the museum. You'll certainly find her there."

I didn't know why she would be there, but I still didn't detect any lies, so going to London would be worth a shot. Looking for her in a museum would be easier than searching all of New York.

"What does she look like?" I asked.

"What does Perseus look like?" Pollux asked.

"He's easy to spot. He's tall, dark eyes, and red hair," I said.

"How red?" Castor asked. "Is he like strawberry blond or like full red hair?"

"Full red hair," I responded, not really knowing the difference.

"Cassiopeia is blond, not so tall, blue eyes," Pollux said.

"There's a lot of people that look like that," I said.

"She's very beautiful," Castor said.

"That's not a very specific trait either," I complained.

"Like really, really beautiful," Castor said with a wink of his eye. "But be careful. She knows how to fight."

I sighed and prepared to leave. I had seeded all the information I wanted the Twins to know and had even learned where to find Cassiopeia. Our obvious next step would be to track her down and figure out what kind of information she could give us.

"And pro tip," Castor said, "flirting with Cassiopeia is a bad idea. She'll kick you in the nuts."

"Thanks," I said, although flirting with Cassiopeia had never crossed my mind.

I stood up, fully intending to leave. I walked around the couch, turning my back to the Twins.

"Wait," Pollux said before I could reach the glass door. I turned around. Castor was glaring at his brother again, who eyed me curiously. "I think I may know what Perseus is doing in India or what he may be after."

I didn't sense any lies.

"But—" Castor complained.

213

His brother held up a hand, and Castor glared at me. "I like you," Pollux said. "I'm sure we could keep in touch, keep trading information."

I knew that meant they wanted to know more about Perseus and possibly about myself. I would have to figure out what else to tell them, but this could become a good alliance.

"What is he doing in India?" I asked.

Pollux smiled. "He could be after the mysterious Prophecies of Alathea, although I'm sure you must have guessed that too." His smile widened. "But I think he might be looking for something else there." My heart beat loudly inside my ears. "If Perseus is as powerful as you claim, then other Star Children will start coming after him. Power gives you more enemies than friends." He set his bowl on the table and paused. Pollux met my eyes, his own were dark blue like the sea outside. "Cassiopeia is most likely his enemy, and so are two others we know of, Draco and Virgo. They probably know how dangerous Perseus is, and they'll fight to stop him." Castor looked at his shoes, his arms crossed over his chest. This wasn't something they had originally been planning to share with me. "Perseus knows he better find new allies soon." Pollux pulled a strand of hair behind his ear. "We heard he was looking for the Pleiades, the seven beautiful Stars that have very strong connections to India. I think he believes they might become good allies."

My heart slammed against my chest. How did the Twins know about the Pleiades? How did they know Perseus was interested in them? I had lied so many times to keep my sisters hidden. It hadn't been enough. Pollux smiled wickedly.

Castor looked up again, half a smile spreading on his lips. "But you probably already knew about the Pleiades," he said. "Didn't you, Corvus?"

My heart sank.

Castor leaned back on the couch with a chuckle. "You shouldn't have lied to us."

The boat maneuvered away from the docks and surged towards the sea. I fell on my side, and something cracked against my upper leg. There was movement behind me. I jumped to my feet and lunged at Castor, who was standing in front of me. I tried to knock him down, but he flipped me around and I landed on my back with a grunt.

"Tell us," Castor said. "How long have you been with the Pleiades? Are they as beautiful as the myths claim?"

The boat made a sharp turn, and I slid toward the window, my back hitting the glass. Dark stars danced in my vision, and when they cleared, Castor stood over me.

"We play fair with those who play fair with us," he said. "And if you don't . . ." Castor balled his fists.

I chuckled. "You should have left them out of this."

I would do anything to protect my sisters. Anything.

"Castor," I said, my voice echoing inside my ears. Castor's gaze became blank. "You want to kill Pollux."

Castor turned to face his brother, who was still standing next to the couches. Pollux looked confusedly at me, then at his brother. Castor pulled out a white carved knife from a hidden belt at his back. He slowly walked toward his brother.

"Castor, what are you—?"

Castor drove the knife forward, but Pollux jumped to the side just in time, falling close to the stairs. The knife grazed his right shoulder, and dark blood stained his shirt. Pollux screamed as he fell on his back.

"Argo!" Pollux yelled.

For a moment I didn't know what he meant, and then it hit me—we were inside the Argo Navis. Before I remembered more from that myth, the Ship took another sharp turn. I hit my head hard against the window and felt the lie dropping. Castor fell flat on his face next to the couches, and the knife clattered away from him, final-

ly disappearing down the stairs on the far side of the room. I scrambled to my feet, leaning against the window.

Pollux turned to me, his face red with anger as his sleeve dripped with blood. "You just want to kill Castor!" My voice was a deep echo.

Pollux's face slackened. Castor, who was leaning for support against the couches, retreated toward the other side of the room. Pollux didn't have a knife. I wondered if he would strangle Castor to death.

"Corvus!" Castor pleaded. "Come on!"

Pollux lunged toward his brother at the same time that Argo gave another sharp turn. I was knocked down once again, stopping my fall with my hands. I faced the window, and the sight outside made my gut twist.

St. Elmo's fire crept over the window surface. I hadn't known the Twins could control that strange phenomenon. Against the window, it looked like twisting blue veins from an invisible ghost. The Greeks associated it with Castor and Pollux saving sailors in a thunderstorm, but I knew that it would not be saving me today. The twirling veins turned an angry shade of violet as they began to cover all of the windows, making the inside of the yacht drown in that eerie light. The waves turned sharp and steep outside, making the Ship go up and down as if we were on a roller coaster. I pushed myself to my feet. Behind the couches, on the opposite side of the room, Castor and Pollux fought each other. Pollux raised his fist to deliver a blow to Castor's stomach. Castor deflected the blow at the same time he kicked Pollux in the leg, making him fall on his back. The blood on Pollux's shirt had turned black with the blue light.

"Stop this, Corvus!" Castor yelled.

I was about to ask him to take us back toward the docks, but the Ship lurched again, making me fall and slide across the floor. My head hit the edge of the table between the couches. I grunted and felt a trickle of warm blood at the base of my skull. Outside, a wave towered above the Ship at least five stories high. The Twins had much more control over the ocean than I had expected. The boat began climbing a large wave that pushed us farther up. I held onto the table, which seemed to be fastened tight to the floor. I gripped the table's leg tightly as we got to the crest of the wave. The Ship's nose pointed directly downward, riding the giant wave. I screamed as I felt my heart floating up to my throat. I held onto the leg even tighter, as if I were dangling off the edge of a building. The boat slid through the wave like a knife cutting through water.

I lost my grip on the table and shot backward, crashing with the window on the other side of the boat. The impact knocked the air out of my lungs. Pollux and Castor had fallen next to me at the window. Pollux had his hands around Castor's neck, strangling him.

"Corvus!" he wheezed.

They would tell other Star Children about the existence of the Pleiades, if they hadn't already. The ship went nose first into the water, and I fell to the floor, hitting my head again.

Dizzied, I stood up.

"You want to stop this!" I yelled at both Twins, my voice deep.

Immediately, the ghostly blue-violet light disappeared, and the ocean surface dropped, turning flat from one second to the next. The Twins stood in front of me—Pollux with his hair disheveled and Castor with his neck an angry shade of red and already starting to swell.

"You tried to kill me!" Castor croaked at me.

Pollux stared daggers at me. "You son of a—"

"You want to keep quiet and stand still!" I said. Both Twins did as I said. "You want to take me back to the shore, to the same place where you picked me up."

"Argo," Castor said. "Take us back."

The Ship turned slowly, and it began sailing toward the dark horizon. The Twins had taken me very far from the shore—I couldn't see the lights from the hotel strip edging the beach.

I thought about my next lie. The Twins needed to forget about the Pleiades and that I was connected to them. They needed to forget about anything related to the Pleiades. They would also forget me.

No.

I wanted them to remember me and what I did to them. I faced the Twins, who still stared at me blankly. Pollux's shirt was wet with blood over his right shoulder. If the knife had been somewhere nearby, I would have made Pollux stab Castor.

"You want to forget everything you know about the Pleiades," I said slowly. "And anything and everything that is related to them."

"We will forget," they agreed simultaneously.

"But you will want to remember me always," I said. Tiny dots of lights finally appeared in the distance. They grew bigger and brighter every second. "You will want to remember that if you ever try to hurt me again, I will *make you kill each other."*

"We will remember that," the Twins repeated.

I stared at the Twins for another long second. Strength swelled within me. I hadn't felt strong in a very long time. The yacht finally stopped. I took in a deep breath and hurried to the glass door. I opened it and rushed outside.

My surroundings blurred around me. I finally stopped, sometime later, under a dim streetlight in front of a closed souvenir store. Across the street was the empty beach. Behind it, the ocean stretched until it met the black horizon. I leaned against the streetlight for support, my legs weak as jelly. My head throbbed, and my hands were shaking.

I fished my hand into my pocket, but only retrieved broken pieces of shells. A lot of them slipped from my sweaty hand and onto the ground. I had spent so much time gathering them. My heart knotted as they crumbled. I let the rest of the pieces fall to the ground, scattering at my feet.

I breathed deeply, my lungs aching. At least I had learned important information, much more than I had set out to get. I had also made the Twins forget about my sisters, and I could only hope that they hadn't told anyone else about the Pleiades. But how had they known about them in the first place? How had they known Perseus was after them and possibly me? My chest tightened with fear.

I looked out toward the sea. It was calm, the waves washing lazily over the beach. The Twins were a lot more powerful than we had thought, and they had Argo. But my sisters were more powerful, I reminded myself. The Pleiades were known as the Water or Ice Maidens. They, too, could control the sea but also rivers, rain, hail, snow, and ice. The Twins had power only in the ocean, but my sisters could use their abilities anywhere.

A violet light appeared above me. I jumped away from the streetlamp. It was St. Elmo's fire again. It looked as if the ghost of a snake were slithering around the top of the light post and I could only see its bright violet veins.

I walked away from the lamp as fast as I could.

• — • — •

I woke up with a start, sitting up. My chest dripped with sweat, my shirt soaked in it. I took a few deep breaths. The room around me was empty. The curtains to my left were closed, and so was the door to my right. The dim light from the bathroom was on, creating a halo around the door I had left ajar.

I pulled my hair back. The Twins knew who I was. I had met them at least once before I lost my memories. I pulled the blankets away from me and climbed off the bed. After wiping my chest with a towel, I changed into new clothes. I grabbed Crater, which sat on the nightstand next to the bed—it was now a tall and slender cup.

At least now I knew why the Twins hated me so much. I had tried to make them kill each other. I realized, with a leap of my stomach, that one of the Twins was prophesized to die, most likely killed by another Star Child. I had nearly made that Prophecy come true. Did they think me capable of doing that to them again? Just as in my memory with Cassiopeia, I hadn't hesitated to hurt them. I shuddered, trying to forget the sense of power I had felt after watching the Twins helpless before my lies. I had wanted to make Pollux stab Castor and hadn't even felt a shred of guilt about that. I pushed my thoughts away. I had to speak to Virgo and Draco. I decided to go to Draco's room first. I walked out of my room and into the hallway. Without knocking, I opened Draco's door and entered. He had left the curtains open, and the light of the moon dimly illuminated the room.

"Draco."

He didn't stir. I hated that he had such a deep sleep. I walked over to him and tried to shake him awake. Something cold and hard prickled my hand. I instinctively pulled it away.

"What is—"

It was a dart. I pulled it out of his arm.

A pinching pain radiated from my back. I yelled, and pulled out the dart from my upper back. My legs turned liquid, and I dropped to the floor. I held onto the Cup as tightly as I could. Two pairs of hands dragged me away.

●————●————●

When I woke up again, the first thing I felt was the warm Cup in my hands. Even though my hands were limp, the Cup was tightly fastened in between my palms. Someone must have taped my hands to Crater. I grunted and realized that I couldn't open my mouth. I probably had a piece of tape there too. It was dark, and it took me a couple more seconds to realize my eyes were covered.

I was sitting on a chair—I could feel my legs tied to it. My chest was tight as I breathed.

I grunted again.

"Oh, look," one of the Twins said. "He's awake."

The piece of cloth was pulled away from my eyes. The room was bright, and it took a second for my eyes to adjust. The wooden walls and floor were dark. The ceiling came to a point in the middle like a four-sided pyramid, as if we were inside an attic. Two triangular windows were at one of my sides, and outside I could see only trees. In front of me, standing side by side, the Twins smiled deviously at me.

Behind them, sitting atop a wooden desk, was Perseus.

CHAPTER 13

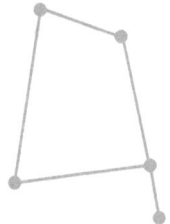

I TRULY HATED THE TWINS.

"Good morning, Corvus!" Castor said. "I'm sure you had a good sleep. No need to thank us. Those darts truly make one sleep like a dead man."

"You traitors," I tried to say through the tape but it sounded like a moan.

The Twins turned back to Perseus, who looked intently at me, like a hunter eyeing its prey. The last time I had come face to face with Perseus had been in Washington Park in New York, when I had tried to kill him and Andromeda had saved him.

Perseus was exactly as I remembered him—tall, athletic, with a sharp jaw and a straight nose. His eyes were so dark they seemed almost black, and his hair was a fiery shade of red. When I had seen Perseus at the park, selling ice cream to children and hungry college kids, he had seemed gentle, kind, and funny as he laughed with his customers. But I knew better. I could see that calculating intelligence inside his eyes, and his strong physique reminded me that among all the Star Children, he was the best fighter. He had nearly killed my friends at Palatine Hill in Rome, and with Algol in his power, Perseus was unstoppable.

"See," Castor said, motioning at the Cup. "We got Crater out of the temple in Egypt. And we also brought Corvus at no extra cost. He's a bit hysterical at times but he can be nice sometimes."

Perseus said nothing, his expression neutral.

"We would have appreciated a warning about Hydra," Pollux glared at Perseus.

"But in any case," Castor looked away from me. "The Water Snake is dead and the Cup is here. Now give us our Prophecies."

Perseus pushed himself away from the desk. His gaze finally broke away from me. He walked behind the desk and opened a drawer. He retrieved an ancient-looking piece of paper. It was thick and ragged around the edges. The words written on it were red as dried blood. Perseus pulled out another piece of paper, one that seemed to have come from a modern notebook.

He handed the Prophecy to the Twins. Castor grabbed the real Prophecy, and they both read the translation that Pollux held tightly. I looked at their faces, anticipating their reactions. I had expected to see them pale with fear or maybe get angry. I imagined their eyes drooping with sadness and maybe some tears. But as soon as they read the Prophecy, both of them opened their eyes wide in surprise. The Twins looked at each other, as if mildly confused but at the same time fully aware of what those words meant. They nodded to each other. Then they ripped both papers to pieces. Behind them, Perseus seemed as bewildered as I felt, but he said nothing. He held another Prophecy and its copy, and I remembered that he had promised the Twins two Prophecies if they gave him the Cup.

The Twins pocketed the pieces of Prophecy, then took the other one. They read that one, too, and were silent for a moment, but they didn't shred it. They folded it and put it away in their pockets. Perseus's eye twitched as he watched the Twins fold the Prophecy and bury it in their mundane jeans.

"It was good doing business with you, Perseus," Castor said with a smile.

"You too," Perseus said, but he wasn't smiling.

"Bye, Corvus," Pollux said with a wave. "We'll see you later." He said it casually, as if we were friends who would see each other the next day for lunch. Both Twins walked out of the room, leaving me alone with Perseus. He closed the door but didn't lock it, then walked over to me. He stood a couple of feet in front of me, towering above me as I sat on the chair. I held the Cup tight. Perseus didn't say anything, he simply studied me from head to toe, as if I were a museum display. I kept my hands from shaking by holding Crater tightly.

Two feet in front of me stood the guy who had caused the deaths of millions of people. He had used Algol to create the worst earthquake Italy had ever seen, crippling an entire country. He was a cold killer who would destroy everything and everyone in his path to achieve his goals. His intense black eyes, like lasers, tried to cut me open with just one stare. How much did Perseus know about me? He had been chasing after my sisters to make them his allies. I didn't remember much of my sisters, but one thing was clear to me—we would never have joined Perseus. From what I *did* remember, we were very intent on figuring out who were Perseus's allies and enemies. We had wanted to hide and cover our tracks—we had been hiding from him.

Had Perseus found my sisters? Is that why they hadn't come after me yet? That thought sent spikes of pain through my spine. Or maybe my sisters were hiding from him. Had Perseus discovered that we had been spying on him?

Too many questions raced wildly through my head. Perseus's dark gaze didn't break away from me. I knew one thing for certain, looking at those piercing black eyes—Perseus knew more about my past than I did, and he would use that to his advantage. He finally stepped forward after what seemed like an eternity. He ripped the tape away from my mouth.

"You just want to let me go." My voice sounded completely normal.

Perseus gave me a small smile. "Your lies won't work on me."

My heart dropped to my stomach. I was truly and absolutely powerless against him. Why was he immune to my lies? No one had ever been immune to them—not even Cassiopeia. Then I remembered something else, something Orion had said when we had last seen him. He had told us that when looking for Lupus, Cassiopeia, and then Andromeda and Perseus, he'd had a hard time using his power to track them. But he never knew why. He thought it might be the Wolf, acting as some sort of shield against our Star powers. But I sensed it was something else—Perseus and his allies were using something to protect themselves from our power.

My heartbeat sped up, thumping wildly against my chest. Being unreadable made Perseus even *more* dangerous than before. With my power, I would have known if he was being truthful, but now there was no way to tell his lies from the truth. I swallowed the lump in my throat.

"You want some water?" Perseus asked.

"What?"

"You seem thirsty."

He didn't even wait for my response. He walked back to the desk and grabbed a bottle of water from the floor, then made his way back to me. He unscrewed the lid and put the bottle to my lips. I drank without complaining; I *had* been thirsty.

Perseus put the bottle down. "At least you seem well rested."

I nodded, trying to squirm from the ropes that bound me. I had no idea why Perseus would care about my sleep. He looked down at the Cup, but made no move to grab it. He cocked his head to one side, then looked back up at me.

"How much do you remember?" His tone was gentle.

"I don't remember anything," I said.

"That's a lie."

"It's not."

Perseus gave an amused chuckle, as if I should have known better than lie to him.

"Do you at least remember why you were looking for the Cup?" He smiled, as if knowing that I did. I reminded myself that Perseus had read all my Prophecies. Knowing that my Prophecies, and the rest of Alathea's book, were nearby made me feel like I had an itch I couldn't scratch. They could have been in the same room as me, hidden under the wooden floor or in a secret compartment in the walls. Maybe Perseus had been bold enough to leave them in the desk drawers. I felt like a restless snake slithered inside me, and it wouldn't stop until I had my Prophecies in my hand.

"Do you remember that Crater is the only way to defeat the Forgotten Star Child?" Perseus said.

I realized then that finding Crater had never been Perseus's ultimate goal. He had known, just as I had, that Crater was the only thing that could defeat the mysterious and monstrous Forgotten Star Child.

"You *do* remember that," he said as he nodded.

I remained quiet. Perseus studied me. He bit on his upper lip, as if trying to figure out how to ask more about my memories without revealing something about my past that I hadn't remembered yet. Could it be that, just like the Twins, I had met Perseus before? I needed to consider that possibility and its implications.

Perseus eyed the Cup again. Did he know that I was the only person who could hold the Cup? His cunning black eyes met my gaze. He knew. Perseus knew that only someone without memories could hold the Cup. If he had known that he would never possess the power of the Cup, then why had he wanted *me* to have it? I simply couldn't believe that Perseus would let one of his enemies have a Star Object of that much power. The puzzle pieces were not fitting together.

"You're confused," Perseus said, crossing his arms. He shifted his weight from one foot to the other. "What do you want to know?"

How had he been able to read me that well? I began to understand why he had been able to fool Andromeda into helping him retrieve the Prophecies. Perseus wasn't just a sadistic killer who murdered people and destroyed entire cities for his own benefit. He was patient, intelligent, calculating, and empathetic. He could be genuinely kind when he wanted to be, if that would play to his advantage later on. Perseus was truly a menace.

"I *am* confused," I admitted, seeing no point in lying about it. Perseus raised an amused brow. "You know I'm the only one who can hold Crater and its power."

"Yes."

"I don't really believe that you would let another Star Child aside from yourself hold that much power." I tried piecing my thoughts together. "You need this Cup, yet you sent us to get it, and you know you'll never possess its power."

Perseus smiled, revealing his perfect teeth. That smile said everything—he was ten steps in front of everyone else because he knew all of our futures. He *was* manipulating us to get the outcome that he wanted. I wouldn't play a part in his game—the problem was that I didn't know how to leave the game.

"I don't need Crater's power," Perseus said. "The only thing I'm interested in is using it on the Forgotten Star Child."

"Because for the first time, there's a Star Child more powerful than you, so you want to kill it," I said with a smile.

Perseus didn't smile back. "The Forgotten Star Child was captured by Cepheus before it killed him," he said. Cassiopeia had told me exactly that. He stared at me, and for the first time, anger flashed behind his dark eyes. "Cassiopeia was the only one who knew where Cepheus had hidden the Forgotten Star Child, but when I captured and interrogated her, she claimed she didn't know anything about the Forgotten Star Child. She said that *I* had been the one who killed Cepheus, although I think I would have remembered that."

I could tell that last part was intended as an accusation. Perseus knew I had lied to Cassiopeia. I remembered Andromeda telling me Perseus had killed Cassiopeia. He'd probably interrogated her before that, only to find out she didn't have the information he needed. We had thought that Perseus had captured Cassiopeia because she knew something about the Prophecies that the rest of us didn't. We had been so wrong. Since the beginning, Perseus had hidden a secret agenda from us. He knew about the Lost Star Child. He knew that Cepheus had captured it before he died and that Cassiopeia was the only person who knew where Cepheus had hidden it. But by the time he captured Cassiopeia, I had already erased her memories. That's why he was interested in my memories. Not only because I knew about Crater but because I was the only person alive who might know where the Lost Star Child was imprisoned.

That meant the Prophecies didn't say where it was, or Perseus would have already retrieved the Lost Star Child while the rest of us found Crater. The problem was that I didn't know how to find the Lost Star Child either. Cassiopeia hadn't told me—she had sworn a blood promise.

"I don't know where the Lost Star Child is," I said. "I really don't."

Perseus looked at me, the anger fading from his eyes. He sighed, and for the first time I noticed the fatigue in his dark eyes.

"Do you remember who you used to live with before you erased your memories?" Perseus looked intently at my face. "Or if you'd met any other Star Children?"

I said nothing.

I wondered again how much Perseus knew about my sisters. How much did my *Prophecies* reveal about my sisters? Did the Pleiades have their own Prophecies? If he was asking me about it, he probably knew something about them. I felt that like a punch in the gut. I had tried so hard to hide them, but that hadn't been enough. Now that Perseus had the Prophecies, there was no more hiding. I wished I had remembered something that would help me know where to find my sisters.

Perseus sighed again and rubbed his forehead. He muttered something under his breath, then he looked back at me, his eyes weary and tired.

"You want some food? I'm guessing you haven't eaten in a while."

"Sure," I said, shifting uncomfortably.

Perseus nodded absently. "I'll bring us some hot dogs."

He left the room, closing the door behind him. For a few seconds, I sat still, my heart beating like a giant drum. I had not expected Perseus to behave like that. He had used his power to kill millions. He had murdered Cassiopeia in front of Andromeda and had nearly killed my friends. He planned to destroy Fate, Destiny, and Prophecy and to unleash Chaos upon the Universe. For a guy of his reputation, I had expected him to torture me, not offer me hot dogs.

Crater! I shouted inside my head.

"Yes?" the Cup answered.

I need your help.

"With what?"

I looked around the room. I didn't think walking out the door was a good idea. Maybe I could escape through the windows. But first, I needed to untie myself.

"I can help with that."

I still wondered if the Cup could read my thoughts all the time. I also didn't know how a Cup would help me free myself of tape, but that question got answered soon enough. Crater began to shift. It remained a cup, but the edges became deadly sharp. I used the Cup to cut the tape, and in less than a minute, my hands were free. I didn't imagine that Perseus would take long to make those hot dogs, so I quickly cut the tape that bound my chest and my legs.

Once I had untied myself, I walked over to the window on the right. I could see branches all around me; it seemed like I was in a house inside a forest. I was at least three stories up from the ground. I opened the hatch of the triangular window and swung it to the side. A cold blast of air drifted inside the room and made me shiver. I could climb down the large tree directly in front of me and then run like hell. I was beginning to swing one of my legs out the window when I stopped myself.

Perseus surely had Alathea's Prophecies somewhere in the house. This would probably be my only chance to find them. But this could also be my only chance to escape Perseus. I was sure that once he found out I had used the Cup to cut through the tape, he would find another way to imprison me. He wanted to know more about my memories, and I had the feeling he might take more extreme measures to force information out of me.

The tree branches rustled lazily in the cold breeze. I took a deep breath, then pushed myself away from the window, raced across the room to the desk, and opened all the drawers. They were empty.

The Prophecies must have been somewhere else in the house.

I quietly walked to the door.

Crater!

"Yes?"

Could you turn into something more menacing? Preferably something I can hit people in the head with?

"I do not appreciate being used as a weapon. That is not my purpose."

You won't appreciate me getting killed either.

Crater was quiet, and I thought it would ignore me. But just then, it began shifting in my hand again as if it were wet clay instead of gold. The Cup grew taller, but it didn't become heavier in my hand. Crater became a very large thermos, probably thirty inches tall, but thin enough to fit in my hand. I imagined that if I hit someone hard enough on the head, it would cause a serious concussion.

I quietly opened the door and walked out of the room, then closed the door behind me. The narrow hallway was empty. To my left was a window, and to my right were stairs that curled down to the floor below. I silently descended the stairs, the thermos clutched tightly in my hand. The second floor was similar to the first, except it had one door on each side. Below me, I could smell burning sausages. I decided to investigate the room on the right. I walked over to the door and opened it, walked quickly inside, then closed it behind me. I startled when I turned around.

The Twins stood in front of me, smiling.

Chapter XXII, Verse II

After such terrible sorrow has befallen the King and Queen,
The Cup shall be moved away from the Castle,
The Silver Wheel to spin once more hiding its mighty towers.
Empty of Souls the Cup shall remain, until a new child it binds to awake.
Through lies and deceit the Cup once more will be discovered.
To ruin and heartbreak it will lead those it has followed,
Or to restore great power buried in secrecy and solitude.

CHAPTER 14

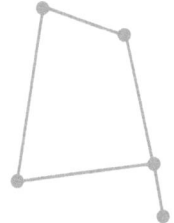

"HELLO AGAIN," Pollux said in a whisper as he crossed his arms.

"Long time no see." Castor smiled widely.

"You treasonous rats!" I whispered.

"The Prophecies are not here," Pollux said. "We've looked everywhere in this house."

I stared hard at them. They weren't lying. Anger rose inside me, and I held the thermos tighter.

"You turned me over to Perseus," I said in between clenched teeth.

The Twins seemed calm, as if I had accused them of eating my muffin.

"Yeah," Castor said with a chuckle. "Since you're the only one who can hold the Cup, we knew we had to bring you here or Perseus would never give us our Prophecies." His forehead furrowed. "We knew Draco and Virgo would never let us take you here, because they would have said it was too dangerous for you." I knew that was true. Virgo and Draco would have tried coming up with a new plan. "We didn't want to bring the others because Perseus might have known something was off, but we knew they wouldn't stay behind."

"So we improvised and used the dart gun again," Castor said with a wide smile. He nervously looked at the door behind me.

"We pretended we left the house. Then while you bonded with Perseus, we searched the entire building."

"And found absolutely nothing." Pollux looked around the barren room.

"You would have left me here if I hadn't escaped," I said, holding Crater so tightly it hurt.

"Probably," Castor admitted.

I sighed. "So, there's nothing here."

"That's what's strange," Pollux said. "This house is absolutely empty. Something is wrong here."

I nodded. "Let's get out of here before—"

The door behind us burst open. I held the thermos up high, and the Twins pulled white knives from behind their backs. We stood side by side. Perseus leaned against the doorframe eating a hot dog. He had another three hot dogs on a plastic plate. Perseus looked at us calmly, munching on his food. He looked at the Twins' weapons, the thermos, and then down at the hot dogs.

"Guess you guys won't be staying for lunch," he said. "All right then. I'll just eat all of these hot dogs myself."

I glanced at Pollux to my right. He narrowed his eyes at Perseus, who walked out of the room. Together, the rest of us slowly made our way out. Perseus began climbing to the floor above.

"So, you don't care if we leave with Corvus," Pollux said, holding his knife tight.

Perseus stopped on the fourth step and turned back to face us. He shrugged. "Well, I can't force you to stay." His black eyes landed on me. "And I got what I wanted."

"Didn't you want Crater?" Castor motioned to the thermos in my hand.

Perseus swallowed a bite of hot dog and smiled. "I told you to bring me the Cup you found in the Egyptian temple." He pointed at Crater. "And you did. I never said I wanted to keep it."

He smiled at us. Fear scratched my bones.

"Well, don't mind if we let ourselves out then," Castor said.

Pollux grabbed my arm and pulled me toward the stairs. I quickly descended them, feeling as if our luck would run out in a few seconds and Perseus would begin to chase us.

On the main floor, we raced down the hall and opened the front door. My feet crunched over branches and dead leaves.

"Argo is waiting for us on the coast," Pollux said, pointing to our right.

I looked back at the house. Perseus leaned out the third-floor window, eating another hot dog. He stared at us calmly.

I hadn't seen Lupus or Pegasus. Could the Wolf and Horse be hidden somewhere inside the woods, waiting to attack us? Perseus's gaze locked with mine as he took another bite from his hot dog.

"Come on," Pollux said as he pulled my arm.

I followed after the Twins as we raced past the trees. I realized we hadn't been in a forest, as I had initially thought. The house had simply been completely surrounded by trees, maybe to offer more privacy. Less than a minute after we had left the house, we stepped onto an empty highway edged by a short metal guard rail. A few yards beyond that, a short cliff dropped into the ocean below. We raced across the highway. I jumped the guard rail and stopped. The ocean was at least thirty feet below us.

"Are we going to—" Before I could finish my sentence, both Twins jumped.

I sighed. I looked at the deep blue ocean stretching beyond me. Dread climbed up my back. Cetus was somewhere out there. Even though I didn't remember him fully, the horror from that experience took over me. That Monster was hiding somewhere in the ocean. I looked back. Perseus was nowhere to be seen, but I still felt like he was chasing me. I took a deep breath and jumped. My stomach flew into my chest as I dropped. I screamed, then hit the surface. The water was cold, as I imagined it would be, and it stung my skin. I swam upward and took a deep breath. I was getting really tired of the ocean, and swimming in general. The Twins were a few yards to my left, and I swam after them. Before I could ask where Argo was, the submarine rose from the water a few yards in front of us, splashing small waves against me. The black metal glistened in the light from the sun.

The hatch opened, and Pollux pulled himself onto the top. He pulled his brother up, then helped me climb to the top of the submarine. I descended the ladder. Thankfully, the inside of the submarine was warm.

"Corvus!" Virgo yelled before throwing herself at me, not minding I was soaking wet. I hugged her back.

"You idiots!" Draco yelled at the Twins. "What the hell were you thinking?"

The Twins smiled deviously.

Virgo pulled back and looked me up and down. "What happened? Are you all right? How did you escape Perseus? Did you find the Prophecies?"

The Twins and I exchanged glances. I looked at Crater, who was still a thermos.

"We should sit down first and maybe eat some lunch," Pollux said. "To be honest, I did want one of Perseus's hot dogs."

"He offered you hot dogs?" Draco asked aghast, as if that was truly unbelievable.

"Let's just go to the living room," Castor said.

A bark echoed from the end of the hallway. Sirius barreled toward me and crashed me against the wall behind me. He howled again and licked my hand.

"I'm all right, boy," I said, thinking that the sea water on my hand must have tasted awful.

"Fine. Let's go sit down," Draco said. His red eyes narrowed at the Twins. "But if you ever pull something like that again, I will roast you like sausages."

"Hopefully you'll turn us into delicious hot dogs," Castor said with a smile, as if becoming a hot dog would be an honorable death.

The Twins seemed at ease with us, so I imagined no one here was prophesized to kill them. I wondered who it would be and for what reason. But that was a question that I probably wouldn't get the answer to. We all walked through the hallways, past the room with aquatic animal bones, toward the living room with the window that faced the ocean. Once there, we all sat down on the couches. Virgo, Draco, and I sat on one couch. The Twins shared the other. I was still soaking wet, but at that point I didn't care anymore.

"So what the hell happened?" Draco asked. The slits in his eyes were still narrowed into dangerously thin lines, even if his voice was calm.

I looked down at Crater. I needed to tell everyone about the Lost Star Child. I was sure Draco had mentioned something to Virgo, but the Twins still didn't know.

I took a deep breath and told everyone what I had remembered about London and what Cassiopeia had told me. Then I recounted my conversation with Perseus. I left the Pleiades out of the conversation. I wasn't going to tell Castor and Pollux anything about them. But I trusted the Twins enough to tell them the truth about the Lost Star Child. They had sold me out to Perseus just to get their Prophecy, but they had it now. And even though Perseus still had their other Prophecies, they had probably realized that he would never hand those over. Their best bet at getting those Prophecies was to help us. The Twins may not have been the most loyal allies, but we needed their help as much as they needed ours.

Once I was done explaining what I knew, everyone was quiet.

"That's why Perseus let us go." I held the thermos tighter. "He never wanted to own Crater. He simply wants to destroy the Lost Star Child with the Cup."

"But then why would he let you keep the Cup?" Pollux asked.

I shrugged.

"He knows we'll go after the Lost Star Child," Virgo said. She met my gaze. "He knows we won't turn our backs on this one."

Draco huffed. "Finding the most dangerous and powerful Star Child . . . of course we wouldn't turn our backs on that."

"Do you guys think Perseus expects us to find this Star Child and kill it using Crater?" Pollux asked. "Does he really expect us to do his dirty work for him?"

Draco scratched his chin where his beard had started to grow. "We could ally with this Star Child. If it's *that* powerful, then it could certainly help defeat Perseus's allies and weaken him."

"But why would Perseus risk letting us find this Star Child so we can then use it against him?" Virgo asked.

"There has to be something we're not seeing," I said. I looked at my friends around the room, then at the dark water outside, pushing my fear away. "Perseus is playing us, and I'm not sure what his game is."

"And we still don't have the Prophecies," Virgo said. "Until we do, we'll continue to be pawns in Perseus's game."

"Maybe the only way to beat Perseus in his game is to play it," Pollux said.

"That's what we just did to find Crater," Virgo said. "And that backfired. We're nowhere closer to getting those Prophecies, and we're about to go on another dangerous mission that may kill us."

We all sat in silence for a moment.

"There's not much else we can do at this point. Is there?" Draco said. "If the Lost Star Child is *that* powerful, then we need to find it before Perseus does and choose what we want to do with it."

Virgo pulled down her sleeves to cover her scarred hands but didn't reply.

"Cassiopeia said that the Lost Star Child wouldn't remain trapped for long," I said. "And I'm sure this memory happened around a year and a half ago." I sighed, clutching Crater tighter. "Regardless of what Perseus is planning, this Star Child will escape its prison and roam free soon. If we don't find it now, then I'm sure it will find us at some point. We can unleash it upon Perseus or kill it with Crater before it can break free, but that choice should be ours." I paused. "Perseus's next rising will be in a few weeks. I would rather take care of this now than later. I wouldn't want to have to deal with both the Lost Star Child *and* with Perseus becoming more powerful."

I looked at the others. Virgo bit her lip, but Draco was nodding.

"Corvus is right. This Monster will escape one way or another. It better be on our terms." Draco looked at the Twins, who nodded, and then at Virgo.

Knowing I had planned this for a very long time made me feel more confident. It had been *my* plan long before Perseus even knew about the Lost Star Child, and I would follow it through.

"This sounds like the most terrible plan we've ever had, friends." Castor said, crossing his arms. He exchanged a glance with Pollux. "But we're in."

"What's in it for you?" I asked.

Pollux smiled. "We've read three of our Prophecies." He paused, dropping his smile. "Helping you is probably the best way to avoid them."

There were no lies in his words, but I knew it wasn't as simple as that. As always, the Twins were playing their own game, but we needed them.

"We don't even know where to start looking," Draco said, scratching his beard again.

"I think I do." I remembered something else from my conversation with Cassiopeia. I turned to the Twins. "Tell Argo to head for London."

CHAPTER 15

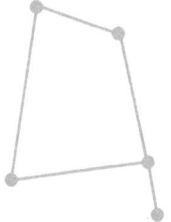

I SAT ALONE in the living room, feeling too alert to try to sleep even though everyone else had already left. We'd had a brief conversation after I had suggested going to London. Cassiopeia had been spending a lot of time in the British Museum before I had erased her mind, so it seemed like the best place to look for the Lost Star Child.

Footsteps echoed behind me, and I turned to find Pollux descending the stairs with two glasses. He walked around the couch and sat next to me.

"Not in the mood for sleeping?" he asked.

I shook my head as he handed me a glass of water. I took a sip and looked at the dark ocean outside. We both sat in silence for some time.

"I'm sorry," I finally said after a couple of minutes.

He raised a brow in surprise. "Why?"

"I . . . I remembered when we first met," I said.

"That wasn't the worst negotiation we've had," Pollux said, then laughed.

I assumed that meant I was forgiven.

"You're the ones who told me that I would find Cassiopeia in London," I said. "In the museum."

Pollux nodded. "I remember that."

"Do you remember why she was interested in the museum?" I asked.

"This was a while ago," Pollux said. "We honestly didn't know that much about her. We never did. She was very hard to track down."

"How did you find Cassiopeia in the first place and convince her to tell you stuff?" I asked.

Pollux looked at his shoes. "The details are not important." He paused. "Did she ever mention the museum to you?"

I shook my head. That's where I had found her—I was sure of that even if I didn't remember—but she had never mentioned the museum.

"Wait," Pollux scratched his head. "I was kind of drunk but I think I remember something." I didn't even want to ask why he was drunk with Cassiopeia. "Before she found out we were Star Children, she told us that she was an art history teacher or something like that." He squeezed his eyes shut and rubbed them. "She said she specialized in Mesopotamia, so she was going to London to do research on that."

"Do you think that may be a clue?" I asked. She could have lied to the Twins.

He opened his eyes again. "It may give us a lead." He shrugged. "The museum is big. It won't hurt to look in the Mesopotamian section first."

"I guess it won't."

Silence stretched between us. Pollux looked out toward the deep black ocean.

"You could have told me that we had met before I lost my memories," I said. A smile tugged at Pollux's lips. "You knew I didn't remember you when we met a few months ago."

Pollux finally met my gaze. "I was hoping you would be less of a jerk this time around."

I huffed. "Sorry to disappoint."

Pollux laughed, then looked out at the ocean again. "I do like you better this time."

"Why, because I didn't try to kill you?"

Pollux shrugged. "You seem more genuine, less wrapped up in your own lies." That was a funny thing to say, considering I had lied to myself to forget everything. "Last time . . . I don't know. There was something off about you." He stared at me, his gaze boring into mine until I looked away. "Your eyes were cold," he said slowly. "There was something bitter about them, like earth hardened into stone."

The glass of water suddenly became too cold to my touch, and I set it down on the table. "How much did you know about me the first time we met?" I asked.

"We knew you were Corvus. Star Children rarely work alone so we knew you must have been with someone else. Although we never figured out who that was." He turned to look at me and I shrugged, pretending I didn't remember. Pollux didn't push me on it. "What else do you remember from that day?"

I looked out the ocean. "I remember you saying I was not handsome or strong so I couldn't possibly be Orion or Hercules."

Pollux laughed. "It was Castor who said that." His lips widened into a mischievous grin. "I thought you were *a bit* handsome." My cheeks boiled with heat. "Although Orion is probably more handsome."

"He is," I said.

Pollux chuckled, then yawned. "I think I might try to get some sleep too. We didn't rest at all last night."

"You were too busy kidnapping me," I muttered.

"Do you have any idea how hard it was to drag you out of Argo and all the way to Perseus?" Pollux asked. "You weigh a lot, Corvus. You should cut down on the tacos."

"I'm glad you had a rough time kidnapping me," I said with a smile.

Pollux laughed. He stood up and walked away. I stayed in the living room a while longer, looking at the dark ocean out the window. I buried my face in my hands, rubbing my eyes. Even Pollux had noticed how cruel I had been before I lost my memories. What could possibly have pushed me toward that violence?

I pulled up my green sweater and looked at the two light pink scars slicing down my torso. I ran my finger over them.

I had fought Cetus. It had killed Darren and nearly killed me. It was strange to think about Darren. I didn't remember his face, nor did I have any particular memories of him, but in that moment, I felt a void in my heart that I hadn't noticed before. I knew he had been human—I just knew. I wasn't sure how to feel about missing someone I didn't remember.

I looked out at the ocean. Cetus was still out there—he had sunk the cruise ship, but he hadn't attacked. The Twins said the Monster was taunting us, but I didn't know why. I didn't even know why the Monster was after us in the first place.

Part of me was glad I hadn't recovered the memory of the attack. Even though I didn't remember Cetus's attack, I was sure it was my most traumatic memory—all the time I had spent in the water recently must have triggered me to remember events from my past. But I still wasn't sure why I had recovered those particular memories. They seemed too coincidental, dropping hints of my past exactly when I needed to know them.

I stood up with a sigh and walked out of the room. I made my way to the bedrooms, which were thankfully far away from the marine skeletons.

I walked to the farthest door on the left, which was our room. I opened the door. The room was empty, as I had expected. It had two individual beds against the wall on the left and a nightstand in between them. To the right was a closed door that led to the bathroom. Next to the door was a small wooden closet that had clothes that always fit us perfectly. I wondered how Argo pulled that off. Out of all the Star Objects, it seemed to be the most complex one, adapting to our individual needs. I took my wet clothes off and took a quick shower, then put my knitted sweater back on and a new pair of pants. I climbed into the bed closest to the door and pulled the covers up.

I didn't feel very tired, but at the same time my body sagged with fatigue. My mind was a jumble of thoughts—the Lost Star Child, Darren, the Pleiades, my Prophecies, Perseus. I remained awake for what seemed like an eternity, staring at the Darkness, the formless, shadowy mist that swirled around me. A pale face with gleaming blue eyes materialized in the dark. I startled awake and turned on the lamp on the nightstand.

I looked around the room as my heart beat heavily. I knew Arianna—the manifestation of Darkness—couldn't appear here. Her power only worked in outdoor places at night. I hadn't thought of her in a quite a while. We hadn't seen her since Palatine Hill, and I wondered what she might have been doing since. I stood up from my bed, knowing I wouldn't be able to sleep there anymore. I walked out of the room, holding Crater.

"*Child of Lies.*"

I nearly stumbled forward. I looked wildly around the empty hallway.

"Who said that?" I asked out loud.

Crater hummed in my hand, but I knew it hadn't been the Cup that had spoken.

"*You will pay the price of your lies.*" The whisper sounded like swishing leaves.

I barged into Virgo's room and closed the door behind me, my heartbeat thundering in my ears.

Virgo sat up on the bed, and Draco looked at me from the large couch right in front of it.

"Can't sleep?" Virgo asked.

"Is there a connection between Argo and Dodona?" The words stumbled out of my mouth.

Virgo looked down at her hands, thinking. In the dark, the cuts in the back of her hands shone brightly, the pulsing light bathing her face in a pale glow. Sirius and Maera slept next to her on the bed. Leo slept against the far wall. The three claw marks on his side had begun to shine. I hadn't seen them pulsing with light before—our scars only glowed once the wounds were fully healed. Leo's pulsed very slowly, in tune with his heart. Aquila stood on a stool next to Leo, his yellow eyes alert as always. His left wing didn't shine, so I guessed his wounds weren't completely healed.

Draco sat up on the couch, still staring at me.

"Yeah," Virgo finally said after a few moments. "In mythology, Argo was built out of oak from the Oracle of Dodona. I hadn't made that connection before." She pulled her blankets up. "The Ship was supposed to have prophetic powers, although the Twins have never mentioned that."

That explained a lot. Was it possible that Argo, and not the ocean, had caused my memories to resurface? After all, I had erased my memories at Dodona and had woken up there afterward. Maybe that forest, and the Ship, had some amount of power over my memories.

I walked over to the L-shaped couch, and Draco threw me a blanket. I left Crater on the floor next to me and lay on the couch facing the ceiling. Was Argo giving me specific memories that it knew would guide me? It was a possibility, and it would explain why the memories I recovered were perfectly timed with everything else that was happening.

"Are you okay, Corvus?" Virgo asked from the bed.

"I'm just—no."

A long silence stretched in the room, until Sirius began snoring loudly. He sounded like a broken lawn mower.

"Is it your family?" Virgo asked after some time. "Your sisters?"

"Perseus knew about them," I said, my chest filling with dread. "He knows about the Pleiades, and I don't know if he already found them and possibly hurt them."

The possibility that Perseus had hurt my sisters made my chest contract as if heavy stones were being placed on it. I had abandoned them. If anything had happened to them, it was my fault. I needed to know where they were. I may have been cruel to Cassiopeia and the Twins, but I had never hurt any of my sisters. If anything, my behavior with them was similar to how I was now. With the one exception when I had lied to Merope, I had been kind to them, always worried about keeping them safe. I had loved them—I still loved them even if I didn't remember much—and my heart ached at the thought they might be in trouble.

"It's all right," Virgo said. "I'm sure they're still looking for you."

"We'll find them," Draco shifted next to me. "I'm sure about that. After finding the Lost Star Child, we should focus on tracking them down, now that we know they exist."

I nodded, my throat knotting. We would find them. I knew that together we could track them down. I was sure I had told them, after my first meeting with the Twins, that Perseus was after them. They were probably just hiding from Perseus, not daring to risk getting caught by him.

Virgo cleared her throat, as if she were trying to swallow something. "In any case, whether you find them or not . . ." She paused. "We'll always be your family too."

My eyes stung with tears.

I smiled. "You guys gave me everything when I had nothing." I tried to keep my voice steady. "I don't think I ever thanked you for that . . . so thank you."

Virgo laughed softly. "It was the least I could do." Draco didn't say anything, but I knew he was smiling too. "I love you guys." Virgo spoke so softly I barely heard her. Warmth spread inside my chest. Draco and Virgo were the best thing that could have happened to me after I erased my memories. I was lucky they had found me.

I thought again of how I had behaved in my memories. What would Virgo and Draco think about me if they knew what I had done? That I had tortured Cassiopeia and almost made the Twins kill each other? I breathed out, emptying my lungs. I didn't feel ready to discuss that with them, not with everything else that we needed to worry about. It still bothered me though—that had been *me*. Not an evil version of myself or a behavior I couldn't control. I had *chosen* to act like that, and I needed to accept it. But that didn't mean I needed to be that person *now*, right? Or would I unconsciously become as I had been before? Was the cold-blooded nature of my Constellation a part of me that I would never be able to change? My head began to throb.

"Virgo?" I whispered.

"Yeah?"

"Could you sing?"

A moment of silence passed, then her song began. Her voice was soft as always. I closed my eyes.

When the night arrives, their souls awake again,
A new moon dark above them, and below the earth barren.

My breaths became deeper, and I could feel my mind clearing. I focused solely on Virgo's song. Her sweet voice was the only thing that could help me fall asleep.

The flames they all follow, for fire is what Stars are made of,
Of home the memories they try to remember, but in the end forget.
Without purpose they roam, but with a hope they walk.

I wondered where she had learned that song. My mind prickled, as if I had heard it in my past. Maybe I would remember, or maybe I never would. It didn't really matter. It was just a song.

Soon they will be born again into a flesh of flames.
Flames that burn white like their souls.
Flames that burn out the brighter they shine.

Virgo's voice faltered a little, and it took me a second to realize that she may have been crying. Why would she cry? Maybe this song reminded her of something sad. For a moment I felt bad that I had asked her to sing, but as I began drifting to sleep, Virgo's voice regained her strength. As I focused more on the lyrics, I realized that they didn't follow a logical order. It was as if Virgo only remembered parts of that song and skipped over all the rest.

Darkness now comes, so their souls must hush.
In silence they will stand, to avoid her gaze.
Only to see how brightly they shine.
For Darkness is the only force that gives light its power to shine.

She started over from the beginning. My muscles relaxed, my head felt heavier, and my mind cleared completely.

Soon they will be born again into a flesh of flames.

Chapter LI, Verse I

The most dangerous child Lost and Forgotten will become.
Once roaming the earth, and feared even by the Gods.
The King shall imprison him inside the black bone,
The one that once belonged to the Generation of Old.
The flames shall free him only if bright they burn around him.
Then the Cup shall restore him into the Monster he once was,
To aid the Prince of Darkness against the forces that once defeated him.

CHAPTER 16

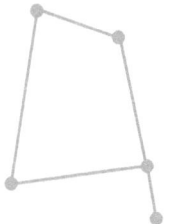

THE BRITISH MUSEUM had a grand entrance. The Greek façade of the five-story building featured large ionic columns that supported the triangular roof. The U-shape led us to the main entrance at the center. Draco, Virgo, Pollux, Castor, and I walked toward it.

Steel-grey clouds hung above us, covering the sky completely. The wind howled softly around us, and once again I was glad for the warmth of my sweater. Thankfully, the closets in Argo had a large collection of elegant coats and jackets, so all of us were well dressed. We had hidden some weapons in our clothes, and Pollux had assured us that, for some reason, Star Weapons never appeared on metal detectors. I also had Crater with me, who had turned into a small thermos that could fit inside my coat pocket.

Several tourists milled around the entrance. Some took pictures of the columns and posed for selfies. To our left stood a big group of children all dressed in bright red vests. Two adults, whom I assumed to be their teachers, tried to make them form three rows.

We fit in perfectly with the crowd, which was usually difficult for us. But today we were just a group of teenagers visiting a museum. We'd had to leave our animal friends behind. Sneaking them into the museum would have been unnecessary trouble. I didn't feel as much distrust for the Twins as I had before, but just out of habit I was on guard and alert.

As we neared the entrance, we passed some lunch tables. Most people had their eyes glued to their phones or tablets.

We climbed up the large stairs that led to the entrance and walked through the glass doors. We quickly passed through the metal detector, which didn't even detect Crater. Once inside, we stopped for a second to admire the vast museum. The entire ceiling was made of glass triangles that let the grey light from outside filter through. In front of us rose a circular chamber, but I couldn't make out what was inside of it. Maybe a special exhibit? The structure, and the rest of the room, was made of white marble.

The museum was full of people. Some groups followed tour guides, but there were also couples and smaller clusters of people who walked around with maps. We made our way to the information booth. Behind the semicircular desk stood a man with black curls talking excitedly to an older couple. We waited behind them.

"Are we sure we should be looking in the Mesopotamian section?" Virgo asked as she looked at the ceiling.

"I think we should start there," Pollux said. "If Cassiopeia mentioned Mesopotamia, not knowing we were Star Children, it must be a clue."

"Okay," Draco said. "So, we find the Mesopotamian rooms first and look at all the objects there."

"What are we even looking for?" Pollux asked. "The Lost Star Child could be anywhere."

An idea popped into my head, and I wondered why I hadn't thought of it before. "Draco," I said as I turned to him. He stared back at me through his sunglasses. "You normally spot Star Children because they emit a different light than humans do, right?

Maybe the object the Lost Star Child is imprisoned in also emits a different spectrum of light."

Draco cocked his head to the side. "I could try that."

"Humans emit light?" Castor asked. "And we emit a different sort of light?"

"Yeah," Draco said. "Every single object, living or non-living, emits light, but most of it is out of the human spectrum. I've noticed that living beings tend to emit the same light that their native planet emits." Draco looked at the older couple, who seemed to have a thousand questions. "Earth emits infrared light, so any being born on this planet will emit the same light. Humans emit a little bit of infrared light that I can detect."

"And what kind of light do we emit?" Castor asked.

Draco shrugged. "I'm not sure how to explain that. I don't think any of us originated on this planet though, because our light is different than anything else I have seen."

"Fair enough," Castor said. "So you could detect if any of the objects here emit a strange light."

"Maybe?" Draco said.

"I still wonder what kind of object is powerful enough to hold a Star Child that is supposed to be the most ancient, powerful, and dangerous one," Pollux said.

"Could it be another Star Object?" I wondered.

"There is no Constellation that represents a coffin or any object where anyone could be trapped," Virgo said. "At least not in Greek mythology."

"But Cassiopeia was interested in Mesopotamian mythology," I said. "So maybe it's an object that doesn't exist for the Greeks?"

"I don't know," Virgo said. "There's no object I know of in the Constellations that can imprison someone."

The elderly couple finally walked away, and we all made our way toward the man. We each grabbed a map of the museum and I asked for directions to the Mesopotamian rooms.

"We have Mesopotamian exhibits on two floors," the man said as he pointed at a map. We needed to narrow down our search more.

"That's great," I said. "But which room would you say has the most ancient artifacts?"

The man turned the map around, which showed the third floor. "We have two rooms that contain our most ancient artifacts. That would be room fifty-four, which dates back as far as seven thousand years ago, and room fifty-six, which dates to six thousand years ago."

"What's the difference between those rooms, aside from the age?" Draco asked.

"The objects from the two rooms were found in different regions," the man explained. "The ones in room fifty-four come from Anatolia and Urartu specifically, and the objects in room fifty-six are from all around Mesopotamia. I would suggest you start with room fifty-six, since the objects are more varied."

"All right," Draco said. "How do we get to the third floor?"

The man pointed at the very far end of the room, past the circular structure. "At the end of this hallway you'll find the elevators."

We walked away from the desk and made our way toward the elevators. On our right, next to the circular structure, was a small store with history books and souvenirs. They had fridge magnets, keychains, bags, pencils and pens, and even some nice mugs that showed ancient Egyptian and Greek art.

"Ohh, look at that one." Castor pointed at a mug that showed an Egyptian mural. "We should get it for Argo."

"Argo likes mugs?" I asked.

Pollux nodded. "It has a collection of mugs. It just likes to collect things in general, but we always bring it mugs when we visit new places."

Castor nodded excitedly.

"Huh," Draco said.

After we had passed the circular structure and the shop, we walked by chairs and tables next to a small cafeteria. The old couple we had seen were waiting for the elevator too. Once it arrived, the couple climbed in first and then us. We ascended to the third floor and came out into a semicircular room. In front of us was the entrance to the first room, which was luckily room fifty-six. We slowly walked in as tension knotted my muscles. The large room—at least fifty yards long—had light green walls and a curved ceiling, also made of glass.

Against each wall locked cabinets with glass fronts displayed ancient objects. Directly in front of me were some tablets with cuneiform inscriptions. Next to them stood the stone statue of a woman. She had no head, which reminded me of the Egyptian statues we had seen at the temple—although the head didn't seem to be broken off, the figure was just made without one, which I found curious. Other glass displays around us had more headless clay figurines.

There were only a few people in the room. We still hadn't come up with a plan to steal whatever object we found. I figured we would plan that later.

"Where do we start?" Castor asked as his eyes scanned the room.

Draco had taken off his sunglasses and held them in his hand as he narrowed his eyes at the display cases in front of us. I hoped no one looked at his eyes.

"Nothing here," Draco said as he motioned at the displays directly in front of us.

We walked to the left. One of the walls featured a Mesopotamian mural. It depicted a large lion that reminded me of Leo against a blue lapis-lazuli background. Draco stared at the mural but then looked away.

At the opposite side was another mural, but this one was made from grey rock and depicted a chaotic scene of little men scrambling as they climbed ladders up a hill while a much bigger figure stood at the top of the hill. I assumed the bigger figure represented a god. Draco eyed the mural but then walked away.

We followed him as he stared at more objects, but none of them caught his attention. We looked at pieces of jewelry, mostly made of gold. There were some clay figurines of serpents and men with eagle and fish heads. We also found a lot of bowls and clay vases. I imagined that the Lost Star Child could be trapped in a magical vase or something similar, but Draco didn't detect anything strange there.

The Twins wandered around next to us, walking the length of the room as they eyed some of the displays. Virgo trailed a bit behind us, reading the plaques next to each display. She constantly leaned against walls or sat down in chairs to catch her breath. She was definitely not all right after what she had done to kill Hydra, and I knew I needed to talk to her about it soon.

I continued to follow Draco as he eyed all the objects in the room. A cold wave of anger rolled through me as I thought of the Lost Star Child. I had erased my memories and forgotten everything about my past just so I could find the Cup and then destroy that Monster. I had been willing to lose everything to prove to my other siblings that I was as strong as they were. Would I be willing to do the same now? I sadly realized that I had fallen into the same problem I'd had before. While Draco and Virgo rarely left me behind, I still resented that Draco hadn't let me go to the battle at Palatine Hill to fight Perseus and his allies. I just wanted to be considered as capable as the rest of my friends, but Virgo had stayed behind with me and so had Sirius. I realized now that Draco had just tried to protect us, knowing that we could have gotten killed. I looked at Draco's neck, which was hidden underneath his coat. The faded bruises still stained his skin. I could have died, but I also could have helped in the fight. I would never know.

I sighed. I didn't think myself as impulsive and reckless as I had been before, willing to erase all of my memories just to prove my worth to others—to gain more power so I wouldn't be afraid of letting them down again. But I still wondered what others saw in me that they felt the constant need to protect me. Or was it maybe something *I* needed to change? If I didn't consider myself strong enough, others probably wouldn't either. I would have to work on that first.

My lies were powerful, I knew that, but I'd always wanted to be good at fighting. Maybe my trauma came from the fight with Cetus. As far as I remembered, that had been the start of all this mess. I hadn't been able to fight and protect my family, Darren had died, and *I* had almost died. I had failed Darren, and I had thought that by becoming stronger I wouldn't fail the rest of my family. But maybe I had been wrong. I was sure I had done everything to save Darren, and though I had failed, I couldn't hang his death on me. And becoming stronger wasn't the solution to feeling left out. I puffed out my cheeks, feeling deflated.

"I'm not seeing anything out of the ordinary," Draco whispered as we stood in front of some clay statues. They looked humanoid, but they were disproportioned—the arms and legs too long, the bodies too thin, the heads big.

"I'm sure something has to be here," I said. "We just have to keep looking."

Draco muttered something that I didn't understand.

"What?" I asked.

Draco shook his head. "It's just something from the Prophecy I remembered." He leaned closer to me, as if he didn't want anyone else to listen to us. "The last line said: *In the end only betrayal awaits, and the loss of everything once gained.*" He glanced at the Twins who were a few yards away. They were looking at a display case with some broken pottery. "They kind of betrayed us when they took you to Perseus, but they might try something else." The vertical slits in his red eyes narrowed. "I feel that last line of the Prophecy still hasn't happened." He looked back at the Twins, then at me. "We're missing something. Perseus would never let us have the Cup and the Lost Star Child . . ."

"You think the Twins might try to give Perseus both? I don't think there's anything else Perseus can offer them, not unless he gave them all the Prophecies, which is something Perseus would never do. He wants the future to himself."

"Let's just stay alert."

I nodded. For some reason, after what had happened with Perseus, I didn't believe that the Twins would turn on us. But then who could it be? I trusted Draco and Virgo with my life, and I didn't think any of our animal friends would betray us. I was more worried about the other part of the last line. The one that said we would lose everything we had once gained. Hadn't the speaking leaves at Dodona told me something similar?

I spotted a small screen against the wall, in between the displays. It showed pictures of excavations where they had retrieved some of the objects. One image showed a grave. It had some skeletons and was littered with broken vases and jewelry. We looked at another glass display next to it that showed jade figures. A twenty-inch bull statue caught my attention, and so did the masks. Another case on the side showed vases of all sizes and shapes, but still Draco didn't see anything out of the ordinary with his superior sight.

We kept moving through the room. One glass case was full of stone tablets with cuneiform script, which to me looked like a jumble of lines. Some of the tablets seemed organized in sections. Each section had a different set of symbols grouped together. Draco studied the tablets carefully.

The next display held some knives and below, a few vases. The three knives were arranged horizontally, pointing to the right. The jade knife at the very top was about the width of my hand. Below it was another knife as long as my forearm. A third knife was black with ragged edges, as if time had cut away the blade. Below them stood three closed vessels. One of the vases was curvy, as if mimicking the shape of a body, and another one was straighter. They strangely looked to be male and female torsos, which gave me a chill. The third vase was smaller and completely circular. Draco turned to this display, and his pupils narrowed so much they almost disappeared.

"What?" I asked.

I looked at the vases again, but then I realized Draco was not looking at them. His gaze was locked on the knives. Virgo caught up to us a second later. She first stared at the vases, but like me, she realized Draco's eyes were narrowed at the knives. Castor and Pollux quickly joined us.

Draco pointed at the black knife, and I analyzed it more carefully. It was around twenty inches long. At first, I had thought that the knife was made of iron or something and had simply rusted black, but now that I looked at it more closely, it was made entirely of a black metal. I didn't know of any metal that could be so dark. The handle was smooth and curved, and the blade looked like the Prophecies of Alathea—like the edges had been burned off, forming ragged curves.

"That metal . . . ," Draco trailed off. "I've seen it before. It was long ago but . . . I think this may be asteroid metal."

"Asteroid metal?" Castor asked.

Draco nodded. "From an asteroid that probably crashed here long ago."

Virgo stepped closer. "I think I've heard of this somewhere. It's very rare, but ancient people considered asteroid metal to be the heavenly metal of the Gods. If they found it, they used it to make sacred weapons." Her brown eyes widened like plates. "But this knife looks strange, almost as if . . . as if it's being consumed."

"What kind of light does it emit?" I asked Draco.

"That's the thing," Draco said. "This knife is not emitting any light—it's absorbing it completely."

"Like a black hole or something?" Castor asked.

"I don't know," Draco shook his head. "I've never seen anything like it. It's literally sucking all the light around us."

"How is that even possible?" Castor asked.

"I have no idea," Draco admitted. "But I think we've found what we're looking for."

"Are there any knives in the Constellations?" Pollux asked.

"Not that I know of," Virgo responded.

"How did someone imprison a Monster in an asteroid-metal knife?" Castor asked.

"How would we even unleash the thing trapped inside?" Pollux wondered.

Virgo cocked her head to the side, to a very uncomfortable and unnatural looking position. "It looks like a candle," she whispered.

"What?" I asked as I cocked my head too.

From that angle it did indeed look like a candle. The handle looked like the body of a candle, and the blade was like a flame. The blade was three times bigger than the handle, as if the flame were growing bigger as it consumed the wax.

I exchanged a glance with Virgo.

"Maybe it's not a knife," Virgo said.

I wished Cassiopeia had been a bit more specific in telling me what we were dealing with.

"This seems too easy," Pollux said.

"You mean, this seems too easy because no giant serpent has attacked us and we haven't drowned yet?" I asked.

Pollux clenched his jaw. "This is wrong. If this is asteroid metal, wouldn't someone have detected that and moved this to some special display? This object doesn't even have a description." He looked around the room. "It's hidden in plain sight."

"But no one can see what it truly is," Draco said. "If you guys had come without me, you probably never would have guessed that the knife is what we're looking for."

Draco was right, but so was Pollux. Something didn't quite fit in.

"What now?" I asked.

"I'm not sure we can just steal this in plain daylight," Draco eyed a couple of tourists behind us who were looking at the clay figurines. "I have a plan. We stay around the museum and keep an eye on the knife. Then when closing time approaches, we hide in the bathrooms. If anyone sees us, Corvus can lie to them. Once everyone is gone, Corvus can convince some guard to open the case and give us the knife."

"I can do that," I said.

We all stood staring at the object for a few seconds.

"How would we even unleash the Lost Star Child from . . . whatever that is?" Virgo asked. "*Should* we even release it?"

"I have an idea," Castor raised his hand. "We should sail to the middle of the Atlantic Ocean, throw that thing into the water, then sail away as fast as we can and hope it drowns and dies."

"It could work," I said, although I still held onto the small possibility that we could unleash it against Perseus to weaken him. We would have to make a decision soon, but without knowing who or what the Monster was, it would be hard.

Pollux exhaled. "We should get some lunch."

"We can go to the first floor cafe," Virgo said.

"I volunteer to go get lunch first," Castor said.

"Me too," Pollux said.

"I'll go with you," Virgo stepped away from the display. "After I eat, I'll go check out the Greek and Roman rooms. I want to see if I can find any myths of what this Lost Star Child could be. I'm sure I can figure it out."

I nodded. That seemed like a good idea. If anyone could figure out who or what we were dealing with, it was Virgo.

"Corvus and I will stay here." Draco put his sunglasses on again.

Virgo and the Twins walked out of the room and disappeared.

"We should also focus on finding your sisters," Draco said. "Once we decide what to do with this." He waved at the knife.

I nodded, my heart beating loudly. "But how will we find them?" I asked.

Draco shrugged. "We could wait for more of your memories to come back, and if not, I'm sure we'll figure something out."

I nodded again. I would be reunited with my sisters soon. That made a burst of joy spread through my chest. Once we found them, maybe we could all work together to steal the Prophecies back from Perseus. At least I had found what I had set out to discover over a year ago—the Cup and the Lost Star Child. But I couldn't get rid of the nagging thought that, somehow, Perseus would find a way to steal both from us.

CHAPTER 17

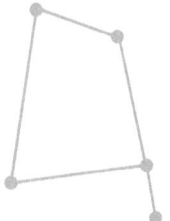

WE QUIETLY SNEAKED OUT of the family-sized bathroom. The semicircular room we walked into was dark and silent. The crescent moon above us created a dim silver glow through the glass ceiling.

Virgo and Draco stood close together. Virgo had covered her scars with a pair of gloves, which she anxiously rubbed together. Pollux looked up at the sky while Castor stared at the wall behind us that displayed an ancient rock mural. It depicted a crowned deity seated on a large chair. The deity had long curly hair and a large beard. Under the mural were stairs that led to the floor below.

The entrance to the galleries was locked by a black metal gate. For the first time, I wished Andromeda were here to help. With a single thought she would have been able to open any of these locked gates, and probably the display case, too, without ringing any alarms.

We waited outside the gate, knowing the security guards would spot us with the cameras and one of them would come here soon enough. To the right, through the metal bars, I could make out some of the Egyptian exhibits. Hanging on the wall were ancient paintings that seemed to depict men and gods standing together. As always, the gods stood at least a head taller than the humans. There was also a large display in the middle of the room that looked like a human skeleton curled into a fetal position as it lay on the rocky ground—probably mimicking how archeologists had found the skeleton. Around it were broken vases, and from the glimmers of light around it, I assumed there was some jewelry too. The Egyptian mummies must have been close by. That made me nervous. I didn't feel comfortable walking past ancient objects that had been taken from graves and temples. If those things had been buried, it had been for a reason. Only at night did that seem more evident to me, when those objects seemed to be restless, even if they didn't move. Or maybe *I* was the one who was restless.

"Anytime now," Pollux said after about three minutes. He looked above the black gate at the camera with its blinking with green light.

Virgo slowly swung a recyclable cloth bag from the gift shop. It depicted some Egyptian gods standing together as they raised their hands to the sun above. Inside the bag was a blanket that showed some mythological monsters. After our varied experiences with Crater, we didn't think that touching the strange metal object with our bare hands would be a good idea. We had decided to wrap it in a large blanket and put it in the bag. Virgo had also bought a Greek book and some souvenirs. She had gotten us all Egyptian ankh keychains. I pulled mine out of my coat pocket and dangled it in front of me. The metal trinket had been painted to look like it was made of gold. I put it back in my pocket, next to Crater. The Twins had also bought the mug for Argo and promised to show us Argo's mug collection when we returned to the Ship.

I looked back at the camera, but still no one came up the stairs to tell us we shouldn't be here. My hands began to tingle. Guards shouldn't take that long. Maybe they had taken a nap or something?

"I wonder what that Star Child is," Castor said next to me. "If it's so ancient."

"I've been thinking." Virgo stopped swinging the bag. "All creatures in the Constellations are based on myths, like Cetus, Hydra, Pegasus, Draco." She looked at him. "I'm still not sure why you materialized as only half dragon."

Draco shrugged. "Not sure either." He tensed slightly, his jaw twitching. I wasn't the only one with a hidden past.

"In any case," Virgo said. "There are other creatures like the Sphinx, the Sirens, and the Chimaera," she paused. "But the most ancient Monster, and one that appears in several mythologies, is the Greek Monster Typhon."

"Remind us who that was." I really needed to review Greek mythology.

"He was considered the father of all Monsters," Virgo said. "He was the only creature that was both a god and a Monster and was said to have been born before any of the eras of humanity." She rubbed her gloved hands again. "He was said to be so tall that his head touched the stars. He had the torso of a man, but instead of legs he had snakes. His human head had one hundred dragon heads coming out of it that emitted different animal sounds. He breathed fire from every head and his eyes glowed red. He had hundreds of different wings and his fingers were also made of snakes."

"Yikes," Castor said.

"It could be something else," Draco said.

"Could be." Virgo looked away from the bag. "But if Cassiopeia talked about a Monster more ancient than humanity itself and the most powerful and monstrous Star Child, then Typhon may be what we're facing." She paused. "In Egypt, that monster was known as Apophis, the serpent of Chaos, but I haven't found any reference to that monster being in the Constellations. But the fact that he was known across several cultures makes me think this is the Monster we're dealing with."

"And we're going to steal him." Pollux gave a small squeak. "I do believe that throwing that thing in the middle of the ocean may be the best we can do."

Castor nodded. "If we unleash it on Perseus, then we unleash it on all of us."

"Yeah," I said. "Unleashing it may not be a good idea after all."

Virgo nodded. "Let's just steal it first. Once we're back on Argo, we'll decide what to do."

"What else do you know about Typhon?" I asked.

Virgo's eyes widened. "Typhon was the father of the Nemean Lion."

"Leo?" I asked, surprised.

"Yeah." Virgo held the bag tighter. "And the father of the Sphinx, the Chimaera, and of Cerberus, the three headed dog of the Underworld, which is sometimes depicted as Canis Major in the sky, and of Hydra and Aquila." She looked down at her shoes. "And he was also the father of Ladon, who is represented by the Constellation Draco."

We were all silent for a few seconds.

"He was the father of almost all the Monsters in the Constellations," I said, feeling a bit breathless.

I glanced at Draco, but his expression was neutral.

"Yikes indeed," Castor said.

"Assuming this is really Typhon or Apophis," Draco said, "then why would his Constellation have vanished from the sky?"

Virgo shrugged.

I was about to ask Virgo if there were any myths of Typhon in other mythologies besides the Egyptian one, but loud steps thundered from the stairs. We all turned to face them. Finally, the security guards had woken from their nap and spotted the five teenagers on the cameras. For a split second, I worried that it might be Perseus coming up the stairs but was incredibly relieved when two security guards came into view. They were both dressed in black. One of them was a head taller than the other. They shone their flashlights in our faces.

"What are you doing here?" the shorter man asked.

"We are supposed to be here." My voice was deep.

I didn't feel the full pain of my scars, it was only a mild ache.

One of their radios spoke. "George, could you please bring those kids down to the control room?"

The taller man, whom I assumed was George, picked up the radio.

"You don't want to answer that." I walked closer to him. "You want to give me the radio."

George handed me the radio with a blank stare.

"Hello," I spoke into the radio.

"Who is this?"

"The five of us are supposed to be here." My voice bounced off the walls, echoing several times. "And all you want to do is help us in anything we ask."

"We want to help," the radio answered back.

I looked back at George and his companion. "You would love to take us to room fifty-six now."

"It would be our pleasure," George said.

They walked to the metal gate on the left. George spoke into the radio. "Oliver, open door to room fifty-three."

The door beeped open. We all walked into the room, and George closed the gate behind us.

"Oliver, could you turn on the lights?" George asked.

Only the lights from the display cases turned on. That was enough for me. We passed by golden necklaces and bracelets, vases, figurines, and human bones. One set of bones seemed small enough to belong to a child. The empty sockets in the skull stared at the glass ceiling above, as if stargazing.

At the end of the room was another closed metal gate.

"Open gate to room fifty-four," George said, and the gate opened for us to walk to the next room.

My heart beat as fast as a galloping horse. If Typhon was really the creature trapped in that strange object, then it was truly the most dangerous and powerful Star Child. Perseus must surely have known what the Lost Star Child was, even if he didn't know where to find it. How would he use Typhon to his advantage? We still didn't know what Perseus was planning, but he seemed to have a plan for everything. As the others had said, it still didn't sit right with me that he had simply let us have both Crater and Typhon. He would have wanted both for himself. I knew he would find a way to get them.

After a couple of minutes, we arrived in room fifty-six. My eyes set on the knives display. I let out a breath, relieved to see that the asteroid-metal object was still there.

"You want to open this so we can get what's inside." I pointed at the display case as my voice hissed in my ears.

George and his companion both nodded eagerly, and George walked over to the display.

"You want to disable the alarms."

"Could you disable the alarms for room fifty-six?" George said into the radio.

He pulled out a small key. The guard inserted his small key at the top of the case and turned it. My heart strained in anticipation. Virgo fidgeted with the bag, while Draco balled his fists. The Twins stood like tightly coiled springs about to shoot forward.

The security guard removed the cover and left it on the floor. The opening was at Draco's height. I looked around, but there were no chairs or stools we could stand on.

"We'll get it," Pollux said.

Castor climbed onto Pollux's shoulders with ease, as if they had done it a hundred times. Castor extended his hand and Virgo handed him the blanket. He leaned forward and grabbed the strange object, wrapping it with the blanket as if he were holding a newborn baby. Castor pulled back and Pollux set him down. My head began to spin with anxiety.

The security guards only stared at us blankly.

Draco looked around the room with his eyes narrowed, as if he expected Perseus to appear from behind one of the displays and charge toward us with a sword. My breathing became more ragged, as if my lungs were freezing.

We all huddled in a tight circle. Castor unwrapped the object but still held it with the blanket. The black metal glinted as it reflected the light from the display case. A piercing pain sliced through the back of my head. Stars danced around me, dark and twisted, consuming all the light.

"Corvus!" Virgo shouted.

I heard my name several more times, but I wasn't at the British Museum anymore.

"Corvus!" one of my sisters shouted in terror, but she was so far away.

I didn't have the strength to shout back as Darkness wrapped around me, and she had a face. It was pale like the moon. Her eyes gleamed like blue jewels, and her black hair spread from her face in tight curls. Darkness smiled at me like a mother gazing down at her sleeping child. Her face vanished, like smoke blown away by the wind. Then I was blown away too, taken by a current to another time, another place. Images flashed through my mind, pieces of my past which were sharp like broken glass. Pain surged through my body, cutting me to pieces. Then his face materialized above me—Perseus's blue-green eyes gazed down at me with fierce intensity. I wanted to scream in pain but couldn't force my lips open. I wanted to die—to be done with the suffering and to forget about the dark hole that plunged my heart in agony.

"He's alive." He flashed a triumphant smile before Darkness pulled me into another embrace.

Chapter XXII, Verse III

The Liar shall hold the power of the Cup,
To restore the forces that for so long were lost.
To strengthen an enemy that Time once forgot,
Or to save one that he holds dear to his heart.
Lightning strikes the sky and ice the sea covers,
When one decision shall determine the Fate of those vanished,
Those that will soon be found chained and bound.

CHAPTER 18

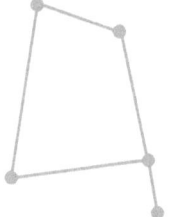

İ AWOKE WİTH A START, coughing. I could still feel the pain in my lungs. I was on my back but turned myself over and vomited the tuna sandwich I had eaten earlier. It tasted as bad on the way out as it had on the way in.

"He's alive," one of the Twins said from behind me.

"Corvus," Virgo gasped next to me. "What happened?"

I couldn't speak. Pieces of my memories still flashed through my mind. I had finally assembled the puzzle. My body trembled uncontrollably.

"I hate him," I muttered.

I vomited again, emptying out my stomach. Pain twisted through me like lightning sizzling in my veins. Rage rolled through me like an avalanche of fire. For the first time, I understood Perseus's plan. I understood the big picture I hadn't been able to see before. Perseus had used my memories against me—he had used what he knew was most dear to me and turned it to his favor. He had played me as the absolute fool. Hate poisoned my heart as if an invisible hand were twisting it. Now I understood why my sisters had never come to find me, why I hadn't seen them since I had erased my memories. Perseus had known I would lose everything and that he would gain it all in turn.

I screamed, not out of pain but out of sheer frustration. I was the Liar, the cheater, and the deceiver. But the only one that had been lied to, deceived, and cheated had been me.

"Corvus," Virgo said with concern, holding my arm.

I looked up at her. She was pale as a sheet of paper, her freckles dark. Her white strand of hair seemed ashen. Draco knelt next to her, his red eyes tracing over me as if trying to find a gaping wound. I was wounded very deeply, but it was not a wound he could see.

The hate tore me apart, but also the regret, the anger, and the helplessness. The Oracle of Dodona had warned me, those stupid leaves had been right—every lie had a price, and the price for this one threatened to rip me in half. Perseus was truly merciless. He knew what this would cost me. He knew this would give him everything he wanted.

I knew what I had to do. The leaves had known what I would do. Perseus most certainly knew what came next. Even the Prophecy at the temple had warned me.

In the end only betrayal awaits, and the loss of everything once gained.

"Are you okay?" Pollux asked from behind me.

I turned. He and Castor looked genuinely concerned, their faces as ghostly pale as Virgo's. Next to them the security guards still stood immobile, staring blankly at the display case.

I stood up, my legs wobbly. Only the pure adrenaline coursing through my veins gave me the strength to stand. Heat emanated from the Cup in my coat as if it were carrying hot coals.

Crater hummed in my pocket. "Our bond could become infected. Your Essence is fuller."

In that moment, I wished I had never recovered any of my memories. I hated myself. I hated me more than I hated Perseus. I extended my hand toward Castor. The object was completely wrapped inside the blanket. The Twins exchanged a glance, but Castor slowly gave me the blanket. Virgo offered the bag, but I shook my head. I placed the blanket with the object inside my coat pocket.

"What did you remember?" Draco asked.

I stared at the wooden floor, which was polished so smoothly I could see my reflection.

"That last part of the Prophecy," I said. "The one inscribed at the temple."

I breathed hard, my lungs failing.

"What about it?" Virgo asked.

I began to walk toward the metal gate. The others stood still for a couple of seconds, then began following me.

"That was meant for me," I said, stopping just outside of the room, right in front of the metal gate. The guards still looked at the display case, their gazes distant. I dropped the lie, and their heads snapped back to us. "I'm the traitor."

I swung the gate close.

"Hey!" George shouted. "What are you kids doing here?"

"Corvus!" Draco yelled as he lunged for the gate. "Tell them to open the door!"

"What are you doing, Corvus?" Pollux grabbed the metal bars tightly.

"Bring more guards!" George shouted into the radio.

Virgo looked at me, only half of her face visible through the gate. She closed her eyes, and a single tear fell from them. Draco's eyes blared red.

"I'm sorry," I whispered. "I'm so sorry."

I turned around and raced away. I had never run so fast in my life. The exhibits and displays blurred past me. I barely knew where I was going, but somehow found the stairs, then I was running down, rushing through the first floor. I was outside, on the cold streets of London. I still didn't have all of my memories, but it was as if my feet and legs knew exactly where to take me—my muscles seemed to have better memory than my mind.

I ran and kept running, through blurry dark streets. They were streets that only my feet remembered. The adrenaline numbed the pain in my lungs and muscles. The heat emanating from Crater kept me warm as I continued onward. At some point, my feet stopped, and I nearly stumbled forward and fell flat on my face. My breaths were heavy, as if I had shredded my lungs, and I nearly dropped from exhaustion. But the pain in my heart, that shattering ache, kept me awake.

The house in front of me was two stories tall, surrounded by thick dark trees on all sides. The main gate had been left open. I stepped inside. This was my house. I just knew it. It was made of red bricks with black gabled roofs and white window frames.

I faced the front door, breathing heavily. I turned the knob and pushed the door open. The house was completely dark. At the end of the large living room was a dark corridor with a large window on the side that showed the backyard—the corridor led to the room where I had interrogated Cassiopeia. Through the dark, I could make out the stairs on my left. I climbed them quietly. Light came from the end of the hallway. The door to the room had been left ajar, and bright light spilled out through the opening. I felt as if I were experiencing everything from outside my body, as if someone else were controlling my movements and I was just floating along.

I walked down the hallway and pushed the door open, making it crash against the wall. Perseus, who had been reading a book on the couch under the window, gave a startled yell. He dropped the book to the floor and stood up with his hands balled into fists.

The fire crackled on the far side of the room. The wall opposite from Perseus was covered with books.

I walked toward the small table next to the couch. Perseus observed me, his eyes blazing like black fire. His red hair was disheveled, and the dark circles under his eyes told me that he hadn't slept well since we had last seen each other. I pulled the wrapped blanket from my pocket and left it on the table, then I pulled Crater out and left it next to the blanket.

I turned to him. "I. Hate. You."

I leapt forward, colliding with Perseus. We fell to the carpet—whirls of red, black, and white blurred around me as we rolled over it. I sat on Perseus's chest and was about to punch him in the face when he pushed me away. I fell hard on my back, coughing.

I stood again slowly, wheezing. Perseus just stared at me as he stood in front of the fire. He seemed amused. I lunged forward again, letting out the last guttural scream my lungs could manage. Perseus caught both of my arms, turned me around, and pulled me toward him, making my back strike his chest. Why was he so damn strong? He wrapped his arms around my torso, gripping my wrists. I managed to turn slightly and drove my knee upward.

Perseus screamed, and we both tumbled to the carpet again, but he didn't let go of me, his arms held me tighter, crushing me. He sat up, his legs wrapping around mine to prevent me from kicking him again. His hands clamped around my wrists like metal chains.

"I hate you," I gasped.

He didn't respond.

"I hate you so much." I wondered why my cheeks were wet. "I hate you. I hate you. I hate you."

I cried. The tears I didn't know I had held for so long spilled out of my eyes like flowing rivers. Those were tears that had been with me since before I lost my memories. Perseus's grip loosened, but still he held me.

"You lied to me," I growled.

I tried to breathe, but my nose was clogged so I breathed through my mouth. The pain was all over my body, as if I was covered in bruises. I pulled away from Perseus with the last bit of strength I had and crawled toward the bookcase. Perseus wiped his cheeks and turned away from me. I looked into the fire, trying to recover my breaths. We were silent for so long that the fire began to die down. It was still dark outside, but I knew that morning would arrive soon. I wished that morning would take away this terrible nightmare, but I knew it wouldn't. This nightmare was the price I had been willing to pay, and now I had to live with it. Only a few stubborn flames still danced with the ashes once the sky began to lighten.

"I hate you," I whispered.

Perseus remained silent for a few seconds, and I knew he was staring at the Cup and at the Lost Star Child—he had known all along that I would bring them to him.

Perseus moved closer to me. He sat at my side, staring into the fire. "I'm glad to see you again."

CHAPTER 19

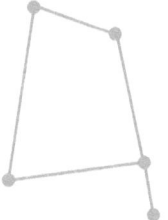

I SCREAMED IN HORROR, *but my screams drowned as another wave washed over my head. I wildly kicked my feet to get back up. I gulped in air as soon as my head broke the surface. The bitter taste of saltwater lingered in my mouth. The sky was completely dark above me, and the waves around me were like molten silver as they reflected the full moon above. The current pulled me away from the coast, far from the cliffside and away from the others.*

"Help me!" I shouted.

"Corvus!" Darren shouted back. I couldn't see where he was. A four-feet-tall wave crashed over me, and I was once again beneath the waves. The water was so cold that I couldn't feel my skin anymore. My arms and legs went numb from the frigid water, but my lungs burned. I tried to hold my breath, knowing I wouldn't last much longer.

I waved my arms wildly, and my right hand slid over the smooth surface of a rock. I tried to hold onto it, to pull myself up, but the rock was too slick with moss and my hand slipped away. I managed to take a deep breath before the current pulled me down again. I wanted to stay close to the cliff, but the waves were so strong that they pulled me farther away. My head broke the surface once again and I took a deep gulp of air, wiping the water from my eyes. A giant black tentacle curled into itself ten yards away from me. I held my breath and tried not to move. The tip of the tentacle was sharp as a spear.

Where had the Monster come from? We had been on our small boat when it had burst from the waves. We'd just wanted to watch the stars above the sea—we didn't get to see the stars in New York.

The tentacle uncurled and smashed down right in front of me, creating a wave that pushed me back toward the cliff. I went under the waves again, and my back hit the cliff wall hard. The force shot the air out of my lungs. I broke the surface, taking frantic gulps of air at the same time that I coughed out water. Our small boat had disappeared. To the left, a few figures frantically moved around on the beach.

"Help!" I screamed.

I couldn't tell if they had spotted me. I tried to swim toward them, but the waves kept pushing me away. More tentacles came out of the water behind me. Was the Monster a giant octopus? It had more than eight tentacles, which were twisted and thick as giant tree trunks. They smashed into the water, creating sharp waves that pushed and pulled me back and forth.

My lungs strained with every breath. A sudden heat filled my chest, and then the heat turned to the worst agony I'd felt. Fire consumed my skin, ripping it off. A tentacle came out of the water right in front of me. Then I was in the air. My screams filled my ears, and I could only see the starry sky above me. The sky disappeared as I hit the water again, and cold cloaked me from that terrible pain.

I tried to kick myself up again but my arms and legs weren't responding anymore, as if they had detached from the rest of my body. The fire in my chest consumed me, burning me from the inside out. My mind screamed at me to get out of the water, and my lungs felt like balloons about to explode.

With the last bit of energy I had, I moved to the surface. I wasn't even sure if I had moved my legs, but soon I was able to breathe again.

I blinked a few times to get the water out of my eyes. I felt heavy, and I wondered how long I would last on the surface before plunging below the waves again.

The tentacles were about fifty yards behind me. A bright white-violet light twisted and curled on the beach. A bolt of electricity sizzled past me and hit one of the tentacles, which curled inward and dipped below the ocean.

Dark grey clouds gathered above the Monster. Those hadn't been there before. Hail, roughly the size of my head, fell from the clouds and crashed hard against the beast. The tentacles twisted wildly, sending spiking waves around me. I found the strength to swim toward the beach, but the blazing fire burned through my veins. No matter how much I swam, the beach still seemed infinitely far away.

"Corvus!" one of the girls shouted from the beach.

A tentacle rose right next to me. It splashed down, creating a wave that pushed me to the side, closer to the cliff. Pain blurred my vision, making flashes of white explode in my eyes.

Another tentacle rose above me.

"Hey!" A shout came from the top of the cliff. Darren stood at the very edge. "Hey, you Monster!"

I could only see Darren in silhouette. The pain numbed away, and my heartbeat echoed inside my ears. It was so slow. The tentacle above me moved away from me, rising high to smash into the cliff.

"Monster!" The scream burst from my mouth, my throat raw with pain. "You want to freeze!"

For a second, the tentacle froze, completely immobile. Then the Monster broke away from my lie, and the tentacle smashed into the cliffside.

"NOO!" The scream tore out of my chest. Pieces of rock blasted away from the cliff. I couldn't see Darren. I swam closer to the cliff, even though all of my instincts were driving me away from it. Rocks

plunged into the water as the cliff fractured and cracked. The tentacles moved away from it.

"Darren!" I shouted.

I frantically swam forward, a sudden burst of energy alight in my body. I couldn't see him. Maybe he had jumped away just in time. Maybe he was still up on the cliff. A figure emerged from the waves. I pushed myself toward it, feeling my heart would tear out of my chest. I held Darren's limp body. I shook him as I pulled him close. Darren moaned, but he didn't open his eyes. Something dark slid on the side of his head, and it took me a second to realize it was blood. I pulled him into my arms, my chest blaring in agony.

The waves spiked up again, and I knew the Monster was close.

The pain blurred my vision, and I struggled to keep myself afloat. I felt like a flaming torch had been rammed into my chest and burned my organs.

"Cetus!"

Perseus stood at the very edge of the broken cliff. His fiery red hair was wild around his head, and his clear eyes were set on the Monster. One of the tentacles rose high above the water.

"NO!" I shouted again, my voice shrill with terror.

Perseus extended his right hand forward. The tentacle, twisting and curling, was only a few yards from the cliff when it became grey and went still. It froze right above Perseus. There was a second of silence. Then the tentacle cracked, and grey pieces fell into the ocean. Water splashed around me as the tentacle crumbled. I tried to swim away but couldn't move as I held onto Darren. I let the current pull me away from the cliff. I looked up again. Perseus knelt at the top and a shadow swirled around him, a black figure made of dark mist—Arianna.

I was too focused looking at them until I felt another stab of pain in my chest. I screamed in horror as the tip of a tentacle embedded into Darren's stomach.

"Corvus!" Perseus shouted. He stood up again. "I don't care what it takes! Make me stronger, Arianna! Now!"

The tentacle ripped away from Darren, and pain swelled in my chest. I held on tighter to him as the current pulled us backward. Three more tentacles rose above Perseus.

Perseus extended his hand. He let out the most horrible scream I had ever heard. I knew it was coming out of his mouth, but it wasn't his. The scream was monstrous—a shriek that could only belong to a demon. Light exploded from Perseus, making my eyes sting. It vanished seconds later, but I could feel my bones vibrating. The tentacles in front of Perseus froze before they hit the cliff. They were grey, the same color as stone. Perseus dropped to his knees. The tentacles cracked loudly. They broke into pieces and fell into the ocean. I held on tightly to Darren as the waves spiked around me. I drifted along. The water warmed as the fire blazed hotter in my chest. I was floating, light as a feather, and for a moment it felt like I was flying. I looked at the Stars, they seemed closer than they had ever been before. Then the pain was gone.

I floated for what seemed like an eternity. The Stars were around me, close and warm, yet distant and cold. A current pulled at me, slowly at first, and then faster. I was falling down into darkness. Something was crushing my chest. The Stars twinkled more frantically above me. I could almost hear them—they sounded like crystals gently clinking against each other, playing a tune.

Fire washed over the Stars as I breathed. Pain cut through my body, and I could barely manage my next breath.

". . . pressure on wound."

". . . we can't . . ."

". . . please don't . . ."

I couldn't make out the voices. I opened my eyes, my vision blurred. I could see only shadows. My chest felt like it had been cut by a flaming spear, but I didn't have the strength to yell out in pain.

*My vision cleared for a moment. Perseus's head hovered above me.
"I think he's dead," one of the girls said.*

*"No!" Perseus shouted. "Come on, Corvus. Don't leave me.
Please don't leave me."*

*A hand gently swiped my forehead, and I felt a kiss there. "Please
don't go," she whispered.*

*"Hang in there, Corvus," Perseus said. His face was white as
the moon above him. His cheeks glinted, and it took me a second to
realize those were tears.*

*I looked up at the Stars. They were so much brighter than I had
seen them. They started clinking again, their crystal-like tune lulling
me to sleep.*

*"You're not leaving me," Perseus said. "Do you hear me? I'm not
letting you die."*

"Corvus!" A ragged cry echoed somewhere to my side.

*I didn't have the strength to answer as Darkness took over me.
It swirled like mist, consuming all the Stars around me. Then a face
materialized from that Darkness—Arianna. I knew it was her even
though she had never shown us her face. As far as I knew she didn't
have a face. Arianna's eyes were bright blue, like shining jewels. Her
hair was jet black as it covered her pale face in curls. She smiled down
at me gently.*

"Hang in there, Corvus." Her tone was melodious as always.

*Then blackness covered me completely—a very different type of
darkness.*

Chapter XX, Verse II

A dark past the Dragon hides, before the new form it adopted.

Its olden days it will try to forget, until by Fire they awaken again.

The Cup shall restore its enemy of old, the enemy once bound to its Soul.

For the Cup it should have guarded, but its power it lost.

The Dragon still slumbers, asleep but conscious,

As the boy fights on to help those that will soon destroy him.

For the Fire still burns, and it shall consume him whole.

CHAPTER 20

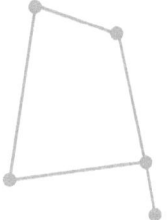

A HAND SETTLED on my shoulder and I startled awake. Perseus looked down at me, his brows knitted together in concern. I realized that I had fallen asleep on the carpet. I didn't even remember being tired, but exhaustion must have taken over me. The sky outside was cloudy, and I couldn't make out what time it was. My head felt heavy, and all of my muscles strained as if I had run to London from Scotland.

"Are you feeling all right?" Perseus asked.

"No." My throat was painfully raw.

I sat up with my back against the bookcase, the world spinning around me. I felt dizzy enough to vomit but knew I had nothing left in my stomach. I wondered what had happened to my friends. Surely they had found a way to escape and were probably back on Argo. Would they come look for me? They wouldn't know where to find me even if they tried. An ache pulsed in my chest, as if thorns were growing out of my ribs and poking my heart until it bled.

I had betrayed my friends. The Twins had never trusted me—they had been right all along. The leaves of Dodona had known that if I found the Cup, I would lose what I had gained. I hadn't realized what that meant until that moment—I had found a new family, people who trusted me and took care of me. I had lost Virgo, Draco, Sirius, Aquila, Maera, and Leo. They would never forgive me. I grunted, feeling like the thorns in my heart were piercing out of my chest

"I made breakfast." Perseus looked toward the door. "I can bring it upstairs if you don't feel like walking down."

"You never came to look for me," I said, letting the anger spread through my veins. "And you didn't let our sisters find me."

"They're all right." Perseus didn't meet my gaze, instead looking at the black tree with white leaves on the red carpet. Was that regret in his eyes? "We didn't know where you had gone." Perseus turned to me, his eyes lighting in anger. "You left no trace, no letter, no nothing." His eyes simmered with rage. "It took me a long time to figure out what you were really up to, but by that time you were already with Draco and Virgo." He breathed out. "Then you tried to kill me in New York."

"Sorry about that," I muttered.

Perseus traced circles on the carpet with his foot. "It wasn't until I read your Prophecies that I pieced everything together." He looked away from me.

"You didn't come find me," I said as anger burned my chest. My scars throbbed. "You could have told me the truth. You could have told me who I was."

Perseus met my gaze. He huffed. "If I had approached you one week ago and told you the truth, would you have believed me?"

"No."

Perseus clenched his jaw hard. "I was glad you weren't at Palatine Hill at least." He sighed. "Your friends tried very hard to kill me."

"You tried very hard to kill *them*."

Perseus shook his head. "I don't understand why they hate me so much."

"What do you mean *why?*" I asked. "When I first woke up without my memories, I was in a hospital, barely alive after you had used Algol to cause a terrorist attack in London that almost killed me!" Perseus's face paled, which made his red hair seem a shade darker. He faced the bookshelf, as if looking for a book that would solve all of our problems. "And then I learned that you're trying to destroy Fate, Destiny, and Prophecy with Arianna's help," I said.

"It's the only way," Perseus said, still facing the books.

"The only way for what?" I stood up on shaky legs, but he still didn't meet my gaze. "To destroy all Life in the Universe and send it back to Chaos?"

"The only way for us to be free," Perseus said. He turned back to me. His eyes seemed to be a swirl of darkness. "Don't we deserve to choose how we live our lives? Why should the Stars and Weavers choose that for us?"

"Because that's how the Universe works! Without Fate, Destiny, and Prophecy, the world would fall into Chaos. These are the structures of Life. Without them, everyone will die."

Perseus stared hard at me. "I don't know who told you that, but it's not true." He chuckled. "You used to want freedom, too, Corvus. When did that change?"

I felt like he had punched me in the gut.

I shook my head. "I don't remember ever wanting that."

"You didn't remember being my brother either."

I looked at the carpet, because I couldn't stand to look at Perseus. "You'll destroy all Life."

"According to whom?" Perseus asked. "Virgo? Who learned everything she knows from the Weavers? They would obviously tell her that so she fights against me, because my plan is to take away their power."

My hands numbed. "How do you know about Virgo and the Weavers?" She had never told anyone about that except Draco and me.

Perseus chuckled, then gave me that same stupid smile—he still knew so much about my past that I didn't remember.

"Yes, Corvus, once we destroy Fate, Prophecy, and Destiny, there *will* be Chaos." His eyes shone with excitement. "Chaos just has a bad reputation, but there's something beautiful about a world where life is led by possibility and probability—a world ruled by randomness."

"You truly are mad," I whispered.

Perseus looked away from me, his exasperated expression once again trying to find an answer in the bookcase.

"It hurts that you think I am." He looked down as he traced circles on the carpet with his foot again. "I'm just trying to make a better world, to give everyone the option to choose their journeys, to choose their endings." He looked back up, his dark eyes as big as an owl's. "Why would you oppose that? Why are you suddenly so attached to Fate and Prophecy and Destiny?"

I took a deep breath. "I don't like the uncertainty." My voice cracked. "When I woke up without my memories—which was a stupid decision, I admit that—I had absolutely nothing." Perseus's arms dangled at his sides. "I was completely and utterly lost. I didn't know who I was, or what I should do, or who I would become, or how I would end." I unclenched my hands, not realizing that I had balled them into fists. "Knowing that I had a Prophecy out there, something that could finally tell me the truth about myself and could tell me where I was supposed to go . . . it gave me hope."

Perseus stood still, considering what I said. At least he was willing to listen as I explained. "Destiny and Fate are not a prison, and neither is Prophecy." Perseus opened his mouth to contradict me but closed it again, letting me continue. "Prophecy guides us. It gives us a glimpse into the future that can help lead the way when we feel lost. It's like a flashlight in the dark, letting us see what's ahead." Perseus himself had been using Prophecy to prepare for the future. I found it ironic, that he was using Prophecies to destroy Prophecy.

"Fate provides a roadmap, Perseus, of all the possible roads and paths that can lead to Destiny. It teaches people that there are no right or wrong choices, that humans can choose without fear of losing themselves because they'll never stray from their paths. Whatever road they walk, Fate will make sure that it leads them in the right direction. And Destiny . . ." I paused, thinking. Destiny was important, it had always been, but I hadn't been able to put it into words before that moment. "It gives a sense of security. That people will end up exactly where they have to end up. They will find their final destination no matter what." Even if Star Children didn't have Fate and Destiny, I knew these were important forces that led people in their lives. I walked closer to Perseus. "If you destroy this, you will destroy everything that guides humankind. We will be lost, and there will be some who stray from their paths and never find them again. It will all be Chaos."

There was a moment of silence, then Perseus nodded slowly.

"I understand your position." He placed a hand on my shoulder. "I understand it completely, and it's a very valid argument. Some people live their lives guided by the Stars, guided by Prophecy to point them in the right direction."

"But?"

"But why should the Stars choose which direction we take?" He paused. "Why do we follow a map instead of creating our own way?"

I clenched my jaw. He truly didn't understand how that would play out.

"People need guidance, direction."

Perseus's grip tightened on my shoulder. I could see his mind gearing, finding new arguments.

"What if your Destiny is to die as a child in front of your parents?" His gaze hardened. "What if your Destiny is to watch everyone you love die before you do? What if your Destiny is to be brutally murdered?" He let his hand drop. "Destiny, Fate, Prophecy—if they're in your favor then that's great, but if they're not, then there's no way to avoid disaster. You're trapped in whatever path the Stars have decided for you."

"And by eradicating the power of the Stars you would solve that?" I asked. "There would still be children killed, and brutal murders would still happen. The only difference is that they would be completely random." I shook my head. "This wouldn't solve the problem, Perseus."

"No," he said. "But it would give people the option to choose."

"To choose what?" I asked. "Do you think people choose to get murdered or see their loved ones die?"

Perseus looked toward the door, as if expecting someone to come rescue him from this conversation. I grabbed his arm and turned him around, forcing him to face me. It felt strange to be so close to him after I had feared him for so long. I still feared him, but I knew he would never hurt me—at least not intentionally.

"I don't understand how Arianna got these mad ideas in your head," I said.

"She didn't," he responded. He pulled away from me. "People will be able to choose instead of having their Fates and Destinies set from birth."

"But what will that actually *change* besides making events occur randomly?" I asked, my tone rising. It seemed stupid that we were arguing about that—having so many other things we could have been arguing about. But I wanted to understand what drove Perseus, what had once driven *me*.

Perseus faced the bookshelf again. I walked around him and stood right in front of his gaze. He narrowed his eyes at me.

"This is about something else," I said. "I don't remember everything about you. But I *do* know that you've never truly been passionate about giving all human beings free will."

A vein strained from Perseus's forehead. I had hit the nail right on the head. This wasn't about saving the world and freeing all living creatures. I knew Perseus enough to know that this fight was personal.

"You're right," Perseus whispered. "I wasn't passionate about giving human beings free will." Fury and grief burned inside his eyes. "Until our brother was killed and there was nothing we could do to save him."

His words stabbed straight through my heart. The memory of Cetus's attack was still fresh in my mind, and I could almost feel the weight of Darren's dead body in my arms.

"It was his Destiny to die on that beach," Perseus said, never breaking his gaze from mine. "Do you remember his funeral?" He stepped closer to me. "Do you remember when we both knelt over his grave and promised we would destroy Destiny?"

"I don't remember," I whispered. "So this is all just for him? All those people dead in Italy, and all the other deaths you have caused throughout the world are just to avenge Darren?" His eyes bore into my face like knives. "I don't think he would have been all right with that." I paused. "There's more to this, isn't there?"

Perseus inched even closer to me. "*I* want to have the freedom to choose!" His lips pulled into a snarl. "I want to choose my own ending! We deserve that." He balled his fists. "We didn't choose the Prophecies we have, and we're all doomed to meet our ends without having a say in them."

It hit me then. How had I been so stupid? "Is this about Andromeda?" Perseus took a step back, as if I had slapped him in the face. "One of you is prophesized to kill the other."

Perseus's face turned as red as his hair. "What if you were prophesized to kill Virgo or Draco? Or if one of them was prophesized to kill you?"

My heart dropped from my chest like a rock. I shook my head. No. I may have betrayed them, but I would never even consider killing them, and I knew they wouldn't either.

Perseus chuckled. "I wouldn't have minded much killing a girl I didn't know," he whispered. "Keeping her alive long enough to recover those Prophecies was a mistake." His voice cut off. "I almost killed her at Palatine Hill." He looked away from me. "Arianna told me that I had to,"—he met my eyes—"that killing Andromeda was the only way I could be free from Algol."

"What?" I asked, dumbfounded.

"You—no, of course you don't remember," Perseus said as he looked at the ceiling. "I can't control Algol. I can't. It's like an infection that's slowly taking over me." He took a step away from me, as if scared he would contaminate me. "Algol is the most destructive Star in the sky, it's—" He took in a deep breath. His next words were barely audible, as if he was afraid ghosts would hear us. "Algol is prophesized to kill every single Star Child that isn't already dead by the time its third rising occurs." He held my arm. "Including you, Corvus, and including all of our sisters." I felt like a tornado was spinning me around the air. "And the only one who can stop me is Andromeda. Unless she kills me, I'll kill everyone else."

"But you didn't kill her," I whispered. "And she didn't kill you."

Perseus shook his head. "I couldn't." He closed his eyes. "I couldn't kill her to end my own curse. If I had killed Andromeda, I would have killed Algol." He opened his eyes and shook his head. "But I couldn't do it, and now I'll have to pay a big price for that." He met my eyes. "Now we'll *all* have to pay the price for what I couldn't do."

I took a deep breath, my hands tingling as they numbed.

"How does Arianna play a role in this?" I asked. I didn't remember much about her, but I knew she was manipulating Perseus from behind the scenes to meet her own needs.

"It's complicated," Perseus said. "Arianna has been taking care of us for a long time." He said that fondly, as if she were part of our family. That made me sick.

"Arianna found us when we were younger, she guided us. She knew I was the one prophesized to destroy everything that *she* had tried to destroy herself for so long."

"So Arianna knows me too?" I asked.

Perseus nodded. "She told me what my future was, around a year before you left. That's when she was strong enough to communicate fully with us." He crossed his muscular arms across his chest. "She told me Algol would kill every single Star Child, because eventually I would lose control of it." I felt as if I had inhaled the ashes from the fireplace. "The only three ways to stop Algol was either by killing Andromeda on Ara, by letting Andromeda kill me, or by completely destroying the power of Prophecy so I could change my future." Perseus tapped his foot on the floor. "Our plan was to kill Andromeda so her blood would give me enough power to kill Algol before it was too late. Then we would destroy Fate, Destiny, and Prophecy. But Ara was destroyed, so even if I killed Andromeda, it wouldn't kill Algol. That option is gone now."

"If you had already killed Andromeda to kill Algol, then why would you still destroy Fate, Destiny, and Prophecy?" I asked.

"We promised on Darren's grave that we would." The words fell out of his mouth, angry. "And that's also the only way we can escape *our* Prophecies." Perseus's tone was solemn. "Even with Algol dead, our Prophecies don't end well."

"Why?" I asked. "What are our Prophecies?"

"I'll show them to you later," Perseus said. "But let's just say none of us has a good ending."

My heart sank inside my ribs. I could deal with that, I told myself. If I was prophesized to die in a horrible way, then I could accept that, because I still didn't think that destroying the structures of Life was worth it.

"In any case,"—Perseus rubbed his red hair—"Arianna began helping us, leading us along. Our plan, which we began about a year before you left, was to find the other Star Children. We knew some of them would help us and others would oppose us." He stared hard at me, knowing I had switched sides. "At the same time, we were looking for clues on where to find Alathea's book. If we knew the Prophecies of every Star Child, then we could more easily move toward our goal." He looked out the window behind me, his gaze distant. "After that, our plan was to find Andromeda, kill her so her blood could free me from Algol, and then destroy Fate, Destiny, and Prophecy so none of us would have to face the rest of our Prophecies."

"Why did it have to be *her* blood?"

"Andromeda represents the sacrifice victim," Perseus said. "Her blood is powerful in any sacrifice, and Ara, the Altar, granted anyone who spilled blood on it a single wish."

"And what exactly would have happened to Algol if you had killed Andromeda?" I asked.

"Its triumph would no longer have been inevitable," Perseus said. "It would have still risen, but it would have been weak enough for us to destroy it before it could kill us." Perseus held my gaze steadily. "But even before we found Alathea's book, Arianna knew that if we destroyed Algol, the rest of you would still face terrible futures . . ." He trailed off. I couldn't help but wonder what terrible Prophecies had made us think that destroying all order in the Universe was the only way out. "Once I regained full control of myself, without the power of Algol threatening us, we would have destroyed Fate, Destiny, and Prophecy. That would have eliminated the power that the Stars have over us and the powers the Weavers hold too. The Star Children, and all of humanity, would be free."

A long silence settled in the room as I pieced together Perseus's plan that for so long had remained an unsolved puzzle.

"But you didn't kill Andromeda," I said, "and now Ara is gone."

Perseus nodded. "I couldn't kill her," he whispered. "I had the knife aimed at her throat but I couldn't bring myself to do it." He took a deep breath. "And now I have to deal with the consequence of keeping Algol. I chose Andromeda's life over the life of millions who died and who will continue to die." He chuckled. "I might have chosen her life over my own when I made that decision."

"So now the only way to be rid of Algol is to . . ."

"To destroy Fate, Destiny, and Prophecy." Perseus's eyes swirled. "Or to let Andromeda kill me." He took a deep breath. "If we destroy the power of the Stars, then Algol will no longer triumph and kill everyone as the Prophecies state because there will be no more Prophecies." He cocked his head to one side. "We will still need to kill the Demon, but we're working on a plan for that." He exhaled. "Algol is like a sickness. I don't know how much longer I'll be able to keep it under control."

The full weight of the situation pressed down on me, and my chest became tight. "Is it worth it?" I asked. "Do you really think it's worth destroying everything just to escape our futures?" I buried my face in my hands and realized that they were cold. Would we have been able to save Darren if Destiny wasn't real? Or would he have died anyway?

I looked back up. Perseus was tracing the lines of his palms. "I don't know if it's worth it, Corvus." He met my gaze. "For me, the only thing that matters is to keep the people I love safe. I failed Darren, but I won't fail any of you again." He said it with such determination that a shudder shook through me.

"How will you even destroy all of that?" I asked. The concept of Destiny, Fate, and Prophecy seemed too abstract to understand how it could be destroyed.

Perseus smiled. "Virgo didn't tell you, did she?" He sounded genuinely surprised.

Virgo had been vague when describing how one could destroy the power of the Stars, and I had never completely understood what she meant when she said Perseus would cut the *Connections* binding us all together in the net of Light.

"I'm guessing you're not going to tell me either," I said.

Perseus waved his hand dismissively. "That's a conversation we can have another day. It's too long and complicated to explain now." He paused. "But I am surprised Virgo never showed you."

I clenched my teeth. How could Perseus know so much about Virgo? Maybe he had read a lot about her in the Prophecies, but for some reason, that didn't sit right with me.

I clasped both of my hands together, trying to warm them. "The others won't stand with you," I said. I knew Virgo and Draco. They wouldn't think that destroying Fate, Destiny, and Prophecy was worth it, even if it saved their lives. The easiest thing for them to do, and truly the easiest solution to everything, would be if Andromeda just killed Perseus and ended all of this mess. That's what my friends would try to do. Then they would face their terrible futures—their Prophecies—and deal with them no matter how bad they were.

"I know they won't help me," Perseus said.

"They'll fight until they kill you."

Perseus nodded. "I'll fight them back. I'll do anything to keep my family alive. Even if Algol continues to rise to power, if we destroy Prophecy, I can change my future. I can kill Algol once and for all without having to spill Andromeda's blood, or anyone else's. We can all be free." He met my eyes, and his dark gaze was so intense I had to look away.

Wind howled outside, and even though the windows were closed, a wave of cold pushed against me.

"I'm sorry." Perseus buried his hands in his jeans pockets. I wasn't sure *I* was sorry. Did I really regret erasing my memories? I looked at Crater, who stood still on the table. I remembered my cruel behavior in my most recent memories—I had changed and I would never regret becoming a better version of myself. Or at least I believed I had improved. "I never should have pushed you to erase your memories," Perseus said. "This is all my fault."

"How could this be your fault?" I said. "My plan was stupid."

"No," he said. "I was more stupid."

I smiled. Perseus smiled for a second, but then dropped it. He licked his dry lips, pulled his hands out of his pockets, and hugged me. For a brief second, the shock froze me. Then I hugged him back. How long had Perseus and I known each other?

Perseus pulled back. He patted me on the shoulder. "I'm the one who pushed you toward doing what you did." He shook his head. "I didn't do it on purpose. I was just trying to protect you."

"I know," I said. "I just felt . . ." I couldn't meet his gaze so I looked down at my muddy shoes. "I just wanted to feel as strong and brave as the rest of you. I wanted *you* to see I was just as strong as the rest of you." I bit my tongue for a second. "I wanted to become strong so I wouldn't ever let you down again."

Perseus's face softened. "You never let us down. But I was stupid enough not to realize that's how you felt."

"I should have just talked to you about it," I said as I looked up. "It was stupid of me to leave like that."

Perseus chuckled. "That would have saved us a lot of hassle."

"I don't know why you think I was braver than you," Perseus continued. "If anything, I have always been reckless. You have a cooler head, which allows you to actually think before you act, and your lies have saved us from so many more situations than I ever have." He shook his head sadly. "All Algol has done is put us in danger." He looked back up at me with a half smile. "You lied so many times to keep us hidden from other Star Children, and you lied so many times to humans so we could survive."

"I don't remember any of that," I said.

"You're the one that convinced Andrew Wood to adopt us all. Before that we used to live on the streets. You always convinced waiters at restaurants to give us free food, and we always managed to get free clothes and free stays at hotels." He looked out the window, his gaze distant. "One time, you convinced the manager at a kids' store to give us each a free Lego set." He laughed. "I don't remember whatever happened to those Legos but we had a blast building them in the hotel suite you lied to get us into."

I smiled. I truly didn't remember anything about that. A soft humming vibrated on the surface of my skin. I looked at Crater. Was I willing to lose the Cup's power to remember who I had been?

"There was another time," Perseus said laughing. "When you accidentally walked into a girls' restroom at the mall and they nearly kicked your ass, so you lied to them to make them think you were a girl too."

Laughter burst from me. It quieted down after a couple of seconds as guilt tore at my chest. How could I be here, laughing with Perseus, when I had left my friends trapped in a museum? My heart throbbed with each beat. What would they do now? They had survived without my help for years before they had found me. But the simple thought of not being with them made me feel like I had carved a void inside my chest.

I looked back at Perseus. He was smiling, but I knew he didn't fully trust me. My relationship with him and the Pleiades would not be the same. After what I had done to my friends, I knew they wouldn't want to see me again. I felt that I didn't belong anywhere anymore.

"Will you stay?" Perseus asked, pulling me out of my thoughts.

"I—yes." I had nowhere else to go.

Perseus smiled. "Good." He bit his lower lip. "I think I should show you your Prophecies. I don't have all of them here but"—he motioned toward the door—"you should know your end."

My heart sprinted. I told myself that whatever my Prophecies were, I could accept them. I took a deep breath as we left the room. I could face whatever the future had planned for me.

CHAPTER 21

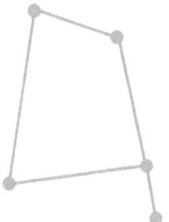

"WHAT?" I shot up from the chair, making it tumble behind me.

I looked down at the white sheet of paper on the table. My hands went numb, and I felt so dizzy that I had to grip the edge of the table. I wanted to believe that the words Perseus had written down on that sheet of paper were false. I wanted to believe that he had only written that to manipulate me. But deep down, I knew it was true—every single word was true. Prophecies were always open to different interpretations, but this one was very clear.

"I will turn into a white raven and kill Virgo?" Horror sank into my heart like monstrous claws digging into flesh.

Perseus had both of his palms on the table, but as soon as I turned to him, he curled them into fists. He nodded slowly. I could have dealt with death or with some horrible injury. I didn't care that much if I was prophesized to die, as long as I knew how I would die. But becoming a raven, driven by greed and cruelty, attacking other Star Children out of spite—killing Virgo because I didn't remember her . . . that was something I couldn't face.

My heartbeat boomed in my ears, drowning out everything else around me. My lungs began contracting, folding into themselves. That was my future, my irrevocable future. Either Perseus, my brother, killed me with Algol, or I would turn into a raven and kill my best friend—those were my only two options. I shook my head.

"So that's it?" I asked. "I will turn into a raven, forget everything, and try to kill other Star Children." My breath rushed out of my lungs. "Kill Virgo."

"And poke people's eyes out if they lie," Perseus said.

"What?" I managed weakly.

"That last line," Perseus said, motioning at the Prophecy. "I'm not sure how to interpret that. Either you become a raven that pokes out the eyes of people who lie, cheat, and betray, or your own eyes get poked out and you remain blind. I'm not sure which interpretation is the correct one."

I stared at the last line, but I may as well have been reading ancient Egyptian hieroglyphs, because the words didn't register in my brain. I shook my head again.

"There has to be another way." I looked up at my brother in desperation.

"There is," Perseus said. "We destroy Fate, Destiny, and Prophecy."

"But . . ."

I fixed my eyes on the paper. The words began floating around, incomprehensible. I closed my eyes. I couldn't face that future, but was destroying Order in the Universe truly worth it? I had the chance to live the life I chose—to save Virgo and to remain as I was, but at what cost? I opened my eyes again, the room swaying around me.

"You don't have to decide anything now," Perseus said, clearly noting my distress. "At the moment we have more important things to deal with."

"The Lost Star Child." I had momentarily forgotten about that.

"That's our priority right now." Perseus folded his arms across his chest.

"It's Typhon. Isn't it?" My hands trembled as I held the paper.

He raised a surprised brow. "How did you figure that out?"

"I didn't." I felt my breath come short. "Virgo did."

Even pronouncing her name made my throat contract. I couldn't bear the thought that I would be the one who killed her. She had nursed me when I had been in the hospital, had sung me to sleep, and had saved me from Hydra—and that's how I would repay her?

"Virgo has always been smart," Perseus muttered. "You can save her, Corvus." Our gazes locked. "You can help me destroy the Prophecies that have doomed her—the Prophecies that have doomed us all. Draco, the Twins, Sirius, Leo . . . they have terrible ends too. We can save everyone if we work together." His gaze softened. "That's what Darren would have liked. He would have wanted us to do everything we could to stay alive and live a good life."

I bit my tongue so hard the taste of iron filled my mouth. I swallowed the blood, my tongue throbbing.

"And how does Typhon play a role in this?" I asked. "How much do you know about him?"

"I know enough. He's the most powerful and destructive of all Monsters. He's not only a beast, he's also a divinity." Perseus leaned back on the chair.

"Yes, I knew that already."

"His Constellation became extinct long ago," Perseus said. He looked at the wooden table, as if he was reading the information off of it. "He allied with Darkness, so the other Stars destroyed him."

"How can an entire Constellation be destroyed?" I asked.

Perseus's face hardened. "The Stars used Darkness." I tried to wrap my head around that concept. "Stars only shine because there's Darkness around them. Without Darkness, there is no Light. Stars have been using Darkness to control our Destinies, and they are using Darkness against each other."

It took me a couple of seconds to process what he was saying. "The Stars are at war?"

Perseus nodded. *"As above, so below.* What happens here on Earth mimics what happens in the Heavens. The Star Children are at war because the Stars themselves are fighting, and have been doing so for millennia."

"How?"

Perseus waved his hand dismissively. "This fight has always existed. You know the Constellation myths. The Stars have been at war since the beginning of time."

"But how does it affect *us?*"

"We're not completely sure," Perseus admitted. "I don't even think the Stars created us on purpose. Their influence is so strong that a part of the Stars, of the Constellations, created us spontaneously in this world." It was strange to think that we had all been made accidentally. I knew that as Star Children we were not influenced by the direct power of the Stars, that's why none of us had Destiny or Fate. But we still had Prophecies that tied us to certain futures, even if the Stars didn't directly control those futures. I wondered if they knew that Perseus planned to eradicate their power. Was there anything Stars could do to stop him? Perseus leaned forward. "What I know is that the Stars are in conflict with each other. They are using Darkness to fight, to become more powerful."

"Like you," I whispered.

He shrugged. "I've made my choices. I made the choice to awaken Algol to save you from Cetus. I made the choice not to kill Andromeda and let Algol grow inside of me. I'm willing to pay the price for my choices."

I felt that last sentence as an accusation. Perseus was willing to live with the consequences of his actions. Was *I* willing to pay the price for the choices I had made?

I took a deep breath. "What exactly do you plan on doing with Typhon?"

Perseus traced his fingers over the table. "If there is any Star Child that truly hates the Stars, it's Typhon. They destroyed his Constellation."

"You want to form an alliance with Typhon?" My lips felt numb.

I had assumed that Perseus would want to destroy him, but he was obviously smarter than that.

"Typhon's Prophecies say he is the only one who can help us achieve victory." Perseus's black eyes gleamed. "Or he will be killed by the Hunter."

"Orion?" I asked.

Perseus nodded. "That's Typhon's Prophecy. He will help the Prince, me, slay Light, or something like that. Or perish by the Hunter's Arrow."

"So he either helps you or dies?" I asked.

"Or both," Perseus said. "Remember that the Prophecies of the Star Children speak of possibilities in our future. One of those possibilities could come true, or all of them could. It depends on what we choose to do."

"If you don't plan on killing Typhon, then why do you need Crater?"

"When Cepheus captured Typhon, he wounded him badly." Perseus absently cracked his knuckles. "Typhon is dying, and we don't have a lot of time left." His eyes met mine. "The only way to save him is using Crater. It's the only object powerful enough to heal him."

"This is insane," I said.

Perseus smiled. "It is, and I need your help." I clenched my jaw hard. "I know you still don't remember everything, and that this seems crazy." Perseus leaned forward. "Don't do it for me, do it for your friends. Typhon will help us destroy the power of the Prophecies and will free us from our futures. You won't have to turn into a raven, and you won't have to kill Virgo. And Algol won't have to kill all of us."

My teeth strained against each other. "How do you even know that Typhon will help you?"

"He isn't prophesized to kill any of us." The way Perseus said that made me think that Typhon was prophesized to kill someone, but not us. "It is prophesized that you will revive him and that he will help us destroy the power of the Stars." Perseus set his hands on the table again.

Silence settled in the room like dust after a storm. Perseus's gaze never left me. I was his brother, but I knew that I was also a potential obstacle to him. We both knew I would never go back to who I had been, and I didn't know what Perseus would do about that.

"Can I see that Prophecy?" I asked. "And all of my other Prophecies?"

"I don't have them with me right now," he responded simply.

I met his gaze—those cunning black eyes. I didn't think it was a coincidence that he had shown me the one Prophecy he knew would convince me to help him. It was a very subtle manipulation, keeping my other Prophecies—my other possible outcomes—from me. He was in control of my future, and unless I fully committed to helping him, he wouldn't let me regain control.

"We need to go to Dodona," Perseus said after a few seconds.

"Why Dodona?"

"Well, it's the oldest Hellenic oracle in Greece," Perseus said. I could feel a history lesson coming on. "It used to be a shrine to the Mother Goddess, Gaia. Back then, it was a sanctuary of healing, and the leaves were the ones who spoke the Prophecies, not the priestesses. The trees were said to have been seeded by the Stars themselves." I could see the excitement in Perseus's eyes, although I didn't know how Stars could seed trees. "Our powers are amplified at Dodona. When we manifest things there, we don't consume ourselves at all. If we want to heal Typhon with Crater, then that's the best place to do it, or else using Crater could be lethal for you."

I now understood why I had erased my memories there. I had known how much energy, how much Light, it would cost to lie to myself. But at Dodona, my power wouldn't consume me.

I nodded. "So we're going back to Greece?"

Perseus smiled. "The girls are already there. They want to see you again. Pegasus and Lupus are also there. They went ahead to make sure no other Star Child was there and to kick out tourists wanting to visit."

The blood in my veins ran like syrup. I would see my sisters again. Shame stained my cheeks with heat. I had lied to Merope, I had abandoned all of them, and I didn't remember what half of them looked like.

"Do they hate me?" I asked.

Perseus's eyes widened in surprise. "Why would they?"

I shrugged. "I left them."

Perseus's shoulders sagged, and his gaze dropped to the table again. "They feel as guilty as I do. They know why you left." That made me feel better, lighter somehow. "You told Draco and Virgo about them, didn't you?" His tone wasn't angry, but the question was still an accusation.

I nodded slowly. I had fought so hard to keep them a secret. They couldn't hide anymore. Perseus didn't respond, and there was no way to know how he felt from his neutral expression.

"I know you're still hesitant about helping me," Perseus said. "But please just think about our family. Everything we have done is to keep each other safe. We couldn't save Darren, but now we have the chance to save ourselves." My heart twisted in pain. "If you heal Typhon, you're one step closer to saving Virgo and escaping our Prophecies."

I bit down on my tongue. I assumed Virgo hated me now that I had betrayed her, but I owed her so much, and if healing Typhon was the way I could save her, then I was willing to help Perseus. My heart pounded painfully as I thought of Darren too. I still didn't remember much about him, but the gaping hole inside of my chest was there. Is this what he would have wanted? Would he have thought that destroying Destiny, Fate, and Prophecy was worth so much death and destruction?

"Please, Corvus," Perseus said. "We can't do this without you."

"Fine," I finally responded. "Let's go to Dodona."

Perseus smiled.

I didn't know if I had made the right choice, but knowing I could save Virgo made me feel strangely calm.

•———•———•

I stood outside Perseus's room, my ear pressed against the door. Perseus was grunting, as if trying to suppress pain. A few seconds later, he sighed with relief.

I pushed the door open and clicked on the light switch. Perseus jumped from the rug, facing me with his hands balled into fists. His room was clean, as always. Even his ancient history books on his desk were stacked neatly. His open curtains revealed the terrace door that let a lazy breeze the house. I didn't see Arianna, but I knew Perseus must have met her outside before she left like a gust of wind.

"Do you need something?" Perseus asked, a bit harshly.

I walked over to him, and Perseus took a step back, as if I had caught him taking drugs. I wished I'd had—this was a lot worse.

I held Perseus's arms. His biceps were thicker, he was becoming stronger.

"How much did you take?" I asked. Perseus pressed his lips together. "How much Darkness did you absorb?"

I looked into his eyes for an answer, then yelped. I jumped back, my heart racing in fear. His eyes—they were black. I shook my head, hoping my vision was faltering. But it wasn't. Perseus's eyes had turned black.

"You—why would you take so much?" I demanded.

Perseus took another step backward, his back hunched as if he couldn't bear the weight of Darkness. I stepped forward again and held Perseus's face. I stared into his eyes. They were black. Not dark brown, but entirely black. They had been beautiful—green at the center and surrounded by pale blue. But now the beauty was gone. He hadn't just consumed more Darkness—it had taken over him. I pulled away and shook my head. I was losing him. Slowly and steadily, I was losing Perseus to Algol's growing power.

"It's still me," *Perseus said. Sometimes I wondered if he could read my thoughts or if my facial expressions were so telling.*

"It's not," I said. "You know it's not."

"Yes, it is!" Perseus shouted.

"You need to stop before—" I was going to say "before it's too late," but it was already too late. It had been years since Cetus's attack. Ever since, Perseus had consumed Darkness little by little, as if it was a thirst he couldn't satiate.

"You wouldn't understand," Perseus whispered.

"I don't understand. All I know is that the more you drink the more we lose you."

Perseus gave a choked laugh. A tear fell from his eye. At least the tear was still clear and not black too.

"I can't stop." He fell to his knees.

"I can see that," I muttered.

Perseus took in ragged breaths, and I wondered if he was having a panic attack. He looked up at me, his eyes pleading. "I'm scared."

I felt like he had twisted a knife into my heart. Perseus had never said he was scared. I knelt next to him as he hugged himself.

"The thirst is so bad," he said. "Not even Arianna knows how to stop this. I don't think she even knew how much this would affect me." He breathed hard, as if the air were full of dust and clogging his lungs. "My thirst is getting more powerful, and every time I drink, Algol grows stronger. I want to stop. I do. But I can't." Another tear fell from his eye. It slid down his cheek and dropped to the carpet. He stared into my eyes. His own were dark pools, as if I were looking at the night sky stripped bare of the stars and moon. "I'm losing control of Algol," he whispered. "I'm scared it will kill all of you, just as Arianna says it will."

I shook my head so hard that my neck hurt. "No." I hesitantly placed a hand on his shoulder. "We'll stop Algol." Perseus nodded, but I could see the fear making his lips tremble. "We will shatter the power of the Stars, and Algol won't have any more control over you."

Perseus nodded again. I couldn't be mad at him. Maybe I was mad at myself. Perseus had single-handedly driven away Cetus while I bled in the ocean. He had saved my life, and it may have cost him his own.

"You won't lose control," I said as I squeezed his shoulder. "If there is anyone strong enough to bear the weight of Algol, it's you."

Perseus looked down at the rug. "You've always been the strongest and the smartest. We will destroy Algol, but until then you'll hold on."

Perseus wiped his wet cheek. He nodded, a new determination flooding into his dark eyes.

"Thank you," he whispered.

"For what?" My words would solve nothing.

"You've always supported me, no matter how monstrous I become."

"You're not monstrous." My voice faltered.

Perseus chuckled. "I killed that man in the car because I was annoyed he was driving so slow. His car crashed and he died."

"That wasn't on purpose," I said gently.

"I electrocuted the man on the ladder fixing the electricity in the building," he said. "I wasn't even thinking about him. I was angry because Miss Lacey gave me a D on the math test, and that poor man was just too close to me."

"That was also an accident."

Perseus nodded, unconvinced. He didn't mention the dozen other "accidents" that had occurred to the people around us as a consequence of Algol. He had never hurt us, but I could see why he was so afraid—he hadn't hurt us yet. He would keep losing control, and before we knew it, Algol would become bloodier and more violent— riots, bombings, massacres, genocides, terrorist attacks, maybe even earthquakes. The Demon Star wouldn't stop.

"I'm a monster," Perseus whispered. More tears spilled from his eyes.

"You're not."

"Then what am I?"

"You're my brother."

Tears spilled from his eyes like an exploding faucet. Perseus buried his head on my shoulder and cried. I hugged him, knowing there was nothing else I could do. The girls were out shopping with Mom, and I was sure Perseus didn't want them to see him crying.

"What's going on here?" Dad asked behind us.

Perseus and I jumped to our feet. Dad stood at the edge of the door, staring at us as if we were strangers to him. His dark hair had wisps of white at the sides, and his brown eyes stared suspiciously at us.

"Nothing," Perseus said. His voice was broken.

Dad raised a brow and walked forward. He opened his mouth to say something, then stopped as if we'd given him an electric shock. "What happened to your eyes?" he asked Perseus.

"They've always been black." My voice rang inside my ears.

Dad's gaze went blank for a second. "Oh, right."

"Nothing happened here," I continued. "We were just . . . playing cards."

Dad nodded. "That sounds fun." He sighed. "I was going to ask if you guys wanted Italian or Japanese for dinner."

"Japanese," I said.

"That's fine with me," Perseus said.

"Okay." Dad walked out of the room calmly. "Hey, Lupus," he said to the Wolf, as if Lupus were just an average-sized husky dog.

The giant Wolf walked into the room after Dad left. He was as tall as Perseus, and his fur had always reminded me of thundering grey clouds. His silver eyes traced Perseus with worry.

"I'm all right," Perseus said. Lupus was smart enough not to believe that. He let out a growl. "I really am."

Lupus growled again, and his ears pricked up. He sat between Perseus's bed and the desk.

Perseus sniffed. He wiped his tears away. Our gazes met again. Fear curled into a knot inside my chest. I wouldn't admit it to him, but I was afraid of his Darkness. Even if Perseus didn't mean to, he could very easily kill us.

"You won't lose control," I said again, and Perseus nodded, this time with more determination. "We will destroy the power that the Stars hold over us. We will build our own future." Perseus smiled, and behind me Lupus gave a low growl of agreement. "Destiny, Fate, and Prophecy will shatter to pieces. We will be free."

Chapter XXVIII, Verse I

They are the Seven Sisters of the Stars, mothers of the ancestors of Mankind.

Together with the Bull they arrived, but their paths shall be cut apart.

With wings like birds the Seven Sisters fly, with the powers of water and ice.

Chased by the Hunter they will be, until by revenge they seek him.

But first another battle to fight, one that they should have fought only once.

In the Sea the Monster awaits them, before with the Bull they reunite.

Twice to fight the Monster of the Sea, and dead or alive they may fly down.

CHAPTER 22

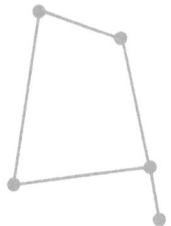

"WE'RE ALMOST THERE," Perseus said next to me.

I woke up groggy, pulling my head away from the cold window and realizing I had fallen asleep in the car.

Crater hummed inside my jacket, its warmth heating my chest.

"Be careful," the Cup said in its strange voice.

I'm not remembering things on purpose, I protested.

"The more you fill the less of my power you can use."

I know.

Hopefully I wouldn't have to use its power much. I placed my head in between my hands. Was I really going to heal *Typhon*?

Perseus's gaze was set on the road. He looked at least a few years older than he had in my memory, his face sharper, his body stronger, his eyes darker. Why had I recovered that particular memory? I couldn't place this one in my timeline like I could with other memories. Most of the memories I had recovered were one year before I'd erased them, but this one felt older. I wondered how many more memories I would recover and what I would do with Crater after I started to become fuller.

I took a deep breath and looked out the window. We had taken a private jet from London, flown to Greece, and were now driving on a single-lane road toward the Oracle of Dodona.

Trees lined the sides of the road, but something was off about them. They were about ten feet tall, and they had so many branches with leaves that they looked like giant shrubs. Around the trees, green and brown vines covered the ground entirely. Some of the vines had white flowers, but they were withered like crumpled tissue paper. The vines became intertwined with the branches of the trees as we continued forward. After a while, the trees and vines and plants became densely packed together. If anyone wanted to cross through them, they certainly wouldn't come out of there unscratched.

Thunder rattled above us, and a few seconds later rain dripped from the sky. The rain was gentle at first, but less than a minute later it seemed like a waterfall was cascading over us. We slowed down as the windshield wipers furiously batted away the rain. I gripped the seat belt. The rain reminded me too much of what had happened in Egypt. Perseus hadn't said anything about the disaster we had caused, even though I was sure he must have heard about it. I also hadn't watched the news. I couldn't afford to feel guilty about that right now, knowing we had harmed people even if we hadn't meant to do it. I didn't want to think of my friends either.

Perseus turned right. To the left the rain battered down onto a bright green field. On the other side were a few small brick houses. Behind them rose a large mountain, its peak shrouded by low clouds. Lightning struck the side of the mountain, and the sound of thunder washed over us a second later. I remembered that the Oracle of Delphi was on a huge mountain, and I wondered why the most powerful oracles were connected to large mountains—either built into the mountain or very close to one.

"Almost there," Perseus muttered. After a moment of silence, he spoke again. "What did you remember about me?"

"What do you mean?"

Perseus didn't meet my gaze, instead keeping his eyes fixed on the road. "You remembered something in that museum. You remembered me. What memory did you recover?"

"Cetus," I paused. "And a few other fragments of random stuff."

. . . *"Come on," Perseus said with a laugh as Maia climbed onto his back for a piggy-back ride . . .*

. . . *"That's you right over there!" Perseus pointed at my Constellation, and my heart sped up . . .*

. . . *"Looks like someone has a crush," I teased Perseus as we walked down the school hallway, his cheeks flushing red after talking to Elle . . .*

. . . *"The girls are going to be so mad at us for eating all of it," Perseus said. I shrugged as I took another spoonful of ice cream . . .*

"The Monster will be back," Perseus said. "He's prophesized to hunt us down. Well, he's prophesized to hunt the *Young Ones.* That's us, the new generation of Star Children."

"He's already back," I muttered. "He was in the Mediterranean, after we left Italy." Perseus's grip tightened on the wheel, his knuckles white. "What else is Cetus prophesized to do?"

"He—like I said, he'll hunt us down. Our sisters are prophesized to fight him again, and he may kill them." He paused. "He's after every Star Child born in our generation."

That meant the Monster was after Perseus, the Pleiades, the Twins, Draco, Virgo, Andromeda, and Orion. In Cetus's myth, the Monster had been after Andromeda specifically. Maybe, when we faced Cetus again, Andromeda would be there too.

"How can we defeat it?" I asked as dread clutched my heart.

Perseus shook his head. "It doesn't matter. That's a problem for another day."

Ahead of us, ruins began to dot the landscape. The two-feet-tall stone fences were barely visible below the grass at the side of the street. Thick moss and vines covered them almost completely.

Perseus stopped the car abruptly in the middle of the road.

"What is it?" A dozen scenarios raced through my mind. My friends had found us and Leo would tumble the car over. Maybe Argo had turned into a truck and the Twins would run us over. Or Aquila would attack us with lightning. Or Draco would set our car on fire.

"I drove onto the wrong road." Perseus began backing up. I let out a breath I didn't realize I was holding. "Thought the entrance was on this road, but it's not."

Perseus turned the car around and drove back the way we had come. Since it was a single-lane road, I wasn't sure we were allowed to do that, but I had seen no cars around us so I guessed it was probably fine.

"Why did you send us to get the Cup?" I asked. "And why would you tell the Twins to take it back to you if you knew I was the only one who could hold it?"

Perseus tensed, his jaw twitching. Even though we had been together for almost a day and had talked at length about many things, I still hadn't asked about that. I realized why as Perseus's gaze darkened—we had both been avoiding this conversation because we knew how much it would hurt.

Perseus didn't look at me. "I was hoping that by the time you recovered Crater you would have remembered me. But that didn't happen." He sighed. "I knew the Twins would figure out that you were the only one who could hold Crater, so they would also bring you to me." Perseus's grip tightened on the wheel. "I also knew it would be hard for you to leave your friends after you remembered me, so I thought it might be better if the Twins just kidnapped you."

I hated how his plan made sense. At least it would have made sense if I had recovered my memories and Perseus would have taken off the weight of having to leave my friends, as I did at the museum.

"But I didn't remember," I said. "So you just let me go."

"I would never force you to stay with me," Perseus said.

I gulped down my fury, trying to hide it from my voice. "You let me live a lie for well over a year."

"A lie *you* created, Corvus."

My heart throbbed painfully, as if it had barbed wire tied around it. I didn't want to feel that pain. I didn't want to confront Perseus about this.

"You let me live in that lie because you knew it would take me to the Cup and to the Lost Star Child," I said. "I know you care about me, Perseus, but this was part of your plan. You would rather risk losing me than losing Crater or Typhon."

The car sped up a bit, although I couldn't tell if Perseus did it on purpose. The rain seemed to pour down louder, as if trying to mute us both. My heart bled with pain as I realized the truth that my words held. Perseus cared about me, but he cared more about his plans. He had used me as a pawn in his game to get what he wanted, and he couldn't deny that.

"I'm not sorry about that." His tone was like ice. "You made your own plans without me, you risked everything you cared about to get to that Cup." I bit down on my tongue. "I just played that to our advantage."

He was right. Why did anger boil in my stomach when I realized he was right? The answer came to me then. I was no better than Perseus. I had used my friends as pawns in my own games without realizing it, and I had hurt them. I had hurt them beyond redemption. Everything that had happened in the last few days had not been Perseus's master plan as I had thought. This had all been *my* plan, and Perseus had just played along. Perseus might not have been my blood brother, and physically we were nothing alike. But we both shared an important trait—I was just as ruthless as him at getting what I wanted. I breathed deeply for a few seconds, trying to ignore the knot tied in my throat.

"You knew we would find the Lost Star Child," I said. "When you let us go, you knew what we would do next."

"I actually didn't think you would find Typhon so fast," Perseus said, and he genuinely sounded surprised. "I expected you to recover your memories soon and knew you would try to find me then. My plan was to find the Lost Star Child together. We knew it was somewhere in London, based on a couple of things you said before leaving. So I had planned to stay there while the girls went to Dodona." Perseus smiled. "I didn't expect you and the others to find Typhon so quickly or for you to come back last night."

"I see." The fact that I had surprised Perseus gave me an odd sense of achievement. But that feeling evaporated quickly. Perseus had left the main gate and the front door of the house open last night. He had been expecting me. He just wasn't willing to admit that. I turned back to look at him, his eyes fixed ahead. It didn't matter that I was back at his side—Perseus was still playing with me. He was still hiding key information from me, and once again, I didn't know where his game would take us.

The car slowed down but didn't stop. I had the feeling we were a bit lost but Perseus didn't want to say it. It would have been good to have a GPS, but the one in the car hadn't worked and neither of us had phones.

"How did you get to London?" Perseus asked after a while. "You woke up in Dodona but then somehow got to London where I—where the attack was."

"I have no idea," I admitted. "What were *you* doing in London?"

"Looking for you," his tone was flat. "London was the last place you visited before you started acting weird, so I thought you might have gone back there, and then Algol just got out of my control that day. After the attack I fled the city."

I still had many gaps in my memories, but at the moment I wasn't very worried about filling them in. The car slowed down after a few minutes as Perseus drove onto a small sideroad that had a few empty parking spaces next to a one-story-tall white structure. It didn't look like a house. It had some bathroom signs so I guessed it was probably just that.

Perseus stopped the car. Two girls came out of the building and stopped a few yards away from the car. My heartbeat pulsed in my fingers. Perseus smiled. Those had to be our sisters.

I swallowed hard.

"It's all right, Corvus," Perseus said.

"I don't remember them," I whispered, barely able to speak.

"It's all right. They remember you."

He got out of the car. I took a deep breath and stepped outside. I had expected a curtain of rain to drench me, but it seemed as if a giant, invisible umbrella was shielding us because the rain didn't touch me. It was still cold though, but my knitted sweater gave me warmth. My breaths created small clouds of mist as I exhaled.

"You've grown taller."

I jumped, turning around. Maia stood facing me. Her hair was longer than in my recovered memory, but still the same fiery red as it had been before. Her face was long with a couple of freckles on her nose. Her forest green eyes seemed to shine slightly. I realized Maia could have passed as Perseus's biological sister.

Another girl peeked from behind her and stared me up and down. "Definitely taller." The girl's skin was dark brown. Her face was heart shaped, her nose straight and small. When she saw me, her lips parted into a wide smile with perfect white teeth. Her long black hair was braided behind her back, flowing down to her waist. The girl's eyes were dark brown, but just like Maia's they seemed to glow. I didn't remember who she was but could feel a tug inside my mind, as if her name was just beyond my reach.

Even though both girls insisted I had grown, they were still a few inches taller than me. They each wore combat boots, black pants, and a thick jacket, as if they were ready to go on a hike on the mountain.

Perseus walked around the car to stand next to me.

"Hi" was all that came out of my mouth.

Both of the girls smiled wider.

"That's the same thing you said the first time you met us," the dark-skinned girl said. Her smile faded, and she regarded me sadly, as if I were a dead corpse they had fished from the river. "I'm Asterope."

"I'm Maia," the red-haired girl said.

I smiled. My chest felt warmer, as if my heart fondly remembered those names. Maia and Asterope stepped forward hesitantly, as if not sure of what to do next. I opened my arms wide and embraced both girls. They hugged me back with surprising strength.

"I love you," Asterope whispered, so low I almost didn't hear her.

I pretended I hadn't heard that because I didn't know how to respond. I had loved them, I knew that. But I didn't completely feel that now. How could I love someone I didn't remember? I pulled back, and they did the same. Asterope's eyes glistened with tears, but Maia's gaze was cold as a forest in winter.

We stared at each other for an awkward second.

Perseus stepped forward. "We should get going."

I nodded, glad to be out of that parking lot.

"Nice work with the rain," Perseus said as he looked up at the sky.

"You did this?" I asked.

"Yeah," Maia said. She turned to Perseus. "We weren't expecting you here so soon."

Perseus shrugged. "Better to get this over with sooner than later."

Asterope nodded. She began walking away from the car, explaining a couple of things they had noticed from the ruins.

"It looks like symbols on the walls," Asterope said as we walked past the white building. "But the rock is so eroded we weren't sure."

Perseus walked beside Asterope, talking excitedly as he asked what the symbols had looked like. Maia walked next to me, her hands buried in her pockets.

"So where exactly are we going?" I asked.

"To the grove of trees," Maia said as she looked ahead. "So you won't get to see the ruins."

I hadn't been particularly excited to see them. I wondered if the grove of trees would make me unlock another memory, just as Argo had been doing. I was scared that would happen. I didn't want to lose my connection with Crater. I hadn't used the Cup yet, but just having it made me feel stronger.

"Do you really think healing Typhon is a good idea?"

Maia winced, then pressed her lips tightly. "Yes," she said after a couple of seconds. "He will help us escape our Prophecies." Her eyes met mine. "We deserve to rule over our own lives. I refuse to accept the futures that were chosen for us."

I nodded.

Maia let out a long breath, mist gathering around her lips. "I know you don't remember much, Corvus. But we really need your

help right now. We won't be able to stop Algol without Typhon."
Her eyes glistened, like wet leaves after a heavy rain. "We'll die if
you don't heal him."

"I won't let you die."

I had let my sisters down too many times—when I had failed
to kill Cetus, when I had left them without a trace. I couldn't fail
them again. Typhon still terrified me, but if my sisters were convinced that Typhon could help us defeat Algol, then I needed to
help him.

"I know you won't," Maia whispered.

I looked up at the grey, misty sky. It seemed like the rain
hadn't touched Dodona at all, and instead it just rained everywhere around the oracular site. Perseus had said that the girls had
worked to keep tourists out. I guessed that heavy rain was good
enough to keep everyone from coming to see some outdoor stone
ruins and old trees.

The scenery around me didn't seem so remarkable, at least
not for a place with so much power. We walked over patches of
green and yellow grass and some vines that grew white flowers.
Oak trees randomly dotted the landscape. In the distance, five
hundred yards to the right, was a steep mountain slightly blurred
by the heavy rain. Maia, however, was looking to the left, about
three hundred yards away, where a dense spot of trees extended as
far back as I could see until it met faraway hills.

"Why weren't you girls helping Perseus at Palatine Hill?" I
asked.

"We were at the Vatican to steal the first part Alathea's book,"
she said. "We knew that the perfect moment to steal it would be
when the entire city of Rome was in chaos. So we took that op-
portunity."

"That must have been quite an adventure," I said.

Maia smiled as she turned to me. "It was. We thought it would be easy—get inside, find the forbidden library, steal the book, get out."

"I'm guessing it didn't go as planned." I placed my cold hands in my coat pockets.

"It did not," Maia said with a chuckle. "We'll tell you all about it later."

She said those words easily, as if "later" meant when we were back home for the night, sipping hot chocolate as we sat around a fire. Maia pulled one of her hands from her pockets, swung her arm around me, and let her arm rest across my shoulders. She had probably done that hundreds of times before, but this time it felt strange.

"I missed you," she said.

I wasn't sure how to answer. I hadn't missed her because I hadn't known she existed until a couple of days ago, so I couldn't lie and say I had missed her too. We passed by a few ruins on our right. They were just slabs of stones scattered on the ground. I could imagine that some of the stones lined together might have been a wall once, or maybe pillars. The dark stones were so badly eroded they looked bloated and disfigured.

"Did you try to look for me?" I asked. "Once I left."

Maia squeezed my shoulder. "We looked like crazy. We didn't find you until a few months later. The Gemini Twins told Perseus about Draco, Virgo, and you working together." She bit her lip, as if unsure of how to continue. "At first, we wanted to go get you, but we knew it wouldn't be that easy. Your friends are very powerful, and since you didn't remember us, we didn't know if you would believe us."

"Did you plan on waiting until my memories returned so I would find you again?"

"Something like that." Maia looked at some scattered stones on our right. "We'd figured out that you'd had a plan before erasing your memories." That last part stung. Maia said it very gently, but that's what made it hurt. She, and all the others, knew I had gone off on my own on a foolish plan. I felt stupid. "Perseus thought that maybe leaving you to it would be a good idea. Then once we found the Prophecies, the first thing we did was piece yours together." She sighed. "We fully understood what you had done once we read them."

I should have told them what my plan was, even if I planned on doing it alone. I could have left a note or something. Maybe I had been too afraid that once they found the note, they would try to stop me.

"I was an idiot." I sighed.

Maia squeezed my shoulder again. "You weren't." She smiled down at me, her curls covering half of her face. "We shouldn't have treated you like a baby, like you couldn't handle the same things we did."

"I just wanted to be able to protect you, like I should have done with Cetus," I said. "I failed Darren." My throat contracted. "I didn't want to fail you too."

"You didn't fail him, Corvus," Maia said. "You did the best you could, and sometimes in life that has to be enough."

I barely managed to swallow. Hadn't Pollux told me something similar a couple of nights ago?

"How did we meet Darren?" I asked.

Maia eyed me for a second with her intense green gaze. "You materialized in Latin America, in Brazil. That's where you were 'born.' Darren found you. You'd known him all your life."

I felt as if Maia had twisted a blade in my gut. I didn't even remember his face. The grief of his loss was a void in my heart, but it was like a hollow shell—present but empty. How could I mourn someone I didn't even remember? I hoped I found a picture of him soon—he deserved to be remembered.

Maia squeezed my shoulder again as we neared the grove of trees. I could see five more people standing at the edge. I knew even from afar that they were my sisters.

CHAPTER 23

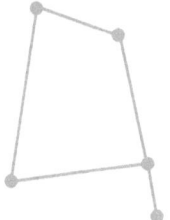

AS WE WALKED CLOSER to them and the grove of trees, I realized how different the Pleiades were from each other. The only thing all the girls had in common was their towering height.

On the leftmost side stood a girl with loose blond hair. She wore a lot of makeup, and she had neon pink clothes that I was sure weren't effective camouflage. Her cheeks were flushed on her round face. As we got closer, I could make out her facial features better. Her thin eyebrows accentuated her big chestnut eyes.

"That's Alcyone," Maia said. "But she sometimes uses the name Rose too."

Next to her stood a girl with shiny coffee brown hair, which was tied in a high pony tail. Her skin was the color of honey. Her cat-like face had arched eyebrows and a short forehead. She had a button nose, and her jewel-like eyes shone like bright copper.

"That's Taygete," Maia said as we moved closer to them. "And next to her is Electra."

Electra had snow-white hair, which fell to her elbows in smooth waves. Then my gaze shifted to her startling eyes—they were a soft purple. Her skin was like carved ivory. Her nose was straight in her elongated face with angular cheekbones. She had a large forehead and thick eyebrows.

"Next to her are Celaeno and Merope," Maia whispered. We were now mere feet away from them.

I had seen Celaeno in my memories. She had been with me before I met the Twins. She had a narrow face with high cheekbones and golden skin. She had her dark hair tied in two braids at the sides of her head. Her eyes sparkled like silver.

I felt a pang of guilt as I looked at Merope. I had lied to her, and she probably didn't remember a thing about that. I swallowed my guilt—I would deal with that later. Her ebony hair flowed down her head in loose curls. Her face was oval and thin, her nose straight and her cheeks a bit sunken. Her eyes shone like two polished sapphires. She looked a bit like Andromeda, but with long hair, and she didn't have that aggressive, distrustful, and cold look that always flashed in Andromeda's eyes.

We stopped in front of the girls, who were all looking at me. I couldn't tear my eyes away from them. Their skin all seemed to have an unnatural glow, and so did their eyes. Virgo had said the Pleiades were extremely powerful, and among the Star Children there was something special about them. Electra slowly walked towards me. She opened her arms with a smile, and I stepped forward to meet her embrace. Then the other girls were around me, the warmth of their bodies spreading to mine. No one said anything. I wouldn't have even known what to say. After a few moments, they pulled back, and we stood silently for a second. Merope wiped some tears from her cheeks.

"Took you long enough," Alcyone finally said, narrowing her dark eyes at Perseus.

"We're here now," Perseus said with a smile. "Unlike you, we can't fly."

They could fly? It probably wasn't an important question at the moment, so I decided to ask later.

Perseus pulled from his pocket a small cloth with Typhon's prison wrapped inside it. Perseus hadn't liked the Greek blanket because it took up too much space, so he had opted for a white piece of cloth instead.

"That thing is giving me weird vibes," Asterope said.

"What is it?" Alcyone said as she cocked her head to the side.

"It's asteroid metal," I said. "That's all I know."

Perseus eyed me carefully. I hadn't told him that before. He turned to Electra. "Did Arianna say anything?"

"She didn't know much either," Electra answered. "She said it was an ancient object but didn't elaborate on what it might be."

"Huh," Celaeno said, stroking her braids. "It must be a very powerful object if it can keep Typhon inside."

"How will we even get Typhon out?" I asked.

"We burn this," Perseus said. "It's in the Prophecies."

"Arianna also said burning should work," said Merope, her blue eyes fixed on the object.

"Where is Arianna?" I asked. "Shouldn't she be helping us?"

I still didn't trust Arianna. I was sure that I had never completely trusted her. Her Darkness was corrupting Perseus, and I knew that she was manipulating him.

"We don't need Arianna for this," Perseus said. "Plus, she can't come inside Dodona." Perseus's dark eyes settled on me. "We just need you, Corvus, and that Cup."

I felt like I had swallowed a golf ball. Perseus made it sound like a challenge.

"What happens after we release Typhon and I heal him?" I asked.

Perseus shrugged. "Prophecies didn't say what exactly would happen. I'm sure we can just figure this out as we go."

That didn't sit right with me. Perseus was a control freak. Figuring out things as he went was not his modus operandi. He was still hiding something, and I wondered if the Pleiades knew about it. He knew exactly what would happen after we freed Typhon, but that was a plan that he didn't want to share with me.

"So where's Crater?" Alcyone said.

I pulled out Crater, which had turned into a golden coffee mug, from my pocket. Perseus stared at the mug suspiciously, narrowing his eyes.

"It likes to change shapes," I said with a shrug.

"Okay then," Electra said.

A howl echoed behind me. I turned to see Lupus and wondered how he could have sneaked up on me. Lupus looked exactly as he had in my most recent memory. His fur was like thunderclouds—dark grey with streaks of white and black. Lupus's eyes were like silver moons. I had heard from Andromeda, Draco, and Orion that his stare could paralyze people with fear, but I didn't feel paralyzed looking at him. The Wolf was a bit taller than me, and he stared down at me with his ears pricked up.

I heard the neigh of a horse and the loud flap of wings. A second later, Pegasus landed right next to Perseus. The Horse was a bit taller than the Wolf, and his coat was completely white. He had a scar that ran horizontally across his left side, right under his wings. I remembered Draco telling me that Aquila had shot thunderbolts at Pegasus. If my memory was correct, Perseus's arm had also been scorched by Aquila's lightning. I turned to Perseus again, but he was covered up tightly so I couldn't see any injuries. In fact, Perseus didn't look like he had been in a deadly fight with my friends only two weeks ago. Thinking of my friends again made my chest swell in pain. Lupus, Pegasus, Arianna, and Perseus had nearly killed them. I remembered Leo's scars, Aquila's injured wing, and the bruise around Draco's neck. I swallowed and felt like pieces of glass were cutting down my throat.

Perseus took a deep breath. "All right, fam, let's do this."

The way he said *fam* made my chest throb, as if my heart remembered the dozens of times he had said that before. He was about to say something else, but a cell phone rang. Alcyone pulled it out of her pocket.

"Oh," she said. "It's Andrew." She answered the phone. "Hey, Daddy!" A muffled voice came through from the other end. "Yeah, we're all here together. . . . You want to talk to Perseus?"

Perseus extended his hand and took the phone. "Hey, Dad." I couldn't make out what Andrew was saying. I felt strange. I knew he had adopted us and that I had lived with him for a long time, but aside from one short memory, I couldn't remember anything about him. "I'll take care of the girls. Yes, we're still in Greece. We're planning on going hiking today. . . . yes, Dad. . . .yeah, I'll tell them."

He hung up the phone.

"What did he say?" Alcyone asked.

"He wants us back in New York soon," Perseus said as he handed her the phone. "He thinks it's safe to go back."

I was about to ask why New York would be dangerous, but then I remembered—after our failed attempt to kill Perseus at Washington Square Park in New York, he had escaped with Andromeda. The very next day Draco and I had found him at Times Square, where Perseus had used Algol to cause terrorist bombings that had destroyed some buildings and killed several people. Draco and I hadn't been hurt badly from the attack—we'd only had minor concussions and a few bruises. But the city had gone into full lockdown.

With everything else that had happened, I hadn't even remembered the attack in New York. Compared to the destruction in Italy, that seemed like a minor incident. I looked at Perseus, who was pensive as he stared at his shoes. I knew now that he couldn't control Algol and that he was scared that he would end up hurting us with it. I wished Virgo and Draco knew that, even if it didn't change their minds. I looked down into my jacket. I still wore Virgo's knitted sweater, and I felt it tightening around me. I didn't deserve to have her protection after I'd abandoned her, but the green sweater was the only thing I had left from her. I still cared about my friends, even if they hated me now.

I wasn't sure what I would do yet, but one thing was certain in my mind—I would fight to protect my family, and I would fight to protect my friends. I didn't know how I could protect both at the same time if they were fighting each other, but I would find a way. And if Typhon was the best way to get closer to that goal—to protect us all from Algol—then I was willing to help Perseus heal him.

"Going back to New York may be a good idea. Is Orion still there?" Perseus asked.

Alcyone nodded. My chest felt cold—Perseus was going after Orion. Even though I didn't particularly like him, he had helped my friends. Draco had mentioned Orion had saved him a couple of times from Arianna's attacks.

"Why are we looking for Orion?" I tried to sound casual but knew Perseus could see straight through me.

Perseus hesitated for a second. "Cassiopeia left a lot of secrets behind." I gulped down hard. "And the only one who can find them is Orion."

"That makes sense." I forced the words out of my mouth.

"Orion knows you, right, Corvus?" Perseus asked. "You met after Palatine Hill." I nodded, feeling sick. "He must think you're still working with Draco and Virgo. That might help."

It took me a second to force my lips to move. "Assuming Draco and Virgo don't find him first."

"They won't," Alcyone said.

Perseus nodded. "We'll have to hurry with Typhon then, and hopefully be back in New York in a few days. Then we'll find a way to capture Orion and get him to find Cassiopeia's secrets for us."

I nodded, not trusting myself to say anything else. Would I be able to betray someone else who trusted me? I began to feel dizzy and pushed those thoughts away. I could worry about Orion later.

"Yeah, yeah," Alcyone said as I focused on the conversation again. "I brought the earplugs."

"Earplugs?" I asked.

Asterope chuckled next to me, rubbing her chin. Her dark eyes were set on the grove. "Trust me, you don't want to hear those leaves spitting out Prophecies at you."

I definitely did not want to hear those leaves speak again. Simply thinking about going back to the place where I had begun all this mess made my hands go numb. Crater felt hotter in my hand, and I could feel it humming with anticipation. I extended my hand to Alcyone. She pulled out two plastic earplugs and gave them to me. I pushed them into my ears. The only sound I heard was the frantic beating of my heart.

I looked at Lupus and Pegasus. Perseus was speaking to them and pointing at the spots they were standing. I assumed that meant they wouldn't come with us but would stand guard.

I looked again at the grove of trees. The oak trees had been planted close together, and they stretched as far as I could see. My heartbeat roared louder. This was the place where everything had started—I had erased my memories here and woken up without knowing who I was. It felt ironic that this should be the place where I reunited with my whole family again.

A hand squeezed my shoulder. Perseus stood next to me, smiling. I forced a smile back. Perseus opened his mouth. *I'm here,* he mouthed. It was only two simple words, but they made my heart twist. I couldn't let my emotions and thoughts overtake me. Not now. I cleared my mind and looked straight ahead. Perseus didn't let go of my shoulder. I was glad for that. I felt that without his hand there I would have crumpled.

Maia stood at my other side. The other girls spread around us.

I took a deep breath, looking again at the trees. They seemed like any normal grove of trees—unmoving, their trunks large and their leaves still. The sky was cloudy above us, making the grove seem darker. I gripped the golden mug tighter.

Alcyone was the first one to take a step forward. The rest of us followed a second later and entered the grove. At first, I didn't feel anything strange or powerful about the grove. It was as if we were just taking a walk in the forest. I looked up, but the leaves didn't move. The ground was covered by grass that hid rocks and tree roots, so we walked slowly. Some of the tree trunks had light green moss. There weren't any animals I could spot around us.

Something in the air around us changed, an ancient power awakening. My bones dissolved to gas. Perseus lost his grasp on me as I fell to the ground. Crater burned in my hand and I bit back a scream. Next to me, Perseus was on his knees, slowly rising. Maia had fallen to my left. I stood on unsteady legs and pulled her up with my free hand.

Above me, the branches swayed, but no wind moved them. They moved as I remembered them—like tentacles. Their leaves fluttered like butterfly wings, frantic to escape their branches. I heard the whispers then. They were muffled, and I couldn't make out what any of them were saying. But I knew one thing for certain—Dodona remembered me.

Chapter LI, Verse II

Born from the first Light in the Darkness,
Raised by the last Fire in the Eternal Sea.
The child of Chaos shall come into this Sphere,
To fight the same war his ancestors once did.
Awakened by the Prince of Darkness and healed by the Liar,
The Forgotten Child once more shall be remembered,
And his children to him shall soon surrender.

CHAPTER 24

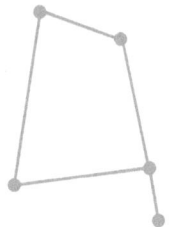

WE PUSHED FORWARD. At first, I wasn't sure why we were walking deeper into the grove, but then I realized that the most powerful spot must have been at the center. I could feel that power—my entire body hummed as if electricity were traveling through my veins and warmth kindled inside me.

We walked in a tight cluster now. Perseus stood at the front, holding Typhon in the cloth tightly. I stood right behind him, and the Pleiades were spread around me. The leaves talked louder as we continued forward. I couldn't make out anything they said, but I could feel their angry tone. Their whispers were aggressive. Dodona was clearly *not* happy that we had brought Typhon here. They knew where this would lead—one step closer to destroying the power of the Stars, the power of Prophecy. Would the power of this grove disappear as well? I clenched my hands as we kept moving.

Crater had turned into a thin wine glass in my hand. It hummed, making every cell in my body reverberate, and it had gotten so hot that my hand throbbed with pain, but I didn't dare let go of it.

The leaves continued to stir. I could feel the power of the grove in my scars. They burned, but for once they didn't hurt. It was a different kind of burning that I hadn't experienced before—a fire that awakened my soul, replenished it. A light shone next to me, and for a second I thought someone had brought a flashlight but then realized that the pulsing white light came from a scar. Taygete had a two-inch scar next to her ear. The bleeding light pulsed frantically, as I assumed her heart did too. I wasn't about to lift my shirt and check if my own scars were bleeding light in full daytime, too, but I knew that they were.

After we had been moving for what seemed like an hour, Perseus finally stopped. Before us was the biggest tree I had seen in my life. The giant trunk could have housed a family, and this tree had a lot more branches than the others, branches that were covered entirely with leaves—the only ones that didn't move—as if feathers coated their naked skin.

The other oak trees still moved around us, their leaves and branches swaying and twisting and their leaves wildly swishing. Perseus walked slowly to stand next to the tree, and we followed after him. My scars burned hotter and so did Crater. The whispers turned to muted screams.

We formed a tight circle before the giant tree. Perseus held the cloth in front of him. Now we needed fire to burn Typhon's prison. I turned to my side, expecting Draco to be there. Pain stabbed at my heart. Perseus pulled a lighter from his pocket and turned to me. I nodded in return, but I didn't feel ready to free Typhon. I held Crater tighter. Freeing Typhon was the only way to save Virgo—to save us all from Algol. Perseus may be a master manipulator, but I knew he wasn't lying. My sisters also seemed convinced that this was our only shot at being free from our terrible futures. But was I willing to pay the consequences that this decision would bring?

Perseus clicked the lighter, and it produced a small flame. The piercing whispers made me wince, even with the earplugs. Perseus placed the cloth, with the strange object still inside it, on the ground. Then he dropped the lighter on top of it. The cloth caught fire as if it had been dipped in gasoline, but the fire wasn't orange or red—it was pure white.

Perseus waved his arms to get our attention and motioned us to step back from the white fire. I took a few steps back, and so did the others. I accidentally bumped into Merope, but she only smiled warmly back at me. She held my arm and pushed me farther back until we were at least ten feet away from the flames. Perseus walked to my other side, looking at the fire.

Around us, the leaves seemed about to fly away from the branches and rain down on us. I didn't know if leaves could kill us, but I didn't want to find out. I couldn't see the cloth or the object—the white fire was too bright. We all stood still, looking at the flames. I tried to ignore the screaming whispers around me, and while the earplugs did help, they didn't block out all the noise.

A massive wave of heat threw me backward and knocked the air out of my chest and the earplug out of my left ear. The whispering screams penetrated me all the way to my soul.

" . . . INSIDE THE PRINCE OF DARKNESS WILL SWALLOW—"

I covered my left ear with my hand, holding Crater tighter than before. I struggled to my feet, not wanting to uncover my left ear. Perseus stood to my right, covering both of his ears with his hands. To my left, Maia, Alcyone, and Taygete had walked closer to the large tree. Electra and Merope were still on their feet to my right. Celaeno and Asterope were covering their ears as they looked at the ground, most likely looking for their lost earplugs.

Perseus bumped into me to get my attention, his hands still covering his ears. He motioned toward the large tree where the girls stood in a line, looking down at the ground. We rushed toward them. I came to an abrupt stop when I realized what they were looking down at.

When I had envisioned Typhon, I had imagined the gigantic Monster that Virgo had described—with fire breathing heads, hundreds of wings, red eyes, the upper body of a man, and the lower body a snake. I was quite surprised to discover a naked man lying on the ground. He looked like any ordinary, sleeping man, although he was uncommonly tall—at least nine feet—and had deathly pale skin and long black hair and beard. His head as a whole, including his large nose and forehead, looked bigger than it should be and featured prominent cheekbones. His torso was lean and muscular, but his chest rose very slowly—he was dying.

Perseus gently kicked me in the leg to get my attention back to him. He looked at Crater, who had turned back into a chalice. I knew what I had to do. Then I realized I had no water to pour into the Cup. I was about to say that out loud when Asterope appeared next to me holding a water bottle. She emptied the water into the Cup, filling it to the brim. It didn't get heavier. Once she was done pouring the water she stepped back.

I turned to Perseus, who nodded in return. With one of my hands still covering my ear and the wailing of the rustling leaves above us, I closed my eyes.

Crater.

"Yes?"

I need to use your powers to heal Typhon. Am I still empty enough to do it?

"You are," Crater responded in its neutral tone. "This forest gives you enough power to heal that creature completely without burning out. But if you heal the Father of Monsters, then you won't be able to use me again."

I considered that. The whole reason I had erased my memories to get Crater was to ultimately get to Typhon. But what would happen if I needed the Cup again to kill someone who threatened us? Or if I needed Crater to heal someone I cared about? But this *would* save the people I cared about, I reminded myself. Typhon would help us escape our Prophecies—he would help me save my friends.

I felt a hand on my shoulder and even without opening my eyes I knew it was Perseus. I had never planned on using Crater for anything else, only for the Lost Star Child. I exhaled and opened my eyes again. Perseus looked at me expectantly. I nodded. I stepped forward at the same time the ground shook beneath me, sending me sprawling to the side. My other earplug fell from my ear. The shrill whispers pierced my ears so loudly that they began to ring.

Tree roots had surfaced from the ground, squirming around me. I covered one of my ears with my free hand, but it didn't help much when the other ear was still uncovered.

" . . . The Old King the Lion will betray . . ."

" . . . then the Hunter will become the hunted . . ."

" . . . in the Darkness the Princess will stand again . . ."

" . . . Prince will regain . . ."

" . . . Weaving one her full-strength recovers . . ."

" . . . Dragon and man, one will kill the other . . ."

" . . . THE LIAR LIES AGAIN . . ."

I screamed as I felt warm liquid come out of my ears. My vision blurred, and I could see only shadows around me. Two pairs of hands, or maybe more, pulled me to my feet.

"YOUR LIES WE OWN!" the trees screamed as one. "YOUR LIES WE RETURN!"

At first, I wasn't sure what that meant, then felt a stabbing pain in my head. I screamed again. I couldn't feel the arms holding me anymore, and the whispers stopped at once. I opened my eyes, not realizing I had closed them. I wasn't in Dodona anymore.

CHAPTER 25

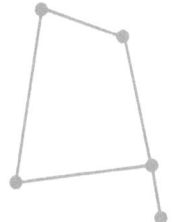

I AWOKE SUDDENLY. *My head felt like my brain had been replaced by heavy rocks.*

"Corvus," Perseus whispered next to me.

"I'm okay." I sat up and looked at our surroundings.

We were in an empty room, about five feet by five feet. Above me, on the wall, was an window that let a cold gust of air in. I shivered. The wooden door in front of us was closed.

"We're in trouble," Perseus said next to me.

This wasn't the first time we had been in trouble, so I wasn't worried.

Perseus swept a hand through his messy red hair. His clear green-blue eyes were wide and alert.

"Where are the others?" I asked. Had Darren and the girls been put in another room? We had met the girls only a couple of weeks ago, after Arianna had led us to them, but we still didn't know them very well.

"They were able to escape," Perseus said. "But you got hit in the head so I came back for you and got trapped too."

"Oh." I stood up, my legs weak. Perseus stood too. He had grown a few inches taller than me, which made me a bit jealous. He was already the stronger one, so why couldn't I be the tall one? "Where are we?"

He shrugged. "I overheard some of the men. They said they could sell us for a good price."

"Sell us to who?"

Perseus shrugged again.

That seemed strange. Why would anyone want to sell children? As eleven year old kids, we were too young to do anything important. The door rattled and swung inside. A bearded man stared down at us. His black and white beard was filthy, as if he had used it as a broom to clean the kitchen floor. I found that funny but didn't laugh.

"You just want to let us go," I said. My voice sounded deeper than normal, almost like an adult's.

The man's eyes became distant, as if he were daydreaming. Strangely, people always looked that way when I lied. I wondered why.

"Yes," the man agreed. "I just want to let you go."

I smiled. I liked when people agreed with me. Perseus and I walked out of the room. The stone hallway, littered with glass and plastic bottles, some cans, and even some rotting food, was filthier than the man's beard. The corridor smelled like several people had vomited there. There were doors on either side. We were passing by the third one when Perseus fell with a grunt, as if an invisible hand had punched him in the gut.

"Perseus!" I said, kneeling next to him.

He breathed heavily. The bearded man also stopped. He still had that dreamy expression as he looked at us.

Perseus pointed at the door on our right. "I can feel it," he grunted.

"You want to open that door," I pointed at the door next to us.

The bearded man pulled a key from his pocket and opened the door. The room was dark inside but for a blinking light that seemed to come from a small flashlight. Perseus took a few deep breaths and scrambled to his feet. Together, we walked inside the room, then stopped dead in our tracks.

We both stared at the source of the light. It came from a little girl in the left corner. When she saw us, she raised her head. She had so many cuts on her hands, which rested on her knees, I couldn't count them. Pulsing white light bled from them in frantic beats. The dim light illuminated her pale face and glinted off the metal collar around her neck. Perseus and I exchanged a glance. She had to be a Star Child—no one else had those scars. Is that what Perseus had felt? He had never felt any other Star Child before, and I didn't know why he would have felt her.

I turned to the bearded man. "You want to let her go."

He stepped forward, pulling a key from his pocket. The girl pressed herself against the wall away from the man. He knelt down to free her of the collar, which dropped to the floor with a loud clank a few seconds later.

"You want to step outside," I told the man.

I walked forward and helped the girl stand, pulling her up by the arms, and then let go of her. She wore a white dress that fell to her knees and featured what I thought were red flowers but were actually bloodstains.

"Who are you?" the girl asked, her voice surprisingly steady.

She held her hands to her neck, which seemed a bit bruised from the collar.

"I'm Corvus and this is my brother Perseus," I said as I motioned behind me.

The girl stared shyly at Perseus, who smiled back.

I wasn't sure what else to ask her. She clearly didn't seem all right, so I didn't want to ask how she felt, and her eyes were wide with terror. Had that man cut her? It seemed like the only way to get so many different bloodstains and so many cuts on her hands. My body flared with anger as I thought of that. Who would hurt a young girl?

"You'll be safe," Perseus said as he stepped forward. "We'll get you out of here."

The girl didn't respond. I extended my hand toward her. She eyed it for a second as if it were a knife, then took it reluctantly. Her hand was very cold compared to mine, as if her bones had turned to ice.

"What's your name?" I asked.

"Virgo," she said.

She was definitely another Star Child. I wondered how she had gotten here. We should probably ask later.

"Nice to meet you," Perseus said.

Virgo didn't respond. I gently pulled her away from the room, toward the door where the bearded man waited for us.

We all walked out of the room. I stared at the closed doors.

"Are there any more kids here?" I asked.

Virgo shook her head slowly. "They took them away a couple of days ago."

"Why didn't they take you?" I asked.

Virgo clenched her dress with her free hand. "I don't know."

I held her hand tighter, which would hopefully reassure her. In the light, I could see the freckles on her face, and at her full height she was a bit shorter than me.

"You want to take us out of here," I ordered the bearded man, who just nodded.

I guessed he didn't like to speak much. People usually repeated my orders when I said them.

The man opened a door at the end of the hallway. We came into a larger room crowded with several men, at least fifteen of them. They either lounged in chairs or leaned against walls while they talked. Virgo pressed herself against me, her face hidden behind her long brunette hair. Her hand gripped mine so tightly that I was sure my blood flow would stop soon. All the men noticed Virgo, and *their eyes trained on us. I didn't think I could lie to all of them at the same time. We made our way across the room toward an open door at the opposite end. I could make out another hallway and stairs leading down.*

One of the men whistled at Virgo. He had very short hair that made his scalp gleam. "And where are you going?"

"Did you find new friends to play with?" another man said as we passed by him. The other men laughed, except the bearded man who was leading us out of the room.

"Where are you taking these children?" A man with braided black hair asked the bearded man. He took a sip from a beer bottle.

The bearded man didn't answer. He continued walking. We were feet away from the door at the end of the room when another man stepped in to block our exit.

"Joshua," a tall, bald man said, "what are you doing?"

I turned to Perseus. Fear swam in his eyes like a hurricane. Virgo pressed herself against me, as if she wanted to bury her face completely in my chest and keep it there.

"We're just going for some fresh air," I said, but my voice sounded almost normal, if a bit distorted. "We'll be back."

The men in the room tensed, their predator gazes narrowing at us. I turned to Perseus again, who nodded in return. He balled his fists, ready for a fight. Perseus had always been stronger than any human man, but I wasn't sure if we could beat all fifteen of them. I did not know how to fight, and I assumed Virgo didn't either.

We would have to make a run for it. I looked at the man who was blocking the exit. I focused all of my energy on him. "You want to move out of our way."

The man stepped to the side with a distant gaze. Perseus and I sprinted toward the open door. Virgo, thankfully, ran at my side.

"Hey!" one of the men shouted behind us.

The new corridor was dark, but a dim glow from the room behind us illuminated the way. We raced toward the stairs at the end of
the hallway that led to the floor below. There was a loud boom behind
us, and one of the walls seemed to explode next to us. I realized a
second later that the men were trying to shoot us.

We ran so fast down the stairs I nearly stumbled but miraculously
kept my balance as I held onto Virgo's hand. I clenched my teeth as we
arrived at the landing and continued to race forward. The new corridor
had rags and blankets covering openings in a ragged mosaic. At the end
of the corridor was a double door that had been left ajar. Light poured
in from the other side, and I hoped that meant the door led outside.

"We need to get outside so I can help," Virgo said.

I didn't know what she meant, but getting outside was our plan
anyway. I didn't hear any of the men thundering down the stairs, which
made me nervous because they wouldn't just let us go. We were only
twenty feet from the door when something knocked me down from the
right. I yelled and Virgo screamed. She knocked the air from my lungs
as she fell on top of me. Sparks blinded my vision, and for a moment
I simply remained immobile on the floor, trying to blink them away. I
grunted, pushing myself to my feet. A tall man smashed Perseus against
the wall behind him. The man seemed to have come in through a giant
hole in the wall to our right. The red blanket that had covered it was on
the floor, and the ragged hole that led outside revealed a barren plain.

"You want to stand still!" I shouted. The man froze just as he
was about to kick Perseus.

Next to me, kneeling on the ground, Virgo screamed as if she had
been stabbed. Perseus doubled over and began screaming too. I rushed
to Perseus and helped him stand as his shouts died down. I turned to
Virgo, who still knelt. She seemed unharmed.

Perseus breathed heavily next to me. His forehead glistened with
sweat. "Something's wrong inside me."

We needed to get out of there. I dragged Perseus by the arm with one hand and I offered my other hand to Virgo. She took it, and I pulled her up. I felt something cut loose inside me, and I knew that the lie had dropped. The man shook his head, as if waking up from a trance, and stepped away from the wall. He looked directly at me and pulled out a knife. "You're dead."

Before I could say another lie, Perseus pulled away from me and jumped forward, knocking the man down. He probably hadn't expected Perseus to be so strong. The knife flew out of his hand and clattered on the floor. Perseus sat on the man's chest.

"Don't you dare touch my brother!" Perseus yelled as he held the man's arms down.

The man began screaming as if Perseus were burning him alive, but I couldn't see him doing anything. I should have pulled Perseus back and run away, but my gaze stayed transfixed on the man. His eyes began crying blood, and he choked on his own screams. He quieted a couple of seconds later. Perseus, his face pale as a ghost, stared at the man, then he stumbled backward and I held his arm, helping him stand upright.

The man wasn't breathing anymore. Blood stopped spilling from his lifeless eyes. How had that happened? Perseus looked at Virgo, his eyes narrowed, as if this were somehow her fault. She held onto my hand and squeezed it. I didn't have time to process what had just happened. I pulled Perseus and Virgo toward the opening the man had come from.

Once outside, the cold wind buffeted at my hair. The clouds above us were dark, and thunder rumbled in the distance. The terrain was flat and barren before us, stretching as far as I could see.

"There," Perseus said, pointing to our right.

About two hundred yards away stood a line of trees. Together, we ran toward it. Virgo broke free from my hand, running alongside me.

CORVUS

Muffled voices from the building echoed behind us, but I didn't dare look back. Perseus ran faster than Virgo and me, so we had to catch up to him. My heart beat wildly, and our flat surroundings blurred together. All I could see were those trees. We were almost there, a hundred yards away and getting closer. I was used to running, so I held up all right, but I noticed Virgo was breathing hard next to me. She didn't stop, and she didn't complain either.

Before I knew it, we were at the trees and running inside the forest. The ground beneath my feet was muddy, making me feel that if I didn't run fast enough, I would sink.

"Wait!" Perseus said.

I stopped, nearly tumbling forward. I turned to my left to face Perseus. He was looking the way we had come from. "Where's Virgo?" he asked.

I looked around frantically, but all I could see were pine trees. We ran back to the tree line. Virgo hid behind a large rock, which seemed to be half submerged in the mud. She looked across the barren land at the shabby concrete building we had just escaped from.

"Virgo," I said as I knelt next to her. "Come on. We have to keep running."

She didn't answer. Her gaze was fixed on the building two hundred yards away where men had started to gather. I could clearly make out the guns and rifles they held. There seemed to be at least twenty men, and more were coming out. The building didn't look big enough to house that many people. Maybe it ran underground?

"Virgo," Perseus whispered. "We have to keep moving. The men will realize that we came here and will follow us."

Virgo didn't answer right away. I looked into her eyes—they held a fierce hatred inside them.

"I can't just leave," she whispered. "I thought I could, but . . ." Perseus and I exchanged a glance. "They killed Ava and Astrid and Stella and Maya and Sienna and Harper and Felix and Ezra and

Lucas and Harry and Noah and Ronan." The names spilled out of her lips like a river. I was sure that if Virgo could shoot fire with her eyes, she would have. "They tried to kill me, too, but realized that no mortal weapon would ever kill me."

My bones turned to ice. What had those men done to Virgo? I looked again at the bloodstains on her dress. With the light outside, the red stains looked dark brown—that blood had dried long ago.

"I can't just leave," Virgo whispered again. "They deserve to pay for what they've done."

Virgo clenched her hands. I didn't know what she could materialize, but I knew I was about to find out. Perseus looked at the men gathering around the building, who were shouting to each other. Then he looked deeper into the forest.

"If we stay here, they'll hurt us all," I said. "They'll capture us again."

Virgo shook her head. "I couldn't do anything chained inside." She placed both of her palms against the rock. "My power only works outside." She looked at me, then at Perseus. "They can't hurt me here."

Virgo stood, making her white and red dress easy to spot for anyone looking our way.

"Virgo," I said, my heart beating up to my throat.

"I thought I could just run away." She looked straight ahead at the men who had already started pointing their fingers at her. "I can't."

She walked forward, slowly making her way toward the men. As soon as they spotted her, they began to advance toward her. Their guns and rifles were pointed at the ground, but it would take only a second to point them at her and pull the trigger. Perseus began to rise, but I grabbed his arm and pulled him down.

"What are you doing?" I demanded.

Perseus opened his mouth, then shut it as he looked at Virgo. I wasn't sure there was much we could do at that point. I didn't want the men to shoot Virgo or take her captive again, but I also didn't want the men to do anything to me or Perseus. If they captured Virgo, maybe we could wait until night, sneak in, and get her out.

The men stopped about halfway between the trees and the concrete building. Virgo stopped, too, about twenty feet in front of them. She stood straight, raising her chin. What was she thinking? Virgo knelt, and my heart gave an aching leap against my ribs. Those men were going to grab her and take her back into that building. She bowed her head as she placed both her palms on the ground. At first, the men stared at each other, equally as confused as Perseus and I.

Then the ground began to tremble. It was subtle at first, like a mild earthquake, but then I heard the rumble, as if the earth was growling. In front of Virgo, the ground split, and from the crack, what looked like a giant snake came out. It took me a second to realize that it was not a snake but a very thick tree root. All around and beyond Virgo, tree roots snapped up from the ground. Some were long and thin, others thick and twisted. The men shouted in confusion. The tree roots were like the tentacles of a giant octopus rising angrily from the ground.

One of the men on the far left raced toward Virgo, but one of the tree roots twisted forward and stabbed the man through the chest. The tree root pushed him downward, and the man lay dead facedown. I screamed and hid myself behind the rock. The ground kept shaking. It was alive and angry—just as vengeful as Virgo.

"Perseus!" I screamed, holding onto his arm.

He was still looking from behind the rock, staring straight ahead, as if he couldn't tear his eyes away from what he was seeing.

The rumbling and shaking stopped abruptly.

"What's happening?" I asked.

Perseus didn't answer. His eyes were fixed ahead, narrowed as they darted from one side to the other. Virgo screamed. Perseus doubled over, screaming as if someone were twisting a knife in his gut.

"Perseus!" I knelt next to him, holding his arms.

I couldn't see any injury or anything wrong with him.

"She's doing something to me!" Perseus shouted.

"Doing what?" I asked, my hands shaking.

Virgo's screams stopped, and Perseus gasped for breath. His face was flushed red. He held onto my arms, his hands trembling. I stood slowly, peeking around the rock. My heart dropped to my stomach. My mind took in the scene in a detached way, as if I were just seeing a picture. The flat terrain was a wasteland of tree roots. It looked as if someone had cut up hundreds of trees and then dug up their roots and just left them scattered. Among the tree roots were gleaming white skeletons, as if the men's clothes and flesh had turned to dust, leaving only their bones behind. The bones were in strange positions, lying all around the terrain. One skeleton had a tree root that had pierced the skull. Another had a root around its neck.

I frantically looked around for Virgo. At first, I worried she might have become a skeleton too, but then I saw movement in the distance. Walking amidst the roots was Virgo. She seemed to be making her way toward the building.

"What's she doing now?" Perseus was standing up now, his big eyes wide. "Come on."

He pulled me away from the rock. Together, we followed Virgo. Walking through the tree roots made my heart shrink in fear. The roots were immobile and twisted as they covered the ground, but I feared that any second they would start moving again like giant wild worms and kill us. I passed by a cluster of bones on the left where two skeletons were so intertwined I couldn't make out which limbs belonged to which skeleton.

We walked to the far right, away from the bones. As we got closer to the building, the tree roots became thinner, and there weren't as many. The ground was cracked and uneven.

"*Virgo!*" *Perseus shouted.*

She stood about twenty yards away from the building. Perseus and I trotted toward her. Virgo stood very still, her brunette hair fluttering with the soft wind.

"Virgo," I gently placed a hand on her shoulder. She turned to look at me, and I gasped. Her face was much thinner than it had been. Her cheeks had sunk, as if she had eaten away the flesh, and her cheekbones stuck out.

"Virgo," Perseus said slowly as if he were talking to a wild animal. "Come on. We should leave now."

Virgo looked away from him, her brown eyes still swirling with hatred. "There's men still hiding inside the building."

"You'll kill yourself," Perseus said, his green eyes gazing at Virgo up and down. "We can't use that much power unless we want to drain and burn up our own bodies."

Virgo eyed him for a second, then knelt on the ground, placing her hands against the dirt. Perseus grabbed my arm and pulled me back a few yards, although there was nowhere for us to take cover or hide. The ground began to shake, the tree roots twisting into life as if they had woken up from a short nap and were ready to keep killing. Virgo groaned. Perseus stepped forward but I held his arm.

"She'll kill herself," he said.

"There's nothing we can do."

Virgo screamed again. The scream resonated across the terrain as if it came from every tree root and every molecule of dirt. Screams wailed inside the building too—screams of terror, pain, and death. Once again, Perseus fell to his knees in pain as if the roots were curling inside of him.

The entire building shook. The screams inside stopped, and Virgo's shouts died down. Roots began to pour out of all the windows, cracks, and openings. They pushed at the walls and curled into knots that looked like a loose weaving pattern. Pieces of wall crumbled away as more roots pushed out from inside, like a monster trying to escape its prison. The second floor crumbled into the first, and the building caved in. But while the building itself became a mound, the knotted roots remained standing like a hollow shell.

The ground stopped shaking, and all the tree roots became still once more. I had been too focused on the house that I didn't see Virgo collapse. Perseus, coughing, stood up and we both walked over to her.

"Virgo?" I knelt next to her.

"I think she's dead," Perseus whispered.

Chapter XVI, Verse II

The Weaving One afraid of her own power.

Her Fate to be determined by none other than the Liar.

Death she shall soon meet, unless the Celestial River she greets,

Into the abode of the Weavers to flee, until her life is retrieved.

Only the Cup shall be able to restore her full power,

But only she can become the master of her own talents.

The Weaving One shall then rise again, to powers unknown to all but her.

CHAPTER 26

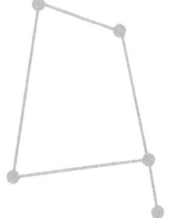

VIRGO'S SKELETAL BODY *lay curled on her side like a fetus. Her hands, arms, and legs had been reduced to nothing but a thin layer of skin and bone. Her face had become a Halloween mask. Her cheeks had completely sunk in, and so had her eyes. They were closed, but it looked like her eyeballs had popped into her skull and left only a thin veil behind. Her lips seemed to have disappeared.*

Perseus knelt next her. "Virgo?" His voice trembled.

A very low whimper escaped from Virgo's mouth. She was still alive, somehow.

"What do we do?" I asked Perseus as my heart battered against my chest.

Even if there was a hospital nearby, we couldn't take her there. Doctors wouldn't know what to do with her, and once they saw her glowing scars, they might turn her over to the government.

"Arianna will know what to do." Perseus looked up at the sky.

The light filtering through the clouds was definitely dimmer than it had been before, but I couldn't tell what time it was or how soon nightfall would arrive. Arianna only whispered to us during the night after it got fully dark. I looked down at Virgo again. I couldn't tell if she was breathing or not or if she would last until the night.

"We should hide in the forest until it gets dark," Perseus said. I nodded. There was nothing else we could do. Perseus leaned down and picked up Virgo. She mustn't have weighed a lot in her current state. Slowly, we walked to the forest again. Our walk was a blur of bones, roots, and dirt. My mind was blank with shock, and before I knew it, we were deep within the forest. We walked for what seemed like an eternity. Perseus and I didn't talk. Our surroundings became darker and darker until the trees became long shadows around us like giant spider legs.

"We should stop," I said.

Perseus nodded. His red hair and pale face were barely visible. I sat next to a tree and he handed me Virgo. "I'm going to look around to see if there's anything close," he said. "I'll be back in a few minutes."

Virgo felt like a fragile doll about to crumble to dust. I held her gently, as if she were a baby. Her body was still warm—I knew that was a good sign. I began humming. Songs had always made me feel better. I had no talent for singing or playing any instrument, but I loved hearing songs.

"Corvus," her voice was barely audible, and for a second I thought I had imagined it.

I stopped humming. "You'll be all right. Someone who can help will be here soon."

She was silent for so long I began to think that I had truly imagined her voice.

"I can't see," she whispered. "I can't open my eyes. I can't feel my eyes."

If her power had burned her flesh and muscles, had it also consumed her eyeballs? I shivered at that thought.

"You'll be all right," I repeated.

"I . . . can't move."

"I know." My arms trembled. "You'll be all right." I paused. "You used too much of your power, but you'll heal and be back to normal."

I didn't know if she would, but that seemed like the right thing to say. The scars on her hands weren't shining anymore. They should have been—our scars always shone at night or in dark places. But it was as if the light within her had extinguished.

"I don't regret it," she whispered. "Even if I die, those men deserved that and more."

She fell quiet again, and I didn't know what to respond. She had been willing to lose her own life to take revenge on those men. I couldn't blame her. They had killed her friends, and only the Stars knew what the men had done to her. I wondered if, someday, there would be someone I hated so much that I was willing to lose my life destroying them.

I began humming again, waiting for Perseus to return. Cold seeped onto my skin from the tree at my back.

"Could you sing?" Virgo asked. There was a long pause. "I like songs."

I didn't know any songs by memory except pieces of the one I was humming. It was a song Arianna had sung to us many times. While Perseus could fall asleep practically anywhere, I'd always had trouble sleeping. So Arianna had sung to me at night, and her sweet voice had lulled me to sleep.

Even though I wasn't a good singer, I began to sing for Virgo.

When the night arrives, their souls awake again.
A new moon dark above them, and below the earth barren.

What was next? I knew the rhythm of the song but not all of the lyrics. I decided to skip over the parts I didn't know and sing only the ones I remembered.

The flames they all follow, for fire is what Stars are made of.
Of home the memories they try to remember,
but in the end forget.
Without purpose they roam, but with a hope they walk.
Soon they will be born again into a flesh of flames.
Flames that burn white like their souls.
Flames that burn out the brighter they shine.
Darkness now comes, so their souls must hush.
In silence they will stand, to avoid her gaze.
Only to see how brightly they shine.
For Darkness is the only force that gives light its power to shine.
Soon they will be born again into a flesh of flames.

Those were all the lyrics I knew from the song, which weren't many. I sang those lyrics over and over again. Perseus returned after I had repeated my lyrics about ten times. He sat in front of me, looking at Virgo's frail body. When I began the song again, he joined in with me. Perseus had a better singing voice than I did. Together, we sang as Darkness cloaked the forest. We sang even when my throat began to throb.

"You remember the song," a sweet female voice said in a whisper. We stopped abruptly.

"Arianna!" Perseus exclaimed as he stood up.

We knew Arianna was all around us—she had no form.

"Virgo is hurt," I said. "What can we do to help her?"

There was silence for almost a minute. It wasn't unusual for Arianna to take so long to answer us.

"Virgo," Arianna whispered. "The Goddess."

"She's dying," Perseus said. "How do we save her?"

Another long silence seemed to last an hour, even though it couldn't have been more than two minutes. Virgo's body wasn't as warm as it had been before. She didn't have long.

"She will fight against you, my Prince," Arianna whispered. "She is prophesized to help the one that will bring your downfall."

I couldn't see Perseus's face, but he had gone still. "I don't care," he said after a few seconds. "Those men hurt her very badly, and now she's dying. What can we do to save her?"

This time, Arianna answered a couple of seconds later, which startled me. She sounded surprised. "You would help those who will fight you in the future?" Arianna paused for a moment. "If she dies now then the Princess will never meet you, and your victory will be assured. But if you save her, then you will fulfill your first Prophecy and escaping from them later will become nearly impossible."

"I don't care," Perseus said determinately.

Arianna sometimes liked to speak like that—talking about Prophecies. We still weren't very sure what she meant but assumed at some point it would make sense. The Pleiades seemed to understand more what Arianna said, but they didn't trust us enough yet to share their thoughts.

"You don't?" Arianna asked a minute later. "If you save this girl, then the only way to escape the Prophecies will be to fulfill them until the end and to choose the prophesized path that will lead you to victory."

"That's all right," Perseus answered.

The trees rustled around us although there was no wind. Arianna did that when she was angry.

"We'll do whatever we have to do to save her," I said, although my voice didn't sound as determined as Perseus's.

Arianna was motionless again. "I cannot save her. Only the power of the Cup would be able to fully restore her."

"And where's the Cup?" I asked.

Arianna waited for a minute. "I do not know."

"There has to be another way," Perseus said.

"Hmmmmm." Her voice flowed around us like a warm wind

current. *"The Weavers may be able to heal some of the damage she has done to herself."*

The Weavers? Weren't those the old ladies who wove, knitted, and knotted Fate together so every human would reach their Destiny?

"How do we find them?" Perseus asked.

There was another silence, this one about a minute long. "The Weavers live at the bottom of the river Eridanus. Any river can connect you if you call on it correctly."

"Where do we find a river?" I asked.

"And how do we connect to it?" Perseus asked.

"If you walk straight to Corvus's left, you'll find the river." She paused for ten seconds. "I will tell you what to do once you get there."

Perseus leaned down to take Virgo from my arms and into his own. I stood up, and we walked as fast as we could in the direction Arianna had indicated.

"How are you feeling?" I asked Perseus after walking silently for a few minutes.

"Should I be feeling something?" Perseus asked.

"Every time Virgo screamed, you did too," I reminded him. "You said she did something to you."

"Oh, that." Perseus paused. "I'm not sure how to describe it. It's as if my body is more awake than before, but I don't know how to explain how that feels."

"ALGOL!" Arianna shouted.

I jumped, and Perseus gave a startled yell next to me. At least he didn't drop Virgo.

"What?" I asked. I had never heard Arianna speak so loudly or abruptly.

"She is an amplifier of Light and has stirred the power of Algol within you," Arianna whispered. "Her near death shall announce the arrival of the Prince, who will awaken when he hears the wail-

ing of her screams." *She paused for a long time as Perseus and I stood still. "You have already fulfilled one of the Prophecies, my Prince. The only way out now is through. You will have to follow the rest of them." There was a brief pause. "Hurry! Take her to the river."*

Perseus and I needed no further encouragement. We sprinted forward. I didn't hear or see the river ahead of us and was worried we wouldn't find anything. A few minutes later, though, I heard the current of rushing water. The noise became louder as we hurried forward, until the river appeared in front of us, cutting through the trees like a jagged road. The water flowed slowly and splashed on the rocks at the edges. The river glinted with silver light as it reflected the light from the full moon. We knelt next to the river.

"What do we do now?" I asked Arianna.

"Call Eridanus—it cannot refuse a call from a Star Child. Tell it to take the girl to the Weavers, then drop her into the water."

"How?" Perseus asked.

Arianna didn't respond, apparently thinking that her answer had been enough. I leaned forward over the water. I didn't know what I was doing and felt driven more by instinct than by logic. I submerged a hand into the ice-cold water, which numbed my fingers.

"Eridanus," I said. "We need your help. Please."

At first, nothing happened. I thought that maybe my idea had been stupid, but then the water began to shine. It glowed dimly at first, as if a lantern had been dropped into the clear water and had suddenly turned on, but then I realized that the light pulsed in slow beats.

"Please take Virgo to the Weavers," I said, "so they can heal her."

I didn't know what to do next, and I turned to Perseus. He seemed unsure, too, and frowned at the shining river.

"Do I just drop her in the river?" he asked.

"I think so."

Perseus leaned forward too. Virgo's face, illuminated by the pulsing river, was like the image of death itself.

I moved closer to her. "Virgo?" I said. "I don't know if you can hear me. But if you can, we're letting you go through Eridanus so you can go to the Weavers who can help you. You'll be all right."

Perseus nodded. "Arianna said that we would meet again. Even if you try to kill me for some reason, I'll be happy to see you."

"Bye, Virgo," I said, strangely sad. I had met her only hours ago. Why was I sad to see her go? "I'll see you again someday."

Perseus gently placed her on the water, which began to pulse faster and brighter as soon as she touched it. Virgo floated for a few seconds, looking like a cadaver. Then she sank. The river burst with light and I covered my eyes, but the light was gone seconds later.

"Is she . . . ?" Perseus didn't finish.

We stared at the water for a long time. It didn't shine anymore but simply reflected the moonlight.

"The Weavers will heal her," Arianna whispered after a while.

We would have to trust her on that. I stood up, my legs trembling. Perseus stood too, and together we walked away from the river. We didn't know where we were heading, and I really didn't care. We had been lost many times before, and at some point, I knew we would find something. Arianna would surely lead us back to Darren and the girls.

"Do you really think she'll try to fight me someday?" Perseus asked after some time had passed.

"I don't know," I said with a shrug. "We saved her, so why would she fight us?"

Perseus shrugged too. "I'm scared of everything Arianna keeps telling us. I'm not sure I want to live in a world of Prophecies, and Princes, and Princesses, and Dragons, and other Monsters."

"Me neither," I said. "But we'll figure it out. We always do."

"Yeah." He sighed. "Even though Arianna was against it at first, saving Virgo was the right choice. Right?"

"I think so," I said. "I'm sure that she would have saved us if we'd needed help."

"I think so too." Perseus sighed again. "Since we saved Virgo from death, maybe she'll reconsider fighting us in the future."

"I hope she does," I said. "I wouldn't want to fight her and get stabbed by tree roots." That seemed like a very violent way to die.

"I want to believe that she'll return the favor someday," Perseus said. "We saved her from death, so maybe one day she'll save us from death too."

I considered that. "Maybe she will."

CHAPTER 27

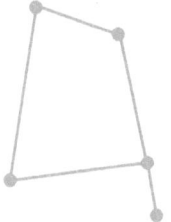

FURIOUS WHISPERING woke me up. My ears rang painfully as warm liquid spilled out of them.

"Corvus!" Perseus shouted distantly.

I opened my eyes, the world blurry around me and full of moving shadows. A few seconds later, Perseus came into focus above me. He pulled me into a sitting position, then looked at Crater, which I still held. The Cup had somehow managed to retain the water inside of it.

The whispers cut out, and the sudden silence startled me. It took me a few seconds to notice the girls spread around us, enclosing us in a circle. Their hands were stretched before them, trembling, as if holding a door that someone was trying to kick in.

"She knew me!" I shouted over my ringing ears. Perseus simply stared at me. "Virgo knew who I was." Perseus's expression hardened as I looked down at the Cup. "This can heal her," I breathed out as I remembered Arianna's words. "The Cup can restore Virgo."

"It won't matter if you end up killing her anyway," Perseus's voice was gentle.

I tightened my grip on Crater. I was the only one who could heal Virgo completely, restoring her power—but I was also the one who would end her life. The image of Virgo's skeletal face flashed into my head. Virgo had used her power to save me from Hydra. Shouldn't I repay the favor?

Perseus held both of my arms, his nails sinking into my skin. "Without Typhon, we'll never be able to escape our Prophecies. He can help us defeat Algol—he *will* help us escape our deaths." His voice was steady.

Behind us, Maia screamed. For a split second, the whispering screams flooded into my ears, then they were quiet again.

"I don't know how much longer we can do this!" Alcyone said in a strained voice.

Typhon still lay motionless behind Perseus.

"Corvus,"—Perseus pulled me to my feet—"this is the only way." He pulled me closer to Typhon. "Virgo will heal eventually, with time, as she has done before. But if we don't save Typhon so he can help us, you won't be able to save her from death. A death *you* will be responsible for."

His words hit me like bullets to the chest.

Virgo had been healing well in the past year. Surely, with time, she would continue to heal. I looked down at the clear water in Crater. But without the power of the Cup, she would never regain her full power.

"Corvus," Perseus said again, urgency rising in his tone. "This is the only way to save her. This is the only way to save all of us." Crater shook violently in my grasp. "Please, I don't want Algol to kill all of you. I want us to live. That's all I'm fighting for."

I let out a deep breath and knelt next to Typhon. Pain sliced through my heart as I moved the Cup closer to his face. Why had Virgo lied to me? Why hadn't she told me the truth? I realized that it didn't matter anymore—I was willing to save her regardless of the answer to those questions. If Typhon could help me escape my terrible Prophecy and if he could help us all escape the power of Algol, then saving him was worth the risk.

Perseus held onto my arm, steadying my grip. He nodded encouragingly. I nodded back.

Crater, I need you to heal Typhon.

"I can heal him," Crater answered. "But not completely. You are too full for that."

I hesitated. I wasn't sure how I could heal someone incompletely. I guessed that healing Typhon somewhat was better than nothing. I leaned forward, staring into his face. For a moment I felt as if I were looking at a man made of white marble—his skin smooth and hard as stone.

I touched Typhon's face and felt awkward as I pulled his chin down. The Pleiades screamed as howls erupted around us. I ignored them. Typhon's mouth was barely open, but I assumed that would be enough. I poured the clear water through his lips. A bit of water spilled out of his mouth and slid down his chin and hollow cheeks. The whispers stopped abruptly, as if Dodona had frozen.

At first, I felt nothing as I poured the water, but once I was done pouring all of it, the pain began. I screamed, dropping Crater next to me. It felt as if my scars were being pulled apart by metal clamps and liquid fire poured into the gaping wounds. An invisible force crushed my bones.

"Corvus!" someone shouted behind me.

The pain consumed me, like a flame inside me burning away my flesh. My heart was on fire, boiling the blood in my veins. Then the pain stopped, as if it had never been there. I gasped for breath.

"Corvus," Perseus knelt at my side, looking down at me. His dark eyes swirled with worry.

"I'm fine," I croaked.

I sat up, my entire body feeling like gelatin. Crater was on my right, a few inches away from me. The Cup seemed to shine with golden light, as if it were made from bits of sun. I grabbed it. For the first time, Crater was cold.

"Whoa!" Electra exclaimed. One of the girls screamed behind me. I jumped to my feet, my head spinning like a wild carousel. Typhon, who still lay on the ground right next to me, twitched. I leaned on Perseus for support, and he held onto my arm. Blood slid down from his ears and onto his neck.

Typhon moaned, then exhaled. His eyes snapped open. Perseus and I took a step back. If he hadn't been holding me, I would have fallen to the ground again. Typhon's eyes were similar to Draco's but ten times more sinister. They glowed bright red like fire. He closed his eyes again. Grunting, he pushed himself up and sat with his back against the large tree. Dodona was entirely silent, as if frightened that Typhon would burn the forest down if a leaf dared to move.

Typhon opened his eyes again. He stared at each one of us in turn. His gaze stopped when he got to me. My bones trembled. He stared at Crater. Then his eyes met my own. His gaze made my eyeballs throb in pain. I had to look away and stare at the ground instead.

I looked up again a few seconds later when Typhon stood. He was two heads taller than Perseus, who was the tallest of us. Typhon cocked his head at Perseus, then looked away. He stared up at the trees above us and then down at the muddy ground. If he felt awkward about being naked in front of nine teenagers, he didn't show it.

"Thank you," Typhon's voice was so deep it stung my ears.

"You're welcome," Perseus said, his voice steady as always.

"Is the King dead?" Typhon asked, referring to Cepheus.

"Yes," Perseus said. He was the only one who seemed to have the strength to respond to Typhon. Every time I thought about talking, my lips and tongue became numb.

"Is the Queen dead?" Typhon asked about Cassiopeia.

"Yes," Perseus answered again.

"What about the golden Dragon?" Typhon asked.

"He's just a boy now," Perseus said.

Were they talking about Draco? He had never mentioned a golden Dragon before. And how could a Dragon become a boy?

Typhon looked up at the sky, as if trying to find a message in the clouds above us. Thunder crackled in the distance. "Then there's still hope," he whispered.

There was a sound like bones splintering and skin being flayed. A thick and large bone peeked up from behind Typhon's back. The bone split into two and extended to each side of him like another pair of arms. The white bone began to grow black flesh that covered it entirely. Then the flesh began to slide down as if it were melting off the bone, spilling onto the ground. It took me a couple of seconds to realize that Typhon was growing himself a pair of wings. They were huge.

I had expected Typhon to turn himself into the horrible mythological Monster I had heard about but then remembered that Crater hadn't healed him completely, so maybe he couldn't become a full Monster yet. Typhon fixed his gleaming red eyes on Perseus.

"The Prince of Darkness," he said. Perseus didn't answer. "Hmmm. There *is* still hope."

Typhon beat his wings so hard that the air knocked us all down. Perseus let go of me and I fell hard on my back with a grunt. There was another wave of air so powerful that it pressed me harder against the ground. Branches and leaves fell on top of me. I covered my face with my arms and rolled to my side.

"Come on!" Alcyone pulled me to my feet.

Her blond hair was dirty and knotted with leaves. She mustn't have been very happy about that. Perseus rose to his feet and placed his hand on Alcyone's shoulder.

"Follow Typhon!" He pointed at the large hole that Typhon had created as he flew away from the forest. The hole, at least forty feet in diameter, had cut clean through the canopy above us. The broken remains of the leaves and branches were scattered on the ground as if a tornado had swept through the grove of trees.

Alcyone nodded. She took off her jacket and let it drop on the ground. She raced to stand under the hole where the other girls had already gathered. Alcyone's back was completely bare. The other girls took off their jackets too. Two lines sliced open in Alcyone's back, as if two invisible knives had cut her. Her back didn't bleed. Instead, a large pair of wings pushed out of her back, as if they had been folded and stored underneath her skin. Wings grew out of the other girls' backs too. Their wings had feathers the same color as their hair.

Alcyone turned to Perseus again. "Tell Pegasus to follow our scent."

Perseus nodded. Alcyone jumped, beating her golden blond wings. She flew out of the forest through the hole Typhon had created. The others flew after her like a flock of birds. I was too dazed to move, until Perseus took my arm and pulled me into a sprint.

"They have *wings*!" I exclaimed as we ran through the silent forest, back the way we had come.

"They're the Pleiades!" Perseus said, as if it was an obvious fact that Pleiades had wings.

I promised myself that when I had the time, I would buy myself some mythology books to study the Constellation and Star myths more. For the last year, I had mostly relied on Virgo's knowledge.

The ground was uneven beneath our feet, and I struggled not to trip and fall flat on my face. I still felt weak, both from the memory I had recovered and because I had used Crater's power. But being in Dodona had helped, just as Perseus had known it would. Even though I had used Crater's power to heal, it hadn't consumed me. The image of Virgo, her skeletal body curled in my arms, flashed through my mind.

"You knew Virgo too!" That realization suddenly struck me. "When we tried to kill you at Washington Park."

"I actually didn't recognize her. I hadn't seen her since we dropped her into the river," Perseus said as we kept running.

A couple minutes later we were out of the grove of trees. Pegasus waited for us a few yards beyond the tree line, neighing. It was no longer raining in the distance, but the sky was still covered in clouds. Perseus jumped onto Pegasus's back with ease. He extended his hand to help me. I grabbed it and he pulled me up on top of the winged horse.

"Follow the girls, Peg!" Perseus said. "We have to catch up to them as fast as we can."

Pegasus whinnied. He turned away from the trees and began running parallel to them. I bumped up and down on his back, feeling that I would drop at any second.

"Hold onto me!" Perseus shouted. I placed Crater inside my jacket and wrapped my arms around Perseus's torso. Pegasus neighed loudly. He jumped up, and his large white wings flapped into the air. I screamed, feeling that my stomach had dropped to the ground.

I wondered what would happen if someone saw us. Two boys riding a flying white horse would certainly be a strange sight. Humans would probably say it was a bird, and even if someone claimed they had seen a flying horse, other people would wave it off as a fake story. That was just how humans worked, I had learned. They didn't very readily accept new truths if those truths shattered the realities they knew. Humans would rather live in a safe lie.

The wind slapped at my face, and I narrowed my eyes, barely able to see what was in front of me. Before I knew it, we were flying inside the clouds, which provided good cover. I had never been inside clouds, and I realized that it was no different from being inside fog. Tiny droplets of water splattered against my face, and the humid, cold air around me was almost suffocating.

"What happened to Lupus?" I shouted above the roaring wind.

"He might have left as soon as he saw the girls flying away," Perseus shouted. "He's fast. He'll catch up."

My vision became blurry, and tears spilled from my eyes. I closed them and let my head rest against Perseus's back. I didn't know how long it would take to get to our destination, and that meant that I had some time alone with my thoughts.

My memory with Virgo had left me weak, more emotionally than physically. I wondered why she hadn't told me the truth. I opened my eyes and looked at Perseus's red hair waving with the wind. He had saved Virgo too, even though Arianna had warned him that Virgo would fight against him and would help bring his downfall. Perseus hadn't cared. Virgo's life had been more important. Then why did Virgo hate Perseus so much? Had she forgotten about us? No, she hadn't. Virgo remembered the song I had sung to her as she died—the same song she had sung to me when I couldn't sleep. My throat knotted painfully.

She remembered.

What had the Weavers told Virgo that had made her turn against Perseus? The Weavers wove Fate together for every living creature. If Perseus triumphed, then they would perish. They had healed Virgo, but they had also turned her against the person who had saved her life. Perseus wasn't as bad as I had thought him to be for the last year. He was the most dangerous Star Child and Algol had killed countless people, but that had been out of his control. Even if his goals caused Chaos, he had good intentions behind them—he just wanted to save the people he cared about.

But I still didn't believe in eradicating Destiny, Fate, and Prophecy and throwing the Universe into Chaos like Perseus did—like I had once believed. There must be a way to keep a balance. What if there was a way to choose? What if we still had Prophecy to guide us, to give hope, to prepare for what's coming, but at the same time we could choose our own Destinies? There had to be an area in between, because neither extreme seemed good for me. Perseus wanted to be free from everything, but I knew there were others like Virgo and Draco who still wanted to have guidance, order, and structure. I was probably the only Star Child who had experienced both sides of the fight—the only Star Child who could find a balance between them. I would fight to find that balance, a balance where I wouldn't kill Virgo and Algol wouldn't destroy us all.

Pegasus descended suddenly, making me scream into Perseus's ear. We flew out of the clouds. Below us, green hills rippled lazily across the ground. They were dotted with trees and shrubs. A highway cut from left to right, snaking across the landscape. Beyond it was the ocean. The water reflected the grey clouds above us, making the sea look opaque.

Perseus looked to the side. The Pleiades flew around us. Their wings were a beautiful mix of red, gold, black, white, and brown. We were all heading for the ocean, but I couldn't see Typhon.

Pegasus descended sharply. I pressed against Perseus, my head buried in his back. I bounced up as soon as the horse touched the ground, then fell back down painfully. Pegasus had landed at the top of a ten-story tall cliff that dropped into the cloudy blue ocean below. The sea stretched as far as I could see. To my left and right, the cliff sloped down to form small hills that enclosed the ocean in a loose embrace. Far on the left sat a narrow strip of beach. There was no one there though, only a red umbrella that had been abandoned in the sand.

I heard the flap of wings and a wave of air slapped me from the right. The Pleiades landed one by one next to us, looking at the ocean before us. Perseus dismounted, so I did the same.

"He's here somewhere." Merope scanned the horizon. "We didn't see Typhon go into the ocean, and he didn't turn more monstrous either."

"Crater didn't heal Typhon completely," I said as I tried to spot movement in the ocean. "That's probably why he hasn't turned into a full Monster."

A loud growl echoed from beyond the cliff. I took a step back, and so did the Pleiades, but Perseus only raised his chin in defiance. Two black wings emerged from the edge of the cliff, then the rest of Typhon's body. Had he been hanging from the cliffside? Typhon crouched next to Perseus. His eyes seemed to have turned a deeper shade of red.

"We need your help," Perseus said. Typhon's red eyes fixed on Perseus with deadly curiosity. "We plan on overthrowing the Stars and the power they have over Destiny. We want to destroy Fate and Prophecy too. We know you want the same, so we could work together."

Typhon cocked his head to the side, his blood-red eyes swirling like pits of hell. "Young but bold." His voice was like rocks grinding against each other. It made my ears throb in pain.

"You're too young to understand what this war fully implies but bold enough to know what to fight for."

"Will you help us?" Perseus asked.

Typhon smiled. His teeth were black, like tiny metal daggers. "No, young one. You will help *me*. Not now." He looked out at the ocean. "There are matters I left unattended before I was captured. But soon, you shall help me, Prince of Darkness." Typhon extended his wings. "Until then."

He jumped off the edge of the cliff and flew above the ocean close to the surface, heading toward the horizon. I wasn't sure if our meeting with Typhon had been a success or a complete failure. Before I could ask, a giant tentacle rose out of the water and slammed against Typhon.

"What the hell was that?" Maia asked.

Typhon splashed into the ocean, and the tentacle went back under the waves. The surface of the ocean turned black. Then the Monster rose out of the water.

My legs froze, and my feet seemed to root themselves into the ground. My mind reeled back to the day Darren had died. The same day Perseus had used Algol for the first time. The day I had nearly died.

I stood frozen in terror as Cetus rose from the ocean.

Chapter XXVII, Verse I

The Seven Seas the Ship has sailed, built from the prophetic tree grove.

An utterance will be made, but only those who listen will remain.

It shall be owned first by the King and Queen and then by the Twins.

To the ends of this Sphere it shall journey, many times in much hurry.

Numerous wars the Ship has fought, against Darkness in its many forms.

Only the Ship shall have the courage to set sail,

Above the mighty waters of the River that leads to the Three Wells.

CHAPTER 28

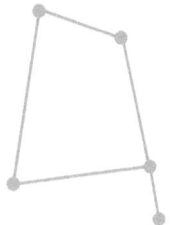

THE LAST TIME we had faced Cetus, I had not seen the Monster completely, only its tentacles. But this time, the full Monster rose from the waves. Cetus had the body of a whale with two giant flippers on the sides. Instead of a normal whale face, the Monster had a frightful snake face. He had three beady black eyes on each side and a huge eye in what I assumed was his forehead. His face had rotten green and blue scales that had algae and other sea plants dripping from them. Cetus opened his mouth and emitted a shriek that sounded like a thousand whales screaming. His teeth were twice as big as me, and his breath hit me like a toxic wave. It smelled as if he had swallowed a ship and all the oil had spilled inside of him. I covered my mouth and nose with my sleeve.

As the Monster rose higher, the giant tentacles spreading out from his neck came into view. Ten of them splashed wildly and created massive waves that crashed against the cliff, the narrow beaches, and the hills around us. Instead of a whale tail, Cetus had two green-yellow snake tails that stretched far behind him. The entire Monster must have been a mile long.

How had Cetus found us here? He may have been attracted by Typhon's presence. Hadn't Virgo said that Typhon was the Father of all Monsters? I didn't remember if she had mentioned Cetus as one of his children.

Cetus's main black eye blinked at us. I knew, as Cetus fixed his gaze upon us, that he remembered exactly who we were. He shrieked again, and my ears felt like they would shatter. In front of me, Perseus went ghostly pale. I looked at the splashing waves around Cetus but found no trace of Typhon.

"Watch out!" Perseus shouted.

Cetus slammed one of his dark tentacles against the edge of the cliff. The impact sent me sprawling to my side, crashing with the rocky ground. I screamed as I felt my stomach dropping, then realized that I was falling. I barely had time to process that before I splashed into the waves. The water greeted me coldly as it fully enveloped me. I kicked my feet and swam to the surface. I gasped for breath and coughed. Behind me, the waves smashed against the cliffside. The top of the cliff had shattered, and a big chunk at the very edge was missing.

The waves pushed me back toward the cliff. Panic rose in my chest, tightening it. The water was so cold it numbed my body, but I somehow stayed afloat, kicking my legs even though I didn't feel them. Cetus seemed more hideous from below. Algae dangled from his scales like rotting hair, and the suckers in his tentacles changed size as if they were giving the air violent kisses when they contracted.

The waves pulled me away from the cliff, closer to Cetus. I was mere yards away from one of its tentacles, but the Monster wasn't focused on me. It was shrieking at Pegasus who flew high above it. One of the giant tentacles rose into the sky and tried to hit Pegasus as an annoyed human would try to slap a bothersome mosquito away. Pegasus whinnied and dove to the left, away from the tentacle.

Another pair of white wings flew from the cliff behind me toward Cetus. It was Electra. Cetus shrieked at her, turning to face her as she flew to the right and circled him. The motion of Cetus turning sent a wave slamming against me. I was underwater for a couple of seconds before I resurfaced, coughing. Electra now flew over the hills, then circled back and flew straight at Cetus. Twisting purple light sizzled around Electra's body. She extended her arms forward and a bolt of electricity shot out of her hands, hitting Cetus right above the main eye. The Monster shrieked loudly, and Electra flew back toward the hills to avoid the Monster's tentacles. Pegasus flew behind Cetus, circling the ocean in the distance.

"Corvus!" Perseus gasped behind me.

I turned. Perseus's pale head and red hair floated above the surface three yards behind me. Blood ran down his temple.

"Are you all right?" I asked. Perseus nodded. His dark eyes brimmed with terror. I swam to him. We were twenty yards away from the cliff, but there was no way we could climb it. I looked to either side but didn't see the beach I had spotted earlier. Cetus's body was so wide that his fins and tentacles blocked our possible exit toward the hills.

"Last time you used Algol's power to turn Cetus's tentacles to stone," I prompted.

In the Constellations, Algol represented Medusa's head, so turning people and Monsters to stone should have been something Perseus could easily do. But I didn't remember seeing him use that particular power ever since.

"I can't do that again," Perseus said, almost in a whimper. "I . . . I lost myself to Algol last time." I looked into his black eyes. Perseus was as terrified of Algol as he was of Cetus. "Most times I can keep Algol suppressed. But if I use Algol's power, if I turn anything to stone, I will lose control much quicker than I was doing before."

I knew he was telling the truth, or else he would have defeated every single one of our enemies by turning them to stone. I wondered if that was how Perseus was prophesized to murder us all, by turning us to stone.

"What do we do?" I asked, the acid panic in my chest rising to my throat.

Asterope, Maia, and Alcyone flew forward. Their hands were extended downward, and as they flew above Cetus, they unanimously pulled their arms up toward the sky. Before us, a giant wall of water rose up. It blocked my view of the Monster completely. The wall rose as high as the cliff and then surged forward toward the Monster. Perseus and I were pushed backward by the waves. The water splashed down onto the Monster, but just as it did, the clear water turned white. The newly formed ice froze Cetus's jaws and the side of his face.

The Monster pulled backward, its tentacles dropping under the surface. The ice clamping its jaws shut shattered into pieces, and the Monster emitted a raging scream. Two of its tentacles rose out of the water again and tried to slap the girls out of the sky. Asterope and Alcyone, who had been flying over the left side of the Monster, dropped down and the tentacle only waved aimlessly in the air. Maia flew right above the Monster. A tentacle surged from the water in front of Cetus and hit one of her wings, spiraling her through the sky behind the Monster.

"MAIA!" Perseus shouted next to me.

There was nothing we could do. We were too far away from Maia to help her, and our powers were useless against Cetus. I knew I couldn't lie to such a massive creature, and Perseus wouldn't use Algol.

From the hills to the right, a sizzling bolt of electricity shot toward Cetus. It hit the tentacle that had slapped Maia down. The tentacle shrunk into the water, curling in on itself. Electra flew far above Cetus, but one of the tentacles rose up to try to hit her out of the sky. From behind us, the remaining three Pleiades flew forward. Merope, Celaeno, and Taygete extended their arms forward. Shards of ice shot from their hands, hitting Cetus on the side of his face. One of the shards embedded into one of his right eyes.

The Monster let out a hollering cry. Perseus pushed me down, underneath the waves. At first, I didn't know why, but then I felt the pull of a giant wave sliding above us, crashing against the cliff behind us. If we had been above the water, that wave would have smashed us against the rocks. With Perseus's hand still on my arm, we swam upward again. I took a gulp of air and looked at the fight still raging with Cetus. Maia was back in the sky, and the Pleiades circled the Monster as they threw electricity, ice, and water at it. Pegasus also flew above the Monster, although he didn't seem to be doing much.

I wondered why no one was trying to come rescue Perseus and me. Then I realized that Pegasus couldn't land on the ocean, or would have a very hard time doing so and then carrying us back up again. The girls wouldn't be strong enough to pull me and Perseus from the sea. Maybe two of them could carry one of us, but we probably wouldn't be flying very fast, and Cetus would surely smack us dead. In that moment, I very badly wished I had wings. My Constellation represented the raven after all, but I had been materialized as a human boy, not a bird.

"Crater!" Perseus shouted to me over Cetus's shrieks. He held my arm tighter. "You can use Crater to kill any creature, right?"

"I can't use it," I said. "I'm too full of memories to use Crater again. I can't use its power, not unless I were to erase all of my memories again." Perseus's big eyes just stared back at me for a second. "There must be something else we can do to defeat Cetus."

Perseus remained silent.

"What do the Prophecies say?" I asked. There must have been something there that could help us. Perseus didn't answer right away. "What do *Cetus's* Prophecies say?"

"We were prophesized to fight Cetus again someday, but I didn't know that would happen *today.*" Perseus looked back at the Monster, whose tentacles rose into the air and waved around wildly to hit the girls and Pegasus.

Ten yards to our right, something soared out of the water. Typhon's black wings beat loudly as he flew toward the hills, away from Cetus and the fight. He didn't even turn to look back. That cowardly Monster. He had left us alone to fight the biggest, ugliest Monster in the Heavens. For a second, I regretted having freed Typhon, but he was still prophesized to help us in the future—I hoped he would. Typhon's figure became a black dot in the distance, and then it disappeared from our sight. We would have to worry about the father of Monsters another day.

I had the feeling that receiving his help would not be easy. We had freed the most powerful and dangerous of all Monsters and I wondered what the price for that would be. How much did Perseus know about the Prophecies that he wasn't sharing with me? He must have known something about Typhon that he wasn't letting on.

I was sure that at least Arianna knew something the rest of us didn't. She had known some of our Prophecies long before we even knew Alathea's book existed. She hadn't shown up once since I had returned, which made me think she wasn't as close to Perseus as we had thought. Arianna had her own agenda, which could very likely come at the expense of our own lives. I wondered why Perseus still listened to her and obeyed her. Maybe the Darkness was so abundant inside Perseus that he couldn't break away from her. Or to a certain extent, Arianna used that Darkness to control and manipulate Perseus.

For what I assumed to be the first time in my life, I felt sorry for Perseus. Typhon aside, he was the most powerful Star Child with Algol, but that was also his curse. Perseus was chained to Algol, that sinister power that threatened to take over him and destroy everything he loved. He was chained to Arianna, too, ever since he had drunk Darkness to save us. I wondered if he would ever be free from her. I held onto Perseus's arm, and he squeezed mine in return.

A sharp wave crashed against us, submerging us for a few seconds before we returned to the surface. Perseus coughed wildly next to me, spitting out water. Then his gaze met mine.

"I'm sorry," he said.

"I thought we already had this conversation," I said. I wasn't in the mood to apologize for all my mistakes. I was more concerned with figuring out how we could swim closer to the hills to get out of the ocean. Cetus had moved farther away from the cliff. Pegasus and the Pleiades were luring him back so Perseus and I could swim either to the small narrow beach on the left or the hills on the right and get out of the ocean.

Another bolt of electricity shot above our heads, hitting Cetus's. Electra's rays of electricity were thinner than they had been before, weaker. The other Pleiades shot fewer shards of ice than before. They wouldn't last much longer. Maybe we weren't meant to defeat Cetus today. Maybe this was a fight for another day.

I pulled Perseus along with me as we swam to the right, getting closer to land. Ragged rocks divided the hills from the ocean. They weren't tall, and I was sure Perseus and I would be able to climb them. The rocks were far, at least three hundred yards away. We would need to swim fast. The waves rolled around us because of Cetus's violent movements, slowing our progress. The Monster moved farther away toward the open sea, away from the land. We could make it. We could all escape Cetus relatively unharmed.

"Corvus," Perseus said as he swam to my right. "I just wanted to say this again. I'm sorry if I made you feel like you weren't strong or brave enough." He breathed hard as we continued swimming. "I was just trying to protect you, but I was being foolish and I hurt you and I'm sorry." He gasped for breath. "I'm sorry for everything else too."

"It's all right," I said, and I meant it. "I'm sorry I left like that."

Perseus nodded. "I just want you to know that whatever happens, you'll always be my brother, and I'll always love you. Everything I've done has been to protect our family." A wave crashed behind us, pushing us forward.

"I know." I coughed out some salt water.

Cetus shrieked again behind us, louder than before. We both risked a glance back. Cetus was slashing at the Pleiades with numerous tentacles. Taygete, Maia, and Celaeno flew in a cluster five hundred yards away from us, close to Cetus's right fin. Two tentacles tried to smash them down but they dispersed and avoided the hit. At Cetus's other side were the rest of the girls, and I spotted Pegasus too. Merope was flying close to the Monster's central eye when a tentacle smashed against her, sending her into a downward spiral. Merope splashed into the water, her wings keeping her afloat. I stopped swimming, and so did Perseus.

"MEROPE!" Electra shouted as she shot electricity at the tentacle that had hit Merope. The tentacle didn't recoil this time.

Time slowed down in the next few seconds. The tentacle rose high above the water, right over Merope, who seemed unconscious as she floated on the waves. I filled my lungs with as much air as I could.

"CETUS!" My voice boomed across the ocean, louder than I had ever heard it. "YOU WANT TO FREEZE!"

The tentacle stopped a yard above Merope. Maia and Alcyone swooped down, pulled Merope away and took her toward the narrow beach. The red umbrella was still there, fluttering with the wind. Electra shot another bolt of electricity at the tentacle that had almost killed Merope, and the other Pleiades flew around it. Ice shot out of their hands in a torrent. The black tentacle froze white. Seconds later, it broke off Cetus's body and splashed into the ocean.

Something cut loose inside me, and Cetus broke away from my lie. Fire burned inside my chest and throat, as if I had swallowed vomit. The Monster turned his attention away from the girls and his big black eye glared at me and Perseus.

Slowly, as if savoring the moment, Cetus began to swim toward us. Its tentacles rose from the water around us and caged us against the cliffside—we still weren't close enough to the ragged rocks edging the hills. The girls flew right above the Monster, shooting ice shards and electricity. From the right, Maia tried to swoop down toward us, but she had to fly to the side, then backward, to avoid a tentacle from slamming her against the cliff. The Monster wouldn't let the girls pull us out of the water. Cetus blinked and began opening its jaws, its rancid, rotten oil breath making my nostrils burn. Cetus rose higher out of the waves.

From the very top of the cliff, a column of fire shot toward the Monster. The orange and red flames hit it right on the forehead, frying its main eye. The fire stopped. The black eye had shriveled and become pale grey. The skin around it was pink and dripping with blood. The Monster shrieked and pulled away from the cliff toward the open sea.

I turned toward the cliff, trying to see where the fire had come from. Standing on the edge, looking straight down at me and Perseus, was Draco.

CHAPTER 29

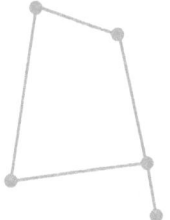

A PIERCING SHRIEK split the sky as Aquila flew forward from behind Draco. The clouds rumbled with thunder, and lightning scorched one of Cetus's fins. The Monster shrieked again, retreating farther into the ocean. Cetus submerged its body, and only its curling tentacles rose above the waves.

I was pushed upward, my feet touching a solid and hard surface. Perseus and I screamed as we jumped into the air, then crashed down on a wooden floor. Water spilled from my clothes like rivers as I knelt. We were on the deck of a medium-sized ship—the ocean waves far below us. A white rail edged the deck, and beyond it Cetus's tentacles coiled through the ocean.

I stood up, coughing out more water, feeling my tongue shriveling with so much salt. A metal door behind us burst open, and out of it came Virgo, Castor, and Pollux.

Castor raced past me and Perseus and stood on the edge of the deck, facing Cetus. "Hello again!" Castor laughed like a maniac. "Do you remember me? You hideous Monster!" Castor continued shouting insults at Cetus.

Pollux stared at his brother, shaking his head. Virgo's gaze didn't break away from me. I hesitantly rose to my feet.

"Virgo? I—"

She stepped forward and wrapped her arms around me, not

caring that I was soaking wet. I hugged her thin figure back and noticed that Pollux studied Perseus carefully. Perseus remained sitting on the deck, looking curiously at me. I pulled away from Virgo and stared into her gentle brown eyes. "You knew me. All along you knew who I was. Why didn't you say anything?"

Virgo bit her lower lip. "You're my friend." Her eyes glistened with tears. "You'll always be my friend."

The boat rocked to one side, and I looked to the right to see that Draco had landed on the deck. His fingers were gnarled and crowned by sharp claws. Had he climbed down from the cliff using his claws? Draco walked closer to me. His orange-red eyes narrowed at me, the vertical pupils very thin and dangerous lines.

"Draco." My tongue knotted in my mouth. "I'm sorry for—"

Draco hugged me so tightly I was sure he wanted to crush my ribs and break me in half. He pushed away from me with a smile a couple of seconds later.

"Nice to see you again, friend," Pollux said from behind Draco. His hair was in a small braid, and his eyes were a cloudy blue.

My eyes darted from the Twins to Draco to Virgo. "You guys don't look very angry with me."

"We're not," Draco said.

"Even though we were detained for an entire night in a cell," Castor said as he walked back to his brother. "I didn't even know museums had prison cells."

"Virgo told us," Draco said as he looked at her, "about your past." His red eyes went to Perseus, who was still sitting on the floor behind me.

I still didn't know why Virgo hadn't told *me* about my past, but she seemed eager to evade that conversation. The boat rocked forward again as the tentacles began to rise tauntingly from the water about six hundred yards from the boat.

With a shriek, Aquila perched on the metal railing. Behind Perseus, Pegasus landed with a loud thud that made the boat sway to the side. Aquila shrieked at the Horse, which glared at the Eagle in turn. One by one, the Pleiades landed on the deck, rocking us from side to side. The tension stretched between us like a rope about to snap in half.

"Well, isn't this a party," Castor said. "We should have brought tacos!"

"That would have been nice," Perseus agreed.

Draco growled at him, but Perseus didn't react. I knew Draco hated him and couldn't blame my friend. Arianna had nearly choked Draco, and Perseus had let her. In turn, Draco had nearly burned Perseus alive. Perseus also eyed the Eagle carefully, because Aquila had electrocuted Perseus and made him fall off Pegasus.

"Wait, wait, wait," Pollux said, standing in between both groups. "I know you guys hate each other and stuff and want to kill each other and blah, blah, blah." He looked toward the open ocean, where Cetus's tentacles were still twisting around. He had gotten at least fifty yards closer to us. "But right now, we all need to fight together to defeat that hideous thing." He glared at the tentacles. "Cetus won't stop hunting us down until we're all dead." He placed both of his hands on his waist. I looked back at Perseus, who nodded. We were the *Young Ones*—the new generation of Star Children that was prophesized to fight the Monster.

"So, what do you say, friends? Do we kill Cetus together?" Castor's gaze traveled back and forth between Perseus and Draco. "Then you can all kill each other if you still want to. Or we can have a taco fiesta or something."

Perseus was the first to nod. He raised his chin. "I'm up for that. Cetus is prophesized to hunt us all down. The best way to defeat him will be to do it together." He stared across the deck at Draco, who turned to Virgo. She nodded slowly.

Draco stared at Perseus. "We'll help you defeat Cetus, with the condition that as long as we're all here we're on a truce. Understood?"

Perseus nodded again.

The Twins smiled widely, their green-blue eyes cloudy like the ocean waves. "I guess we'll need the weapons!" Castor said excitedly.

The Twins walked back through the metal door and disappeared as they descended the stairs.

"I can shoot electricity at Cetus," Electra said.

Aquila shrieked, indicating that he too would be glad to shoot lightning bolts at the Monster.

"The rest of us can shoot shards of ice as we fly," said Alcyone.

"I can breathe fire," Draco stepped forward. "But if Cetus gets away from the cliff then my fire won't be able to reach him."

"You can ride Pegasus," Perseus said.

Draco hesitated for a second, then nodded. The Horse stomped one of his hooves on the floor. A howl echoed from the top of the cliff, followed by a deafening roar. We all looked up to see Leo and Lupus. They stood ten feet apart, looking down at the assembled crowd. They must have understood we were all in a truce, or else they would have already tried to kill each other. I couldn't make out if they were happy or not. Draco took a step closer to Virgo, glaring at the Wolf who had paralyzed him weeks ago.

"Lupus can help too," Perseus said, bringing the attention back to him. "Just as he can paralyze people with fear, he could paralyze Cetus. But his powers won't last long with the Monster."

Perseus looked out at the sea, where the scales from Cetus's head rose out of the ocean like knives. Cetus was getting closer but still biding its time. Maybe it was unsure if it would be wise to fight against all of us at once.

"I don't think Leo, Sirius, or Maera will be able to help us much," Draco said with a sigh. I hadn't seen Sirius, but assumed he was around somewhere.

"Leo should be able to help," Perseus said, looking at Draco. "He is the Golden King. He can lend strength to others, even if he can't fight himself."

Draco blinked in surprise.

"He can?" Virgo asked.

Had Leo always been able to do that? Why hadn't he told us? Then again, he was a lion, and I couldn't understand roars and growls. I tried to remember if I had ever felt stronger or more powerful around Leo but couldn't think of any particular occasion.

Draco and Virgo exchanged a glance. They had both known Leo for at least two years. Based on Leo's mythology, we knew his skin was almost impenetrable, except for Lupus's claws, and he had massive physical strength. The most important Star in his Constellation, Regulus, controlled anything that had to do with royals—ascension, assassination, and anything else related to kings and queens. Regulus even ruled over presidents, leaders, and politics in general. But I didn't remember anything about Leo or Regulus lending strength to others.

"Did you read that in the Prophecies?" Virgo asked.

Perseus nodded. "I thought you guys knew."

Draco and Virgo exchanged another glance. "I'll ask Leo if he can help, I guess," she said.

The Twins burst out of the door carrying a large array of weapons. Perseus's eyes widened like donuts when he saw all the bone weapons. I was sure he hadn't seen so many of them before.

"Just a quick note," Castor said. "These are *our* weapons. After this fight we want them back."

Perseus clenched his fists, but nodded anyway.

Castor handed Draco an eight-foot-tall spear. He looked at the girls. "We have three more swords, so who wants them?"

The seven girls shared a silent conversation between them. Alcyone, Asterope, and Taygete stepped forward. He gave the three girls the three swords.

Pollux exchanged a glance with his brother. "We can control the ocean waves," he said to Perseus and the Pleiades. "We can stay here in Argo and use the waves to attack Cetus."

"I'm not sure there's much I can do," Virgo said, folding her frail arms over her chest.

"I can't be of much help either," Perseus said.

"But in mythology," Virgo said. "Algol, representing Medusa's head, is what turned Cetus to stone and killed him."

Perseus looked at her for a few seconds, then shook his head. "I can't do that."

Virgo opened her mouth to respond, then closed it, eyeing Perseus carefully. No one had ever seen Perseus use that particular power except us siblings. We were also the only ones who knew that if he were to turn Cetus to stone, Algol would completely take him over, and the rest of us would end up dead. Even though I wanted to explain that to my friends, I knew we had no time to discuss that now.

Perseus looked at me. "Virgo, Corvus, and I will stay on the cliff with Lupus and Leo."

I wanted to say that I could help in the fight, too, but then realized that there was really nothing I could do. I could probably lie again to freeze Cetus for a few seconds to give the others some time to attack him, but I couldn't fight the Monster directly. It made me feel slightly better that Perseus would also stay out of the fight. He was one of the most powerful Star Children, but even he couldn't fight against Cetus.

The boat rocked as a wave slammed against us. Cetus was now three hundred yards away and slowly getting closer.

"We'd better get going," Maia looked at me and Perseus. "You can all take Pegasus up to the cliff."

I turned to Draco and Virgo. I desperately needed to tell Virgo about my Prophecy—that *I* was the one who would kill her. But that I would find a way to escape that future. I wanted them to know that I didn't completely believe in what Perseus was doing. I wished I could tell them that, together, we could find a way to escape from our deadly Prophecies but that we could still find a balance between Chaos and Order. People could choose certain Fates, or certain Destinies, and still have Prophecy guide them, but their Destinies wouldn't have to be set from birth. We could all choose a better future and ending for ourselves. I had no idea how I would do that, but I knew that if we worked together, then we would find a way.

"There's so much I have to tell you," I walked closer to my friends.

Draco patted my shoulder. "You can tell us all about it when this battle is over."

"But—"

"There's no time now," Draco squeezed my shoulder. "But we'll definitely catch up later." He turned to Virgo, who nodded. "There's things we have to tell you too." Draco smiled at me, his teeth white and sharp. "We'll talk later, Corvus."

Draco walked away from me and toward Pegasus, followed by Virgo. One by one, the Pleiades jumped into the air and extended their wings. The girls flew above Argo, still not nearing Cetus. Next to me, Perseus motioned to Pegasus with his head, and we both walked toward the Horse. Virgo and Draco were already on top of him. Perseus jumped on with ease, then extended his hand to help me up. Draco rode at the front. Behind him was Virgo, then me, then Perseus. Virgo wrapped her arms tightly around Draco, and I hugged her in turn. She was so thin, I felt my arms would cut through her stomach. She had been looking healthier in the last few months, but she was frail as a twig after saving me from Hydra.

Perseus's strong arms wrapped around me, crushing my ribs a little. Pegasus whinnied and jumped into the air, flapping his wings. My heart lurched forward. I couldn't see where we were going with Virgo's hair fluttering around my face. Seconds later the Horse landed again, making us bounce up and down. I descended after Perseus, then helped Virgo down.

I looked up at Draco, who held his spear tightly. He flashed a smile at us. "I'll be back soon." Pegasus jumped into the air and flew away from the cliff.

To my left was Lupus, and at my other side, next to Virgo, was Leo. The two animals glared at each other but then set their eyes on the ocean. There was a bark behind me. I turned to see Sirius and Maera wagging their tails.

"Hey, boys!" I knelt down and hugged Sirius by the neck. He licked my cheek, then let out a whimper. "Missed you too."

I couldn't leave my friends behind. I *wouldn't*. I would find that balance—a way for all of us to triumph. Sirius slowly backed away from the cliff. I couldn't blame the dogs. Cetus's head had risen from the water again, but neither his tentacles nor his large snake tails moved to attack.

"How did you find us?" Perseus asked Virgo.

She smiled, as if he should have known. "Argo was built from wood that came from Dodona. It's connected to the sacred grove of trees. The Ship can communicate with the Twins and knew that you were in Dodona. We sailed Argo around the coast and planned on going to the Oracle. We honestly didn't expect to find you here."

I looked at Perseus, who had his eyes set ahead. If he had read the Prophecies, then he must have read a mention of this battle. Enemy Star Children working together to defeat the Sea Monster—that was significant enough to be mentioned somewhere. I was sure of that. Then why hadn't Perseus said anything? I remembered what he had told me just minutes before. He would get to his desired outcome and would do whatever was necessary. Did that include not telling us the truth? Maybe if the rest of us knew what was about to happen, we would avoid that particular prophetic outcome and fulfill a different Prophecy.

"Leo," Virgo said, pulling me out of my thoughts. "Is it true you can give more strength and power to other people?"

Leo turned to look at her, his golden eyes cold as metal. I wasn't an expert in feline facial expressions, but even *I* could tell that this was a subject Leo didn't want to discuss.

"We might need your help," I told Leo, who regarded me with that same icy expression.

"Come on!" I heard from below. I looked down to see that Argo had turned into a small, metal submarine. The Twins were peeking at Cetus from the hatch. The Monster still hadn't tried to attack, and everyone was waiting for him to come out of the water.

"Come fight us, you filthy, fat whale!" one of the Twins, probably Castor, shouted.

The tentacles twisted and splashed against the water, but Cetus still didn't rise. Was it waiting for everyone to draw closer so it could strike?

The Pleiades were to the right, circling the hills. They were out of Cetus's reach but still close enough to attack. Pegasus and Aquila flew in circles to the right. Was Cetus waiting for us to strike first? Virgo turned to Perseus, probably realizing that Leo wasn't going to tell her much.

"Are you sure Leo can lend strength?" she asked.

Perseus nodded. "He's the Golden King, the King of Beasts. According to Alathea, he has control and dominance over other beasts and Monsters."

Lupus stepped to the left, away from the Lion, as if he was scared of experiencing that dominance himself. I wondered again why Leo had never used that power. It would certainly have been useful the first time we fought against Perseus at Palatine Hill.

Cassiopeia had said that several Star Children had materialized at the same time. That was us, the *Young Ones*. But Argo, Crater, Leo, Sirius, Maera, Aquila, Pegasus, and Lupus could have been much older than us. We had no idea how old they were. For some reason, I got the feeling that out of all the Star Animals present, Leo might have been the oldest.

In front of us, Cetus was still waiting beneath the waves. His body had submerged deeper into the ocean, as if he had decided that fighting all of us together might not be a good idea.

"He's about to leave," Virgo said.

Perseus shook his head. "We can't let that happen." He clenched his jaw tight. "He's hunted us for too long. If we don't kill him today, he'll kill us another day."

Leo let out a small growl, which sounded like a tired sigh. The Lion took a step forward, glaring at Perseus, who shrank away from Leo's golden gaze. Leo stepped on the edge of the broken cliff and stared directly at Cetus, his lips pulled back in a snarl. His teeth gleamed white.

Leo roared.

It was a roar unlike anything I had heard before. It was deep, as if it had come directly from Leo's soul. The roar echoed in the distance, and even the sea beneath us rippled.

Cetus surged from the ocean, revealing its entire gruesome body again. Its central eye was scorched and dripping with blood. The Monster opened its huge jaws and shrieked back, the force of it nearly tumbling me backward. The acrid smell of oil burned my nostrils so badly I coughed.

I turned to Leo, who stood tall as he faced Cetus. I didn't know what he had done, but it seemed that the King of Beasts had provoked Cetus to fight us. Leo definitely had some secrets that he hadn't shared before, but hopefully he would use his powers more from now on.

"HELL YEAH!" one of the Twins shouted from below. "Let's fight!"

Chapter XVIII, Verse II

The Young Ones the Monster of the Sea follows,
In revenge for the harm inflicted by those who fought before them.
A new battle raged above the waves, only if enemies join their strength.
Like Sun and Moon, and with Fire and Ice they shall unite,
Those that once for each other felt much despise.
One life shall be restored, and another one will be taken,
But only one with enough power shall be able to take aim.

CHAPTER 30

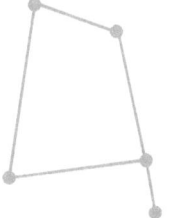

PEGASUS FLEW ABOVE Cetus, close to its face. A column of fire shot from Draco as he sat on the Horse, hitting Cetus right above his eyes. The Monster shrieked as it tried to move away. A tentacle rose from the water and the fire stopped as Pegasus swooped down to avoid the tentacle. Cetus's skin smoked, and even from the cliff it smelled like burnt fish.

Pegasus circled Cetus, trying to avoid the giant tentacles. He swerved to the left, then down and up again. Just as Pegasus flew behind Cetus, a ball a fire flew from Draco and hit Cetus in the back of the head. I had never seen Draco spit out fireballs. Cetus shrieked again, and the rocky ground underneath me trembled slightly. A tentacle passed inches from Pegasus. The Horse swerved down and flew back toward the hills. I could see a few flames behind Cetus and assumed that its skin must have caught fire.

Cetus began to descend, probably wanting to douse the fire on the back of his head by submerging it in water. He didn't get the chance to do it. As soon as he started diving down, a massive wave rose below his chin, pushing his entire body upward. Below me, close to the cliff, Argo was still a submarine. Castor and Pollux stood at the top, their arms extended toward the waves. They kept pushing the water upward, lifting Cetus's body farther above the surface of the sea.

Cetus waved his tentacles and snake tails madly, and I was afraid a wave would knock down the Twins atop Argo, but miraculously, the submarine remained almost immobile as sharp waves slammed against it.

Six of the Pleiades, except Electra, swooped down toward the sea. A tentacle came dangerously close to Alcyone as she flew in front of the Monster. She slashed her sword to the side and cut the tentacle, which retracted, but the others waved wildly in the air, trying to keep the girls away.

Lupus stepped forward, nearing the edge of the cliff. He howled toward the sky. The sound made my bones vibrate, and my heart beat five times faster than it normally did. The tentacles went still. Cetus's jaws froze as they had begun to open, revealing jagged black teeth. Cetus froze, the black eyes at its sides blinking desperately.

The Twins made the water rise higher around the Monster, enveloping Cetus, then let it splash on top of the Monster. All of the girls extended their arms toward the falling waves. The water solidified, creating a white layer of ice covering all of Cetus's body. Around it, its tentacles were frozen mid-motion and its face petrified in a shriek. Even the waves close to the Monster had frozen, as if time itself had stopped around it.

Electra and Aquila flew close together, coming from the right. Aquila flew higher toward the clouds. Thunder rumbled loudly inside them. A thick bolt of lightning twisted toward Electra. She caught it with her left hand, then used her right hand to direct it toward Cetus's snake tails. The electricity that came out of her hand split into different directions. She created a net of electricity that wrapped around the snake tails behind the Monster, frying them black.

"Come on," Virgo whispered next to me.

Next to me, Lupus whimpered. The ice began to crack, forming fissures that broke through the smooth white surface. The snake tails at Cetus's back lashed to the sides, but they moved a lot slower than they had before, dripping dark blood. The ice cracked more, spreading through all of Cetus's body. The Twins climbed back into the submarine, and the Pleiades, Pegasus, and Aquila flew away from the Monster.

"No, no, no," Perseus muttered next to me.

The ice around the Monster shattered, falling into the ocean like giant hail. Cetus opened his jaws wide and shrieked again, making the ground shake underneath us. Pegasus came from the left and flew above Cetus again. Another ball of fire flew from Draco's mouth and hit the Monster right above his three eyes. Cetus bellowed in pain and rage as the fire turned to smoke. A tentacle rose behind Pegasus, its sharp point aimed at the Horse. Aquila shrieked and lightning hit the tentacle, which immediately shrunk back. The Pleiades flew far above Cetus, just below the clouds. Shards of ice, which were sharp as knives, plunged down toward the Monster. One of those shards hit Cetus in one of the left eyes. The Monster shrieked and rose higher, its tentacles waving at the sky as they tried to hit the Pleiades. One of the tentacles grazed Asterope. She swirled downward for a few seconds. Taygete dove down steeply, caught Asterope, and pulled her upward again.

Pegasus and Draco returned to fly above Cetus. Pegasus flew farther up to avoid a tentacle that nearly hit his left wing. Then the Horse swooped down again and Draco shot another fireball at the Monster, right on its three eyes. Cetus shrieked once again. When the fire began smoking, Draco shot another fireball on that same spot with deadly precision. Cetus pulled back toward the open sea. The smoke cleared a little, revealing a big ragged hole on the Monster's skin. Three smaller holes seemed to penetrate into the Monster's skull where its three eyes had once been.

Electra and Aquila flew down from the clouds, both of them throwing lightning and electricity on each side of the Monster's head. Aquila, with a shriek, aimed at the hole Draco had created. The lightning made Cetus's skin ignite again. Electra shot forks of lightning to hit different tentacles that threatened to knock her sisters out of the sky.

Pegasus swooped down again from the left. Cetus's body suddenly swung to the side, and Pegasus whinnied before swerving sharply, barely avoiding the Monster's jaws. Pegasus flew upward closer to Cetus's right side. Draco held his spear tightly, aiming at the burnt hole in the Monster's skin. He pulled his arm back as far as he could, then threw the spear. The white spear sailed in the air for a few seconds and went right through the middle black hole where one of the eyes had been. Only half of the spear went through, while the other half stuck out.

"Yes!" Perseus said next to me.

Cetus bellowed in rage, like thousands of drowning whales. Electra shot a bolt of electricity at the spear, which seemed to be a good conductor. The spear didn't sink farther, but the electricity disappeared inside the Monster. Cetus's shrill wail pierced my ears. His tentacles slammed hard on the water. I didn't see Argo anywhere and hoped the Twins were all right. Cetus swung around sharply as it continued to shriek.

"Get back!" Perseus shouted.

I turned around and raced backward. Leo leapt further inland, and Lupus rushed before us. I ran between Perseus and Virgo. Ahead of us, I spotted Sirius and Maera, who were at least a hundred feet from the cliff. Sirius howled. The ground beneath me broke apart. I fell down, the rock underneath me cracking and trembling.

"Corvus!" Perseus shouted next to me.

I scrambled to my feet and stood just in time to see a giant tentacle rising above me. It sliced downward. I knew I wouldn't have time to move, the tentacle was so wide that even if I jumped to the side it would still crush me.

"No!" Perseus shouted. He leapt forward, standing in front of me. He extended his right hand toward the dark tentacle, which stopped right above his head, then turned ash grey. There was a moment of silence that stretched into eternity, then pieces of grey tentacle broke off and fell around me. I scrambled to my feet and pushed Perseus to the side a second before a large piece of stone broke off and crushed him. We fell hard on the ground, facing the ocean. Cetus had destroyed the edge of the cliff where we had just been standing.

Perseus grunted on my left. I knelt at his side. He clutched his chest, as if he were having a heart attack. His face was a mask of pain, and he doubled over.

"Perseus!" I moved closer to him. He had lost control.

"I—" He choked off.

Another tentacle smashed down somewhere behind me. The impact sent me crashing onto my back, yellow and black stars dancing in my vision. My tongue tasted like ash, and my head throbbed. I sat up quickly just in time to see the ground beneath Perseus break off.

"NO!" I jumped forward, trying to catch him, but Perseus had already fallen far below my reach. I stared in shock as he splashed into the waves below. The ground shook underneath me and I slid forward. I would have fallen to the sea if a hand hadn't gripped my arm. I dangled off the edge for a second before looking up to see Virgo straining as she held my arm. I used my free hand to grip the rocky side of the cliff. Virgo moved backward, pulling me up. I scraped my hand as I used my strength to pull myself up. I crawled away from the edge of the cliff and knelt on the ground.

I glanced down at the water below and let out the breath I had been holding. Perseus's red head bobbed up from the waves, looking up at me. I couldn't see his eyes but knew they would be swimming in dark terror. He had used Algol again. My heart thundered inside my ears. He kept saying he wouldn't use Algol anymore, that he would do anything to stop its spreading influence. But his family was more important to him—*I* was more important to him than losing himself to the Demon Star. Perseus had saved me so many times, risking his own life and the lives of so many others. I would find a way to help him—I would do anything to destroy Algol's power before it took my brother from me and killed us all.

A giant wave rose fifty feet in front of Perseus. The wave rose as high as Cetus and slammed against the Monster, pushing him a few yards away from the cliff. Electra and Aquila shot lightning and electricity all around the Monster's body, but Cetus didn't shrink away. It didn't even shriek in pain. The other Pleiades, from high up in the sky, let loose their shards of ice, but there were a lot less now than the dozens they had summoned before. I couldn't see Pegasus, until I spotted him lying on his side on the narrow beach strip. He wasn't dead—his wings still flapped—but I assumed he had been hit. Draco was standing over the Horse, but I couldn't make out what he was doing.

Cetus frantically waved its tentacles. One hit one of Alcyone's golden wings. She was shot to the right, and Taygete and Celaeno flew toward her to catch her before she fell to the ground below. Both girls grabbed Alcyone by the waist and arms and carried her away.

"Corvus!" Virgo grabbed my arm and pulled me backward before another tentacle slammed against the edge of the cliff. We both fell backward. Next to me, Virgo screamed. The very tip of the tentacle had pierced her stomach, right below her knitted sweater. The tentacle pulled away, making Virgo gasp as drops of blood splattered from the tentacle.

"NOOO!" I scrambled toward Virgo and pulled her farther back as a column of water rose right next to the cliff. It pushed Cetus back, away from the cliff. The Monster sliced at the water with its tentacles, making water splash on top of us.

"Virgo!" She lay on her back, her hands over her wound. Blood slipped in between her fingers like a rushing river. "No, no, no, no, no."

I pressed my hands over hers, pushing down as I tried to stop the blood flow. Virgo screamed. Her brown eyes met mine.

"Corvus," she said weakly.

"No!" I shouted. "I can do something, I can—"

What could I possibly do? Virgo was bleeding out fast and we had nothing to heal her. Sirius howled in anguish as he raced toward us. His ears were thrown back, and he licked Virgo's cheeks.

"It's all right," Virgo said. She gave me a gentle smile.

"You're dying!"

"It's all right," she whispered. "Corvus." She held my cheek with her bloody hand. "I never told you the truth about your past because I believed you could help us. You're one of the few people Perseus listens to. I knew you could convince him to change his mind. I—" A thin line of blood slid from her mouth. Leo roared as he got to us, his front paws scratching the ground as if he were trying to dig up a healing elixir. "I haven't read the Prophecies," Virgo whispered as the line of blood slid down her cheek. "But the Weavers knew you were the only one who could change Perseus's mind. You're the only one that can keep Order in—"

She coughed out blood.

"I'm not letting you die!" I pulled Crater from my pocket, holding it out. Crater had turned into a small chalice.

Crater! Can you heal her?

"If you empty yourself completely, you can use my full power."

So I can heal her?!

"With my full power, you can both restore a life and take a life."

Restore a life.

Take a life.

Crater was thinking more clearly than I was.

"No!" Virgo shouted. She held my arm, more blood flowing out of her mouth. My free hand still pushed down on her wound, but her blood spilled in between my fingers. "Did you listen to anything I just said?" She coughed again, and Sirius licked the blood from her cheeks, whimpering loudly. "You're the only one who can convince Perseus to keep Order and not destroy Fate, Destiny, and Prophecy. If you erase your memories again, then Perseus will obliterate everything!"

"I don't care."

In that moment, I didn't care about Fate, Destiny, and Prophecy. I didn't care about Order and Chaos or about Light and Darkness. For the first time, I knew I was able to do something that could save all the people I loved.

Restore a life.

Take a life.

I knew exactly what I had to do.

CHAPTER 31

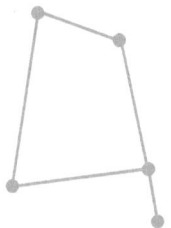

I WOULD NOT GET to talk to Draco later, and I wondered if I would ever talk to him again. I wouldn't get to tell Virgo and Draco the conclusion I had come to—that no extreme was good. We couldn't have absolute Order and structure, but we couldn't have complete free will and Chaos either. I desperately wanted to tell Virgo about my Prophecy—that I was helping Perseus not because I believed in him but because I wanted to find a way to escape the horrible future that had been written for me. I knew that I could have convinced both my friends and my family to find a balance between what they all wanted—but that would not happen anymore.

Had Perseus known how this battle would end? Is that why he had apologized to me again, so he would be at peace that we had forgiven each other for our mistakes? He must have known what I would do—it was surely in my Prophecies, the ones he hadn't shown me. This would lead him one step closer to victory. It had been part of his plan all along. He may have had good intentions, but he was truly a scheming mastermind.

I was about to lose everything after I had gained it all back—the leaves of Dodona had warned me I would lose it all. My friends and my family would both be lost to me. Even though I would forget, everyone else would remember what I had done, and that made my heart twist in pain. I didn't want them remembering this without me. I wanted to live knowing what I had done—knowing that my lies were as powerful as what everyone else could materialize and that I could use them to save the people I loved.

Maybe I was still trying to prove myself worthy. Maybe I was trying to finally show everyone that I could fight instead of letting everyone else fight for me. For the first time, I was the only one who *could* destroy Cetus, and I was the only one with enough power to save us all. I wouldn't save us by sheer strength or by fighting—my lies were the only thing that I needed.

Every lie comes with a price.

Dodona had warned me.

I frantically looked around me. Inches away from where I knelt, to the right, a piece of the ground had broken away, and the water Cetus had splashed over us had created a small puddle. I slid Crater through the puddle and filled half of the Cup with water. That would probably be enough.

"Corvus, no!" Virgo's voice was weak. Her face, so pale I could see the veins in her cheeks and in her forehead, was as white as the strand of hair on her head. I would finally be able to help Virgo—to return the power and strength she had lost.

I looked up to the left. "Lupus, howl when I tell you to." I turned to the Lion at my other side, whose golden eyes were fierce like fire. "Leo, I'm going to need you to lend me strength."

I wasn't sure what kind of strength Leo could offer, but any amount of strength would be good enough. Sirius whimpered next to Virgo, his dark snout smeared with her blood.

"Take care of Virgo and Draco." I scratched Sirius on the head behind his ears. His deep brown eyes seemed to glisten as he pushed his ears back.

"Corvus, don't." Tears streamed from Virgo's eyes. "I don't care if I die. I'm so weak I'll never be useful for anything again. But you can change the outcome of this war and prevent more bloodshed."

I leaned down and kissed Virgo on the forehead, her skin was cold and wet. "I don't care." My cheeks felt warm and I realized I was crying too. "Leo, help me out."

Leo growled.

Power burst through my veins, but it was a different sort of power than I had ever felt. My mind cleared of all doubts. Determination flooded through my heart. I felt no more sadness, and my heart didn't twist in pain. My heartbeat slowed to a steady rhythm. I knew what I had to do and I wouldn't let anything stop me. I didn't focus on what I would lose. I turned my full attention to everything I would win—Virgo would live, Cetus would die, and my friends and family would finally be safe from the Monster that had haunted us for so long.

"I just want to forget," I said. Even though I knew I had spoken, I couldn't hear my own voice, as if I had gone mute. "I want to forget everything I have been." My breath caught, and I forced the silent words out of my lips. "I want to fully forget myself." The ground beneath me trembled as a shriek erupted in the distance. Virgo whimpered underneath me. Crater sizzled in my hand, and its power vibrated through every cell in my body. "I want to forget everything about me. I want to forget everything I have ever been." My voice was completely silent in my ears.

I could feel a leak in my hand letting my memories spill out into the Cup.

Crater, save Virgo. Heal her completely.

I leaned forward and poured the water through Virgo's lips. Her eyes were closed, and her chest had stopped moving.

My grip was steady on the chalice. If it wouldn't have been for Leo's strength, I probably would have spilled the water all over the ground. I finished pouring the water through her lips, but Virgo didn't move. Sirius gave a whimpering cry and licked her cheeks and forehead. Leo's gaze didn't break away from her.

Why was she so thin? I wondered. Had she always been like that? She must have had some sort of health disorder or a disease. Leo growled at Virgo. She gasped for breath, and her brown eyes opened. Her eyes were a very beautiful color of brown, like milk chocolate. She had freckles on her face too. Leo turned to me and growled again, his foul breath attacking my poor nose. I jolted, coming back to my senses. The girl next to me breathed out slowly, as if taking her first breaths in years. The giant Lion motioned with his paw at the puddle.

The puddle. The filthy water. The Cup.

Fragmented thoughts flashed through my mind, and I filled the Cup. The ground beneath me shook, and when I turned, a horrific Monster was staring at me with three bleary black eyes. One of them was bleeding. The Monster was just beyond the cliff, about twenty yards away from me. I stood, my legs steady.

The puddle. The filthy water. The Cup. The Monster.

The big grey Wolf stepped next to me and gave me a nod. I turned forward again and focused solely on the Monster that seemed to be a mix of whale, snake, and octopus. One side of its face was scorched and had a spear poking out of it. I wondered how that had happened. I was so close to the edge of the cliff, yards away from it. My mind was slipping away, but I knew what I had to do.

The Cup. The Monster.

I raced forward, and thankfully the water remained inside the chalice. The Monster opened its huge jaws as if to bite the side of the cliff and swallow us all. Behind me, the large Wolf howled, the sound reverberating in my bones. The Monster froze. Its two remaining beady black eyes blinked frantically. I was ten feet away from the edge of the cliff. Down below I spotted a metal submarine, and three figures atop it. One of them had fiery red hair, and the other two were blond. A tentacle had frozen above them, a yard away from smacking the submarine to pieces.

Strength flowed through my legs as I kept racing forward. I was five feet away from the edge. What were those winged figures flying above the Monster? They looked like giant eagles. Were those human bodies attached to the wings?

The Cup.

The Monster.

I looked away from the sky and fixed my gaze on the Monster, whose jaws were open to welcome me. The Monster could have swallowed an entire cruise ship without a problem.

I jumped from the cliff, screaming.

Kill him.

I threw the entire Cup into the Monster's mouth. It flew in between his black teeth and disappeared inside of him. I would have fallen inside the Monster, too, if one of those flying creatures hadn't grabbed me by the waist and pushed me away to the side. I couldn't make out what it was and saw only a blur of red feathers. Two strong hands carried me away from the Monster's jaws just as it snapped its mouth closed. The Monster emitted a soul-crushing shriek like a thousand lamenting whales.

"Corvus!" The thing carrying me shouted. It sounded female. I slipped out of its grasp and fell. I screamed. The sky above me was full of dark clouds. Thunder rumbled inside of them like twisting white veins.

Then everything went black.

Cold wrapped around me. I welcomed the cold—it was a familiar feeling.

———•———•———•———

I opened my eyes. A circular white light gleamed above me, so bright that my eyes stung and I had to close them again. I grunted, feeling a sudden pain that seemed to emanate from every single one of my bones and muscles.

I opened my eyes again and blinked several times, letting my sight adjust. In front of me was a blue curtain. People talked somewhere behind it. I couldn't make out what they were saying, but something about the hushed tones and the way they spoke conveyed a sense of urgency.

I realized I was lying on a bed, its white blankets covering me completely and a soft pillow cradling my head. I moaned, feeling my head burst open in pain. I raised my right hand to touch my head and realized that my hand and arm were bandaged. How had that happened? The curtain in front of me swung open. A young nurse stepped forward and swung the curtain closed again. She smiled at me.

"How are you feeling?" Her accent was British. How had I gotten to England?

"What happened?" My throat felt sore and dry, as if I had been walking in the desert without water for a week.

The nurse's smile vanished. "There was a terrorist attack. We recovered you from the debris of a fallen building." She scanned my face, as if assessing the damage. "You weren't seriously hurt, but you have a broken leg and some broken ribs. You also have a minor skull fracture."

"Oh." I didn't know what else to answer.

"Olivia!" someone shouted from beyond the curtain. The nurse turned.

"I'll be back soon." She didn't spare me another look as she slid behind the curtain, leaving me alone again.

Terrorist attack? I didn't remember that. I didn't remember being in England either. What was the last thing I remembered? I searched my memories, but an intense pain made my vision blur. I moaned, my stomach twisting so badly I nearly vomited. I must have had a very severe concussion if I had no memories. I had heard of that before, somewhere. What was this called? Amnesia? Surely I would remember at some point.

Corvus.

The thought penetrated my mind like a flash. I remembered my name, at the very least. It was a strange name, I realized.

I closed my eyes, sighing. Maybe I should try to take a nap. I didn't know what else I could do. I heard the curtain slide open again and expected to see the nurse when I opened my eyes. I was surprised to find two teenagers standing in front of me. The girl was sickly thin, and I wondered if she had some medical condition. Her cheeks were sunken in her gaunt face, making her cheekbones look as if they were about to slice through her skin. She had dark freckles splashed across her face. Her eyes were a gentle color of brown, like hot chocolate. Her ash brown hair fell to her elbows, and her arms and legs were thin as twigs.

The boy standing next to her was half a head taller. His short, light blond hair was disheveled. He had a straight nose and a sharp jaw. I couldn't see his eyes behind his sunglasses. The boy seemed athletic—he had a lean torso and strong, muscular arms.

"Do I know you?" I asked. Maybe they were my school friends? Was I a high school student or maybe a college student? The boy and girl seemed no older than eighteen. I was probably around the same age.

The girl smiled fondly, as if she had known me all of her life. *"No, we haven't met before."*

Her expression and words seemed contradictory, but I didn't argue.

"My name is Draco," said the boy.

"I'm Virgo."

"Draco like a dragon?" I asked. They had names as weird as mine. "And isn't Virgo a zodiac sign?" Both of their accents were American. Was I American too?

Virgo smiled wider.

"How much do you remember?" Draco asked.

"I have a concussion," I said, "and some bad amnesia. So not much."

Draco nodded.

"It's all right," Virgo said. "We'll explain everything."

The nurse returned. She gave a startled jump at seeing Virgo and Draco. "Visitors are not allowed."

"It's all right. They're my friends," I lied. My voice sounded deeper. That was strange. Then I remembered—every time I lied, people believed me. "They're allowed to stay here."

The nurse's stare went blank for a second. "Sure. They can stay." She walked away again.

Once she was gone, Draco sat at the edge of the bed, as if we were two old friends catching up. I wondered again if I had met them before. They said I hadn't, but by the way they acted they seemed to know me.

"Do you remember your name?" Virgo walked to the right side of the bed and stood next to me.

"Yeah, it's Corvus."

Again, both teens smiled.

"All right then, Corvus," Draco said. "We'll get you out of here soon. These people won't know what to do with you, and if they see your scars, you're toast."

I remembered that my scars shone in the dark. I didn't have any particular memories of that but simply knew it. But how did they know about my scars?

"We'll make sure you heal," Virgo said. For some reason, I trusted my health to her more than to the nurse.

"Okay."

Draco nodded at me, his smile gentle. "You'll be all right."

I had no idea who those two teenagers were, but I trusted them.

Virgo's smile seemed nostalgic. "We'll take care of you."

I smiled back.

Chapter XXXIX, Verse III

The Monster of the Sea rises again to kill the Young Ones he once fought.

No power shall be a match for the Monster, and no strength enough.

Only with lies he shall be defeated, the lies the Liar once told himself.

One last lie the Liar speaks before he meets his own fall,

Then to return with the Dark Prince to learn again all he once knew.

His mind now empty, and the power of the Cup restored,

The Liar shall turn against those whom he has now forgotten.

CHAPTER 32

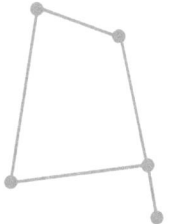

I STARED AT the wooden ceiling above me. A colorful glass hummingbird hung from it, right above my head. The bird was frozen midflight.

I sat up, realizing I had been asleep on a bed. Right in front of me was a mirror. My face was thin, as if I hadn't eaten in a long time—my cheeks were sunken, and so were my eyes. To the left was a large window. I startled when I looked to the right.

"Hello?" I choked up.

A boy, around seventeen or eighteen years old, sat on a chair facing me.

"Hey," he said.

The boy had fiery red hair, which was disheveled as if a whirlwind had passed over it. He had dark circles under his eyes, which were so dark they seemed black. The boy had a sharp jaw and a bumpy nose. He wore a tank top, revealing his very muscular arms. He wore black gloves that reached up to his elbows.

"Ummmm . . ." I wasn't sure what else to say. Where was I? Who was he? Who was *I*? Had I been in an accident and had amnesia or something? My heart beat in panic as I realized I didn't remember anything about myself.

"It's all right, Corvus," the boy said with a gentle smile.

"Is that my name?" I asked.

The boy's smile disappeared. "Yeah," he said, the veins in his arms bulging out. "I'm Perseus."

"Have we met before?"

Perseus smiled. "We're brothers." I looked back at my own face in the mirror, then at Perseus. "Not biological brothers," he hurriedly said. "But we've been brothers all of our lives."

"Oh," I scratched my head, my brain sizzling as I tried to remember *something*. "Were we adopted or something?"

"Kind of," Perseus said. He pulled a piece of paper from his pocket and unfolded it, and it took me a second to realize that it was a picture. He hesitantly handed it over to me. I took the picture in my hands and stared down at it. Three boys smiled back at me from the picture. One of them was Perseus, with his bright red hair. The boy next to him had dark skin and a bright grin. I stood in between them. I looked much younger. All three of us stood close to each other in front of a large tree.

"Who's he?" I pointed to the dark-skinned boy.

"That was our brother Darren," Perseus said. Grief flashed in his eyes. "He died a few years ago."

I stared at the picture for a few long moments. I didn't remember Perseus or Darren—my own adopted brothers. I handed the picture back to Perseus, feeling uncomfortable. Perseus took it and put it back in his pocket. There was a moment of silence. The light coming from the window to the left made a rainbow on the right wall, next to a closed door, as it refracted through the hummingbird.

"What happened to me?" I asked. "Was I in an accident?"

"Umm. Kind of."

I didn't know what he meant by that. The silence stretched between us again like a tight wire. Perseus pressed his lips together, as if he wanted to say so many things but was holding back a torrent of words. A few veins popped out in his forehead.

440

"Is there anything you want to tell me?" I asked.

Perseus gave a choked chuckle. His cheeks turned fiery red. "You wouldn't remember anyway." The veins in his muscular arms seemed about to burst. "Do you want to eat something? You've been out for quite a while."

"Sure." I wasn't hungry, and I was afraid to ask how long I had been unconscious, but I wanted to get out of that small room. Perseus stood from the chair. I swung out of the bed and pushed myself up to my feet, feeling dizzy. I was wearing a dark T-shirt and some black sweatpants. Perseus held my arm to steady me and we slowly walked to the closed door at the end of the room.

"Thanks," I said. His grip was strong. I noticed a small table that had been directly behind Perseus. On top of it was a golden chalice and a green sweater. "What's that?" I asked as I pointed at the chalice.

It seemed to be made out of gold and looked completely out of place in the room. Were Perseus and I rich? I found no other explanation for having a golden chalice.

"That's Crater," Perseus said, his tone sharp. That told me he didn't want to talk about the chalice, as if it were cursed or something. The olive-green sweater was folded next to the chalice. I grabbed it and slowly put it on. I wasn't sure why, but it simply felt right. Perseus eyed my sweater suspiciously but said nothing. Maybe he didn't like green. He opened the door and we stepped into a large circular room with a domed glass ceiling. The rest of the building was made out of wood, like a modern-looking cabin. Right in the middle of the room was a circular table with several chairs around it. There were people gathered around the table—I counted seven girls. They were talking as they drew something on a whiteboard to the right.

A growl rumbled on my side and I turned, then gave a startled jump back. Lying against the wall was a very big Wolf. Its eyes were like two silver rings. The Wolf whimpered at me. The girls at the table became silent and turned to me. Perseus motioned me to walk towards them.

"Hi," I said as we stopped in front of the girls, unsure of what else to say.

"These are our sisters," Perseus said. "Maia, Alcyone, Asterope, Merope, Electra, Taygete, and Celaeno."

"Nice to meet you, or see you again, I guess."

"Nice to see you again too," said the girl with dark skin. Her eyes glistened with tears, and she turned back to the table. Old pieces of parchment and other sheets of paper were scattered across its surface. Strangely, all of them had only seven lines of text. Maybe the girls liked poems?

I looked at the whiteboard and tried to make sense of the pictures taped there. The first one that caught my attention was a drawing someone had made with black charcoal. It showed a Monster with the upper body of a man and the lower body of a snake. It had the head of a man but with fangs and horns, and from his neck sprouted two dragon heads that breathed fire. On his back, the Monster had three pairs of wings. Atop the drawing was a single word: *Typhon*.

Next to him was a picture of a girl. At first, I thought she was one of my sisters but realized that she was someone else. The girl had long black hair and light blue eyes. Her face was lean and her nose small. Her ears stuck out a little bit. Above that picture was another name: *Andromeda*. She sat on a bench at a park, her gaze dreamy. It seemed as if someone had taken the picture without her noticing.

Next to her was another picture, which showed a guy around nineteen or twenty. He was tall, towering at least a head above the other people on the sidewalk around him. He wore a tank top that showed his arms, which were thick as tree trunks. He looked even stronger than Perseus. His hair was like midnight, and his jaw so sharp it almost cut through his skin. His nose was straight, and his eyebrows thick. His eyes were a very bright amber, almost yellow, which reminded me of a lion's gaze. Above his picture was the name *Orion*.

Typhon, Andromeda, and Orion were all within a red oval. With the same-colored marker, someone had written *TARGETS*.

Below them were another two pictures. One showed a beautiful woman around thirty with blond hair and clear blue eyes. Her face was heart-shaped, and her cheekbones high. Above her was the name *Cassiopeia*.

Next to the woman was a man who seemed the same age as Cassiopeia. His skin was a soft shade of brown. He had long, curly black hair and a shabby beard. His eyes were piercing blue. His name read *Cepheus*.

A blue circle enclosed them, and below them read *DEAD*.

Those large words made my heart flutter. I looked back at Perseus. He was staring at me expectantly, as if those pictures would make me remember something.

"We thought this would help explain everything better." He motioned at the board. It took me a second to realize that they had probably set up the board for *me*. I wondered what kind of things my adopted siblings needed to explain to me.

I looked back at the board. There was another circle with more pictures inside it. One showed a boy with blond hair and sunglasses, another showed a very thin girl with flowing brunette hair and freckles. There was a Lion with golden eyes, and a large Golden Eagle. Another picture was of a pair of twins who stood on the deck of a boat, waving at the camera. There was even a picture of a Boxer dog. A purple circle enclosed all of them but with no text or names.

"Who are they?" I asked as I pointed at the pictures enclosed in the purple circle.

Perseus's fists clenched. The girls turned to him. His eyes were dark with anger, and his face seemed to have hardened into stone. I was sure he would grab the purple marker and write *THEY SHOULD BE DEAD*. It seemed like Perseus hated them, so I guessed that maybe those people were our enemies. The large Lion definitely didn't look very friendly.

"They're—" He sighed. "You lived with them for a while."

"You seem to dislike them," I commented.

Perseus nodded. "We've fought each other a couple of times. We have—we're driven by different ideals and goals." Perseus seemed about to say something else, but the red-haired girl intervened.

"I made some hot dogs," she said as she walked over to Perseus. She had five hot dogs on a large plastic plate.

"Thanks," Perseus said as he grabbed the plate. He pointed at the board. "We'll explain more about all of this later. You should eat first." He looked toward a glass door on the other side of the room. "We can go eat outside."

"It's cool, right?" the blond girl asked before we walked away. "It took us like an hour to find the pictures and set it up."

"It is very cool," Perseus agreed. He turned back to me. "Having pictures will make explaining easier. We'll do that later though. Maybe tomorrow morning."

Perseus pulled me away from the table and we made our way to the door. He swung it to the side and we stepped outside. There were pine trees all around us as far as I could see. Perseus looked back at the building. Right next to the door was a ladder that went up to the roof. Perseus, still holding the hot dogs with one hand, climbed the ladder. I followed after him. The ladder took us to a small wooden terrace with a few chairs. Behind it was the domed glass ceiling. The girls were still standing above the table and pointing at the board. The terrace had a wonderful view on the other side. The house stood at the top of a large hill, and the terrace rose above all the treetops. Around us were small mountains and hills entirely covered with trees.

The sky was a dark shade of blue—the sun had already set behind a large mountain behind us. Perseus motioned at the two chairs that faced the trees. We sat down. Perseus offered me a hot dog and I took it but didn't eat it. The bread warmed my hands. Perseus swallowed the other four hot dogs in less than ten minutes, but he didn't take off the black gloves to eat. I looked up at the sky as it turned darker. The wind was cold as it blew around us, but it didn't bother me—my green sweater was warm.

"There are many things I need to explain," Perseus sighed. "There's a lot you need to know before you fully understand what happened to you and what our family is trying to do."

"Okay." My heart beat faster with anticipation. The hot dog had gone cold in my hands, but I still held it.

"We don't live in a world where we choose our futures," Perseus began. "We live in a Universe where Stars choose our futures for us through Destiny, Fate, and Prophecy."

"That sounds . . ." I wasn't sure how that sounded.

"Awful?" Perseus looked up at the darkening sky, which was almost black.

"I . . . I guess. So there is no free will?"

"Nope."

I considered that. Why couldn't we choose our own futures? Didn't we have that right?

"And how do Destiny, Fate, and Prophecy work?" I asked.

Perseus kept staring up at the sky where stars had begun to shine like diamonds encrusted in blue silk.

"Let's start with Destiny," Perseus sighed. "It's unalterable. Destiny is practically the outcome of your life—the destination at the end of your journey. You get there one way or another, no matter what happens." He leaned back in the chair and looked at me. "Fate is a bit different. Humans can have many different Fates that lead them to their Destiny."

"Huh."

"Look at it as if you were a traveler," Perseus said with a smile. "Let's say you want to get to New York. You have a map, and you notice that many different roads and paths will take you to New York."

"So, New York would be the Destiny and all the roads and paths are the Fates that take me there," I said.

"Exactly," Perseus said with a smile. "But without free will you can never stray from those paths." His expression became somber. "We can't wander freely, and we can't choose a different Destiny, say Los Angeles or any other place."

I let my head wrap around that idea. Had I known all this before and forgotten?

"But where do Destiny and Fate come from?" I asked.

Perseus looked back up at the sky. "The Stars control Destiny."

"How?" I asked, looking back up at the twinkling stars. I knew Perseus must be telling the truth. I didn't think there was a reason for him to lie about this, but the idea was still hard to grasp.

Perseus rubbed his hair. "The Stars, the Planets, they're alive," he paused. "They have a consciousness, just as we do. They're millions and billions of years old, and their consciousness is much more powerful than ours."

"How?" That was a strange idea.

Perseus cocked his head to one side, as if unsure how exactly to explain that. "I'm not sure," he admitted. "The Universe is alive too, all of it. This world is just full of life, and life takes many different forms."

I nodded.

"Everything in the Universe is made of energy," Perseus continued. "Everything. The Stars, their Light, they emit the most powerful energy in the entire Universe. The energy of the Stars is powerful enough to materialize thoughts into physical objects or actions." I didn't completely understand what Perseus was saying, but I didn't interrupt him. "The energy that the Stars emit materializes the Destiny of all living creatures." He looked at me expectantly.

"I'm not sure I understand that," I said.

Perseus smiled. "It's all right. It will make sense as we talk more about it, so don't expect to understand everything tonight. What you have to know now about the Stars is that the energy they have is powerful enough to materialize Destiny."

"Okay." I looked up at the twinkling lights in the sky. "Do Stars materialize Fate too?"

"Not really," Perseus said. "Those are the Weavers."

"Who are they?" I asked.

"The Weavers are three immortal women," Perseus said. "As their name implies, they weave." He spread his arms wide. "Everything is connected. The entire fabric of reality is woven together as one multidimensional net. The Stars dictate Destiny, and the Weavers use that energy, that power, to weave the Fates that connect all of us."

That didn't make a lot of sense to me and gave me a slight headache.

"What about Prophecy?" I asked.

"Prophecy allows us to look into the future," Perseus said. "Humans use Prophecy to look at their Fates or to know their Destinies." He smiled at me. "But for us, Prophecy is different."

"Us?" I asked.

His face was less visible now, as the sky had darkened and turned almost black.

"Take off your sweater."

"What?" I was sure Perseus must have seen me shirtless before if he was my brother, but I still felt uncomfortable.

Perseus laughed. "Just do it."

I hesitantly reached down, then pulled my shirt and sweater above my head. There was a sudden white light. I screamed as I realized the light was coming from my chest. "What is *that*?"

Perseus laughed again. He took off his shirt too—light shone forth from a line on his stomach. It blinked in a steady rhythm.

"We're not human," Perseus said.

"What are we?" I asked, my heart galloping like a wild horse, which made the light on my chest pulse faster.

"We're Star Children," Perseus said with a smile.

"Star Children." I looked up at the Stars. "How . . . ?"

"The Stars are divided into Constellations in the sky," Perseus said. "Each Constellation controls a different Destiny." He paused. "We're still not completely sure of how, but we know that each of our Constellations materialized us into life."

That made little sense. How could we come from a Constellation and materialize into people? I tried not to think too much about that logic.

"You said that Prophecy was different for us. Why?"

"Because Star Children have no Destiny or Fate," Perseus said. "We only have Prophecies that speak of possible outcomes that may happen in our futures. So we're somewhere in between Destiny and Fate, I guess."

I looked down at the light coming from my chest. It pulsed in tune with my heart—just like a twinkling star.

"What we've been trying to do," Perseus continued, "is to destroy Destiny, Fate, and Prophecy."

"Why?" I asked.

Perseus smiled gently. "Because we all deserve the freedom to choose our own futures."

I considered that. "I guess that makes sense." Perseus smiled wider. "But wouldn't that destroy the Stars or something?"

Perseus shook his head. "I don't want to literally destroy the Stars, just the power that they, and the Weavers, hold over the future. The net of reality would still exist, but instead of the Weavers weaving our futures, every person would build their own path. And instead of Stars deciding our Destinies, we would all have the freedom to choose our destination. If there is no Fate or Destiny, then there would be no Prophecy either, so all Star Children would be free from our Prophecies."

I nodded. "And how are we planning on destroying all of that?" I asked.

"Darkness," Perseus said.

"How?" I asked. This was all too confusing. "Isn't Darkness bad?"

Perseus looked back up at the sky. "Why do Stars shine?"

I looked up too, seeing how they twinkled brighter now that the sun was completely gone. "They shine because there's Darkness around them."

"Exactly," Perseus said. "Darkness came before Light, and without it, the Stars wouldn't shine. The Stars have used Darkness for millennia, taking control over Destiny."

"Hmmm," I said. "I'm sorry. This is hard for me to understand. So there was Darkness before Light?"

Perseus exhaled. "It will all make sense. I promise." He patted my bare shoulder affectionately. "Maybe I should have started explaining things from the *very* beginning." He looked up at the stars, his eyes dark as night.

I pointed at the Stars. "I have the feeling I used to know the names of the Stars and the Constellations too."

"You did," Perseus said. "It's all right. I'll teach them to you again."

He said the word *again* as if long ago he had taught me all about the night sky. Maybe I didn't completely understand who or what I was or how the Universe functioned, but I was certain Perseus would explain everything to me—he seemed eager to teach me.

"So what's the very beginning?" I asked.

Perseus squeezed my shoulder as we both looked up at the Stars. "*In the beginning there existed only Chaos, the infinite Abyss. The endless sea of Darkness, untamed and unbroken . . .*"

ACKNOWLEDGMENTS

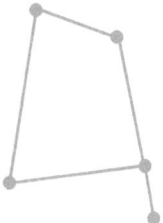

IT FEELS INCREDIBLE that less than a year after publishing *Andromeda* I was able to publish *Corvus*, and that was thanks to all the support I've had from so many people.

I want to thank everyone at The Writer's Ally who have used their expertise to make this book the very best it can be. Ally Machate, thank you so much for your advice and for helping me navigate this journey. Harrison Demchick, I don't think I'll ever be able to thank you enough for everything you have taught me as my editor and all the dedication you have put in to help me grow as a writer and improve with every single book. Julie Haase, thank you for helping me polish my writing and bringing it to another level.

I also want to thank Emily Hitchcock and Clair Fink. Thank you for your patience, for all the advice you've given me, and for helping me navigate the publishing process.

To Augusto Aguilera and everyone at D'signLab for another beautiful book cover: thank you for all the support you have provided and for every single beautiful design you have made to help me promote my book.

I'm grateful to have so many amazing friends who have supported me along the way. To my Mexican friends: Alejo Isaza, Ana Sofi Guerrero, Mel Ruiz, Val D Ibarra, and Pam Ross—thank you for being there since the very beginning. To my friends at Rice: Gargi Samarth, thank you for being an amazing friend and always supporting me. Sam Lydon, thank you for being the best beta reader. Josselyn and Yessenia, thanks for being the best Latina roommates. To my O-Week family: Everett Adkins, Hamza Saeed, Claire Morton, Priyanka Patel, Mark Mutugi, Jerry Templeton, Julia Li, and Yoshwa Kyei—you're the best. To Lingkun Guo, Daniel Koh, and Abby Dowse, thanks for all your support. Thanks to everyone at Hilton Lab: Rosa Guerra, Erik Teran, Mario Escobar, Daniel Brenner, Hailey Szadowski, and Dr. Isaac Hilton. And thanks to the A-team at Brown: Jess Krom, Monica, and BJ & Shirley Fregly. To the awesome team at Lilie: Dr Hesam Panahi, Kyle Judah, Taylor Anne Adams, Patrick Ray, Sophie Randolph, Mercy Harper, and Micaela McGlone, thank you for helping me apply my entrepreneurial skills to publishing a book and for being so supportive of my writing. Thank you to AD Andracchio, for all your support.

To my family, who always continues to support me: Mama, thank you for being a role model for me and for encouraging me to do my best. Papa, thank you for being my #1 fan and for teaching me to always chase after my dreams no matter the risk. Caro, for being my sister and best friend, thank you for always being there for me in the highs and lows. Abu, the kindest person I've met, thank you for always cheering me on.

And thank you, dear reader, for following me along in this journey.

ABOUT THE AUTHOR

AT SEVENTEEN, Sofi became the youngest published author in Mexico. She is the author of "The Lost Origin" and "Star Blood" series. She won the award "Writers of Tomorrow" and was named one of the most influential women in Mexico by *Quién* magazine at nineteen.

Sofi wants to keep one foot in the future and get involved with technologies that are making fiction turn into reality through science. She holds a BS in Bioengineering from Rice University and has worked at Hilton Lab doing research in epigenetic engineering and synthetic biology. Sofi currently works in venture capital to find startups working to transform the world.